I would like to dedicate this book to my readers. To the fans who have celebrated Found and encouraged me to forge ahead in writing Forsaken. It is your enthusiasm that drives me to write every day and get The Conduit Chronicles in your hungry hands.
Thank you for your excitement and the valued time you spend diving into the world of the Conduits with me.

A NOTE TO READERS

I have added a few extras in this novel to help immerse you back into *The Conduit Chronicles* right where *Found* left off. If you feel that you need a refresher, please take the time to read Ophelia's letter to Aremis, located at the front of the book.

In addition, I have included other resources at the back of the book: a Glossary, a map of the trio's travels in *Forsaken* and pedigrees that you may find useful.

I hope these items make it that much easier to leap back into the Conduit world and its fantastical characters.

I also want to note that everything in the book is fiction, including the stories and legends inspired by the various aboriginal tribes I include in the story.

I have never been in contact with these tribes; therefore, all of the descriptions, names and cultural references I make are strictly from my wild imagination.

FORSAKEN

THE CONDUIT CHRONICLES

ASHLEY HOHENSTEIN

A LETTER TO AREMIS

Dear Aremis,

I know you are gone and will never read the words on these pages, but I needed to say goodbye nonetheless, and in my own way. During my years as a therapist (which seems oh so long ago!) I asked my patients to do this many times—write to their deceased loved ones, that is. Turns out it's harder than you think to write words you know will never be seen.

I miss you. I miss our talks; I miss your wisdom and guidance. I miss your arm hooked in mine, consistent and strong, like a pillar in a time when I needed it most. The night that Hafiza fell, I lost you, the closest thing I ever had to a father.

But during our time together in that grand castle, I gained so much more, and that is going to be what I choose to remember and honor.

From the moment Lucas and Elias whisked me away from my quiet life in San Francisco, it was as though someone had taken the world and turned it inside out. If I'm being honest, though, the transition started before that. It was during my visit to Chicago to see Eleanor, my mother, that my world began to shift. I never could've imagined that a collision with a stranger there could lead to the events that would follow. I knew at the time that that run-in was special; I couldn't get Elias' golden-hazel eyes out of my mind.

Then Lucas entered my life and we had a year and a half of happy "normalcy." Truth be told, I'd never had an ounce of peace until the day Lucas moved into my apartment. Of course, hindsight is 20/20 and I now know it was Lucas' Conduit gift of camouflage that brought me peace from my "curse"—my uncanny and utterly debilitating ability to absorb others' emotions and unintentionally compel them to share their deepest and sometimes darkest secrets with me. But Lucas was able to shield me from the onslaught, from the continuous noise and the pain. He became not only my protector, but my best friend—and I thought I was ready for more, when everything changed the night Yanni found me in San Francisco.

As you know, I suddenly found myself on the run in a foreign country; everything I knew up until that moment would be shattered by new truths. I would never see my mother again; I would never go back to the career I'd built in my beloved Golden Gate City. To the rest of the world I was dead.

Aremis, I remember the first time we met. Di—that spritely little goddess of love—was taunting me and you stepped in, as you have done so many times since, and calmed me. In the center of the great courtyard of Hafiza, in that ancient fortress, you took my hand and introduced yourself. I remember the warmth you radiated on that day and every day thereafter. (Pun intended!)

Lucas and Elias would sit me down less than twenty-four hours later and blow my already cracked reality apart. They told me I was a Conduit, a piece of a world greater than the one that I knew existed. My "curse" was my gift; it was a power, not a hindrance, they told me. Later, the ever-eccentric Rand would help me harness it—but you helped me come to terms with it and that was just as important. I learned I was in the middle of a war, a feud among Conduits that had been going on for centuries. The barbaric Nebas were out to get the peaceful Conduits, and I'd already been identified by one of their two dark leaders, Yanni and Esther. I was terrified. But you were always there to hold my hand and encourage me to see my own strength.

I met so many people in the castle: Winston, my quirky personal chef who could boil anything from the inside out. Di, the giggly goddess of love and all-too-stoic warrior. Ying, my petrifying mentor who could manipulate metal. And Rand, the whimsical and flamboyant developer of my gifts. How lucky was I that a Conduit who expressed similar powers to my own was there to guide me. But I have to admit Rand made me a little nervous, and I was happy you were there to cheer me on and walk me through the halls of the magical Hafiza. (Who, I was to learn, had a great sense of humor!)

I learned about my new world and all the wonder that was in it with your arm hooked into mine. I don't think I could've been as brave without it. Your reassurance and efforts with Winston to create an outlet for me to escape if—and sadly, when—the fortress fell definitely made me standing here today possible.

More importantly, you taught me things about myself that I couldn't see. Because of you I've been able to push past fear, to let destiny take the wheel—sometimes.

That night in the tunnel while Hafiza was under siege by the Nebas, your words gave me the fortitude to continue on. They gave me the wisdom to transform my relationship with fear. And I can never repay you for that. Not only did you save my life, but you gave me a new lease on it.

I keep seeing the look on your face when you told me to run while you protected me from Esther; it stays with me always. I also see the look on Rand's face when he spared me from Yanni. You two were my keepers, my heroes. Because of your sacrifice, I am here today.

That awful night changed me. You changed me. When I arrived on that riverbank to see Lucas and Elias waiting for me I was no longer the woman who had entered the tunnel on the other side.

The battle isn't over. In fact, some battles have just begun. Today I struggle with my feelings for my companions more than ever. I love Lucas. He is my constant, my guardian. Life feels easy and fun with him. But he's hiding something, and it scares me. Elias pulls me to him emotionally and physically. I can feel our bond like I can feel my arm. He feels like a home for my soul. But I don't know him, and how do you place your soul in the hands of someone you barely know?

I replay your words in my head all the time: "When you realize you are safe to just be you, the *true* you, then and only then you will understand that it isn't about choice."

It reminds me of something the Oracle Aurora said to me when she tracked us down in Portugal before we left for Easter Island. She said, "Destiny is futile to fight, so give into it and enjoy the journey."

I haven't quite mastered your words of advice, but I'm increasingly aware that so much of this voyage that I'm on is out of my control.

I can thank you for that awareness and sense of surrender. You taught me there is peace in letting go of things you can't control. So, I conclude this letter with letting go of the pain I feel at your loss. I'm letting go of the regret I feel for putting you in danger. I'm letting go of the grief I feel when I remember I'll never see your face again or feel your arm hooked into mine.

Today I take your wisdom and your memory, and I let the rest go.

Your dearest friend,
Miss Ophelia

PART I

ELIAS

I watched as the old woman's eyes glazed over. She was channeling something or someone. I took a few moments to study my surroundings. The hut was small; the grass roof was dilapidated, and strips of light filtered through the cracks. I looked down at the dirt floor I was seated on and then back up at my hostess —she was still in a trance. I noted the countless clay pots of all sizes and shapes strewn about the crude shelter. Some were quite large, and others were broken. I wondered why she held onto the broken fragments. *Perhaps they held some ritualistic meaning?*

She began mumbling in a language I did not recognize; it was not native to this island. I was quite sure because I had spent countless hours studying all the languages and dialects of the Rapa Nui—on Easter Island—the remote Chilean outpost in the middle of the Pacific Ocean.

I heard her mutter a few phrases that sounded distinctly like Asagi, and I wondered if she had accumulated some of our language over the years from her ancestors and their interactions with Alistair and his family. By all accounts, as I understood it, Alistair and his kin had been visiting these people for nearly two thousand years.

I thought about the last time I saw Alistair, or at least what was left of him, enveloped in flames. Then my mind drifted to the image of his dear friend Emerson, whose body I last saw being hoisted up by Yanni's henchman Salzar that same night outside my hotel room—just moments before Emerson had given me vital clues that have determined the critical steps I have taken during this search. That fateful night led me here. To an obscure village, investigating aboriginal languages in an attempt to decipher Alistair's journals and find a place to unite my people.

The woman's eyes rolled back into her head and then her demeanor changed completely. She was now staring at me. Intensely staring at me.

"Your spirit is pure, but you are a doomed fatota." She pointed at me with her crooked finger. "Moai Kavakava told me about you—that you would come for answers. Answers I do not have."

"Who has the answers?" I asked.

"It is not that simple. If it were, I would not be necessary."

"What is a fatota?"

"If you don't know the ways, it doesn't concern you."

I tried a different tack. "Who is Moai Kavakava?" I had versed myself on what little there was to know about the Rapa Nui culture. Moai Kavakava was a spirit expressed as a man.

She looked at me suspiciously as though she knew I knew more. "You know Moai," she said plainly. Then she pulled a wooden figurine from a long chain around her neck. It had been hidden by her blouse. The figurine was thin, with a long face, and it had the undeniable features of Alistair.

I nodded in agreement with her. "I knew Moai Kavakava." I did not disguise sadness in my voice.

"Knew?" she said. She then got up and walked over to me in a curious crouch, staying on my eye level, watching my every move. She got so close that I could feel her wispy grey hair tickling my forehead. I said nothing, just kept her gaze. After a long while she sat down and crossed her legs.

She put her index finger in the dirt of the floor and traced a circle while mumbling more words I did not understand. Then she reached up with her thumb and placed it squarely in the center of my chest, she began chanting continually growing louder—more rhythmic. She closed her eyes and rocked where she sat, her thumb still firmly planted on my sternum. I could not tell you how long we sat there—I dared not disturb her rituals; I needed her cooperation. As it was, it was amazing that she was willing to entertain me at all. I thought it was going to be more difficult to get an audience. But the tribal people south of Hanga Roa had been eager to welcome me. It was, as the old woman had said, that they had been expecting me. Someone knew I would come. This obviously left me with questions, but somewhere in my soul a calm voice said "trust," and I decided to listen. I did not have much choice.

"You will come to see me for three days—on the third day I will give you answers and questions." She held up her hand with three fingers and pointed at each one. Then she stood and went to the other side of a work table. She was putting the dirt from her finger into a clay bowl. I watched her gently dust it off then scrape the bed of her nail with a stick. She grabbed a small bundle of what looked like crushed leaves and muddled them into the bowl as well.

"Take this." She handed me a sheet of linguistic symbols. "Moai said you may need our markings."

She waved her hands at me in the fashion that suggested I should leave—quickly. So I stood up, brushed off my backside and exited the way I came. A small congregation of villagers stood just outside the hut.

Although the old woman spoke good English, the other villagers appeared to only speak Pascuan, the native tongue of these parts. I paused outside the door and summoned my best Polynesian accent, racking my brain for the sentence I wished to articulate. Only a single word came to mind. "Name?" I uttered, gesturing back at the hut. I said it in Pascuan, but they all looked at me as though I could have been speaking in tongues. A voice from inside of the shelter shouted out.

"You may call me Alalli." All of my onlookers nodded in unison, as though they now understood what I had said. Many of them repeated

5

the name Alalli. I started walking slowly through the crowd, following the path I had taken on foot to get here.

A small girl and a medium-sized dog with black and brown spotted fur fell into step beside me. She grabbed my hand and I gently clasped hers in return. She had an angelic smile and was probably no older than four years of age. Dark, thick hair framed her round face. She smiled up at me as we walked, trying to keep time with my step. So I slowed to meet hers. Her dog trotted alongside us, periodically lapping her free hand with his big clumsy tongue.

The duo escorted me all the way to the outer boundary of the village. I wondered if she would have the sense to stop there. When she let go of my hand, I was relieved. I knelt beside her and put my hand on my chest. "I am Elias." Then I pointed at her and said "Name?" in Pascuan, hoping for a better response this time.

She picked up on my communication immediately and put her hand on her chest. "Lalee," she said, then reached down and put her hand on the mutt's chest and said "Pikuu." This simple exchange made me smile so wide my cheeks hurt. I put my hand on her shoulder and repeated "Lalee," then patted the patient pup on the head and said "Pikuu."

Lalee clapped with delight—then put her hand on my shoulder and said "Elias." She was so tickled, she erupted with laughter. I laughed with her. She ran back to the village center as fast as her little feet could carry her, with Pikuu jogging beside her. When she was almost out of view she turned around and waved at me. I waved back, before continuing to walk the rest of the way back to a vehicle I had stowed a short distance outside the village, in a clearing near the main road.

My head was busy with thoughts. I was happy to have the walk to organize some of my more pressing questions. *Is this woman really able to give me answers?* I had thought this journey was going to be an arduous one. I imagined I would have a difficult time tracking down persons willing to assist me. *Does she really know my questions? And could it be a coincidence that her name, Alalli, means mother in Asagi, the Conduit language?*

OPHELIA

J had my pen to paper again. I'd written in the journal Elias gave me in Serpa, Portugal, every day, trying to honor my experience and the people I'd met during my time in the fortress Hafiza. I was jotting down all I could remember about Winston this time. The way he moved and spoke—both awkwardly! His odd sense of humor—dry and at times indistinguishable as such. I thought about his impeccable cooking and my mouth watered.

Then the image of Hafiza up in flames filled my mind's eye and I had to hold back tears. I didn't even know who'd made it out alive. Winston and the others were most likely dead—that was why I felt I had to write down everything I could remember about their lives.

We'd arrived on Easter Island two days earlier. The house Elias put us up in was massive. Different than the one we stayed in in Serpa days earlier. This one didn't have a giant veranda with an amazing view. It was more of a secluded compound. *Is Elias protecting me from the world, or the world from me?* I thought.

My meeting with Aurora the Oracle had me wondering what major role I was going to play in this war. Aside from encouraging me to stop fighting my destiny, she alluded to the fact that that very destiny of mine was going to impact the Conduit war that had been raging for several hundred years. It must be in an Oracle's job description to be vague though, because aside from a few other ambiguous statements, she didn't mention whether or not my role would help Elias and the Pai Ona defeat the Nebas. My blood boiled slightly at the thought of that evil organization of Conduits—led by Yanni and Esther—who killed my dear friend Aremis and left the fate of the others unknown. I took a deep breath, then let it out slowly.

I finished what I was writing and put my pen down. I fanned through the pages of my journal, realizing this was all I had left of my time at Hafiza: memories of friends I'd lost and would never see again. We knew for sure that Aremis was gone, and Hafiza herself had been blown to pieces. Two beautiful souls had been brutally taken from this earth—and I felt to blame.

Before I could wallow in my guilty feelings any longer, I heard a knock at my bedroom door.

"Come in."

Lucas peered around the corner. "Ready?"

I'd almost forgotten our plans.

I put my grandmother Lilith's photo in the journal to hold my place and jumped off the bed with anticipation. I looked at Lucas, took him all in. He was wearing tight gym shorts that left very little to the imagination. He didn't bother with a shirt. His perfectly trim body —with deep olive skin that sheathed tight muscles and a large frame— brazenly dared me not to stare. His brown hair had grown out some since we left San Francisco; it now fell just above his shoulders in a masculine wave. He often wore it pulled back these days, but it was hanging loose and free today. His warm brown eyes were watching me—until I finally pulled my gaze away.

Lucas had agreed to continue with my combat lessons. I hoped that I could somehow channel some of the mojo I had captured while studying under Ying, the master of metal, while at Hafiza. I'd been progressing nicely while under his guidance; I'd really started to feel like a contestant on American Ninja Warrior—invincible. Now I wasn't sure.

I followed Lucas outside. It was a little muggy, but thankfully not too hot. I pulled my strawberry mane from my face; it too had been unkempt for a while and was now long enough to graze my lower back.

I looked around the backyard. Lucas had decided that this part of the property would serve us best. It was vast, just like the house. If I had to guess, I'd say we were on at least two acres. The grounds were well manicured, though, with a huge rectangular lawn and cropped grass. We were encompassed by a large security wall, but you could hardly see it behind the trees that hugged the lawn's perimeter.

"Okay," he began, "so first I want to teach you a jab, specifically a right-hand jab."

I looked at him, eagerly anticipating direction. Ying had focused on what Lucas called a "fencing technique" while he trained me. Lucas on the other hand was more skilled in hand-to-hand combat. "Get both your hands up by your chin, one leg in front of the other. Like this." He gestured down to his legs. I mimicked his posture: hands up, legs staggered.

"Good, good, Olly. That looks about right."

I dropped my hands to my sides. "About right? I want to get it right," I demanded, repositioning myself. Lucas responded by making some minor adjustments to my stance.

"Looks perfect. Now let's see if you can do anything with it. This isn't going to be any of that sissy fencing crap you learned in Hafiza. We're going to wrestle!" he said as he smiled devilishly, adding, "Just so you know, I'm intending to make contact if you don't utilize the evasion tactics I taught you yesterday."

I sneered at him. I was too busy concentrating on my body place-ment to make a snarky comment back.

I nodded, and he stepped forward. I countered by stepping back-wards and sideways. This part reminded me of my lessons with Ying. Lucas would move and I would react defensively just as Ying had taught me. I kept my eyes on Lucas', but I couldn't read him, as usual. Still, I peered into his eyes nonetheless.

Again, he advanced and I darted right. We circled around about twice before I detected a slight shift in his demeanor. He was going to strike.

His cheek pulsed once and I intuitively knew this was a clue to his intent—he'd make his move. This time when he stepped forward I shifted left and advanced, catching him off guard for a fraction of a second—enough time to plant a hard-right jab to his left ear.

My wrist jarred under the impact of the blow on my bare hand, and I had to take a deep breath to keep from whimpering in pain. Lucas, however, looked stunned. He spun around on his heels—and was now facing me with a menacing stare while progressing swiftly in my direction. I quickly took two steps back—I wasn't sure what to do after I landed a blow. Ying had spent most of my lessons teaching me evasion tactics, not offensive ones. I realized I felt completely unequipped for this form of combat.

Lucas filled the gap between us in less than a second and I closed my eyes, anticipating impact somewhere on my face. I'd never actually hit anyone in my entire life—at least not with my fist. *Why shouldn't I expect to be hit right back?*

Lucas erupted into laughter. My eyes shot open. "What is this?" he said, barely formulating words between the bellows coming from his stomach. "Great jab, by the way. My ear is still ringing. But your next move can't be to fumble backwards and close your eyes, Olly." He laughed even harder. I let out the breath I'd been holding in and giggled gently. My pride was a little hurt, but Lucas' laughter was so contagious that I couldn't help but join him, even if it was at my expense.

After a minute, I nudged his arm. "Okay, okay, so you have to train me on what to do after I plant a punch."

"Apparently." He tucked me under his arm and pulled me close. "Let's start with what *not* to do. Never close your eyes in a fight." He held back another chorus of laughter—a smart move on his part, because I was starting to seethe a little from the embarrassment. *I knew better, than to do that.*

"Cut me a little slack," I protested. "I've never punched anyone before. I was surprised that my hand hurt, and I didn't know what to expect next," I added sheepishly. Lucas caught on that I was feeling fairly humiliated, and quickly changed his approach.

"It was a great hit; you should be proud," he said. "And yeah, fighting with fists can hurt you just as much as the opponent if you don't use proper mechanics. That's my fault. I should have warned you." He noticed I was holding my wrist. "Does it hurt?"

"Yeah. Apparently more than your face."

"I don't know about that." He tugged at his ear. "Still ringing over here." I smiled. "Oh, so that's funny?" he teased.

I smiled even bigger. "Only a little."

Our banter was interrupted when we heard the front door open. We figured it must be Elias returning home from one of his forays. I wondered what he'd been doing, and if he was successful. I knew it must be important; he'd been extremely secretive about his plans so far.

Lucas snapped me back to the present. "Well, let's see if Viraclay can't patch up that wrist and we can discuss strategies for after you land the first punch," he said as he directed me into the large foyer and down the hall to the kitchen.

Elias was grabbing a cold beer out of the fridge.

"I'll take one of those," I said as I sat on the barstool at the break-fast bar. I considered Elias' nickname for a moment, Viraclay—it meant "miracle" in Asagi. I didn't particularly care for it; I couldn't exactly say why though. Maybe it was because whenever Lucas said it, it sounded condescending.

"How was the lesson?" Elias asked as he handed me the beer he'd opened for himself and reached in for another one.

I put the chilly bottle on my throbbing wrist and it felt good. "Short," I huffed. "We spent most of the morning working on my Asagi, and just started dueling a few minutes ago." I took a sip of my beer, set it down and began palpating my wrist with my free hand. It was pulsating, with sporadic sharp pains shooting in either direction. I squeezed it hard and felt an odd sensation radiate up my arm: a tingling warmth while almost feeling cool simultaneously.

"She laid one punch on me and hurt her wrist," Lucas chimed in.

Elias was immediately at my side. "May I see that?" he asked as he gently moved my hand aside and began massaging the area. More of the tingling and the throbbing subsided. Thank goodness Elias was using his healing touch to mend any damage I'd done. After a moment it was as good as new.

"Now aren't you going to fix Lucas' face?" I said mockingly, knowing Lucas was already right as rain. By now I understood that the perks of being a consummated Conduit included expedited self-healing, in addition to super speed and strength. Not to mention a little extra shimmer to their skin, along with each Conduit's own special flavor of magic. Basically, a Conduit was the equivalent of a superhero. Luckily for us, Lucas' special gift was camouflage—a very useful tool when you're hiding from a homicidal duo that is hell-bent on killing you and everyone you love.

"I do not believe I possess such a skill," Elias cracked as he pointed a thumb in Lucas' direction and tried to suppress a smirk. Over our last couple of days on Easter Island, I'd noticed that Elias seemed to be relaxing around us, allowing himself to joke and interact with both Lucas and me in a more lighthearted way. I laughed, while Lucas stared at Elias for a moment before adjusting his gaze back on me.

"No one needs to mess with perfection," he said coolly, caressing his cheeks as he spoke.

"Exactly," I replied as I laughed even louder.

ELIAS

"*P*ie – own – ah. Is that right? I don't say it right, do I?" I could hear the smile in her voice from the other room. Lucas and Ophelia had been working on her Asagi vocabulary all morning. I was always surprised to see how quickly she picked things up. The Conduit language was not an easy vernacular to acquire. My father called it a living language—it was always growing, absorbing and modifying. True, the foundation always remained the same, but in order to remain useful over the passage of time, it often had to mutate. She was ascertaining the nuances beautifully. Lucas would say a word and Ophelia would over-enunciate and then laugh at herself. *Oh, how I loved her laugh.*

"Why are you smiling?" I heard her say to him.

"What? Sure, you said it right, Pai Ona," Lucas replied, definitely goading her. She laughed again. "Now what does it mean?"

"That's easy—they're the good guys. You know, the Conduits that *aren't* trying to hunt us down and kill us."

There was a moment of silence and then Ophelia spoke up once more. "I've been thinking, Lucas. Why do people call the great painter by so many different names—Dalininkas, Malarin, Chitchakor? Aren't they all the same entity?"

"Yeah, they're all referring to the same guy. I think it's comparable to Jesus and Christ and Lord and blah, blah, blah."

"Lucas." I noticed her telling pause after addressing him—by now I knew it meant that a more difficult question was to follow.

"Olly," Lucas replied.

"I remember hearing almost everyone in the castle refer to 'the great creator' or just 'the painter,' but you never do. Why is that?" I listened closely, intrigued by her perception here. I had also noticed this. He waited a few seconds to answer.

"Dalininkas, Malarin, Chitchakor, the great painter, whatever name you use doesn't matter; they all mean one thing to me—deserter. If this guy, the creator of all things, painted our lives as they were meant to be, then why is there so much loss? Why do some of us experience so much fucking pain? Did he just forget about us? He forgot about me a long time ago."

I grabbed my satchel and threw it over my shoulder, all the while thinking about how Lucas' insight into the painter explained a lot. The house we were staying in was expansive, an enormous complex of rooms and hallways. It was far more space than we needed, but it was on a large piece of property about a thirty-minute drive north of Hanga Roa, the island's main town, thus providing us with the perfect amount of privacy.

I sighed. It felt like the attack on Hafiza had happened years ago, when in fact it had only been a matter of days. I was amazed at how well Ophelia had acclimated. You could see it in her eyes; something had shifted in her since that night at the castle. She was now a fortress herself. I loved her newly developed fortitude, but I sensed it made Lucas nervous. She was no longer the woman he knew from their time together in San Francisco; she was no longer in need of his protection per se, at least not the kind he had grown accustomed to imparting—the stifling kind.

Nonetheless he had all of us very well shielded; I hoped it was enough to have kept any tails from following us across the Atlantic.

I just needed time—and that was the one thing I had little to spare while we were on the run. I needed time to collect enough information to complete the translation of Alistair's journals and determine the safest possible location to hold the Conduit summit. This summit was the only chance I had to save Ophelia from her doom, a fate prophesized about when I was a child.

I had hoped that when the Oracle Aurora found us in Portugal it was to tell me something had changed in her vision, but she had only confirmed that our fates were still the same. If Ophelia and I consummated, she would either annihilate our kind or finally end the war. This meant we were condemned to deny our union until I could alter her fate.

Hosting the summit and uniting the Pai Ona was the only way that I could sway the outcome in our favor and save the woman I loved.

I paused in the hallway once more, so I could hear her pronounce the word 'lasteea.'

"Laaast-ea. No, that doesn't sound right. Laas-stea. Was that right?" She waited for Lucas to respond, but he was silent. "Answer me!" she demanded his aid. "I think you're just a terrible teacher. I'm going to ask Elias for help."

Lucas laughed, and I heard what sounded like a playful jab to the torso. Then she called for me. "Elias, I need your help. I need a real teacher!"

I heeded her plea, even though I was running behind. I quickly rounded the corner into the large living space, which included the kitchen, dining nook and a cavernous common space with vaulted ceilings. "I would love to be of assistance," I began, "truly, I would, but I must be off to attend to another errand today. I will be home by supper." I waved at them both and headed toward the foyer.

As I opened the door I heard Lucas ask her what lasteea meant.

"It means love; possibly something even deeper than love," he replied when she kept quiet. *Definitely something deeper,* I thought as I shut the door behind me.

I MADE THE DRIVE TO THE RAPA NUI VILLAGE IN SILENCE, ACCOMPANIED only by a host of questions. *Would I see Lalee again today?* I had so enjoyed the simple, pure moments of kinship and joy we had shared the day before, thinking of her brought a smile to my face.

Still smiling, I let my thoughts drift back to Ophelia. She was so beautiful, her long, wild pale red hair framing porcelain skin dotted with faint freckles. Her lips were always a soft pink, they framed my favorite part of her, her smile—it was wide and friendly, accented with an adorable dimple in one cheek. Her green hazel eyes lit up when she smiled, adding an irresistible allure and charm.

I desired nothing more than to be with her on the sofa back at the house, at this very moment, introducing her to our world. But instead I was *alone*, in a car, chasing my father's dream for the summit. The word *alone* stung, like salt in an open wound. That familiar resentment I had started to harbor for this mission began to simmer again in the back of my mind—for the loss of my parents and the life of seclusion I was forced to endure to complete my father's undertaking. I hated feeling anything less than admiration for my mother and father, for all that they had done. With a shake of my head, I quickly dismissed my frustration as I parked the car in the same clearing I had left it in the day before, and walked the quarter of a mile through the jungle to get to the village.

There she was—all two and half feet of her. Beaming at me, jumping and waving. She had waited patiently for me to reach the village boundary before running up and hugging my legs. I nearly tripped as I tried to reach down and pat Lalee on the back, a minimal but appropriate reciprocating gesture. Simultaneously I scratched behind Pikuu's ears, and he leaned into my legs as well. That was it— their unevenly distributed weight sent me down to the ground, with the two of them toppling on top of me.

Lalee giggled heartily, and Pikuu quickly repositioned himself so he could give me a thorough licking to my face. I erupted in laughter at the ridiculousness of it all—yet at the same time it felt like such a 'normal' and enjoyable moment that others have among their friends and family—not something I was often blessed with.

After a few minutes Lalee and I both lay on the grass out of breath and our abdomens sore, with Pikuu panting between us. A woman's voice carried across the clearing and sang out Lalee's name—we sat up. I saw a short, rustic-skinned woman traipsing our way. She was smiling, but behind her smile was concern. I could not blame her— her young daughter was rolling around in the grass with a strange man. I quickly stood up and brushed myself off. Lalee did the same, and as the woman closed the gap between us Lalee took my hand in hers and yelled back to the woman. "Elias!" she blurted. It sounded adorable coming out of her tiny mouth with her thick accent and bell of a voice. The woman stopped a few feet away, still smiling. There was now less fear behind her eyes, but she was clearly uneasy. Lalee repeated, "Elias," then beamed up at me.

I put my hand to my chest and repeated "Elias" as assuredly as possible, then pointed to the village and said "Alalli." I wanted to make certain she knew I had real business to attend to in the village.

It was then that realization and relief set in around the woman's shoulders. She put her hand to her chest and said, "Ualee."

I repeated her name back to her, and she smiled much wider. I took a moment to examine her more closely. She could not have been taller than five foot. She was not stocky, but not thin either. Her long black hair had been whipped up into a tight bun on top of her head. Her attire was traditional for that area—a long, loose wrap skirt with a basic tan tank top. When she smiled I noticed she was missing at least three teeth, although she had managed to keep her two top front ones. Her eyes were warm and welcoming, and as I glanced down at the adorable Lalee I saw the resemblance.

Lalee began to walk and pull me forward. I now had an entourage as I entered the village center. Before I could make my way to Alalli's hut, Ualee took my arm and drew me toward a smaller structure of the same makeup. I ducked to enter and realized that this must be their home. Lalee was ecstatic, jumping up and down and picking things up and saying words in her native language to describe each item. I just nodded and smiled as she paraded about.

Ualee rummaged through a basket, and after a moment turned and handed me a few leaves. I unwrapped them and found several pieces of dried fish. I smiled graciously and said "thank you" in Spanish, hoping she understood me.

She did and nodded enthusiastically. It was so interesting to me, the contrast of this particular village in comparison to the rest of the islanders. Most of Easter Island's inhabitants spoke Spanish and had for many years now. Some even spoke some English. There were still a few dialects of Polynesian languages floating about, mostly in tattered pieces. But this village, tucked away from the beaten path, was courageously holding on to as much of their Rapa Nui heritage as they could, including the Pascuan tongue. I wondered if that was why Alistair visited this village—or perhaps it was the opposite, perhaps they held onto so much of their culture *because* he visited.

What will happen to them now? I wondered. Now that he would not be returning. I shook the unsettling feeling that particular reality brought. *Maybe they would stay the same?* After all, I had had to go to extreme lengths to hunt down their whereabouts. Thank goodness for Google Earth. I had scoured hours of satellite footage to pinpoint a settlement in this jungle. The village was tiny, well camouflaged with its thatched roofs, and completely surrounded by thick vegetation. This was not a tourist location—these were a few people holding onto their traditional ways fiercely and choosing seclusion as their tactic to do so. I was certain the local authorities in town knew of their settlement, but from what I had dug up, it appeared that someone paid a hefty amount of money each year to keep them undisturbed. It was very likely that Alistair had been the benefactor that made this possible.

I had not gotten to know Alistair well before his untimely murder in Chicago, but the more I researched his work and travels, the more respect I gained for him and his family. I was not certain what his motives were for visiting the aboriginal people he did over the years, but if as a consequence a few people got to quietly protect their way of life—well, that was a beautiful thing.

A nudge from Lalee brought me back to the present. I took a bite of the fish to find it was delightfully smoked. I made the universal

"Mmmmm" sound, and Lalee clapped in approval. I unfortunately was not hungry, so I rewrapped the fish and placed it in my satchel. Ualee appeared satisfied with this exchange and was ready to escort me to the priestess' hut.

The rest of the villagers waved to me as we passed; some even stopped their dealings to welcome me. I did my best to acknowledge everyone I saw out of respect for their courteousness.

The old woman's voice reached my ears as we approached. "Give me a moment Mr. Elias." I patiently waited outside her door with Lalee, who was still beaming at me. I thought her cheeks must hurt by now. *She might be the most charming young girl I have ever met*, I thought. She was like a beacon of innocence in a world that writhed with a viciousness and iniquity I knew all too well.

Soon I sensed a faint smell of smoke coming from the shanty. Its fragrance was not familiar to me.

"Enter, Mr. Elias," the old woman's throaty voice commanded. I let go of Lalee's hand and waved goodbye as I ducked under the entry curtain and into the small circular room. "Sit." I followed her direction as I looked around the room again. The same small clay pots littered the space, except this time I viewed them through a rather dense screen of smoke.

I chose not to speak, because it did not seem appropriate. The old woman said nothing more for a long time. She just stared at a bowl that contained burned fragments, and every now and then she would reach into a box, pull out some kind of dried leaf and place it in the fire.

The smoke built up as she did this. I was starting to find it hard to breathe when she finally stopped looking at the fire and turned her gaze to me.

"What do you know about circles?" she asked. The question caught me off guard. It was so simple, *but it could not be that basic, could it?*

"They are round, continuous," I instinctively replied.

"Ahh, they are unbroken," she said matter-of-factly. She threw more dried leaf on the small fire.

Since the silence had been broken, I thought I could ask my own question. "What is it that you are burning?"

"Is that important to you?" she asked, but she did not wait for a reply. She just shook her head and answered. "It is grass from the Motu Nui—grass that lay near the nests of the manutara. Do you know of these things?"

I nodded. "Motu Nui is the island where the manutara birds lay their eggs. It is tradition for a man to steal an egg from the manutara and bring it back to be declared champion, the tangata-manu."

"Oh, you did your homework," she said sarcastically.

I looked down at my hands, feeling chastised, because that was precisely what I did. I had conducted a ton of research, hoping that it may help me find answers. I now felt silly; what could the internet really tell me about a culture?

"No matter." She waved her hand. "You will have read about Make-make and the birdman, no doubt. They are different, but the same. This is circles."

I tried to follow her train of thought, but I was rather lost.

She continued. "I know Makemake, you knew Makemake—we are a circle." She handed me a handful of the dried grass and pointed to the contents of the burning bowl. I threw them in. She repeated. "We are a circle."

This was how the day proceeded. A lot of smoke and much discussion about circles. I left wondering what answers I could truly get from this woman. I was grateful that she had given me the sheet of symbols, a virtual codex of their language, the day before, because that would at least help me translate Alistair's journals.

The highlight of the day had really been my time with Lalee and Pikuu. They were waiting for me as I left Alalli's hut. *Have they waited there all day,* I wondered, *listening to the priestess' rantings and smelling the wafts of smoke as they billowed from the curtained entrance?*

Lalee rambled on about something in her language. I did not understand a word, but her flamboyant gestures and hilarious expressions kept me laughing. Pikuu chimed in with his own commentary,

<del>20</del>

barking at times as she carried on with her story. I pondered what this beautiful soul would grow up to be. *Will she stay in her small village, or venture far beyond?*

We soon reached the clearing and she bid me adieu. I waved until I could not see her anymore, my heart full.

LUCAS

"What did Ying teach you about eye contact? You can do better than this," I encouraged her.

Her eyes narrowed and her shoulders set. *Now we're talking,* I thought. I clapped my hands, signaling her to advance.

Her eyes stayed focused on mine. I felt the intensity of her stare; it was almost intimidating. She moved forward three steps, filling the gap between us, and then without hesitation she lifted her left leg to kick my right side. I blocked her. She quickly rebounded and countered with a right hook. Once again, I blocked it. I saw her frustration build. She moved fast, though—faster than I thought she could.

She spun backwards then darted to my right where she kicked me with a reversed strike. Her foot hit me just below the knee. My leg immediately buckled. She didn't wait for me to recover. Instead she spun back around and followed up with an elbow to the ribs and then a knee to my gut. All in a matter of seconds. Then she graciously gave me a moment to regroup.

"That was… good," I said as I straightened my pummeled body, my voice a little shaky as I spoke, and I realized that was way too good for an unconsummated Conduit—an Unconsu. It was one thing to see her move with extraordinary speed when she was fencing with Ying, and another thing entirely, actually underestimating her speed and feeling the impact on my own body. I had seen how Ying, a master of warfare, had been surprised by her ability. I understood now. She was exceptional. And she didn't even know it.

She heard the strangeness in my tone and began hounding me for answers, asking, "What? What did I do?"

I considered telling her the truth—that her proficiency worried me —but that would just worry *her*. I decided not to say anything.

"Nothing. You just got me," I said as I threw my hands up in defeat.

ELIAS

I lay in bed sleepless, considering my day in the village. When I had decided to carry out the quest to find a summit location, I could have never expected it would lead me to the remote corners of the world, investigating aboriginal languages, smoke and circles. I had been so close to answers before Alistair's murder. I knew those answers were hidden in his journals, and deep in my soul I knew that however roundabout this may seem, this was the way to get them. Someone out there knew I would be looking for this information; they had paved my way. If I was going to trust that voice in my soul, then I would have to own this experience and trust that whatever comes out of my time in these villages was part of the process. Whatever ritual or discussion of shapes—I would trust that this was part of the way that had been paved for me.

When I closed my eyes I saw the priestess spreading more of the dried grass onto the fire. I could almost smell the smoke, taste it even.

Then it occurred to me—I had seen that grass before. But I had mistakenly believed it was a herb. I shot out of bed and bent down to retrieve my small lockbox from between the mattress and box spring. I engaged the lock and the lid popped open. Inside were the items I had stowed away the night Alistair had been murdered and his apartment set on fire.

I felt the three leather sacks—I could easily distinguish between the contents of each. I had held these items more times than I could remember. One sack held three large crystals, a second contained a black sand, and the third enclosed what I had assumed was a herb—but as I pulled it open, the texture and consistency confirmed that it was the dried grass from Moto Nui.

I fastened the small sack with the contents in it and rolled it between my fingers, feeling and hearing the grass crumble.

What did this connection mean? I decided I would bring the items to Alalli's attention the next day.

I felt hope—true hope—swell-up in my chest. Perhaps I was closer to answers than I thought.

LUCAS

I heard a rap on my door. "Come in," I responded, a bit annoyed. It was too early for Olly to be up, so I knew it had to be Viraclay. Elias' nickname, "miracle," meant something of reverence to most Conduits. It was a bit much for my taste—if anything, his unusual conception just proved how incredible his parents were. Sorcey and Cane had performed the miracle of creating him when no one believed it was possible, and now we were all left with the oh-so-noble Viraclay.

He slowly opened the door and stepped into the large room. This whole place was huge. I wondered if that was on purpose or purely coincidental. *Was Viraclay flashing his wallet?* If so, it was unnecessary —Olly didn't care about those things.

"What is it?" I asked. He hadn't asked for help or advice since we fled Hafiza. Although he hadn't said anything yet, I was pretty sure we were on Easter Island for more than just evasion. He was researching something or someone, and my gut said it was about this special summit of his.

"I need your assistance?" he said, more of a question than a statement. My ears perked up and I turned to face him instead of the window where I'd been watching a chimango caracara, a local bird of prey.

"Really? What's so trivial that you need *my* help?" I said curtly.

He ignored my tone; he was a pillar of self-control—irritatingly so. It took a lot to get under his skin, or at least for him to show it. I on the other hand, well, I was a hot head and I didn't try to hide it.

"I am expecting a delivery of various IDs and passports today at the local post office in Hanga Roa, but I have a conflicting appointment. Would you consider picking up the package for me? It arrives in an hour. Ophelia will most likely still be sleeping."

I had nothing else going on. I looked back out the window where the bird was and realized it had moved onto better things; I couldn't see it anymore.

"Sure. What name is the package under?" I stood and walked to the dresser to grab a shirt.

"The last name is Willace. They should not require identification." Elias turned to leave and paused at the door. "Thank you," he said, then softly shut the door as I went to brush my teeth. Maybe while in town I'd take the time to grab a local snack for Olly to try when she woke up. If I remembered correctly, banana po'e could pass for a decent breakfast. As I mulled it over, I heard the front door shut and I assumed Elias was off on his mysterious errand. Fine by me.

I knew Olly would be thrilled to try local cuisine, especially because she'd been cooped up for the past few days. I was getting more excited as I finished combing my hair into place. I spritzed on some cologne so I'd smell good when I got back, then headed out the door myself. It was a crisp morning—not cold, just fresh. I could've used the other rental car that Elias supplied for us, but a run sounded better. I needed to burn off a little of my eagerness anyway.

I ran at my usual clip—arriving at the city center fifteen minutes later. The drive would've taken longer. I decided I could take a few minutes to get my bearings and figure out which restaurant looked like it served the freshest food.

After a few short laps around the town I decided on a quaint place that boasted authentic local dishes—the smell wafting from the kitchen had my mouth watering. I meandered into a tourist shop while I waited for 9 a.m.—opening time at the post office—to roll around. I picked up a silly miniature figure of one the famous Easter Island statues and decided I would buy it for Olly, too, since I wasn't sure if she would get to see the actual monuments on this trip. We had the time for sightseeing; I was just being hyper vigilant after what happened at Hafiza.

The thought no sooner crossed my mind that I heard a familiar voice. It had been years since I heard her speak, but I knew it was her. My body immediately stiffened. I felt the hair on the back of my neck stand on end.

It was Nandi. Shit! We hadn't seen anything indicating she was still tracking us since she'd attempted to abduct Olly from Hafiza. *How has she found us?* I wondered. Then I realized: I needed to get to Ophelia and conceal her—now!

I turned and saw the back of a woman's head. That was her; she was right behind me. *Does she know I'm here? Is she baiting me to run back to the house and expose our location?* At this point I didn't care. I just needed to get out of there.

I replaced the shitty gift back to its resting place on the shelf, and took a deep breath, tuning in to hear what the conversation between Nandi and the cashier was about. It sounded innocent enough. Nandi was asking how long he had lived on the island. Small talk. I solidified my camouflage tight around my body, hoping it would shield me from her immediate detection. Then I ran, faster than I had ever run before.

ELIAS

I was pleased that Lucas had easily agreed to procure the additional IDs I had arranged for us two months ago; they were important to our ongoing mobility. I had sent the package on a wild goose chase in the attempts to throw off any would-be assassins. From Hafiza, I had sent it to Turkey, then Germany, Canada, Taiwan, Australia, and seven different states in the U.S. before its eventual arrival here on Easter Island.

I knew we would end up here in due course after Emerson gave me the list of tribes Alistair had visited around the world. It had already become clear to me that we could not stay in the confines of Hafiza for long. Ophelia had expressed too many extraordinary qualities. The other Conduits of the castle were growing uneasy and I was not certain I could maintain our secrecy from the outside world; and the fewer people knew about her gifts, the better. Furthermore, I had grown increasingly aware that it was likely we had a traitor in our coterie.

Of course, I had not expected we would be ambushed in a castle siege where I likely lost many dear friends and almost got Ophelia killed. That was a shock.

I took a deep breath and let it out slowly—I could never share these pains with Ophelia, or Lucas for that matter, but that last night in Hafiza ailed me, in many ways—I would even say it broke me. I took another deep cleansing breath. There would be time to grieve. I did not know when, but there would be a time to let this all go. There had to be.

I forced my train of thought to circle back to the task at hand as I walked from where I had stowed the car. It was day three of my convening with the priestess Alalli. Today she would give me answers. I let myself smile at that, to feel joy with that. I was not certain what answers she had to give, but she knew I was coming and I suspected she did have pertinent information that could help me determine the summit location that Alistair had been working on. The codex alone confirmed that many of the markings in his journals came from the Rapa Nui language; if nothing else, I had already gotten what I came for.

I stepped around and then through some thick jungle vines that had fallen from the canopy to the floor. A few steps further down, the trees thinned and the tropical vegetation opened up to reveal the east edge of the village.

I picked up my pace, excitement bubbling up in my chest. I was also eager to see my adorable escort again this morning. Sure enough, Lalee had been waiting; she waved when she saw my head pop up from out of the foliage and into view.

I began to lift my hand and wave back when something in the corner of my eye caught my attention. It was moving quickly and quietly in the brush. I turned to face the commotion and the air arrested in my lungs. It was a manticore—it was Vivienne.

Her huge body—that of an Amazonian-size lioness—stood poised to leap, her paws the size of basketballs and her violent scorpion's tail whipping enthusiastically behind her furry torso. Fringed in an auburn mane, as lush as any male lion's, were the fierce eyes of a lethal mercenary and the wicked razor-sharp smile of my huntress.

I looked back at Lalee standing so innocently, so eagerly waiting for me, and prayed that by the strokes of Chitchakor she might be spared, then I ran. I ran as fast as my legs would carry me, knowing that it would take a miracle to outrun Vivienne.

I heard her pouncing behind me, a soft chuffing laugh escaping her mouth. She loved to play with her prey—I knew this folly and arrogance would be the only chance I had to get away.

I pushed even harder. I had to warn Ophelia; I had to save her.

I dodged and wove through the jungle terrain.

I could just see the roof of the car when I felt a ripping of my flesh, as her talons tore through my back and scraped my scapula, swiftly followed by the distinct pain of bone fracturing in my shoulder. I dared not cry out, however, knowing this was part of her game.

I grabbed the Dirk of Inverness from my calf where I kept it sheathed, and invoked the invisibility charm—thus cloaking it in magic. My mother had bequeathed the dirk to me shortly before her murder. It was an ancient and powerful weapon called a Rittle, and it could temporarily paralyze an individual with a single nick of the blade. Most living Conduits believed weapons such as this had been long since destroyed.

When I turned around to strike, she was not there. In the manticore's place, high above my head, flew a massive eagle—a thunderbird. Vivienne had changed forms.

"Oh, piss!" I yelled as I dove down, below the thicker vines. I began army crawling. She could hear me and mostly see me, but in this form she would need to land on top of me and then pull herself out of the lower hanging trees without disturbing her massive wingspan. I was feet away from my car, but once in the open I would be easy pickings for her. *Will she wait me out or transform again?* I wondered, and no sooner did the thought cross my mind than I heard her soft voice and the footfalls of a human.

"Viraclay," she hissed. "Crawling on your knees is so unbecoming."

I immediately stood and faced her, the dirk still invisible in my right hand.

"Vivienne, I rather enjoy crawling when I find it necessary."

"We have never formally met, but apparently my reputation precedes me." She smiled. She was naked. Her form was that of a beautifully curvaceous woman with long wavy auburn hair that surrounded her face and fell just above her pink nipples.

"I could say the same for me," I suggested.

"An assassin must know her target; I would hardly call yours a reputation." She was slowly filling the space between us as I was deliberately trying to make my way to the vehicle.

"No matter, I was never one for celebrity," I said casually. "Are you here to kill me or capture me?"

"Either."

"Then I suppose we must be getting on with it," I said flippantly, hoping it irritated her. I saw something flash across her face for an instant, and then it was gone. A moment later her eyes started to morph, melding into a lime green—but I had no time to see what she would become this time.

I turned to run and heard her step forward, so I swirled around brandishing the dirk, and smoothly sliced her across her transmuting chest.

I knew from experience it would take a few moments for the dirk's power to take effect and paralyze her. She was still not aware that I had injured her in the slightest as she continued to mutate and claw for my body. I finally slipped out of her grasp, but not unscathed. Once more, I felt her claws rip into my flesh. Then the assault stopped and I maneuvered my way into the car's driver's seat. Vivienne's horrific figure stood frozen in the clearing, rendered as one-half human, and the other half a chilling scaled creature with long curved claws. I shuddered to think what she had intended to transmute into.

I hit the gas in reverse and thanked Malarin, the great creator, for his strokes.

LUCAS

I made it back to the house in seven minutes. Before entering, I took a moment to calm my demeanor so I wouldn't frighten Olly when I asked her to get ready to leave. I didn't know where the fuck Elias was, but I wasn't going to wait for him. He could track us down later—somehow. I smiled at the thought. Maybe this was perfect. Viraclay couldn't find us unless I wanted him to.

I entered the house as collected as I could. "Olly!" No answer. "Olly?" I repeated, feeling panic rise in my chest. *Was I too late?* "Olly!?" I yelled it this time.

"What?" she asked sluggishly as she trudged down the hall, rubbing her eyes, wearing that adorably sexy nightshirt. Her tangled, strawberry-colored hair bounced on top of her head in a messy bun. *Damn, she's beautiful*, I thought, *but not now, Lucas.*

I stopped and grabbed her shoulders. "I need you to focus." I said it to myself as much as to her.

She looked up at me blearily.

"Go pack your things, Olly. Don't ask questions. Don't shower or brush your teeth, just grab what you need and get dressed. Meet me out here in the foyer in five minutes. We are leaving."

Suddenly her face was filled with alarm.

"Now," I said decisively.

She turned to comply—ran back down the hall to her room. I went to my own room and grabbed my bag, stuffing it with another set of clothes, some paperwork and what cash I had. The rest could be replaced.

I paced in the foyer until she met me with her things.

"What about Elias?" She looked concerned.

"He'll meet us later." I tried to sound as sincere as I could, knowing there was a huge possibility that we wouldn't see him again, then added, "Trust me."

She nodded and I grabbed her arm and the keys to the SUV Elias had rented. I knew exactly what to do.

We got out the front door and I saw the tan sedan Elias had taken on his errand flying down the gravel road. *Shit!* I thought. He skidded to a stop in front of us.

"Get in!" he ordered. He was collected, but there was serious alarm in his eyes. I hoped only I detected it. *Had he seen Nandi too?*

Olly and I simultaneously got into the back seat. I wasn't letting her out of arm's reach.

Elias put his foot on the gas and we sped off back the way he came.

"Vivienne is here," he said coolly. His eyes met mine in the review mirror and I now understood the alarm.

"Head east," I said. "Find a dense part of the jungle and park the car. I can get us off the island." Viraclay looked at me curiously but didn't hesitate.

ESTHER

I looked around the cluster of shanty dwellings. What a pathetic existence. Vivienne had cordoned off the villagers, backed them up to a pocket between two houses.

"Is that everyone?" I looked at her sternly. What a disappointment —she let Viraclay get away. "Are you certain?"

She nodded, afraid to speak. *As she should be,* I thought. *She is a failure.* I would deal with her later. Yanni stood next to me, by the entrance to the largest building in the center of the settlement.

"She is in there, my beloved. The crone wouldn't speak to me. Perhaps you will have more luck." He kissed my right temple.

I looked at my Atoa, my partner, my Yanni. He was so brilliant, ferocious and handsome. I admired his strong cheekbones, the way they strengthened the rest of his features: deep, dark—nearly black— irises that stood out brilliantly against his rich, olive skin; thin lips that parted into a wide wicked smile; and his sharp nose—*like his tongue,* I thought. His hair sat on his head in a curly chaotic crop. I loved running my fingers through it. I reached up and played with a kinky tendril.

"We will see what I can do," I said, smiling at him.

"What shall we do with them?" He pointed at the huddled mob of villagers. Some of them were crying and wining. A young girl stood with her dog, apart from the rest, staring at me intently. Her look was almost a challenge. *That girl has spirit,* I thought. *She probably would have done something with her worthless human life.*

I walked closer, my curiosity piqued by the odd aura about the youngling. She didn't break her gaze; in fact, quite the contrary—she squared her shoulders as I approached. I laughed aloud.

"Look at this one." I pointed at her. I noticed she had cuts and bruises on her arms and legs.

"She is a fighter," Vivienne added.

I laughed again. When I was a few feet from the girl, her dog began to growl and snap his bared teeth at me. They were a pair of fighters.

I squatted to be at the girl's level. "What is your name, child?" I purred. She looked at me hard and didn't answer. I stood and turned to deal with the priestess, while giving Vivienne orders over my shoulder. "Kill them. All of them."

I made eye contact with the child once more, then added, "Save this one and her dog for last, so they can watch."

Then I disappeared into the hut, and Yanni followed. The crone was in the center of her chamber, praying.

"Where are they, old woman?" Yanni hissed at her.

I looked around—it was a worthless hovel. A disgusting corner of this earth occupied by filthy peasants. I shook my head in disgust. I put my hand on Yanni's shoulder, informing him that I would be proceeding with the questioning. The old woman peered at me through her disheveled hair and out her knowing eyes.

"What is your name, woman?" I attempted my most sincere sentiment in the question. I could tell she was not fooled. *Fine by me,* I thought, *I can save the performance for a more malleable audience.* She said nothing. I stepped closer to her—and she stepped back.

"What is your name?" I demanded.

"I do not share my name with demons," she spat.

"I see." I closed my eyes for a long moment, pretending to think.

"You think me a demon?" I circled her as I spoke. When I came back around to where she could see me, I gestured to my body. I was draped in a long crimson silk dress, which I considered very flattering. My black hair brushed the backs of my calves—I adored the sensation as I walked. "This looks like the vessel of a demon?"

I stopped and stood in front of her, so she could take in the entire sight of me. "Those are not kind words," I said with a mocking pout. I turned to Yanni, who was shirtless by my side. "Yanni, my love, this dear woman thinks we are demons." I walked to stand behind him now, purring in his ear. "Why would she think we are such a thing? What have we done to deserve such accusations?" I shook my head as if in dramatic disbelief.

"Esther, little people cannot be blamed for their ignorance in the presence of gods," my love opined, his voice equally as depraved as his smile when he spoke.

"You are right, darling," I sighed. "Demons are messy..." I stepped out from behind Yanni and again stared down the crone as I continued. "...Irrational... " I stepped toward her slowly. "...Facetious..." I maneuvered myself behind the old woman and placed my hands on her shoulders. "...Creatures." I pushed her toward the entrance of the hut as Yanni moved aside, allowing us to pass by then he followed. "Demons... " I continued. "...Do not have the resolve or skill to slaughter an entire village in a matter of moments without its inhabitants making a single sound." I whispered the last word in her ear just as we stepped into the crisp air outside the hut.

I felt her knees buckle and I lifted her with my hands still braced on either side of her shoulders. She began to weep openly as she looked upon the faces of every man, woman and child in her village. All thirty-four of them were beautifully strung up, upside down so that the blood from their precisely cut throats could drip together into a medley of dirt, rocks and sticky fresh blood along the village road. I nodded at Vivienne in approval—I thought, *she may find herself in my good graces once more. How swiftly and efficiently she works when needed.*

The old woman tried to fall to her knees again, and this time I let her. "Demons are not that clever," I concluded. "Now, let me ask you again—and this time I expect an answer or your fate will be worse than death." I kneeled down and brushed the nasty matted hair from her round brown face. "Where is Elias Kraus?"

OPHELIA

$\mathcal{W}$e had parked the car along the road and were hastily making our way to the dense jungle in front of us.

"Trolls?" I scoffed. "As in the big angry barbarians that live under bridges and demand payment?"

"Yes. Fucking trolls," Lucas replied without a hint of sarcasm. "Trolls are portals that can shuttle you to anywhere in the world—and just like in fairytales, they demand a price for safe passage."

I stood there, my mouth agape. I looked to Elias, expecting to see a nod of assurance. But his face was ghostly white and he seemed just as skeptical.

"Lucas, I have never heard of these trolls you speak of, not from my parents, nor from any other Conduit I consort with." Elias shook his head in disbelief.

"Of course you wouldn't have. Most Conduits stopped using their services after the last open battle three hundred years ago. Some Pai Ona felt that the trolls were favoring the Nebas, and rumors spread." Lucas waved his hand in the air nonchalantly. "You know how that goes, and business has declined for the trolls."

Elias stepped in front of Lucas. "If that is indeed the case, then why on earth would we utilize their services?" Elias' voice was slightly elevated.

Lucas moved around him. "Because I know a *guy* and we're in a bind."

The two of them were moving faster than usual—I understood the urgency, and I was doing my best to keep up, but I was struggling.

Elias stopped and crossed his arms. I was grateful for the opportunity to catch up. "What do you mean you *know a guy*?" he demanded. "Enlighten me before we proceed."

Lucas paused and waited a moment before he turned around, probably trying to regain his composure. He didn't like being questioned—especially not by Elias.

"We don't have time for this!" Lucas growled, then decided it was useless to argue with Elias and relented. "Six hundred years ago, when troll channels were still widely in use, Yessica and I stumbled upon a troll being mugged by a powrie. Yessica hurtled herself between the two beasts before I had a chance to figure out a plan, or better yet, convince her to stay out of it."

He turned to me to explain the next part. "Yessica was a receiver of light—she was called a Lantern. She could absorb it and essentially blind you with massive amounts of luminosity... light simply radiated off her skin." He seemed to say the last bit to himself. "She was my sun, my Atoa."

He quickly shook off the reverie and continued. "Trolls don't care for light—and powries really hate it, so the powrie ran off and the injured troll lay there, bleeding to death. Yessica demanded we escort the troll to Sorcey and Cane's home in New Zealand to be healed by his mother." He gestured to Elias.

Elias always winced when his parents were mentioned. It made my heart hurt for him. He had lost them so violently, so suddenly. Everyone who ever spoke of them did so with massive respect and reverence.

I wanted to change the subject, to ease his pain. "What's a powrie?" I asked.

"They're headhunters, assassins," Lucas answered. "Hired by all sorts of assholes who can't do the job themselves. Yessica and I had interrupted an assassination attempt on the troll. But Sorcey worked her magic and the troll was as good as new. Ever since, she's been eager to help me whenever she can." Lucas started walking again. "Her name is Fetzle, and she would never double-cross me."

Elias assaulted Lucas with questions. "When was the last time you spoke to Fetzle? What kind of magic does she use? How do you know it will not set off any alarms with Yanni?"

"Look, Viraclay, the way I see it, we don't have much of a choice here. We are currently being hunted by Vivienne and Nandi, the jet we chartered to get here is gone, and Olly can't travel as fast as we can on foot." He gave Elias a once-over, like he was sizing him up, not sure he could run fast enough either. Then he continued. "I last saw Fetzle two years ago, just before I travelled up to San Francisco to help you out with Olly. She clearly didn't trigger anything then, because it was an entire year and a half before we were detected." Lucas spun around sharply. "And I don't know what kind of magic she uses—it's troll magic, and these portals crisscross all over the world, and have done so since the beginning of time. So I doubt the magic will set off any alarms. Satisfied?" He threw up his arms and continued moving.

Elias didn't say anything for a while, and I didn't know what to say so I kept my mouth shut.

"Very well. How do we arrange passage?" Elias sounded slightly defeated.

"We're almost there." Lucas pulled a coin out of his pocket and began flipping it in the air. "This medallion is like a transit pass. I can call on Fetzle whenever I like, with the right conditions."

"What might those be?" I asked.

"Exposed tree roots." He pointed at the horizon of trees just ahead. "We should find something in there, don't you think?"

I nodded and quickened my pace to try and meet Lucas'. Elias had positioned himself just behind me. I was sure it wasn't because he couldn't keep up with Lucas, but more likely to make sure no one came up from behind. The edge of the jungle fast approached and my heartbeat quickened. It was clear Lucas thought we were in good hands, but all the stories I'd heard about trolls as a child were scary. *And what on earth is portal travel going to be like?* Not to mention I could feel the uncertainty radiating off Elias like heat off a wood stove in December.

We got to the wall of trees and Lucas navigated us about ten feet into the jungle. He knelt down and brushed away some leaves, exposing several large roots. He placed the coin on the flattest root surface he could find and started reciting three words in Asagi. The roots began to tremble and bulge. The tree shook violently, and Elias grabbed my arm, pulling me back from the convulsing arbor. Lucas continued to recite the three words while concentrating with his eyes closed.

The tree was shaking so wildly now that the ground was vibrating. Then it suddenly stopped and a loud, high-pitched voice trilled from inside the belly of the trunk, though I couldn't make out what it said. Lucas jumped back and positioned himself in front of me, so that I was flanked by both men. I felt anxious. *Is something wrong?*

The trunk shook again with shrill laughter, and a huge figure manifested in the tree's shadow. The figure stepped into the light and continued to grow.

The thing was enormous both in girth and in height. Its individual legs were each the size of the tree trunk it had just materialized from. Its skin was clear white, almost translucent, but it looked like she had been rolling around in the mud, because there was dirt all over her body. I wouldn't have known it was a female if Lucas hadn't told us in advance. She had no hair and no genitals, and her torso was slim and muscular. My gaze followed her form all the way up to her face. Her eyes were huge—more than half her head was consumed by her eyeballs. I caught her stare and saw her pupils were a teal blue, piercing and inquiring. Her giant right arm, which to that point had been dragging on the ground, slowly drew up and pointed a titanic finger at me. I noted she only had one finger and what looked like a thumb.

Then her petite voice chirped something, and Lucas responded with a laugh.

I nudged him. "What did she say?" He laughed louder.

Fetzle leaned down and got one of her eyes really close to my face, examining me. "Saydwhothisshe? Thissmelldingfunny?" It all came out as one weird word. She took a deep inhale through her mouth. She was close enough for me to notice she didn't have a nose or nostrils. *Is she smelling me through her mouth?* I heard Elias chuckle behind me.

"Did she just say I smell funny?" I nudged Lucas again.

Fetzle's face got closer to mine, and she took another whiff. Her giant finger pushed me aside and she peered into Elias' face.

"Whatsyou?" Again, she inhaled, getting a solid whiff of Elias without my stench in the way.

"Hello, Fetzle. My name is Elias Kraus. I understand you met my parents, Cane and Sorc..."

Before he could get the last syllable out, she had him on her shoulder, twirling in circles and jumping up and down, yelling something neither English nor Asagi. Elias looked like he might get sick.

Lucas interceded. "Fetzle," he started. She paused. "You might want to be gentle with him. He is Unconsu." She immediately stopped parading about—but didn't put Elias down.

"ApologeezSorcayCanechildren." She patted Elias' head with her thumb. He looked uncomfortable. A giggle escaped my mouth. Then, all of us erupted with laughter. After a moment the chorus died down. "FetzlemelovingmySorceyCane." She shrugged her shoulders. Elias leaned in and she took another big whiff of his scent. "YousmellingSorcey."

"Thank you, Fetzle. Would it be too much to ask—that I might be returned to the ground? I am getting rather ill up here with all of the commotion." Even in this shaded wooded area, I could tell that Elias looked a little green. A flash of disappointment swept across the troll's face, but she conceded and put Elias down.

"Thank you." Elias nodded as his feet stabilized onto solid ground. Fetzle smiled and her lips rolled up, exposing four rows of needle-like teeth, which had been previously hidden in her mouth. Chills ran down my spine. I didn't know what she used those teeth for, but I was sure it wasn't for a vegetarian diet. No one needed choppers like that for a fresh salad.

"Fetzle, we need your help." Lucas wasted no more time getting to the point of this little reunion. "We need to get far from here, and quickly. What are the portals like today? Can we travel safely?"

Fetzle looked past him and set her gaze on me again. "Whosethisshe?" she repeated.

"Sorry, my name is Ophelia Banner. I'm friends with Elias and Lucas." Fetzle looked at the two men wearily and then back at me.

"Frendzbethis?Smeldingfunnylikes-soursandsweets-notsso-goodthisbe." She transitioned into addressing Lucas in Asagi. Elias looked alarmed and pulled me closer.

I whispered, "What is she saying? Did I offend her? Do I really smell that bad?" I lifted up my arm and tried to find out for myself.

"No, you do not smell funny, you smell amazing," he quietly gushed. "She is explaining that trolls read auras, and your aura is questionable to her."

"I think that's even more offensive," I said.

Elias stepped forward positioning me behind him. He was attempting to safeguard me in case something went awry. He interjected himself into the discussion Lucas and Fetzle were having. Whatever Elias said seemed to defuse the situation. Fetzle took one more enormous breath, closing her eyes as she inhaled.

"AwesnowsIseesits-thismaybesnotsobads." She leaned in. "Hellos-OpheliasBannersthsisFetzle."

I smiled my huge nervous smile and tried to remember to breathe.

"Notssogoodsdaytotravel-manytravelers-manyslimeybeingstoday," she said with a sigh. "Yousandthiscouldsstayinmeshuttletodays-then-travelswhenclean."

Elias looked at Lucas despairingly. It was obvious he wasn't sure if that was a good idea. But they also couldn't have a conversation about that in front of Fetzle, afraid they would offend her. They were trying to communicate with their eyes. Truth be told, I had no clue if this was a good or bad idea. The only one of us who had even the slightest clue as to what to expect was Lucas. I, for one, trusted him. Elias apparently didn't. After a long stare-down, Lucas won.

"Fetzle, we would be honored to stay in your shuttle," he said with a smile.

ELIAS

How in the world have I allowed Lucas to coerce me into this? I
wondered. Though I had not had much choice, had I?

Portal travel seemed painless enough. My face was still tingling,
and my toes felt warm, but as far as I could tell there were no long-
term discomforts or deformations. I held onto Ophelia's hand with a
firm grip. It was completely absent of light down here in Fetzle's shuttle, as she called it. It smelled moldy and stagnant. Lucas steered us in
the dark, presumably led by the troll's hand, or at least that was how
we had entered the portal. I heard the footsteps ahead stop, then
Ophelia hurtled forward and nearly fell.

"Lucas," I whispered. "Will we be kept down here in the dark?"

"Why, Elias, are you afraid?" he sneered just as a very dim light
appeared above our heads. It was, for lack of a better word, oozing
from the ceiling. A second light appeared, then a third and a fourth
until the entire ceiling looked like a sky full of gelatinous stars.

"WelcomestoFetzlesshuttle," Fetzle said as she gestured her hands
above her head and twirled in a circle. It was still very difficult to see
where we were or what the contents of the shuttle truly entailed. I
could see that it was a huge cavern, with shadows strewn along the
walls.

The jelly-like stars continued to multiply, and slowly but surely the room took shape. It was most certainly a cave, an enormous one at that. Huge stalactites dripped from the ceiling. In the center of the floor was a hole with some dim embers smoldering inside it. Shelves lined the furthest wall, with rows and rows of an assortment of objects—some identifiable and some unknown. I looked up once more at the odd lighting. As I did so, one of the long oozing illuminated strings recoiled.

"Fetzle, what is the... substance above our heads?" I tried to phrase it as politely as possible. Ophelia looked up, then stumbled backwards in alarm when she realized there was something amiss about the way it hung.

"Fetzlesfriendstheybe," our hostess said as she reached up and touched one with her large finger. It responded by wrapping itself around her digit. "Wormsglowingworms."

"Worms!?" Ophelia gasped, although she may not have meant to even say it aloud.

Fetzle swiveled her huge head around to peer at Ophelia. "Fetzlesaysworms," she said firmly. Then she began mumbling something to herself. The mumbling got louder and louder as she continued.

"I'swillstakesmagicsIthink."She nodded enthusiastically."Fetzleswilltakemagics."

OPHELIA

"*I*'swilltakeamagic," Fetzle asserted again.

Lucas leaned into me and whispered, "Trolls take magic currency as their tolls—anywhere from a totem, spell or a deposit of magic from each traveler. Fortunately for us, Fetzle still feels like she owes me for saving her life, so we don't have to pay a toll."

He paused while Fetzle trudged past us looking for the stash of magic she'd collected from others. "The interesting thing is that they can temporarily manifest the magic of others."

"Looksheresitbe!" Fetzle giggled with enthusiasm. She had a bell of a laugh that tickled your ears and sounded like it should be coming from the body of a five-year-old, not an enormous she-troll. We all watched as she joyously traipsed over to us, plopped down and gently unzipped a backpack that was probably of normal size but looked tiny in her hands. "LookswhatFetzlegets." She held the contents of the pouch out for us to see. It just looked like a bunch of small crumpled pieces of paper to me—but I nodded excitedly to show her I was impressed. I looked at Elias and he shrugged his shoulders, confirming that he, too, had no idea what the fuss was about.

I watched as she gingerly took one of the pieces of paper and dropped it into her enormous, menacing-looking mouth. She smiled a big toothy smile and, as if a switch had been turned on, when she spoke, her speech sounded normal.

She pointed to the ceiling. "Those are glow worms, Fetzle's friends," she said, giggling again. "Yay! Fetzle is just like all of you!"

"What kind of magic is that, Fetzle?" Elias inquired, pointing at the bag.

"Oh, I don't knows. It is very old." She put her thumb on her chin to gesture she was thinking. "Fetzle thinks it was from before the falls of Listy."

"What is Listy?" I wondered out loud.

Fetzle slapped her knee and the cavern shook. "You do not knows about Listy?" She shook her head in disappointment.

Lucas spoke up. "Fetzle, Olly is still very new to this world and all of the different creatures that inhabit it."

The troll just shook her head again. "Come sit by the fire. Let Fetzle tell you about the greatest trolls' city, Ophelia. Fetzle will talk abouts Listy and some other important things."

Lucas and Elias looked at each other skeptically but they weren't going to protest our hostess' request. I followed them over to a huge bench seat that was positioned beside the large fire pit. The seat comfortably fit the three of us. It squeaked as we adjusted ourselves, and it occurred to me that this particular bench seat probably originated from the cab of a truck.

Fetzle hadn't sat down yet. She was gathering more wood under one arm and rummaging through a pile of what I would assess as junk with the other.

"This be Fetzle's sinkhole treasures," she said. "Things sink and Fetzle collects them up. I's looking for my story chair," she shouted over her shoulder. "I have not had companys in many more years. Fetzle can't remember where I puts it. There is only one chair good for stories." As her search progressed, she found the large logs under her arm cumbersome and decided to scuffle over and dispatch them onto the burning embers. The wood ignited immediately, sending thousands of brilliant sparks into the air. I held my breath as I admired the beauty of the drifting illuminated particles above us. It was majestic with the glowworm backdrop.

Fetzle squealed and I jumped. "I found it!" she called out excitedly.

She came hulking over to the fire pit, dragging a pickup truck behind her. The tires were flat but she maneuvered the vehicle easily until she got it in just the right spot next to us. At which point she plopped down into the bed of the truck, filling the entirety of the space easily with her large frame. The metal creaked under her weight, but it didn't buckle.

"It was right there. Right where Fetzle lefts it." She was so pleased. I smiled back at her. "Is everyone comfortables?" Fetzle asked.

"Yes," we all stated in unison. I smiled a little to myself. For once, we all were on the same page. Imagine that.

"Let's begin, then. Once upon a time..." The troll paused, then giggled. "Fetzle is just kidding. It was not once upon a time—it was twenty-one hundred years ago! Fetzle was a young girl. Fetzle's father Spitzle and my mother Tazzle were peacefully watchings over the troll kingdom, and had been for over two thousand years. Trolls were happy, many peoples paid our tolls, the nasty powries were not attacking our shuttles. It was a good time to be a troll: lots of trades, safe kingdom, and we were friends with the Conduits. Fetzle lived in Listy, the only tunnel center in the world. It was a wonderful place to trades magics. Yous would call it a city."

"Where was Listy?" I interrupted.

"In the Atlantic Ocean. Humans call it the Bermuda Triangle. Silly humans; we named it Listy first." She scoffed. My eyes got big— I wanted to follow that rabbit trail, but decided that might be rude. Plus, I was actually more intrigued with the direction Fetzle was going with her story. "Fetzle thinks Listy was the most beautifuls city in all the world. Shuttles all over. Fetzle remembers lots of trade markets full of treasures. More treasures than any troll's hearts could desire. Fetzle was happiest then, except for Pladzal." She almost growled his name. "Pladzal had beens courting Fetzle for years." She spat at the ground. "He was gross. Fetzle's father liked his ideas, but Fetzle's mother knows better. She sees his grossness and in troll families mothers do choices for your marriage. Fetzle's mom could smells Pladzal's stinky auras. She says, 'No troll queens should marry a desperate troll man,' is what she says. Fetzle was fine with her judgments because I thoughts Pladzal was ugly and talked funnys.

"So Fetzle stayed looking for her partner and peace still stayed in Listy. Then four hundred years ago Fetzle and hers mother Tazzle were shuttling to islands and a powrie attacks! The firsts attacks for mores than two thousand years." She put her hand up. "Don'ts worry, we made it.

"But all things changed. Trolls had to go back to guardings big shuttles. Fetzle's mother sadly decides to order all young female trolls to reports to a faction officer."

I interrupted again. "Just the females? Why not the males?"

"Young female trolls are strongest; more than wimpy mens! We are fastest, larger and smarter." She giggled. "Males are short and fat, their legs are stubby and they don'ts have the big strength." I nodded that I understood and she could continue. "So, Fetzle was sents away to a faction close to Rome. It was boring—all days and nights we did nothings but watch. Theres be no shuttles, no magics, just watch for powries. For one hundred years we watch, and then they attack! Hundreds of them, more than any troll can counts—through every portal. All of Fetzle's faction dies, only I survives. Fetzle transports back to Listy, to make sure my family was survived too. But they were not okay. Listy had tumbled into a portals vortex—a hole of magic— no tunnels, no trade, no trolls; just a giant swirling vortex. Fetzle founds no survivors." A single giant tear cascaded down the troll's cheek.

I wanted to march over there and hug her, but I had no idea what troll customs were. I thought the polite thing to do was to stay put.

"Everyone's gone but Fetzle and stinky Pladzal and trolls whose thinks Pladzal is smart. But Fetzle knows he's nots smart. Fetzle starts to think maybe Pladzal planned the first powrie attacks on her. To clear the city Listy of strong female trolls." Fetzle threw her fist down, crumpling the metal on the tailgate of her truck chair. "Fetzle gets so mad when I thinks about it. Pladzal says we should get married and Fetzle says no and Fetzle runs and hides."

Fetzle looked down at her hands shamefully. "It's Fetzle's fault the trolls helped the Nebas. If Fetzle was not afraid, if Fetzle wasn't sad about her family's dying, I coulds have stopped the trolls' helping in the opens war three hundred years ago. Now Conduits and trolls are not friends, and no one trades magics or rides shuttles. Fetzle has no friends. Except Lucas—Lucas is Fetzle's friend."

"Yes, I am, Fetzle," Lucas assured her. "And so are Ophelia and Elias."

LUCAS

$\mathcal{I}$ watched Olly closely throughout this conversation. She was so charmingly adaptable. She might be surprised at first, but then she soaks it all in, never missing a beat. A lesser person would be terrified in this situation, but not my Olly. She blew me away.

She'd always been resilient, even back in our San Francisco days, but something had happened to her since the fall of Hafiza. She seemed to have a newfound strength, one that grew by the day. On one hand, it was sexy as hell; on the other hand, I was uneasy navigating through this unchartered territory. There were new rules with this new Ophelia, and I didn't know them yet.

I'm just relieved she isn't falling apart, I thought. But then another part of me spoke up. *Am I* really *happy she isn't falling apart? Wouldn't I be happier if she needed me to console her? To be her rock again?*

I dismissed the thought; I was better than that. I just wanted her to be happy. My Olly deserved happiness. But then the second voice spoke up once more, asking, *Is she really your Olly anymore?*

OPHELIA

a fter a long silence, Fetzle spoke up. "Now thats you know about Fetzle, tell me. How do yous three end up calling me in Easter Island?"

I looked at Lucas, who in turn looked at Elias. "Well, Viraclay," he said, "why don't you start by explaining why we were on the island to begin with?"

Elias didn't hesitate. "It is simple, really. We have been evading Yanni and Esther since they laid siege to our safe house in Europe. I thought I had taken all the appropriate measures whilst covering our tracks when Hafiza fell, but I was wrong."

"What is this Hafizas?" Fetzle interrupted.

"Hafiza was a haven my parents constructed many years ago. She was a good friend," Elias said mournfully. The look on his face made my heart heavy as well.

"A havens?" Fetzle gestured to her surroundings. "Like Fetzle's shuttle? Safes and magical and home?" As she said "home" she seemed to realize how sad she would be if she lost her shuttle, with its magical glowworms and her comfy truck chair. She placed her giant thumb on Elias' head and patted it softly. "Fetzle is sorry yous lost your Hafizas."

We all sat there awkwardly until Fetzle stopped petting Elias and she spoke again. "Hows do these naughty Nebas find yous?"

Lucas answered. "That's a good question. I'm wondering if I shouldn't take over the evasion tactics." It was a statement that got a hard glare from Elias.

"No, thats is silly," Fetzle interjected. "If Elias can'ts hide from them, hows would yous?" She said it so matter-of-factly, I had to hold back a giggle. She shook her head again. "Fetzle thinks more likely that they are using magics, Fetzle thinks."

"What kind of magic, Fetzle? What kind of magic could help them divine our location?" Lucas asked eagerly, ignoring her earlier dismissal.

"Thats be a good question." Fetzle tapped her big finger to the right side of her head. "Fetzle thinks, not divining rods, no. Fetzle thinks not crystals. No. Fetzle thinks perhaps a hairsy charm will help hides yous. Yes! Fetzle thinks a hairsy charm will do the tricks for hiding." Fetzle clapped her hands and bounced up and down with wild satisfaction. "A hairsy charm will stops those nasty divinations."

"What is a hairsy charm?" I asked.

Fetzle stopped doing her happy dance immediately and looked at me as though I was deaf and dumb. "Fetzle tells yous about the hairsy charms, yes she does." She got up purposefully and walked down a corridor of shelves. I heard jars moving and metal clanging together.

Fetzle came back smiling a wicked smile. As she walked toward the fire, she quickly swiped a hair from Lucas' head. He gave a surprised yelp. "What the hell, Fetzle?"

"Fetzle must show somehow, Lucas. Of course, I show with yous." Lucas rubbed at his scalp and scowled at her behind her back. She leaned down in front of me—between her two huge fingers in her right hand was Lucas' hair, and in her other two fingers was a small braided necklace. She handed me both.

"Fetzle got this hairsy charm from an angry poppit for passage." *What is a poppit?* I thought. I let it go for the moment, though, as the troll continued. "Poppit says braid the hairsy charm with one peoples hair. But poppit does not know what Fetzle knows—braid with two hairs and peoples can feel each other's. Ophelia could knows where Lucas be." She gestured for me to go on. "Braid with yours hair." I didn't respond right away, so she spoke again. "Now."

I quickly plucked a hair from my own wild mane and looked at the necklace. It appeared to be braided grass. The knots weren't that of a traditional braid. I wasn't sure where to begin or if I needed to mimic the knot structure for it to work. I was also positive I couldn't successfully do that, so I took the open end and began a normal braid, intertwining Lucas' and my hair onto the set knots. Immediately I felt an odd sensation. There was tingling in my fingertips as I wove it together, simultaneously my skin lit up with goosebumps. Fetzle began clapping wildly, as though she could see the magic working right in front of her eyes—for all I knew, she could.

When I was done, I looked up and saw all three of them looking at me intently.

"Puts it on!" Fetzle shouted. "Lucas, Fetzle says puts it on hers. Puts it on her wrists. It is too big for hers little stringy neck."

I touched my neck self-consciously. Lucas stood up and looked at me. "Don't worry, you have a beautiful neck, Olly," he said. Here, let me have it." He took the necklace and wrapped it three times around my left wrist before tying it off and sitting back down. I was waiting for something magical to happen, but I had not felt any other sensations.

"Rubs it together!" Fetzle said, frustrated with my ignorance. She demonstrated rolling the string together between her two fingers. So, I did just that, and then magic truly happened. It was hard to explain, but my face must have expressed my awe because both men leaned forward in their seats.

"What do you see?" Elias inquired eagerly.

"It isn't something I can see, it is more something I can feel," I said as I tried to hone in on the feelings. It was as though I could sense Lucas' proximity, his direction. I'd describe it as a smell, but that wouldn't be an accurate description either. It was like when a cartoon character gets carried away by a wafting scent in the air—like a faint trail that led straight to him.

"Lucas, do you feel anything?" I asked. But Lucas shook his head no.

LUCAS

After Ophelia tried to describe the effects of the hairsy charm several times without success, she gave up and decided it was time for bed.

I kissed her on the forehead as she curled up on a large circular pillow on the cave floor. "We'll play with it some other time, Olly. We got the gist, right?"

She smiled up at me. "I got the gist—you're magically broken."

I laughed. "I guess I am."

I walked over to Fetzle and tried to ask her a question as politely and as quietly as I could. "Fetzle…" I put my finger to my mouth. She leaned in closer. "Are you sure no one can detect us down here?"

She abruptly put her hands on her hips. "Lucas! Fetzle knows hers shuttle is invisibly with magics." She pointed behind me. "Fetzle already tolds Elias." Then she walked down a dark corridor and her huge figure disappeared into the shadows.

I looked in the direction she had pointed to see that Viraclay had found his own corner to pass out in. Looking at him, then around the cavern, got me thinking about this morning and how close Vivienne and Nandi got to catching us—to hurting Olly. It was all I could do not to walk over there and kick him. *What was his plan?* If it weren't for me, we might all be dead. Yet here he was, still insisting on calling the shots.

I found my own corner of the cave to stew in. I wanted to replay the last few days in my head and see if I could nail down where it all went wrong.

Why is Nandi tracking us? I wondered. *She can't be working for the Nebas. It makes no sense; she hates them for killing her partner Huan. No, there is no possible way she would be employed by Yanni or Esther. She must have her own agenda. But what does that agenda have to do with Ophelia? And clearly Vivienne is doing minion work for Yanni and Esther—but how had she found us? How did either of them find us?* My head was pounding with questions.

OPHELIA

etzle's shuttle didn't have any truly comfortable places to
sleep. I ended up in a fetal position on an old papasan
chair cushion. *Who knows where she got that from,* I thought. It smelled
weird and was lumpy. Fortunately, at least the cave temperature
stayed moderate throughout the night; that fire pit had done its job.

After who knows how many hours on the cushion, I stretched and
twisted my torso. I opened my eyes to see Fetzle's large mouth inches
away from my face; she was taking long, deep breaths.

Finally, she declared, "Yousstillsmellsfunny-Fetzlethinks." Apparently, whatever magic pill she had taken last night had worn off.

"Sorry," was all I could think to say.

I looked over to where I'd seen Elias turn in the night before. He
was gone. I quickly scanned the room, hoping to see him or Lucas. I
knew they wouldn't leave me, but it still didn't mean I wanted to sit
there and have an awkward conversation with Fetzle about my aroma.

"Is it morning?" I asked. The light of the shuttle's cavern hadn't
changed. I looked up at the glowworms as I stretched.

"Fetzlesaysyes." She nodded approvingly.

"Sure is, sleeping beauty," a friendly voice chimed in. "Fetzle says
the portals are clear today. We were just waiting on you to finish your

beauty sleep before our hostess here obligingly escorts us to Colombia." Lucas smiled his charming smile at me as I got up and brushed myself off. My stomach growled. All we'd eaten were the beef jerky and crackers that Elias kept on hand in his bag, in case of an emergency.

I guess that paid off, I thought.

Again, my stomach growled, loudly.

Fetzle heard it. "Yousgetsfoodssoon," she said, then tapped me on the head with her giant finger.

"WheresinColombiadoesFetzlestakeyous?"

"Campo Alegre," Elias answered. Lucas raised an eyebrow at him but didn't say anything. I wondered if they'd spoken about the plan before I'd woken up, or if Lucas was hearing it as I was—right now.

"OhsColombiasgoodsforshuttles," Fetzle said as she sauntered toward the way we'd entered the day before. "LotsoftreesFetzlethinks." She stopped for a moment and turned around. "Aresyoucomingtocolombia?"

We realized that was our cue. The three of us quickly fell in behind the troll. We entered the dark passage.

"HoldsFetzlesfootLucas," she instructed. I couldn't see anything, but I felt Elias holding my left hand and Lucas holding my right. I wasn't even sure when they had latched on.

I heard Fetzle say, "Thisgoodbyesfornow," then the air around my face vibrated and got heavy. My body was spinning, or perhaps falling, and then our portal journey was over. We were standing in a humid tropical forest, the sound of running water in the distance and not a troll in sight.

LUCAS

"*D*o you know where we're going, now that we're in *Campo Alegre, Colombia?*" I asked as Viraclay began walking. My tone and the stress I put on the name of our new location hinted at my annoyance.

He didn't turn around as he spoke. "Yes. I secured a country bungalow that should meet our basic needs while I run a few errands."

"And where will these 'errands' lead us after Colombia?" I asked the question expecting him to dismiss the answer.

"Costa Rica," he replied plainly. The hair on the back of my neck stood on end. That was almost the last place in the world I wanted to go.

I considered prodding further while Viraclay was in a loose-lip type of mood, but was interrupted by Olly chiming in. "Should I be looking out for snakes?" she asked.

I turned around to see her sheepishly stepping over vines and around large, long tree limbs. Her face was a study in concentration as she watched her footing.

I held back a laugh. The woman wasn't afraid of the Nebas but was leery of a few little snakes. "Yes, probably," I replied honestly. "I could carry you, if you prefer."

She looked up and gave me her "the fuck you will" face. "Or not." I shrugged.

"I just wanted to know what threats I should be looking for," she said. "Besides the Nebas, that is." She'd returned her eyes to the ground.

"We are less than a quarter mile away from the house, according to my coordinates here," Elias added.

Well, that was convenient. Who was I kidding? Elias had things planned out to a T. I didn't know how much being found by Nandi and Vivienne botched up his plans, but he'd been playing it very cool.

"Show me the coordinates and I'll scope it out ahead," I suggested, solely for Olly's sake. I didn't want her to go into a panic attack about the jungle. She was less than thrilled.

"Very well," he relented. I caught up to Elias and looked at the printed coordinates along with our current ones, which he held in a GPS device that scrambled every ten seconds.

Then I was gone, sprinting through the forest. It felt good to stretch my legs. I was able to locate the house in about three minutes.

He wasn't joking about it being basic, I thought at first glance. Something about it reminded me of the house Yessica and I had in Monte Patria. I forced myself out of my reverie, though, did a quick perimeter check, and sped back to them.

"It's there." I pointed straight ahead. "Maybe a ten-minute walk from here." I looked around Elias to Olly. "Looked snake-free along the way," I teased. Her shoulders fell from around her neck ever so slightly.

"I have another favor to ask, if I may?" Elias handed me the GPS. "Can you run into Campo Alegre proper and purchase some food and drink? While you are there, pass this device off to anyone who will take it." He paused when I didn't respond right away. "If this is too big of a task, I can tend to it as soon as I disarm the security system I had installed on the property."

I was going to do it; I just enjoyed watching him squirm. "I've heard Olly's stomach growling since Fetzle's place," I said. "I wouldn't want her to wait until you could get to the city and back to provide a meal for her—it could be all day." I shrugged nonchalantly. Of course, it wouldn't take him all day, maybe just an hour or so more than me, but I couldn't resist the dig. Plus, this would just be one more favor he owed me. I was keeping track.

He nodded and kept walking. I waited for Olly to catch up, and I gave her a hug and kiss on the cheek. "Want anything in particular?"

"You know me, whatever the locals are eating." She swatted at a mosquito. "And maybe some bug spray."

OPHELIA

*T*he jungle finally thinned out as we reached the house. It was quaint compared to our last accommodations, but I didn't care.

"This is it, right?" I asked when Elias didn't say anything as we entered the yard.

"Yes." He turned to look at me. "I know it is small, but I was able to purchase it with cash, and more importantly, without questions." He was suddenly directly in front of me, his hands on both of my shoulders. "We will not be here for long."

"Honestly, it looks fine to me. Probably way bigger than my apartment in San Francisco." I smiled at him. "I sure hope there's an AC unit in there, though. It's humid as hell out here."

He laughed. "Yes, I had the selling agent install one in each room. Now wait here. I have to disarm the security system."

"I won't move a muscle," I said as I swatted at a mosquito the size of a small bird. Then Elias was gone and I took a moment to really assess the house. It was completely surrounded by trees, the yard around it was lush, and I could hear running water coming from somewhere nearby. The exterior was painted a simple beige color, and it had a tiled-roof top. It appeared to be just one story from my viewing angle, with a lot of windows. There was an awning that encompassed the house, and under that was a brick patio. Various pieces of weather-worn patio furniture littered the space. I heard a door open and saw that Elias had made his way inside and was welcoming me through two French doors.

"It needs to be aired out, but I think it has potential." He moved out of the way and let me into the small family room. It was definitely stuffy, and because of the humid climate, there was a mildew smell in the air.

I began opening the window shades and saw that the patio went entirely around the property. When the blinds were open the space looked larger. Elias turned on the AC unit that was installed above a large window near the front door. Cool air wafted through. I opened up two of the windows to push the hot air out.

The kitchen was small but had all of the necessary equipment. There was a dining nook with a cute brown table for four, and the living room had three pieces of wicker furniture for seating and some end tables—but no television.

I liked its rustic simplicity. "It's perfect," I said as I looked down the hall. "How many bedrooms?"

"Two bedrooms, two bathrooms. Your room will be the master down the hall and to the right."

"And you and Lucas will share a room?" I said reluctantly.

"Of sorts. As you recall, he does not sleep—and I will be gone most of the time during the day. We will manage," Elias assured me.

Must be nice not to have to deal with all these human hang-ups, I internally sneered. *Nothing like being around a Conduit to make a girl feel fragile.* Here I was, always needing food and sleep. I felt like a baby. Consummated Conduits like Lucas didn't need any of that stuff. They ate when they wanted to enjoy the food, but not for sustenance.

I looked at Elias skeptically, because although he wasn't Consu, he wasn't like me either. His parents had miraculously conceived him. This meant he was exceptional in his own way. He'd inherited his mother's gift of healing, and he could move much faster than other humans—than me. The way I saw it, the only things we had in common physically was the necessity for food and sleep.

Nonetheless, I wondered how the roommate situation was really going to go; both men really liked their privacy, and they had trouble keeping it civil for even a few minutes in the living room. I decided not to worry about it, they were adults.

I peeled off my bag from across my shoulder. I was feeling disgusting. Between sleeping in a troll's cave and the stickiness of the jungle, I was way overdue for a shower. It dawned on me I hadn't showered the day before either, since Lucas had evacuated us as soon as I woke up.

"I'm going to turn on the AC in my room and get in the shower," I called out to Elias. I stood in the hallway for a minute looking for the light, since there were no windows. "Is there a laundry room?" I asked.

"We have a washing machine and a clothes line."

"That'll do." I was traveling around with only three sets of clothes. If I had any more, I might have just thrown the ones I was wearing away.

"Leave your clothes outside the door and I will start a load of wash," Elias suggested as I made my way down the hall to a door on the right.

"You don't need to do that," I hollered. I closed the door behind me, suddenly exhausted. The poor night's sleep at Fetzle's had not been enough to recharge my batteries.

"Please leave them by the door. I insist," he hollered back.

My legs and arms felt heavy. I threw my bag on the ground and stripped off my filthy clothes. I cracked the door slightly to throw them into the hall, then shuffled off to shower. My room was tiled just as the rest of the house was, and the cool squares felt great on my feet. I switched on the AC unit as I entered the bathroom. It was small, with a single vanity, toilet and shower stall. I turned the water to cool, and stood under it, letting it wash away the stink.

After a luxurious thirty-minute shower I crawled into the queen-size bed. The blankets were musty, but of a light enough fabric so as to not feel heavy or hot. I didn't even bother putting back on any clothes to sleep in; the bed was calling my name. I quickly fell fast asleep.

～

I WAS BACK IN THE HUGE COURTYARD OF HAFIZA. I LOOKED DOWN AND saw a branch tickling my calf. *That's odd. There were no plants in the courtyard*, I thought. But I felt the distinct sensation of something on my leg. I swiped at the bush and somewhere between my dream state and my conscious mind I became aware that I wasn't in Hafiza, and this wasn't just part of my dream.

My eyes shot open. It was dark in my room. I felt the scuttle of multiple tiny legs on my thigh, I screamed and jumped out of bed.

I was as naked as a newborn and pressed up against the wall when Lucas and Elias barged into the room to save me from the imminent threat. I still hadn't found the light switch, but someone did. When it flipped on and the room illuminated both men were staring at me. I mean gawking, taking it all in.

"It's in the bed!" I yelled. "Stop staring at me and get it."

Elias threw back the sheets and sure as shit the biggest spider I'd ever seen was sprawled on the mattress; apparently, it had been enjoying a good snuggle with yours truly.

I screamed again and involuntarily shook all over as though I was still trying to get it off me. I was still not aware of the spectacle I was creating in my birthday suit.

Lucas walked over, picked the creature up and let it crawl up his arm. He had no threat of being poisoned by a bite—Conduits were impervious to that type of affliction.

"Stay away from me. Take it outside. But don't hurt it," I added at the end.

"Oh, don't worry, Olly. I'm just going to take this fella outside and ask him his secrets," Lucas joked. "Like how did he get so close to that gorgeous naked body, and of course, I'll remind him he's not welcome in here again—you're spoken for."

I was now intensely aware of my bareness and of the tension it was creating. Adrenaline gone, humiliation swept in.

Lucas exited, but not without giving me one more yearning look. Elias threw me the sheet while he tried to politely avert his eyes.

"I will leave you to get dressed," he said as he closed the door.

I collapsed to the cool tile floor and let it ease the heat of the embarrassment that had enveloped my body. I'd learned a valuable lesson. When in the jungle, check your sheets—always check your sheets. And don't go to bed naked. I felt ridiculous.

LUCAS

I was putting away the dishes, wondering what I'd do the rest of the evening. Ophelia had slept most of the day, until the spider incident, of course. I chuckled to myself—what a beautiful woman she was—and boy, was she embarrassed. There was no need for that as far as I was concerned, nothing at all to be ashamed of with a figure like that. Olly was curvy in all the right places. I couldn't get those round hips and plump breasts out of my mind.

Regardless of her humiliation, she did alright at dinner, but afterward made a lame excuse about wanting to hang out in her room and read the rest of the night. *She'll be over it by tomorrow*, I thought.

Elias stepped into the kitchen. I'd been meaning to talk to him about what we were really doing at these out-of-the-way locations. Now seemed as good a time as any.

I put the last dish in the cupboard and turned to face him. He was wearing his bag—he never put that thing down. *He probably spooned it while he slept.*

I dried my hands as I spoke. "What are we really doing here?"

He leaned against the island in the kitchen, obviously prepared for this conversation. "We are evading the Nebas and keeping Ophelia safe."

"Sure, that's part of it. But you're running 'errands' all day." I used my fingers to make air quotes for 'errands,' emphasizing that I knew there was more to them than what he was telling us. "You obviously have another agenda. You had those IDs shipped to Easter Island months ago, so you knew we'd be there eventually. It's fine if you don't want to tell Olly what you're up to, but at least fill me in a little, so I can be ready for whatever might be coming our way."

I hated being in the dark. I'd been on my own for too long to comfortably fall in line with Viraclay's plans. The only reason I had kept my cool this long was because of Olly. I had to keep her safe. It was my job—my purpose. If that meant I had to bounce around the globe while Viraclay ran secret errands, I guessed I could tolerate that, as long as I knew the general plan. Besides, he was toting the bill, drawing from the cavernous wealth his parents had accumulated over many centuries on this planet. I had my own nest egg, but I bet it couldn't compare to the Kraus fortune.

He stood there for a long moment, debating what was classified information and what was acceptable to share.

"You know I have been working on my father's summit plans since he..." Elias swallowed hard. "He bequeathed the task to me. I was in Chicago, tracking down leads for a safe location, when I literally ran into Ophelia and everything changed. I have reason to believe that the places where I have arranged safe houses while we evade Yanni and Esther may hold clues, or possibly be potential summit locations."

I had to admit I was surprised he'd divulged that much. I thought about what I knew about the summit Cane had been planning. It wasn't much. Cane felt that if he could unite the Pai Ona and the Poginuli that wanted justice for their dead, that maybe we could finally end the Conduit war. I, for one, felt the whole effort was a waste of time. But if Viraclay here wanted to rally the troops, *who was I to say anything?* I knew he didn't trust me, but I thought I would press for more. "Why would you think these locations are important?"

"I have my grounds," he said curtly. "They needn't concern you." I'd hit the information wall.

"Alright," I said, retreating a little. "And you don't want Olly to know anything about these errands?"

"I do not see any reason to inform her at this time. She is still acclimating to this new world, and with the siege of Hafiza and the loss of Aremis—I do not wish to add any more to her plate at present. Besides, there is nothing either of you can do to assist me in my research."

"What do you do on these errands?" I asked.

"Again, that does not concern you. I am simply following up on leads." He shifted on his feet. "The way I see it, Lucas, this is a victory for you. I am preoccupied, allowing you to monopolize Ophelia's time. You get to spend her waking hours keeping her company and keeping her safe."

"When you put it that way, I think I'm getting the better end of this deal," I laughed. Something flashed across Viraclay's face. I wasn't exactly sure what it was; he was incredibly disciplined. I slapped him on the shoulder. "You keep up your research, dear Viraclay, and I'll take care of our beloved mistress." It was a little below the belt, but all this diplomacy between us had been getting to me. Truce or not, we still didn't like each other, plain and simple.

He nodded.

"Take the bed. I got the couch," I said as he entered the bathroom. I didn't need a bed anyway, and I intended to go on a few runs throughout the night. Running kept me occupied, and I felt better knowing the perimeter was secure.

OPHELIA

J sat in the bay window of my room with my journal and the little leather pouch full of leaves that Rand had given me the last time I saw him—the last time anyone saw him alive.

I still hadn't shown Lucas or Elias the bag. I couldn't really explain why either, except that for some reason it just didn't seem like I needed to. I wondered if it was my way of maintaining some kind of control of something. There were still so many questions about my future, about the war going on—so many things I couldn't change or have any say in. But this little leather sack was mine. I could protect it and its contents. It was my secret. In a world where everyone had secrets they were keeping from me, I could keep this single secret for myself.

I told myself that I'd know when it was the right time to reveal it to the guys. Sometimes I even believed it.

I wasn't hurting anyone by not sharing what Rand had given me. If he'd wanted me to tell Elias or Lucas, he would've asked me to. Rand wasn't one for mixed messages; he was very blunt—almost too blunt.

I started writing. This time I wrote a letter to Rand. He had been an important mentor, a Conduit with a similar gift to mine. He'd helped me harness and appreciate what I had always thought of as my "curse," and for that I would be forever indebted. Not to mention the fact that he'd saved my life—twice. I would never send the letter, of course, because it was likely I would never see him again. But I wrote it anyway, because it made me feel better.

ELIAS

J was up early, ready to track down the small Tukano Tribe I had located a few kilometers from our safe house. I chose this particular tribe because it bore similarities to the tribe on Easter Island: small, traditional, and to most of the world, hidden. I thought about Lalee and her family. My heart twanged with worry, then I shook it off. She had to be okay. Vivienne was hunting me. I had run; that was all I could do, I assured myself, then I redirected my thoughts. I wanted to accomplish what I needed to here in Colombia quickly, and keep moving. It seemed highly unlikely that anyone could have traced our travel through the troll portals, but I was still on edge.

The Tukano people were different than the Easter Island aboriginals in many ways. But perhaps the biggest difference was in how the inner workings of the tribe functioned. The men of the tribe married women from other tribes—which meant that one village could have many languages spoken throughout. This made deciding which Tukano language I should study very difficult. So I learned several basic words and phrases from the five main dialects in the region. I trusted that was enough. I hoped that by the grace of Malarin's strokes I would find that this tribe was also expecting me, somehow.

I took everything with me, all the articles from Alistair's study. If I was fortunate enough to notice similar items such as the grass clippings again, I did not want to come unprepared, as I had with Alalli; I would never get that opportunity again. I could not put that village in danger again by returning. It would be devastating if they were hurt by my association. I thought again of Lalee and Pikuu, and I let a smile touch my heart.

I slung my satchel over my shoulder and gently closed the door behind me. Lucas was on the couch, reading some book he had found. I waved at him as I made my way out the front door.

He did not bother to wave back. I pulled out my map and a compass. I expected it would be about a thirty-minute walk if I took my time.

I SMELLED THE COOKING FIRES BEFORE I SAW THE VILLAGE. I WAS traversing the jungle when I heard some brush behind me snap under someone's weight. I turned to see three young men, bare-chested, with painted faces, clearly unhappy about my presence. Two of the men carried long staffs, while one had a bow, but he was not drawing it—that was a good sign. I put my hands up to show there was nothing in them. I tried some words in one of the Tukano dialects I had rehearsed. The men did not respond to the greeting, so I tried two more, and on the third there was at least a glimmer of recognition. I asked as best I could to see their leader. That prompted them to quickly flank me and nudge me in the direction I was already going, all the while saying nothing.

We entered the village, where several small thatched huts were strewn about in no particular order—at least none that I could tell. Some were closer to others, and fires were lit in between many of them. Women and children, along with the occasional man, were gathered between the buildings. They were all very curious about the pale stranger who was being escorted among them.

We stopped at a large clearing amongst the buildings. One of the men disappeared into the passage between two dwellings, and when he returned there was an older gentleman with him. His skin looked darker than the rest—it was a deep caramel color. His hair was also longer than that of the men who had escorted me here, and he was adorned with an elaborate necklace.

I repeated my greeting, the one that had appeared to work with my escorts. He looked at me stone-faced and unmoving. The young man to his right began to speak very quickly, and I caught a few words: *danger, alone, and back*—and I wished I had studied the languages more comprehensively.

I put my hands up in the "surrender" gesture again and then pointed to my bag. I had kept the only photo I had of Alistair's family on me, in the event that seeing him would spark recognition and communication. I slipped my hand into the bag and the three men took a defensive position. I said "no danger" multiple times, attempting to put them at ease as I pulled out the photograph.

I presented it to the leader, who still had not said a word. He took it and looked it over, but I could tell instantly that he did not know anyone in the photo. My heart deflated.

I asked, "Do you know them?" just to be certain—and he shook his head no. I looked around and took a deep breath. There were several eyes upon me, viewing our exchange.

A woman came up behind the leader. She was very pregnant. She met my gaze then turned away, but first she whispered something in the older man's ear, and he promptly pointed me back into the direction whence I came. As I turned around, I heard him speak a few words I was familiar with. "Leave, do not return." I knew better than to protest. I was certain this man did not have answers for me, anyway.

This meant I was back to square one. The bigger problem was that I did not have the resources to do proper research here—I had not managed to install a secured internet connection at the bungalow. I would be fumbling around in the dark. Perhaps we could leave for Costa Rica and come back to Colombia when I had found another potential tribe.

I was mentally chastising myself for not having prepared alternatives to choose from. I was so certain this tribe fit the mark that I let my hubris get in the way. We were nearly to the spot where the men had picked me up when I heard a woman's voice ring out over the sound of crunching brush underfoot. The men stopped, and the young pregnant woman agilely found her way to my side. She looked like she was going to go into labor any moment, and yet she could still move nimbly through the jungle.

She must have been the leader's wife, the way the three men heeded her command. In a different Tukano dialect than her husband spoke, she said "hello" and laid her hand on the pocket of my bag from where I had drawn the photograph.

I again pulled it out. She pointed at Ruit, Alistair's grandfather. She said something I did not understand, then she pointed to Alistair and said a word I recognized as Asagi: *pealatunic*, which meant magic.

I repeated the word and asked her where her tribe was located.

She pointed east and said it was half a day's walk. I thanked the young woman profusely while she nodded excitedly. She then turned to go, and my escorts followed her. I stood there, immensely relieved, and thanked the strokes of Dalininkas.

LUCAS

"*A*re you ready for your combat lesson today?" I asked as I sat on the end of her bed. It was important that Olly could defend herself. I'd been hesitant about anyone teaching her to fight when she first began her lessons with Ying at Hafiza. I believed I'd always be there to keep her safe. But the siege proved that may not always be the case, and she needed to feel confident in her abilities to protect herself.

"I thought we could start with the fun stuff first," I teased.

She rubbed her eyes and looked up at me blearily. "Really?"

"Yes, really. Are you in, or are you too chicken?" I gestured chicken wings with my arms.

"I'm not afraid of you," she stated.

"Alright then. Brush those pearly whites and get your ass out of bed. It's a beautiful day; we'll duel outside."

I admired how attractive she was even in the morning, with her sleepy eyes and untamed hair. Crazy strawberry-colored waves framed her adorable face, highlighted by her freckles and her delicious plump lips. I took a deep breath, trying to calm myself. Then she threw the blanket off her body and exposed her gorgeous legs. I swallowed hard. Her nightshirt was short, though not meant to be seductive—but she didn't need to do a thing to seduce me. Elias and I were still honoring our truce that neither of us make any moves on her for the time being, so I took another deep breath, refrained from some inappropriate flirting, and left the room. "See you in a sec, stems."

"What?" I heard her mumble as she headed to the bathroom.

I ignored the question and opted to do a quick jog—it was either that or take a cold shower. I'd be back before she could change and meet me in the yard. I took off on a hard sprint. The trees whipped against my face as I ran. It was a perfect distraction. I felt the blood retreat from my lower extremities and back to my head, so I could think—really think.

By the time I made it around to the house I was clearheaded and ready to focus on training.

ELIAS

*I*t is so odd the way a destination seems to take forever to get to when you have not been there before. That was how I felt walking to the second Tukano village. It was hot, and I feared moving too quickly, afraid I would miss clues of the village's where-abouts, since all I was going on was the young woman's gesture to the east and the approximation of a half a day's trek.

She had not steered me wrong. I arrived at the border of the extremely small settlement—perhaps half the size of the first—several hours later.

Unlike the last village, I was not greeted by armed sentinels. I smelled the settlement's cooking fires and saw evidence of agriculture before I spotted the thatched buildings clustered together. The same busy work was being done throughout the structures, but no one even bothered to look up from their tasks. I passed the third dwelling before someone approached me. He was young, no older than thirty, and very dark-skinned, with striking light-colored eyes. His entire torso and face were painted with colored clay, and around his neck were several ornate necklaces.

He stepped in my path and then spread his arms wide—I was not certain what to think, because the gesture appeared to be the welcoming of a hug. But I did not want to offend him if that was not the true meaning, so I did not do the same. After we stood there in silence for a long minute, he came closer and pulled me into an embrace. I reciprocated and felt the tension in my shoulders subside. *This was a very different greeting than that of the last tribe.*

He put his hand to his chest and said "Reedta."

I mimicked his gesture and said "Elias."

He indicated for me to follow him. We walked past all the other homes and beyond the crops that were being tended to a larger house that was secluded from the others. Upon entering I could smell several aromas in the air—dried blood and burnt flesh were the most pungent.

He sat at a small fire and patted the ground to his left. I followed his lead and sat.

He began chanting. The language was clearly the dialect that the young woman spoke and I barely understood, but once more I heard bits of Asagi strewn throughout the chant.

We sat and I listened. Dusk approached, and since I was not certain how I would traverse my way home, I was beginning to get a little anxious. When I thought I was going to have to interrupt—and I had no idea what the repercussions from that might be—I started to sweat. Just before I could not wait any longer the chanting stopped, and the young man simply stared at me.

After a few moments, he stood up abruptly, walked to the house's entrance, where he beckoned, then handed me a large white stick.

Reedta tried his best to articulate what I translated to mean "Come back tomorrow." I attempted to return the stick, but he firmly placed it back into my hands and repeated his instruction to come back the next day.

I walked slowly back through the village as I processed what this might mean. I looked at the stick; there was nothing remarkable about it. As I reached the edge of the village, I tried to approximate the best way home. I pulled out the safe house coordinates and my compass and decided there must be a more direct path than backtracking the way I came. I turned around one last time before disappearing into the now shadowy jungle. Reedta stood in the center of the dwellings, waving an enthusiastic arm. I was once again reminded of my short time in the Rapa Nui village, and I found myself hoping Lalee was okay.

OPHELIA

*L*ucas had gone for a run, so it was just Elias and me on the porch. It was a nice night for the jungle—*only* a few mosquitoes the size of hummingbirds and humidity that could challenge the thickness of tomato soup.

I looked at the can of beer I was drinking. "Club Colombia," I said aloud.

"Do you like it?" Elias asked.

"Not bad. I prefer my wine, as you well know. But a cold beer in this heat is pretty nice."

"Agreed. Solute!" He raised his beer can to toast mine. I let my eyes stay on his face a little longer after our cheers. He was a handsome man. He kept his sandy blond hair on the shorter side and had recently been leaving a little stubble when he shaved. I liked it. I liked it a lot. His piercing golden-green eyes still captivated me. He wasn't as muscular as Lucas, but he was still very fit, and tall. He had to be about six-two. I was intensely attracted to him.

We sat there listening to the sounds of the tropical wilderness around us. It wasn't scary or savage-sounding, like I expected. It was tranquil.

"So where do you go all day?" I asked. Elias didn't say anything. "Is it top secret? Because I thought we were on an open-door policy now."

"No, it is not a secret necessarily. It is complicated. I am not sharing very many details with Lucas either." He paused again. "Truth be told, I do not know exactly what I am looking for."

"Do you have an end game in mind?" I asked.

"I do. I am trying to track down information about where we can carry out a summit to unite the remaining Pai Ona."

I remembered what Aremis had said about the summit. Elias' father had started the planning of a large congregation of the Pai Ona, with the intention to unite them and end the war. Now the burden was Elias' to bare. "That sounds like a tall order. Why are we looking here in Colombia?"

He paused again, longer this time, then said, "Wait here." He walked into the house and immediately returned with his bag in his hand. I hadn't even noticed that he didn't have it on him before that moment. That thing was glued to him.

"I have not shown anyone else these findings," he said as he pulled out the contents of the bag.

My heart skipped two beats as I considered what that meant; he was letting me in. Really letting me in. I scooted closer.

"My associate was killed," he continued, "quite likely for this information." I looked at him intently as he spoke. "These are the encrypted journals of a Conduit who had the skill of mapping. Mapping is the ability to locate places that would otherwise be unlocatable. Precisely the type of location we need to congregate thousands of Conduits."

He opened each journal and fanned through the pages. "The author of these books had the answers I needed, but he died before he could give them to me. Now I am following his last known whereabouts, hoping to decipher the markings in these journals in order to find our summit location."

I put my hand on his shoulder. "That sounds like a nearly impossible task." I realized I sounded very pessimistic, and I felt bad.

"It is indeed." His eyes met mine. "But my father told me once that things only appear impossible because others have not conquered them yet; pave the way and others will follow."

I smiled at him and he reciprocated with his warm, sexy grin. I felt my abdomen light up with butterflies. I couldn't feel the electricity that we shared when we first met anymore because I was so shielded by Lucas' gift. But that didn't stop good old-fashioned attraction. I missed the tingling sensation from his touch, though. It had become a familiar buzz, a reminder of our deep connection. We were bound to each other, and the electricity was proof of that.

Thinking about my bond with Elias reminded me of my attraction and love for Lucas. I had purposefully been ignoring my feelings for both men. So much was going on around me, so much change and chaos, that I didn't have time to fuss over my love life. Fortunately the tug-o-war the two suitors had been actively participating in for my affection had also subsided since the siege. I was grateful.

"Can we keep these journals between us?" he said as he filed them back into his bag.

I nodded, and then he was off replacing his satchel back to wherever it had been. I took a deep, exasperated, sexually frustrated breath, melted back into my chair and sipped my beer.

ELIAS

*I*n my head, I replayed our time on Easter Island many, many times, attempting to deduce how they found us. Not only the Nebas, but Nandi—who I still had reason to believe was not in coterie with them, but acting on her own accord. Naturally, as I pondered our narrow escape from there, I had to speculate on the safety of the Rapa Nui villagers, at which point I found myself plagued with worry and guilt. I knew it would be dangerous for them if I tried to initiate contact—and honestly I was not even sure how to do that from our current location in Colombia—so I simply had to hope that Dalininkas had graced them with good strokes.

It was a vicious cycle that was not conducive to a good night's sleep, and the previous night was no exception. Yet my mission had to continue, and so I was up early and on my way, white stick in hand, to pay my second visit to the Tukano Tribe.

Reedta was standing right where I had left him. It took me only a quarter of the time it had taken me to get home the previous night. I had left clear markers along the trail, so I would not need to speculate my path for the remainder of the time we spent in Colombia.

When I was a few feet away from where he stood, Reedta turned and headed in the direction of his hut.

This time when we entered, he took the white stick from me and placed it on a large wooden table with etched carvings on the surface —what I assessed was an altar. He sat down once more and insisted I sit across from him, not beside him as before.

I expected him to say something, or perhaps chant, but he was silent. He pointed at my satchel, and I realized it was a perfect time to present him with the contents of the leather pouches; perhaps he would recognize something in them.

I reached in and pulled all three out very slowly, then laid them in front of him. He opened each one up gently, carefully examining the contents and then concealing them once more. After he had examined all three to his liking, he shook his head no, said several words in his native tongue, then looked at me curiously and simply said, "Loktpi."

I knew the word; it was the name of a magical key. The only story I had heard about it was when I was a young boy. I did not recall all of the details, but in the end the Loktpi was lost. The creator of the key had broken it into five pieces and dispersed all of the parts. Before he dismantled it, however, the Loktpi was said to open any door—no matter how complicated the lock was, or the magic used to fasten it.

I pointed at the sacks on the ground and repeated the word as a question, "Loktpi?" Reedta shook his head again. Then he got up and grabbed a small woven basket that contained a heap of red dust. He threw a handful of the dust into the air, filling the room with a strong fragrance. I had never smelled anything like it before. It was a sharp smell, floral and bitter all at once. Reedta threw another handful into the air, this time while singing gleefully, "Loktpi, Loktpi, Loktpi!"

I let him finish his charade. When he sat back down I gathered up the leather pouches, disappointed that he didn't identify any of the items, and put them back into the security of my bag.

The rest of the day was full of more chanting, the meaning of which I had no idea. Reedta had me join him in a few dances, and when the evening loomed near he dismissed me, this time with a large rock. Once again, he followed me to the village center and waved goodbye.

LUCAS

"*Y*ou want to make dinner tonight?" I asked as Olly jotted down her grocery list. I remembered how she used to love to cook in our little San Francisco apartment.

"Yep! I have to admit," she said, "I'm getting a little bored. I like routine and all, but we wake up—and you have my breakfast and coffee ready. Then you lead our Asagi lesson. Then we have lunch—then we do our combat lesson. It's been the same exact thing every day—aside from the occasional emergency escape, of course. I'm going to shake it up with some good home cooking." She handed me the list.

"Alright," I said, putting my hands up. "I'm not complaining. I love your cooking. Mind you, I can't promise this corner of the world will have all of your desired ingredients, but I'll do my best."

"I trust you will." She smiled.

"Do I get to know what's on the menu?" I looked at the list of ingredients, not sure what to make of it.

"Nope, it's a surprise." She smiled bigger.

"Okay, okay, enough said. I'll be right back. Keep the doors locked." I kissed her on the cheek.

"Yeah, yeah, yeah—hurry up," she scolded playfully. "I'm going to start on the onions." Olly went to wash her hands in the sink.

I picked up my pace comfortably maintaining a sprint. It took me about 15 minutes to run into town, where I had to slow down and move at a human pace while I gathered the groceries. Her list was long, so I figured I might have to stop by the larger store in town if the smaller market I preferred didn't carry everything. All in all, I estimated it would take me about an hour total when all was said and done. I looked at my watch; I was going to try and beat that time.

It was a little game I liked to play with myself, along the lines of the saying, "Your competition shouldn't be with others, just be better than you were the day before"—or something like that. I still liked to compete with others, but when no one else was around to contend with, this worked. I guessed Olly wasn't the only one who got bored.

So, when I was strolling up to the house fifty minutes later, I was pretty damn proud of myself. Until I smelled blood.

I dropped the grocery bags where I stood on the porch and slinked around to the side of the house. I couldn't hear anything. I peered through the kitchen window, and all I could see was Ophelia sitting at the island. I let my shoulders relax. I knew I hadn't felt anyone else penetrate my shield, but there was no doubt about it, I smelled blood. I walked back to the pile of groceries, picked them up and tried to act casual as I opened the front door.

The smell was more pungent in the house. Ophelia looked up from her book.

"Took you long enough," she chided jokingly. "I had time to read a whole chapter."

She got up and I noticed she had a large Band-Aid on her left index finger. "What happened?" I pointed at the finger while I started putting the groceries away.

Olly leaned against the counter. "I'm a klutz and I cut my finger while I was dicing the onion. This just proves I haven't been spending enough time in the kitchen. I'm losing my touch," she said as she put the spices in the cupboard.

I went to toss the grocery bags in the trashcan and as I opened the

lid I saw a dishcloth covered in blood. I turned to look at her, mortified. *She must've cut herself bad,* I thought.

I didn't want to fuss over it, because she would just get defensive
and say she could take care of herself. But I worried she might need
stitches.

"Let me see it," I said.

"Are you going to insist?"

I nodded,

"Well, then go get another Band-Aid in case it starts bleeding again
when I take this one off."

I followed her directions. Then I gingerly removed the bandage,
simultaneously calculating how I'd convince her she needed stitches
without a fight.

But when I examined the cut it was not only no longer bleeding,
but it was oddly small.

"Oh, thank goodness the bleeding stopped," she said. "See, I told
you it wasn't that bad. Just a lot of blood."

I looked up at her, skeptical. There was no way such a little cut
produced all of that blood.

"You know I hate the sight of blood," she said. "Can we wrap it up
again in case it decides to break back open?"

I nodded, and she noticed my peculiarity. "What? What's wrong?"

"Nothing. Just glad you're okay." But something *was* wrong. I just
didn't know what.

ELIAS

$\mathcal{F}$or the sixth day in a row I went to see Reedta, but I still did not know very much. Although he had started teaching me the symbols for the Tukano language, and I was excited to see that many of them appeared in Alistair's journals.

Oddly enough though, on this day he sent me home early without an item. At the end of our previous engangements I had carried home and then returned a white stick, a rock, two feathers, a basket woven from vines, and a turtle shell. But on my sixth visit, I received nothing. I wondered if this meant I had graduated from some sort of initiation ritual. As we said our goodbyes, Reedta moreover insisted that I not come to the village until after the sun was directly above us in the sky tomorrow. This was another oddity, since I had been arriving to the village around 8 a.m..

I was still building a rapport with him, so I agreed to everything and left.

On my walk back to the safe house, I thought about what he had told me so far. I had learned that he was the shaman of his tribe, and that he spoke two languages—he was very proud of that. He was a young shaman, because his predecessor had died before his time. All things considered, I liked him, albeit I did not understand most of what we did throughout the day, and I was anxious for more answers. He had an ease about him that led me to believe I needed to trust the process—so I did. I was keeping detailed notes about the written language; I figured if nothing else, this would be one huge step towards deciphering Alistair's codes.

LUCAS

I watched her move. Again, something was different. I couldn't put my finger on it, but it was as though she was screening me out. I could feel a thin barrier between her body and my gift. I tried repeatedly to move in closer, to fill the gap, but I couldn't.

At least three times over the past few days I considered telling Viraclay, but I wasn't sure what his response would be. I definitely didn't want to tell Ophelia, concerned it could scare her—if she wasn't doing it intentionally.

Another thought tugged at me. *Maybe I'm afraid she won't need me anymore, or worse, that she would purposely shut me out.*

"What are you staring at?" she teased.

I shook off the disturbing thoughts and redirected my focus to the present.

"I was just thinking that you could do better," I taunted.

"What? That's been our best spar since I started!" She paused, then a huge smile spread across her face. "But you bet your ass I can do better." She squared off again; sweat was glistening on her lightly freckled forehead.

"Are you sure you don't want a quick breather?"

"I'm sorry—who am I talking to here? The guy who just challenged me, or the man who likes to baby me?" she jeered. Then stepped back and threw her hands up in the air, in a dramatic gesture of frustration.

"Alright," I relented, "but this time I won't go easy on you."

"Right." She rolled her eyes and resumed her defensive position. I felt the divide thicken. I was so alarmed by the sensation that she caught me off guard—my alarm was quickly replaced with pain in my jaw as she landed a spinning kick to the left side of my face.

"Oh shit!" she gasped. "Lucas, are you okay?" She looked frantic. "I didn't think you'd let me land that kick. I was taking advantage of whatever was distracting you."

She was palpating my face where it stung, and suddenly I felt tingling and warmth—the same sensation I'd felt the night Viraclay had healed me outside Hafiza. *Was she healing me?* I wondered.

I shook the feeling off. "Good move," I said casually. "I deserved it. Don't worry, I have my head in the game now." I drew my shoulders back to reassure her. "I'm fine. Seriously, try harder," I chided. "If you ever get another chance like that, I want to be on my back."

But the truth was she was exceptionally strong, and her kick hurt just as badly as any other blow I'd taken in battle. This brought up a whole different flurry of concerns, but I shoved them down this time. It was obviously not the right time to let my distractions get the best of me. I waved her on and she didn't hesitate, ready to strike me again.

AFTERWARD, I TOOK A LONG SHOWER. I SPENT MOST OF IT THINKING back—counting how many days it had been since I'd noticed the change in Olly. I was sure I hadn't felt this when we were still at Hafiza. I thought it might have started the night of the siege. I'd seen a difference in her almost immediately afterward, but I assumed that was from the trauma of the incident, an unfortunate hardening that happens when you lose people you love. There was no doubt that the siege left its mark, but this was bigger than that. This was power—and it was almost as if my own power was being used against me. I was baffled and frightened, two things I hadn't felt in a long time.

Viraclay had been out running his secret errands, but as I stepped out of the shower and toweled off I could hear Olly talking to someone, so I figured he must be home. I'd decided that I was going to bring this little problem to his attention. I doubted that with all of my years on this planet he knew any better what we should do about it than I did. But I didn't want to put Olly at risk because my pride said he was a young asshole who deserved to be kept in the dark.

I needed all hands on deck if this was going to become a serious issue. I pulled on my jeans, a belt and a plain white T-shirt before heading down the hall and into the dining room.

"You took such a long shower, I got hungry," Ophelia spat out with a mouth full of food. "Elias brought home some empanadas from Campo Alegre, and he was hungry too... and since you don't need to eat, we started without you." She swallowed what was left in her mouth. "Sorry, that wasn't polite, talking with my mouth full. Help yourself, there's plenty."

I walked past them and into the kitchen.

"You mad?" she hollered at me.

"No, I'm just not hungry." I was never hungry, but I was thirsty. "Wine?"

They both said nothing for a long minute, then Olly spoke up. "Sure."

I didn't wait for Viraclay's reply. He would follow her lead. I grabbed three glasses, filled them with a heavy pour and carried them to the table. I was banking on some liquid courage before I sat down with Elias. I wasn't sure how I felt about confiding my concerns to him.

Hell, I wasn't sure how I felt about talking to him, period. Our truce was important for Olly's betterment, but it was awkward as hell —and I still loathed the kid. I shook off my misgivings—reminding myself this was all about Olly.

"How was your lesson today?" Elias asked her.

"It was good, but this guy," she said, pointing at me accusingly. "He was distracted—I got over on him more than once."

Elias raised an eyebrow in my direction inquiringly.

"I wasn't at my personal best," I said, trying to act sheepish. The rest of the explanation could come later, out of Olly's earshot.

Viraclay's stare was unchanging, though; he was perceptive—maybe too perceptive. He knew something must be wrong.

I shrugged.

"Maybe I'm just getting that much better," Olly said, then erupted into a boisterous laugh—she didn't believe that for a minute.

We all laughed, and I was relieved to see Viraclay didn't press the conversation any further.

They ate, we drank and by ten Ophelia was hugging us both good-night and heading to bed. If she thought it was odd that Elias and I were staying up together, she didn't mention it.

He waited a long time before he spoke. I'd decided I would let him ask me about the lesson; it would tell me a lot about what he was capable of picking up on, or if he was simply deducing.

"How was today's lesson?" he repeated to me, but this time he emphasized the word *today's* in such a way that indicated he expected further explanation.

"Interesting," I said plainly. I took a fraction of a second to decide how I would try to explain what I was feeling. I'd been mulling it over all day, but now none of my hypothetical conversations sounded right. So, I just dove right in. "She's getting stronger—significantly stronger."

Viraclay still said nothing. The man was patient. I had to give him that.

"She seems faster too," I added. "I know she's a quick study, but there's something else."

Finally, his icy exterior broke slightly. "Elucidate."

"She has another barrier on her, one I didn't place." If he was shocked or frightened, his face didn't betray him. I continued. "I can't lift it, I can't move it and I cannot penetrate it."

"So, let me recapitulate what you are insinuating, Lucas. Ophelia has increased her strength and speed, in addition to commanding her own shield?"

I nodded. "There's more. I think she's healing herself too. There

97

was an incident where she cut herself the other day. It was almost healed within an hour—and it was a bad cut."

As soon as I said it all aloud, I felt like a fool. Either I was going crazy or Olly was somehow transforming into a consummated Conduit without consummating—one that also happened to demonstrate gifts similar to my own. *Maybe I was spending too much time with her. Maybe I wasn't getting enough alone time, time to clear my head.*

"I know it sounds ridiculous," I offered. "I can't imagine anyone penetrating my shield—I've had her so closely guarded, it's as if she's wearing a Lucas skin."

He chuffed under his breath.

"What's funny?" I demanded.

"I was agreeing with your description," he said.

"So then, what could it be?" I probed.

"Something far more dangerous than an invader. Ophelia is Sulu," Viraclay asserted.

I felt the color drain from my face. Yes, this was far worse.

OPHELIA

"Where are we?" I murmured.

Lucas looked my way and motioned for me to be quiet. I could hardly see a thing. I felt the distinct familiarity of déjà vu. "Where's Elias?"

"Ophelia, be quiet or they'll hear us," he demanded.

Who was they? I wondered. We were in a muddy tunnel.

I lost control of my footing and slipped, then slid down a long shaft, but I couldn't scream. I landed alone in a huge cave. "Lucas?" I whispered, but he said nothing. There was a small flame opposite where I stood—in the largest part of the cave. "Aremis?" I called. It had to be Aremis.

I walked toward the flame but it danced away. I started to run toward the tiny light, but as soon as I would get close enough to be able to see anything around me it would jump aside. It finally stopped at a large rock. I knew instinctively to push the boulder aside. *I've done this before*, I thought.

Behind the rock the passage opened up into a vast cavern with huge stalactites everywhere. The small flame flew up. I looked after it, and when it reached the cavity's ceiling it grew into a massive fireball.

Suddenly the whole place was illuminated, and I saw that I was no longer in a cave, but a large room, and the stalactites weren't pillars anymore, but people—Conduits I knew.

Lucas and Elias stood in the center of the chamber, and beyond them stood Winston, Ying, Di, Nara and Valerian. Rand was the furthest away, almost out of sight. I looked to my feet and saw a pile of ashes, and without anyone saying it, I knew they were Aremis' remains.

The fireball grew larger above us. Then I felt a cold hand touch my shoulder, and a familiar soft, sultry voice whispered in my ear. "Kill them. Kill them all," the voice said. It was Esther, and she had control of my body. I had no choice but to kill everyone.

The fireball began to dive toward my friends, and my eyes watched in terror as it descended onto everyone I loved, knocking them to the ground. It landed on the cavern floor and incinerated their unmoving forms.

Esther laughed. "Good work, my pet," she purred in my ear.

"I saw exactly who you were the day we met," Yanni hissed in my other ear. "A killer."

I shot up in bed, my heart pounding wildly, tears streaming down my face. "It was a dream, only a dream," I said with relief, assuring myself over and over again.

I had been having the same dream repeatedly since Hafiza had fallen. At first I'd wake up screaming, but recently I was able to contain my terror when I was startled awake.

I was covered in sweat. I threw off my blankets, got out of bed and turned on the light. *What did the dream mean?* I wondered. It was always the same sequence of events, and always the same outcome. Then I stopped mid-thought—wait, there was something different this time.

Aremis wasn't in the center of the room as he'd been before—he was already in ashes at my feet. I scrambled over to my journal and jotted down the change. I didn't know what this connoted, but if it might mean anything at all, I was writing it down.

The adrenaline finally subsided, and I was back to being just plain exhausted. I crawled back into bed and promptly fell asleep.

ELIAS

J was grateful for the opportunity to sleep in. After the conversation Lucas and I had had the previous night about Ophelia and her advancing gifts, I had found myself restless.

Having the morning free for the first time in a week, I decided to pop over to Campo Alegre to grab a few essentials I had run out of, like deodorant and toothpaste.

I was in a small convenience store when I saw the television behind the counter flash a familiar landscape. It looked like the village I had been visiting on Rapa Nui. My heart warmed at the thought of Lalee and her family.

"Sir, can you please turn that broadcast up?" I asked as I pointed to the television, and the clerk acquiesced.

The reporter was speaking in Spanish as she described the brutality of a massacre that had occurred in the isolated village on Easter Island. The female voice went on to say that everyone in the village had been beheaded, even the animals—all except for a lone survivor, a young boy who had been playing outside of the settlement. A picture of a small male child flashed across the screen. "He returned to the village to find the bloodbath, and ran until he was seen on the streets of Hanga Roa, nearly seventeen kilometers away," the reporter detailed. "Authorities are baffled as to the cause, but will be updating the public as leads surface."

My heart sank and my throat went dry. I dropped my things on the counter and made it outside just in time to vomit in the trash bin by the door. Their fate was worse than I could have ever imagined. They were all dead: Lalee, Ualee and Alalli, even Pikuu. *I led Vivienne to their doorstep and now they are all dead,* I berated myself. *She killed them all—an entire village of innocent people.* I vomited again, with tears rolling down my cheeks as I pictured Lalee's beautiful face being torn from her fragile body. I started to shake violently. I wanted to scream. I wanted to kill Vivienne. I felt waves of rage pounding my body—a sensation I had only felt one other time in my life, when my parents were murdered. I was tired of being on the losing side of this war.

A steely resolve came over me. I had to complete this scavenger hunt and find a safe place to regroup before anyone else could get hurt, or killed, because of my quest. I regained my composure and returned to the clerk's counter, paid for my items and ran back to the house.

OPHELIA

I heard the front door open. Lucas was home with me, and I'd thought Elias was gone for the day. It was too early for him to be returning. *Something must be wrong*, I thought.

My bedroom door wasn't quite closed as I got up to go see what was going on. I could hear Lucas and Elias talking in extremely hushed tones. *They were obviously trying to keep something from me if they were whispering.*

We'd agreed that we were a team, that there'd be no more secrets. I was just warming up to the idea of sharing with them my gift from Rand. I'd realized I wasn't being fair, keeping something from them while expecting them to be fully transparent with me.

But their conspiratorial tone changed everything.

I couldn't quite hear what was being said from my room, so I moved as quiet as a mouse down the short hall until I could make out words.

"I'm sure it was a message." Lucas stated.

"I would concur," Elias agreed. "We cannot tell Ophelia though. It would only make things harder for her—it would certainly alarm her."

"Alright, I'll buy that. But in that case you have to agree with me that we also can't tell her about what she is," Lucas bargained.

What I am? I seethed. *These jerks are keeping secrets* about *me,* from *me?* The anger burned hot in my chest.

There was a long pause in their conversation, and I was worried they'd discovered me listening in and dropped the discussion.

Then Elias spoke. "Fine, we will keep both things from her for the time being."

I was dejected. I'd really thought we were building trust, working as a team, making decisions together—especially after Elias told me about the summit and his agenda of visiting these remote locations. I turned and walked back to my room, not so quietly. I wasn't worried about them thinking I overheard them, not anymore. I was evaluating my position and my next move. I'd meant what I'd said when I demanded we start acting like a team. I was tired of being manipulated, even if it was what these two felt was in my best interest. So I was going to start making some of my own decisions.

ELIAS

"I will be back shortly," I shouted to Lucas as I walked out the front door. Truthfully, I did not know how long my rendezvous in the Tukano village would be, but the day was nearly halfway over already.

I ran there this time. I still had so much pent-up angst about the devastation of the Rapa Nui village, it felt good to expel some of that energy physically.

I was slightly winded when I reached the village border. I became alarmed when Reedta was not at his usual post, welcoming me.

My anxiety eased some when I saw other villagers shuffling about in their daily duties. Still, I walked faster than usual as I made my way to Reedta's dwelling. There was a curl of smoke rising from the hole in the roof, and as I entered the hut I saw Reedta at the far end, hovering over a pile of items and chanting. As I moved closer, I realized it was the five items he had sent home with me over the first five days we had met. He did not stop his ceremony to greet me, so I stood back a few feet and waited patiently.

Then he rose from his crouch and stood in silence for a moment before turning around and speaking fluent Asagi directly to me.

"I have seen it," he said. "They are coming here. The blood leads them. You have to go to the mountain god—leave immediately or others will die." As he spoke, all I saw were the whites of his eyes; his irises were rolled back into his head. "The secretive one knows where the mountain resides. He will lead you there. She is wiser than you know and her power grows quickly. You can do nothing to slow it down. Follow the circle, and when the time is right you must sacrifice."

Then the atmosphere in the room changed, and Reedta's eyes were back to normal. He resumed his speech in his own language mixed with broken Asagi.

"You must go now," he urged. "I read it in the earth." He grabbed something from the altar and handed it to me. "Take this, it may help."

It was a piece of hide. When I unfolded it, I saw it was covered in symbols with their drawn meanings besides them—a key of sorts.

"Go now." He pointed to the door. "Before you kill my people."

I bowed a solemn thank you and ran directly into the jungle. I would find a different way home. I could not bear to lead Vivienne to another village for her to slaughter.

PART II

OPHELIA

*E*lias had come back flustered, which was alarming, since he was always so stoic. He explained to Lucas and me that we needed to leave immediately for Costa Rica. He'd already chartered a jet and pilot from the local airport. *How is he so efficient with our travel plans?* I wondered. *He should've been a travel agent.*

I quickly packed my things in my room, and when I re-entered the conversation just a few minutes later, I was a little confused.

"Where are we going?" Elias demanded.

"It was your silly witch doctor that told you *I* needed to decide where in Costa Rica we'd go, correct?" Lucas sounded annoyed.

"Indeed," Elias conceded.

"What did he say exactly?" Lucas insisted.

"He said you knew where the mountain god resides, and that we needed to find him."

"Well," Lucas cleared his throat uncomfortably. He was sweating. I'd never seen him that way. "My dad is in Costa Rica, and he's a Vulcan." Riled, Lucas threw his arms in the air.

I didn't know whose jaw was closer to the ground, mine or Elias'.

"Your *dad?*" I asked.

"Yeah, Olly, my dad. You didn't think I just appeared out of nowhere, did you?" He was snarky with me this time—and he was never snarky with me, no matter what we discussed. He paused, then continued. "I'm sorry, I didn't mean to be a dick. It's just that I haven't seen the old asshole in years and I'm not exactly looking forward to the reunion."

"What happened? Why haven't you talked to him?" I asked, bewildered. *Why hasn't Lucas mentioned his father before? For a man with so few allies, why would he keep a family member at a distance?*

"Can we just get to the plane and I can explain during our flight?" he moaned.

"Sure," I relented. "But you'd better know I'm not letting this go." Lucas didn't answer.

As soon as the plane was at its cruising altitude I reminded Lucas I was waiting for answers. "Lucas, spill it! What the hell is up with you and your dad?" All this time I thought I was the only one in this trio toting around parental baggage. Eleanor popped into my head. Even though she'd driven me crazy when we'd spent any time together, I hoped she was doing okay. According to Lucas, she and her husband Simon had grown closer after Lucas had orchestrated a car accident to look like I had died. He had also arranged for Eleanor to be financially set for the rest of her life. I was grateful for his foresight; he knew I'd want her to be well provided for. But I never got to say goodbye, and as difficult as our relationship had been, I still loved my mom. She was the only parent I had ever had.

He poured himself a drink from the very well stocked minibar on the jet, and I brought my attention back to him.

"Give me a minute, alright?" he asked. I hoped he wasn't just stalling.

Elias entered the cabin from the cockpit as I sat down next to Lucas. He chose a seat a few rows back. He had still said very little since we'd boarded the plane.

Lucas cleared his throat in that awkward way once more. Then he began. "I was born on the island of Thule in 1175 A.D."

I gasped. I knew he was old, but hearing his birth year out loud was staggering. His expression mirrored his embarrassment, as though I'd just realized he was way too old for us to ever date. I tried to appear nonchalant, but it was too late. "Yeah, Olly, I'm a little bit older than you." He tried to smile, but it looked painful.

"You still look great," I playfully said, trying to lighten the mood.

"Yeah, thanks." He rolled his eyes and continued. "Thule was inhabited by Picts, a Celtic people. My dad's name is Vosega, and my mom's was Grannus. My parents were happy. The Pict people worshiped them and their gifts. Vosega is an earth Elemental—a Conduit that can create volcanic activity, and my mom, she was a Calentar, like Winston. Her gift only worked on water though, unlike Winston's; he can heat anything from the inside out. So they dubbed her the 'goddess of the mineral baths.'"

"Did you like living on the island? I mean, did you just live with the locals?" I asked.

"It wasn't so bad. The island was an alright place to grow up. We lived in an elaborate chateau inside the mountain. Being an earth Elemental meant my dad could manipulate everything about the mountain itself—the soil, rocks and even magma. My parents thought they'd be safe in Thule, far away from all of the panic taking place around the world. It was evident at this point that the Conduit assassinations had begun again."

I pondered what it must've been like—growing up as Lucas did. A thousand years ago, his parents in hiding. When Elias and Lucas had shared the history of the war I was now in the middle of, it felt distant, removed. I hadn't even considered that Lucas had been in the middle of this conflict for centuries. I was trying to wrap my head around all of this as Lucas continued.

"Then pixies showed up in the summer of 1185. Turned out Thule was a pixie nesting colony. Every 788 years—yes, before you ask, that is an exact number—the fucking island is overrun with a herd of horny depraved pixies." Lucas took another drink. "My parents had no idea. Odysseus had described some insignificant 'little people war' he witnessed on the island during his travels over twenty-three hundred years earlier. Turns out it wasn't war—it was mating." Lucas visibly shook with disgust. "Something you can never unsee."

"Just slow down," I demanded. "What the hell are pixies? And just to clarify, you *are* referring to *the* Odysseus?"

"Yes, I'm talking about the lost Greek guy." Lucas rolled his eyes, then continued. "Pixies, my dear, are the mythological equivalent to a severely roided out teenager—but during mating season they become extremely volatile. They are usually boorish thugs, but the hormone cocktail makes them four-foot-high homicidal maniacs."

"I still don't get it. I mean, what do pixies do?"

"On a good day, they are the bouncers of the sprite world. They specifically keep the water sprites in check, prevent flash floods or even tsunamis, shit like that." He took another swig from the bottle he was brandishing. "They have some kind of freezing power in their fingertips. I don't know how or why they became the keepers of the water sprites, but they're definitely equipped for the job. Any water sprite gets out of hand and *BAM*! Frozen—at least temporarily."

"Okay, so a bunch of zealot pixies show up. Did your family leave?" I had my suspicions that this story had a far sadder ending than just packing up and moving.

"Not exactly. I mean, we may have, eventually. But we didn't get the chance. The pixies arrived, started destroying shit and assaulting the locals in the valley where most of the Picts lived. My dad wanted to help *his* people out. He was trying to evict the pixies himself. My mom would've preferred to just go. After two weeks of fighting with the little bastards, we weren't getting anywhere. More and more just kept coming. I was only ten, but I remember thinking it was a lost cause."

Lucas slumped back into his seat and I knew we were getting to the bad part. "My mother was down by the mineral springs outside the mountain, taking a bath," he recalled. "The pixies hadn't ventured out of the valley, so we hadn't thought to arm ourselves while in or near the chateau. I heard her scream—it was abruptly choked off. At the time, I was in the chateau. I yelled for my dad and darted outside. But it was too late. Her body was completely frozen, and about thirty pixies were dismembering her." Lucas swallowed hard. I moved closer to him and put my arm around his neck. "I charged after them," he continued, "but they were fast. By the time I reached her body they'd already rescinded the ice and lit her body parts on fire." I saw a tear cascade down his cheek and I hugged him tighter.

Elias spoke up. "Where was your father?"

"That blubbering idiot eventually came barreling out of the chateau in a frenzy, but like I said, by then it was too late. He hunted down the murderous little assholes and killed all of them one by one, but none of it felt like justice to me. She was gone." Lucas was looking past me and Elias.

"So, you don't like your dad because he wasn't there to save your mom?" I asked. "I'm sure he wished he'd been there."

"No, that isn't why we don't speak. Even as a child, I recognized how much he beat himself up over her loss. He and I left Thule—we became nomads, wandering from one mountain range to the next, all across Eurasia. We were traveling through what is now Pakistan on our way to the Hindu Kush Mountains when *she* appeared. Oya." He said her name with disdain. I sat silently, patiently waiting for an explanation.

Lucas took another long drink, swallowed, and still didn't continue. Naturally, I prompted him with a nudge of my elbow.

He started again. "I was fifteen by now. Life wasn't great, but dad and I'd found a rhythm. Oya had to show up and ruin all of that." Lucas' brow furrowed in distaste as he recalled the fated encounter.

I interjected. "Who is Oya?"

"Oya," he said sardonically, "is an attention-seeking whore who bewitched my dad and monopolized all of his attention from the moment they met."

I nodded slowly. The trained therapist in me was screaming all kinds of clinical words and tactics to use to help my wounded friend —but I stayed silent.

"She manipulates lightning. She used to spend most of her time in

South America, but her Atoa was murdered and she found herself on the other side of the world. My dad decided to haul her around with us, and they began an affair."

"Your father found happiness with another Poginuli? That has become common amongst the broken," Elias stated. Lucas darted a menacing glance at him.

"It was too soon. My mom had only been gone five years. I was still a boy; I still needed him. He didn't understand." Lucas sneered at Elias once more. "So I left. Having no one was better than enduring a halfhearted attempt at parenthood from a distracted father. I warned him I'd go, but he didn't believe me. I snuck out one morning while the two of them were too busy in post-coital bliss to realize I was gone. I joined the Varangian Guard, and I've not spoken to him since."

I didn't say anything, and I think Elias was apprehensive about opening his mouth again on the subject. We sat there for a while in silence. All kinds of thoughts ran through my head. *Poor Lucas, to lose his mother at such a young age.* I felt bad that he'd been so angry and lost as a teenager that he left his dad. *What is the Varangian Guard?* Perhaps most importantly, I was wondering how on earth this reunion was going to go.

I felt the plane start to descend and my stomach squirmed.

ELIAS

*I*t was dusk when we landed and found a cab. Once again it appeared that we had evaded our tail. I tried to take some deep breaths. It felt like it had been hours since I had truly inhaled and exhaled. I was usually quite calm and collected, and although I was seemingly in charge of our agenda, I felt everything but. From trolls to stalkers to our current refuge.

I had to admit the location was ideal for my errands in Costa Rica. The Boruca Tribe I was interested in conferencing with was not far from where Lucas was taking us.

I was strategizing my plan while Lucas spoke to the driver.

"Para aqui, por favor." He put his hand on the driver's shoulder. I was reminded that Lucas and Yessica had spent many years in Central and South America. His accent was perfect.

"How do you know Vosega is here? I asked. "There are over a hundred volcanoes in Costa Rica."

"Trust me, he's here," he snarled as we stepped out of the vehicle. We were in front of the Turrialba Volcano National Park entrance sign. The gate was closed.

"But how do you know?" Ophelia asked. She had read my mind,

and I was glad she decided to insist he answer the question—he was more responsive to her.

Lucas paid the driver and began walking toward the huge sign. "There are some telltale signs that Oya is back home in Venezuela, and I have to assume that Vosega isn't far from her. My curiosity got the best of me when I noticed that Lake Maracaibo was back to its glorious self a few hundred years ago. Yessica had been trying to get me to reconcile with dear old dad for centuries. I humored her about sixty years ago and investigated my hunch. Oya was home alright. Yesi and I meandered around Venezuela, but none of the volcanoes were demonstrating Vosega's usual behaviors."

That was the first time I had heard Lucas use Yessica's nickname since she had disappeared. It affected me in a sentimental way. Like smelling fresh-baked chocolate chip cookies, it took me back to my childhood.

Lucas continued. "He has specific habits; they're very telling. When I was younger, I kept my ears open for strange volcanic activity. He likes to show off—he's full of hot air." Lucas chuckled to himself.

It must be difficult for Lucas to keep up this stoic exterior he has insisted upon, I thought. He may not have meant to—in fact I was certain he did not intend to—expose the vulnerable man underneath it. But he had inadvertently done so by mentioning that he had tried to follow his father's whereabouts, perhaps make certain he was okay. My heart softened for him ever so slightly.

Lucas continued as we walked, slipping under the gate and ducking into the lush landscape. It was getting dark; I hoped he was comfortable leading us through this terrain.

"Vosega likes to be revered," he explained, "but not feared. He keeps his eruptions showy but not fatal. He wants the people to appreciate his power without fleeing for fear of their lives. Turrialba is perfect. He's active enough that they closed the park and he has his privacy, but not so busy that the nearby villages or cities have evacuated."

"Okay, so let us assume your conjecture is correct. How do we make contact with your father?"

"That's the easy part. I just need to find the right alcove. Some of the landscape is created naturally, but when it's created by an Elemental, there are distinct indicators. Each Elemental has his or her own signature. Vosega loves blister caves."

"What are blister caves?" Ophelia asked. "And what is an Elemental?"

"Caves are formed in all kinds of ways. Blister caves are domed in shape and occur from a bubbling and then cooling of lava," Lucas answered. "And an Elemental is a Conduit who controls one of the four elements: earth, wind, water or fire."

"Aren't blister caves all over the world?" she prodded.

"Yes. And Vosega has been all over the world." He paused and smiled. "There aren't nearly as many blister caves as lava tubes; feel free to mention that when you meet him." Lucas laughed as though it was an inside joke.

"We are looking for a cave then?" I confirmed.

Lucas nodded, but it was almost imperceptible in the dim light and the dense vegetation. I silently hoped that we would find it soon so that we were not ambling in the dark.

"We're close. I can smell him," Lucas said. Just as he announced our proximity, I felt the earth beneath my feet turn upward. We were inclining.

"Over here!" he shouted from the top of a small mound. "The entrance is here, under this bush. Olly, follow me in. I'll catch you." With that he slipped behind the shrub and was gone from sight. I did not hear a calamitous landing, so I presumed he had landed safely.

"Alright, Ophelia, he will catch you and I will be in short pursuit," I said assuredly.

"Did I ever tell you that I hate enclosed spaces like caves? They're dark and confined; two of my least favorite things," she rambled nervously.

"We would never let anything happen to you."

She nodded rapidly, and it occurred to me that this might remind her of the tunnel escape from Hafiza. I hesitated, afraid of how a reminder of that night may affect her. But she squared up her shoulders and moved so quickly that I was unable to give it another thought. I waited, listening. When I heard nothing, I too slipped down into the cavern.

It was pitch black, but the fall was brief, so I estimated that it could not be a very deep cave. I landed awkwardly on a large stone. Ophelia grabbed my arm.

"Well, now that we're all here, let me knock," Lucas said mockingly.

Completely in the dark, we waited. I held my breath. Beside me, Ophelia was huffing heavily.

"Vosega! It's me, Lucas. Show yourself," Lucas announced, while under his breath, he whispered, "Asshole."

Then all was quiet.

OPHELIA

*M*y heart was beating wildly in my chest. I'd not felt this afraid since the night Hafiza fell. Maybe it was the cave, maybe it was the smothering darkness. Whatever it was, I was moments away from a full-blown panic attack. I squeezed Lucas' hand hard, while Elias held firmly onto my shoulder.

All of a sudden, light erupted in the dark space as a hot orange glow oozed from the crevices below us. It took me a moment to realize that it was lava. Flashes of terrifying disaster-movie scenes zipped through my mind as I imagined falling into the boiling molten mass. I adjusted myself onto the only solid stone I could see.

It was terrifying and stunning all at once, as thousands of tiny lava veins twisted and pulsed through the cave's floor. I followed one of the veins until it arrived at the pillar Elias was standing beside. I met his gaze. He wasn't showing fear, but I could sense his bewilderment. The cave itself was very large—not deep, but wide—and it appeared to have many corridors leading from the main chamber.

One of the largest tunnels lit up and the silhouette of a man appeared. He was tall, with broad shoulders and long, wavy fiery red hair. He didn't have a shirt on, and his bare chest glistened with sweat. His pants were tight, showing off the muscular legs they shrouded. A thick smoke billowed behind him, creating an odd softening effect on the lighting in the room. Curious shadows danced along the stalactites hanging above.

No one said anything. The silhouette stepped into the large chamber, and from that range I could confirm that he was undeniably a very handsome man. His masculine face was dominated by a strong jaw, and wide eyes perched on chiseled cheekbones.

Finally, he spoke. "Lucas?" His voice was deep and raspy, with an accent that was unfamiliar to me. It wasn't English-sounding like Elias'; instead, it was more eastern European.

"Vosega," Lucas asserted. The older man filled the space between them faster than I could've imagined and was now holding his son's expansive shoulders. The two of them had brawny body frames in common.

Lucas let go of my hand. I stepped back beside Elias, not sure what this reunion would consist of, but very aware that we were still surrounded by hot lava. Lucas removed his father's hands, but Vosega ignored the gesture and drew Lucas in closer for a very awkward hug.

I guessed that Vosega must've had Lucas in a pretty good vice because although he didn't reciprocate, he also didn't remove his father's embrace.

When Vosega had gotten his fill he stepped back, and only then seemed to realize that Lucas had not come alone.

"I am Vosega," he said to me and Elias. "Any friends of Lucas' are welcome in my home. What say you to a glass of honey mead?"

"Vosega, this is Olly." Lucas paused. "I mean Ophelia. And this is Elias." He gestured to both of us casually.

I reached forward to shake his hand. "Hello, Mr. Vosega. You can call me either Olly or Ophelia—it's just a pleasure to meet Lucas' father."

Vosega grabbed my hand with both of his; it was a strong and assuring kind of handshake. He also made intense eye contact with me, the kind that makes you hope you don't offend the person if you have to look away first. "Ophelia." I kind of liked how my name sounded in his raspy deep tenor of a voice, and found myself blushing.

He turned to Elias. "Elias Kraus?" he asked. Elias nodded as he took Vosega's hand. "I knew your parents well," the Vulcan said. "They were good souls. I mourned their passing deeply." Unlike myself, Elias didn't turn away from Vosega's intense stare. It seemed as though they were having a silent, intense exchange.

Lucas interrupted them. "Where is the mead?"

"I beckon you, follow me," Vosega said as he turned and started down a different passage than the one he'd come in through. I watched where I stepped. The lava continued to ooze in the cracks between the stepping stones. "You would have found an untimely end should you have pursued that entrance," he said, gesturing to his point of entry.

I shook slightly at the thought. Lucas grabbed my hand. I thought it was to assure me that I was safe, but I realized that perhaps I was his rock, his assurance. I squeezed his hand tighter and clasped both of our hands with my other one. Elias slowly trailed behind. He looked deep in thought, as he often did when his parents were mentioned.

"I was not expecting guests," Vosega said. "I must ask you for your forgiveness. The sight of my residence is unsatisfactory."

The same flowing lava glow followed us through the long passage. It made the tunnel warm but not stifling. I wondered what would've awaited us had we entered through the other passage.

No one else spoke the rest of the walk. The air got noticeably lighter as the tunnel widened and revealed a great hall. I hadn't gotten a good look at the mountain when we'd entered the national park, but I figured this must be the belly of the volcano itself.

I looked around. Huge stalagmite pillars stood erect along the walls. Long crimson drapes cascaded and billowed from one pillar to the next, creating an enchanting, ambiance. In the center of the hall was a massive fire pit, deep and wide and surrounded with marble.

Large pieces of ornate eighteenth-century furniture were scattered around the space. All kinds of colors and patterns covered the over-sized pieces. *For a bachelor, he sure has impeccable taste*, I thought. To my right was a huge bath. The water steamed and smelled slightly of sulfur, but not to an offensive degree. To top it off, the hall was lit by three giant, clear cauldrons hanging from the ceiling; all were full of more magma.

"This place is spectacular," I asserted.

"I am pleased that you find it agreeable, Ophelia. Please sit." He waved his hand to the area near the fire. "I will prepare the mead."

Both men assumed their usual positions on either side of me. The couch I'd chosen was big enough for the three of us, but I thought it looked a little silly that there were four other seats about the fire pit, and all three of us were sitting on one. Apparently, I wasn't the only one who found it ridiculous. When Vosega returned with four large steins of mead in his hands he stifled a laugh.

"Please do not feel that you must sit on a single sofa. I have many, and I can even procure more upon your request."

I took the opportunity to move, as did Elias. I wasn't abandoning Lucas, but I thought I could be of more help to him if I could study his expression and give him some reassuring nods. He reluctantly let go of my hand. I took a seat across from him in an overstuffed and very comfortable plush velvet piece. From there I had a great view of both him and Elias.

Vosega handed each of us our stein, then took a seat to my left. I was kind of disappointed that I didn't have a better view of him, as I would've liked to make a better assessment of him in the more-vibrant light.

Each of us took a long swig of our drink and waited for someone else to break the silence.

Vosega spoke up again. "So which one of you bribed my son to finally call on me?" He pointed at me. "It must be the beautiful lady." He winked at Lucas. "Unless you have come to tell me you have changed your preferences?"

"No," Lucas said flatly. "We were in a bind and I had a hunch you were here in Costa Rica."

"All this time, son, I assume you did not bother to follow my whereabouts?" Vosega asked.

"I didn't really," Lucas fibbed. "But I also didn't really want to accidentally run into you somewhere." Lucas was trying to sound nonchalant, but the pain was evident in his face. He'd been following his father to make sure he was still alive.

"I have kept my ear to the wind," Vosega said, "doing my best to keep track of where you were. Listening for news of your safety." He looked down at his mug. "I am sorry for Yessica."

Lucas' face stiffened to stone and for a moment I thought he might pounce on his father.

I wasn't ready for this meet-up to go south so soon, so I spoke up quickly. "Can we get a tour, Vosega?" He reluctantly took his eyes away from his son. I didn't know if he would be angry at me for interrupting, but it was worth the risk if it kept these two from duking it out.

"Of course, Ophelia. "How rude of me to not suggest that sooner." Vosega stood and gestured toward a long passage. "Shall we? By all means, bring your mead."

I noticed Lucas didn't stand up. I paused.

"Go," he whispered, waving me on. "You've seen one volcanic chateau, you've seen them all." I waited, wavering between staying with him or following his father. "Seriously, I could use the moment," he smiled, and I decided he was probably right.

LUCAS

I walked around the chateau while Vosega gave Ophelia and Elias the formal tour. It reminded me of the place our family had lived in, in Thule, with lots of different chambers, hidden exits and opulence. It wasn't as cozy as our home had been; it was my mother who had made it warm. I remembered her smile and it stung —she was so kind to me and others, the perfect mom. I shook off her memory, as I'd been doing for years.

Vosega must've been here a while in order to have created this large a residence.

I looked for signs of Oya's presence, but I didn't see any obvious markers. If they were still an item, she obviously spent most of her time somewhere else.

As we would need to spend some time here, I chose a small room at the end of a long hall, separate from the others. It was simple and all that I needed during our stay. I threw my bag down and sat in the chair, it was comfortable enough.

Lava dripped through minute crevices of the wall, creating a snug, homey ambiance. Childhood memories crept to the forefront of my mind. I hated reliving my youth, I hated seeing Vosega again, I hated being here! Anger coursed through me. "Fucking Viraclay and his village toadies! How'd I let him talk me into this?" I said it out loud, hoping it would relieve some of the tension and frustration I felt, but it didn't help at all.

I decided that I'd find things to do during the visit. I'd stay busy with perimeter checks. *How will I keep Olly's questions at a minimum, though?* I thought. I really didn't want to have the therapist in her analyzing my daddy issues. I'd postpone our combat lessons, just until we left Costa Rica. I was hoping that would be sooner rather than later.

Yeah, that will work, I thought. *Then we'll move onto other things and she'll forget all about this.* I let my shoulders relax. *Just a few days. I can do anything for a few days.*

OPHELIA

"*L*ucas, remember that one time your mother boiled the winter's rain in Thule?" Vosega slapped his knee and the hall shook a little. "Those Picts didn't know what to do with themselves! We laughed so hard."

Lucas smiled. He wanted to fight it, but apparently the memory was too good to shun for foolish pride. "Yeah, that little old lady kept telling the village folk that the last battle was days away," Lucas added.

I'd never recalled seeing Lucas smile so wide before. Obviously recalling his mother was good for his soul. I had a thought while he and his father spoke. At first I had to admit that I'd dismissed Grannus' powers as sounding somewhat trivial, because she could *only* heat water. But the thought of being showered with boiling rain had me reconsidering my judgment. Maybe no Conduit power was trivial.

Vosega got up and poured us another round of mead. "Viraclay!" he said heartily. I noted that when Vosega said it, it wasn't with the spiteful undertone Lucas used. He went on. "Did your father ever tell you about the time we scared the living daylights out of a Viking village?" Vosega was laughing so hard I thought mead might come out of his nose.

"I am not certain I have heard this one," Elias said as he leaned in.

"Oh, my paint strokes. I thought we had given a handful of Scandinavian Vikings a heart attack. It started when Cane came to visit for a fortnight." Vosega's grin was still stretched across his face. It reminded me of Lucas' smile. "At the time, I was camped out in Katla, a volcano near the southern coast of Iceland. There were a few small settlements in the area." Vosega snuck in a sideways glance at Elias, then continued. "Your father, the kindest of our people—you know I used to say it was his heart that made him a giant..."

Then Vosega poured some of his drink on his hand and splashed it on his face, and Lucas and Elias copied the gesture, so I did the same, although somewhat more awkwardly. When I opened my eyes, all three of them were looking at me. They erupted into deep exuberant laughter. I had to laugh at myself too. I made a mental note to ask about the gesture at a later time.

When the men had wiped the tears from their eyes, Vosega continued. "Big heart or not, your father could also get gargantuan. So needless to say, after hours of mead and laughs around my fire, we were frisky young men again. Ready to challenge each other and our gifts. A duel of sorts. The wager was that I could not grow faster as a mountain than Cane could as a giant. He stumbled out of the cave and began expanding so fast I think he might have shit his pants." Vosega looked at me quickly. "I am sorry." I waved him on. "He grew, and he grew, and I started spewing lava like it was my own penis pissing into the wind."

He looked at me again and this time I replied. "I'm a woman, not a fucking nun." This caused the room to erupt in laughter once more and I think mead might've come out of a few noses.

"She is a feisty one," Vosega said. "I can see why you both love her." A hush fell over Lucas and Elias. I wasn't going to have that.

I chummed up right next to Vosega and sat on the arm of the chair. "Cheer up, boys," I cracked, "otherwise I might decide to stay here with Vosega where the mead comes easily, and boy, can he make me laugh!"

Vosega caught on. "Geez, I am falling in love as well!" he teased. I kissed him on the cheek and then went back to my seat.

"So, you're pissing lava in the air and Cane has shit himself?" I reminded him.

"Yes! A proper duel! Well, Elias, your father sees me jumping ahead in the challenge and he wouldn't have that. By now he is as big as seventy elephants stacked tall. He begins digging. Dirt is flying like an avalanche and boulders are cascading down into the valley. I don't know how long we went at it. Teasing each other so. I don't even remember which of us won. But the next morning when we meandered into the village, the local folk had begun to prepare for Ragnarok, because many of those town folk had seen Loki dig his way out of the mountain the night before."

Vosega hit his thigh again, making the cave tremble as laughter billowed out of everyone's bellies. "I don't think that town was ever the same."

After the laughter died down, I thought about what Lucas had said just before we entered the cave, about Elementals' signatures and how Vosega's was a blister cave.

"Is your signature a blister cave?"

"Why, yes, it is, Ophelia."

Lucas' eyes got wild and knowing, and I should've taken the hint, but I didn't—I'd obviously had too much mead. "So then whose is the lava tubes? Those are the more common cave formations around the world, aren't they?"

Vosega's face flashed red, and the room shook violently. My eyes must've been as big as saucers because Elias rushed over to me.

Vosega began muttering words I didn't understand but I got the drift—he was definitely cursing. Lucas was trying to stifle a smile. Finally, Vosega's words became coherent. "Fucking Stalt, motherfucker." Then he turned to me. Elias was shielding me with his body.

"Do you know who signs with lava tubes, Ophelia?" he asked, exasperated.

"Stalt?" I guessed.

"Do you know this venomous hoarder?" he questioned, peering at me closely. Elias was still sitting on the arm of my chair between us.

"No—you're the first Elemental I've ever met." The mead was giving me liquid courage.

"He is swine!" Vosega spat the words. "He spends no time with the mountains or the people. He just defiles the mountainside with his ostentatious signature—lava tubes. He has the nerve to call himself 'The Vulcan'—all mountain Elementals are Vulcan!" He pounded his chest with his fist. "I am Vulcan!"

Lucas couldn't help it; he laughed out loud.

Vosega clutched his chest. "Did my son put you up to this?"

"Well, he definitely inspired the question," I admitted. "I had no idea you would be so offended." Elias relaxed and took his seat. I was grateful for his response and decided I would tell him so later.

"What, Dad, you can't handle a little taunting?" Lucas jeered. "I know Ophelia can appreciate a good joke."

I could and did. But I should've known better. I'd seen that look in his eye. I should've known that he was setting me up.

Vosega was still halfheartedly muttering under his breath when he decided to forget the whole thing. "More mead?" he asked. With that, he got up and refilled our glasses.

ELIAS

Thus far Coast Rica was turning out to be the most challenging of the destinations Emerson had given me. I replayed that night in my head—nearly two years ago, in Chicago. The stench of Alistair's charred remains still nipped at my nose. I wondered if Emerson—Alistair's oldest confidant and the one who had connected me with the now-deceased master Mapper in the first place—somehow managed to survive that terrible night himself—if he had freed himself from Salzar's vice. I would be forever grateful for his brief assistance. He was the reason I had gotten this far. Had Emerson not given me the names and countries of the five tribes Alistair had visited in the year before his death, I might still be at square one. Instead, I had already made contact with two of the tribal villages, and was hopefully close to locating my third.

However, I felt as if I had spent all the previous day wasting time. There were many indigenous tribes in Costa Rica, and although Emerson had named the Boruca as the tribe Alistair visited here, it made no sense—they were too acclimated to modern society. They were so well integrated that I found some sample Boruca text on the internet—and it did not look like any of the symbols in Alistair's code.

It simply did not feel right. All the other tribes I had researched were far more isolated.

Yet I had not been able to track down any obscure villages, ones that were secluded from large populace, not a single one.

Because of this I had reluctantly decided I would ask Vosega for help. Of course, I would not let him know the inner workings of my mission, but he had been in this country for some time—it was likely he could help me narrow down my search for the proper tribe.

I had heard Lucas leave the chateau earlier. I knew Ophelia would not be up for another hour or so. Now seemed as good a time as any.

I walked into the huge hall and took a seat. As I expected, Vosega made his way to the fire to keep me company. It was traditional in these situations that a host should give their guests companionship as often as needed; in turn, a guest was not to take advantage of this allowance. That was the interesting thing I was noting about Vosega—his sheltered lifestyle kept him in somewhat of a time capsule. He observed older traditions, because it had been centuries since he had enjoyed the company of strangers or guests.

"Good morning, Viraclay." I welcomed how different my nickname sounded coming from him, in contrast to how his son typically spat it out.

"Good morning, Vosega," I replied. "Thank you for the comfortable accommodations. My bed is very suitable."

"Is it? You seem to be up early for a man who slept well."

"Very astute. I am well rested, but in need of assistance. I preferred to ask for your help in private."

He nodded.

"I am not certain what Lucas has told you about our being here."

"I assure you, my son tells me nothing. Perhaps you will inform me?"

"Well, I am afraid I cannot disclose much—for your safety, of course." I had to be careful not to insult him by insinuating I did not trust him. "I have reason to believe that an aboriginal people of this region may have some answers for me concerning a codex I came across—one that I desire to transcribe."

He nodded again. "I see. I know my people very well. I have been here for over seventy years."

I pulled out the sheet of paper I had ripped off many years ago when I showed Emerson my findings from Alistair's apartment, fishing for a lead.

As I handed it over to Vosega I explained why I thought it was the Boruca Tribe who could help me decipher the code it contained.

"This is all you have?" he asked, looking suspicious, but he decided not to follow that line of query any further. "You have been misinformed. The Boruca people had nothing to do with the crafting of these markings."

My shoulders fell in despair.

"But this here," Vosega said, leaning over and pointing at a small symbol that looked like an upside-down F. "This symbol resembles markings I have seen drawn by the Cabecar people." He smiled. "They also happen to be my favorite local tribe. I have visited them many times. They are true mountain people and appreciate my gifts. That is not very common anymore. Come to think of it, it has probably been thirty years since my last visit. I could take you to them."

I readily agreed, thinking this was either a beautiful happenstance or an unfortunate mistake. I decided I would chance the latter in the hopes that Vosega would make my Costa Rican errand that much easier. I had found some Talamanca text online, but it was difficult to distinguish between the Bribri people and the Cabecar, hence why they had been lumped into one indigenous group called the Talamanca.

"Follow me. I have a direct line to them," Vosega said excitedly. "There was a time when I frequented the villages on top of the Cordillera de Talamanca mountain range." We entered into Vosega's room, and behind a large tapestry was a dark tunnel. "Do you need a light?" he asked.

"It would be appreciated," I admitted.

"Here." He handed me a small candle lantern and snapped his fingers together to create a quick spark. He smiled. "It doesn't always work. I can't control fire. I just run hotter than most." He laughed, and I had to admit Vosega was growing on me.

We began to walk—I noticed the tunnel was surprisingly smooth. *Probably a lava tube*, I thought, but I dared not ask considering how Ophelia's question was met a day earlier. Instead I queried, "Who exactly do the Cabecar think you are?"

"A descendant of Iriria, their earth goddess." He paused for a second, chuckling to himself. "Who knows, maybe I knew her. But whoever she was, she has long since left these lands."

"Do you believe all legends, gods or creatures are either Conduits or Swali, the half-children of Conduits and humans?" I asked.

"Don't you?" His back was to me, but I could sense his contemplation. He went on, "Let me put it this way, I have yet to run into a story that didn't anchor its origins in our people."

I did not doubt a word he said. It was what my parents had always told me. I guessed, over the last few weeks, my world had been expanded even further than I had imagined.

"What about all of the mythological creatures?" I asked. "Like the troll I met a week back. How does she fit into our world?"

"Those creatures were painted in the first strokes, just like us. Humans were the last to be created, and Malarin wanted to keep them innocent, so he painted their lenses different than ours. My father explained it to me as such. Have you heard of color blindness? It's that strange phenomenon that some humans live with."

"I have heard of it, yes."

"Humans were created with magic blindness. They can sense that it exists, because it is all around them. So they make up stories to explain the sensation. Sometimes they even see magic happen right in front of their eyes. Depending on their origins, they may recognize it as such or simply shrug it off. My father believed that those who 'saw' some of the magic in the world were either Unconsu or Swali—that always made sense to me."

"Is that what we are, magic?" I asked. I had never put much thought into what one would call a Conduit's gift. It was just part of our makeup—like our hair or hands. Vosega had a very different perspective than my parents had; he was much more ethereal about our world. I wondered if my parents had been that way before war ensued, before their time on this earth had hardened them.

"Magic is as good a word as any, I suppose," he said. "Asagi might have a better word for it. But humans like that word, and I find that I prefer it as well." He turned to look at me. I could see his strong features in the candlelight, their long shadows stretched across his face. "I met your father and mother many years ago. They came and warned my wife and I about the tumult that was coming our way. They may have saved our lives at the time." He paused, and I could see he was trying to figure out how to say what he was going to say next. "I have spent much of my life in caves, secluded. But your parents, they lived for something—for the betterment of our people. They saw many die and worse still. If I had lived as courageously as they did, I would find it hard to see magic in the world still, as well."

I swallowed hard.

Vosega turned around and continued walking. After five minutes of silence, he spoke again. "We are just about there." I had been trying to watch my surroundings, so I could retrace my steps if need be, but I was afraid that would be difficult to do. The entire trek was one long slick cave with random offshoots. "Can you smell it? The air has thinned. The ascent begins here." He pointed at some steps in front of him.

He began to take the steps three at a time. I followed in short pursuit.

There must have been hundreds of stairs. I was winded when we reached the top, where Vosega casually moved the earth by putting his hand on the ceiling of the cave. The dirt and rock fell away and exposed a brilliant blue sky. The fresh air flooded my lungs. I welcomed it.

Vosega climbed out, then offered me a hand. The view from the top was breathtaking. Nothing but green mountains as far as the eye could see.

"Come, the village is this way."

We began heading east, traversing the landscape fairly easily along a narrow path. I turned around at one point and noticed some offerings that lay next to a large rock close to where we had emerged from the mountain. The path, I surmised, had been created by the villagers when they came to worship Vosega, or whatever they thought his name was.

Vosega caught me staring. "See, I told you, my people."

We walked for another fifteen minutes or so along the mountaintop path until in front of us appeared a large, round, reedy structure surrounded by gardens and a field that had been freshly burned. A woman watched as we walked past, but said nothing.

I thought about how we must look. Vosega bare-chested, his wild red hair flowing in the breeze, and me, dressed in shorts and a casual button-down shirt, with mere stubble on my chin and short-cropped hair.

"Vosega?" I called. He stopped and turned to face me. "I have to admit, you actually look like a mountain god, but I look like a tourist. Is this going to be an issue?"

He waved his hand aside. "No, these are my people. Trust me." His confidence was reassuring.

"The Cabecar are a matriarchal society. They don't live in a village per se. They have a community up here, but think of it more as a farming collaboration. I am going to introduce you to Tuludi, their medicine woman, if you will. In other words, she calls the shots."

"Do you speak their dialect of Chibchan?" I knew from my research that many of the local Costa Rican people spoke a dialect of Chibchan.

"Yes, fluently. Plus, they have picked up some Asagi words. The historians want to give credit to a Mesopotamian influence, but I know this particular tribe has roots with Asagi origins."

"Did you teach them?"

"No. I have only been here for seventy years. They were speaking Asagi long before that."

"Who taught them?"

"I don't know. Maybe it was Iriria?"

Obviously Vosega was not concerned with the Asagi overlap, but I was because it was likely that Alistair and his family had something to do with this development. I was excited. This meant we were on the right track.

We passed people at four more dwellings, all with the same nonchalant response to our presence.

"No one visits this village," Vosega explained. "Strangers are assumed to be gods, and they believe they shouldn't approach a god unless they are acknowledged. I will acknowledge them on our way back through."

"I see."

We reached a larger settlement that had several structures on the property.

"Here we are," he said. "She will come." We stood there, waiting.

A young woman came out from behind a smaller building carrying a basket of green beans. She had long black hair held back from her face by a leather band. She wore a top and skirt both made out of leather, as well, she was slender, with tan skin. When she saw us, she stopped in her tracks and stared. Vosega nodded his head. She set the basket down and walked over to the two of us. She pulled a small woven-grass doll from a belt at her waist, where it had been attached. Vosega took it and examined it. Then he opened his arms to embrace the young woman. No words had been spoken, but she reciprocated the gesture.

After the exchange was over, the woman spoke in Chibchan. I picked up on a few words but waited for Vosega to properly translate. We stayed where we were as the woman left and ducked into another building on the property.

"She says Tuludi died eight years ago, that she is her daughter and the current medicine woman—her name is Tulaswaga." He quickly put his hand up. "I know it means 'gift' in Asagi. She is going to prepare a small meal for us to partake in with her. At which point I will explain that she is to acquiesce to whatever request you may need of her while you are visiting."

"Who will you tell her I am?"

"I don't need to tell her anything. She just told me, you are Sibu's son." He looked at me curiously. But I had no explanation to give him. *Who is Sibu?* I thought.

OPHELIA

*I*t was my third day sitting by the fire with Vosega while the guys scurried about—Elias on his secret mission and Lucas scouring the landscape, pretending to scan the perimeter for trackers; of course, we all knew that was just an excuse to avoid time with his dad. I didn't mind being alone with Vosega. He was a pretty good host and he had no reservations about sharing information with me. Either Lucas had not warned him to be sparse with the intel or, more than likely, he just didn't care. My only request would've been that Vosega put on some damn clothes. He traipsed around his mountain chateau with very little attire on, and needless to say, I understood where Lucas got his delicious physique. I had to be very mindful of my gawking.

"Ophelia!" I jumped slightly at his thunderous assertion of my name. I thought I'd been alone with my reveries and hadn't realized he'd reentered the hall. "Would you like some mead this morning? I have a special batch that I just finished brewing for eyok."

"What is eyok?"

Vosega stopped mid-step and stared at me with sincere bewilderment. "What have they been teaching you?" There was disgust in his voice. "Eyok is an integral part of our existence. It's a ritual that builds relationships." He shook his head again. "When times were proper, and you had the companionship of a guest, you would exchange stories. It is how histories are passed down, and it demonstrates *beau geste* to your company—an opportunity for them to build their own legacy."

I wasn't sure I had a story he would enjoy, but I was eager to hear about any tales Vosega found pertinent to our history. "I would love to coalesce over eyok," I said, smiling at him excitedly.

"In that case let me prepare the gilly mead and some cheese and bread. Will that satiate you for breakfast?" he asked.

I nodded and followed him into the kitchen area, for lack of a better word. It was a designated space that held several giant barrels full of an assortment of meads home-brewed by Vosega, as well as a large cooler of sorts. It definitely wasn't a refrigerator, but instead just a simple stone box with a heavy animal pelt buckled to the top. Inside was a large block of ice and some perishable meats and cheeses Vosega kept on hand.

"What is gilly mead?" I asked, figuring it wasn't what we'd been drinking the last couple nights.

"Gilly mead is a fine drink," he said affectionately. "Sweet and warm and thick, but with less alcohol than regular mead, so as not to get us too sloshed before noon." He walked over to a metal barrel I hadn't noticed before. It rested on top of two metal plates, and the plates were stacked above a small pool of lava.

"Is that keeping it warm?" I asked.

"Yes, I keep this lava circulating and slightly cooler than the other magma in the mountain. The tungsten plates prevent the steel barrel from melting and conduct the heat evenly into the cylinder." He poured the gilly mead into a large wooden stein and handed it to me. It steamed and bubbled slightly. "Now wait to drink it, give it a moment to cool."

I nodded and, very carefully, took it to a seat beside the hearth and set it down. I returned to the kitchen area to see if he needed assistance with the cheese and bread, but it was already displayed on a beautiful redwood chopping board. Thin wedges of fragrant cheeses lay alongside small oval-cut baguette slices. My mouth watered with anticipation.

"Take your seat, young lady," he chided. "I can handle this." Before I could sit, a small table appeared in front of my chair with the plate of food and my stein on it. By the time I was seated Vosega was already lounging and had taken several sips of the gilly mead in his mug.

I went to reach for my own mug, but he cautioned me with his hand. "A few more moments." He adjusted himself slightly in his lounger and looked at me intently. "Tell me what you think of the deep orange cheese. It is one of Oya's favorites. Imported all the way from Marseille, France."

I took a piece of the cheese and a slice of bread in my hand, and politely maneuvered it into my mouth, then I nodded vigorously with approval.

Vosega chuckled. "I am glad you like it. Now that we are settled, I would like to go first, if that does not offend you." I shook my head. "Wonderful—it is custom that the host entertain first. And then I will request a specific story from you."

My eyes got wide as I wondered what type of story he could possibly request from me. He must've noticed my demeanor change because he quickly added, "Don't worry, it is customary that the guest share only what he or she is comfortable sharing."

I smiled nervously.

"Shall we drink first?" he said. "Your gilly should be cool enough." I swallowed my mouthful of food and cleared my throat, prepared to chime in with a toast.

We raised our glasses and I repeated a phrase I'd heard Vosega use over the last few toasts. "To the strokes. May they favor your passage!" After we spoke that in unison, we both settled back into our chairs and I pulled my legs in tight under me, ready for a story.

Vosega began. "Today I will tell you my favorite story, that of the three brothers and the forging of The Rittles. The great painter, creator of all strokes, began with three. Three brothers as they were: Fih, Tindle and Priloc. Fih was the most mischievous of them all. He liked to manipulate his own strokes, pervert lines and separate the whole. Tindle was a creator. He enjoyed blending the painters' strokes together and creating bonds, objects and beauty. Priloc was a lover. He loved all that was—all Chitchakor created was perfect in his eyes—and when strokes were broken, interrupted or perverted he would mend all manner of things.

"So it went that as Malarin painted the first strokes, Fih defiled them, Tindle created with them and Priloc mended them.

"Malarin saw this in his children and thought, this is good together they balance the strokes. They create and destroy, and this continues the strokes and the melding of colors. This was before Fih created the first colors of the grey. So it was. For centuries Fih, Tindle and Priloc danced during the daylight along the never-ending strokes, creating new creatures and mending broken bonds, with the occasional separation performed by Fih. When twilight would descend, the brothers would retreat to their own private sanctuaries.

"Fih loved the woods. He resided inside the Ikkell Forest, where huge Toaglin trees shrouded Fih's home from sight. Toaglin trees are so large that you can fit six large waterwheels lying down at their base, whilst their branches expand beyond the clouds." At this point Vosega paused. "Do you know what waterwheels are? I mean the big ones that were often stationed beside an abbey or an inn." He shook his head, as though he was frustrated with his description. He began using his hands for assistance, spreading his arms out wide and then shaping a moving circle with them.

"Yes, I know what waterwheels are, Vosega," I said with a little eye roll. "They move flowing or falling water and create a form of power for a variety of things, like mills. And by your hand gestures I'm assuming these are some *big* water wheels," I teased.

He looked at me and nodded approvingly.

"So all of this translates to a big ass tree," I said.

He laughed. "Several big ass trees, actually." He went back to using his story voice, which had a somewhat more mesmerizing, majestic tone than his casual, small-talk voice. "The leaves of the Toaglin trees were the size of large quilts and as soft as a rabbit pelt. They littered the forest floor, and thus Fih slept peacefully upon the floor of the Ikkell Forest amongst the Toaglin trees.

"Now, Tindle preferred the caves of the Yiqueth Desert. This desert was to the east, where the winds stayed warm and colorful. The sand of the desert was a brilliant mix of purple, red and yellow. The wind was a vibrant green, and Tindle enjoyed the shapes the wind and the sand created together. Tindle lived there in a cave called Cataphet. This was no normal cave; Cataphet was a place of sand deep beneath the world's surface—with miles of rooms and caverns. Cataphet could speak, and was Tindle's greatest friend." Again, he paused. "Caves can say amazing things." He smiled wildly with his eyes.

I couldn't hold back a chuckle. "I bet they do. Is it a secret language?" I asked, half-joking and half-curious.

"No, not a secret," he answered seriously. "But you must listen very carefully to hear it." He put his hand around his ear as though he were listening to it right where we sat.

There is so much to this world that I have yet to learn about. I sighed. *I'll have to put the language of the caves on my list.*

"And Priloc resided by the ocean," Vosega continued. "He loved the vastness of her body and the curve of her waves. As the waves broke along the shore, he was reminded that all things can break and also be mended. Priloc would lay on a log with his toes in the sand. The water droplets would tickle his toes, then rush back to their mother, the sea. It was a spirited game they played. And if the water got carried away and swept him into their tide, the log he lay upon would gently sweep him back to shore."

Vosega adjusted himself in his seat and continued. "It was one twilight when Tindle decided to follow Fih into Ikkell. At first it was because he imagined his brother was lonely. Fih didn't share the forest with a companion the way Tindle did with Cataphet or the way Priloc shared his home with the ocean and her children—Fih was alone.

"Tindle worried for his brother, for he believed it was not good to spend the span of night alone. So he followed and he kept silent, believing that perhaps Fih had a secret friend, one he did not wish to tell his brothers about. After hours of walking under the Toaglin leaves, Fih stopped and Tindle sank behind a tree root, careful not to be seen. He waited for Fih to speak to his secret friend. He heard nothing but the rustling of the giant Toaglin leaves. For hours he heard rustling and adjusting, and his curiosity was besting him, but he dared not look beyond the root, afraid that Fih would see him and grow terribly angry.

"It is unclear how long Tindle waited beneath the root of the Toaglin tree, but at some point during the span of the night he fell fast asleep. When Tindle woke Fih was gone. 'It will not hurt much to see what made all the commotion last night,' Tindle said aloud to himself.

"So he climbed over the root to the place he last saw Fih standing beneath the Toaglin trees. As he stood, he saw an indentation beneath the leaves. He scurried down to the brim of the hollow and pulled back the closest leaf. His mouth slacked, agape. It was a cavity full of objects Tindle had never seen before. Tools Tindle had never laid his eyes upon until now. Anger and disappointment bubbled up inside of him. Why would his brother hide such things? Why would his brother create such things without Tindle's guidance? Some of the objects appeared sharp—and dangerous.

"Tindle resolved that he would discuss this with his brothers, together, as one. He took one of the giant Toaglin leaves and began stacking the unique objects into the center. When he had collected them all, he hoisted the leaf and its contents over his shoulder and began the arduous journey back to the meadows of Amawin, where the three met each dawn. As he bounded over the last hill that led into the meadow, his brothers ran to him. Fih and Priloc had been afraid when Tindle was not there to greet them as he always was. But for Fih that fear soon grew to anger when he recognized a Toaglin leaf upon his brother's back.

"'Where have you been, Tindle? Did you find the dawn okay?' Priloc asked as he looked his brother over.

"'He has been guileful!' Fih pointed at the leaf. 'What have you here? From my den, no less.'

"Fih tore at the leaf, and the unknown objects tumbled out and onto the grass.

"'Fih, what are these creations?' Tindle yelled back vehemently. 'You keep things from your only brothers?'

"Priloc looked aghast between the two, sad that one brother stole and that the other brother coveted secrecy.

"'Tindle, you have your Cataphet, and you, brother Priloc, have your ocean and her children. I have my treasures, which I procured, or made myself!' Fih tapped on his chest with the palm of his hand, emphasizing with pride that they were his objects.

"Priloc spoke up. 'But Fih, we are not painted to covet, we are not painted to take or to separate.'

"'Says who?' Fih growled. 'The great painter?' Then Fih picked up the most menacing object he had acquired. It was a long shaft, pointy at both ends—and ominous. He put it to Tindle's throat. 'You are only jealous because I created too. You believe only *you* can create.'

"Tindle's voice was shaky when he spoke. He had never experienced a blade before, and although it was new to him, he was aware it presented danger. 'Fih, my brother,' he said. 'Perhaps you are right. Perhaps I was jealous. But now I see these objects are of your creation and of such beauty. Perchance that we may paint them into the strokes together?' Tindle reached for his brother's hand to assure him of his intent. 'I only want to create with you, bond as brothers, keep no secrets and continue to dance across the strokes together.' Tindle's voice was pleading.

"Fih then took two steps forward toward his brother, anger still bubbling up inside him. Tindle fell to the ground as he stumbled over the pile of objects that had fallen from the torn leaf, which no longer adorned his back. When Fih saw Tindle splayed out amongst his hidden treasures—his prized possessions—he could not contain his rage. He bent down and slid the sharp end of the staff across Tindle's neck until blood poured out of him in every direction.

"Priloc, frightened, harnessed the power of his beloved friend, the ocean, and with a wave of his hand he expelled Fih over the Rabfed Hills and back to the beginnings of the Ikkell Forest with a strength he never knew he had, and never possessed again. Then he knelt beside his bleeding brother. Tindle's blood poured out as billows of colorful paint onto all of the cursed objects crafted by Fih. Priloc drew his brother close and began to mutter a binding so full of love and so fastened by intent that by Chitchakor's strokes Tindle was healed.

"Then, because Tindle had nearly died and Priloc had given all he had to save him, they slept.

"When they woke it was once again dawn, but Fih had not returned. They gathered the cursed items, including the staff that had pierced Tindle, and they walked to Cataphet."

I exhaled long and loudly, and Vosega paused. I hadn't realized I'd been holding my breath.

"I'm sorry! I didn't mean to interrupt you," I admitted contritely. "That Fih was a real bastard!"

"Yes, he was," Vosega agreed, and then resumed, satisfied with the fact that I was now breathing normally again. "Priloc and Tindle walked for miles and miles, both still weak from heartache and loss. When they reached Cataphet, she wept when she saw her Tindle, and swore she would defile Fih should he ever attempt to call upon Tindle whilst he resided in her caverns. Tindle assured her that was not necessary, but she still swore it so. Tindle and Priloc then travelled as deep as anyone ever had before into Cataphet's tunnels, and then they travelled further still, so deep into the surface of the world that their breath held no color, no strokes were to be seen. It was here that they laid the cursed objects. They were no longer Fih's; Tindle's blood had bonded them to the world, to his own creation. Priloc's love and mending of his brother Tindle had hinged them to the blessed painter's strokes, where all things begin and end."

Vosega looked at me to make sure I was still following him. I nodded quietly, then he continued. "But there was something more, something venomous that was trapped inside the objects from Fih's malice: a poison that was bound to them, deep within their essence, that made them lethal. So Priloc and Tindle knew the objects must remain hidden, because such things are bound to insidious actions."

There was a long pause and I sat thinking. Thinking about what I knew about The Rittles, and what I'd heard about Fih from the story

Aremis had told me weeks ago—the story of the painter who created all things through long, continuous paint strokes.

"But they don't stay hidden, do they?" I asserted.

"No, they don't," said Vosega, "and neither does Fih stay expelled. Otherwise we would not be here today. Isn't that the way of it? That good relies upon evil to exist. That there could be no day without night, or any paragon for what is right if we don't have a precedent of what is wrong. You cannot value something fully if you have never lost it."

I sat there in silence once again, taken aback by his outburst of wisdom. I felt some bitterness swelling inside me too. It was as if in a way he was dismissing Aremis' death or even his wife's death as a necessary evil. I wanted to press on with questions about the story, but I was suddenly overcome with resentment. Resentment of all evil things—of their existence and any rationale for it. Angry at Vosega for suggesting they deserved a place in this world, for implying that they were a necessity.

ELIAS

J spent most of the prior day with Tulaswaga, learning about Sibu and why she insisted I was his son. I heard all about how Sibu created the earth and taught the Cabecar people how to sustain themselves.

I had the sneaking suspicion that the legend of Sibu was somehow associated with Alistair and his family. The origin of the entity made no difference. What did matter was how she felt about my appearance in the village. Just like with the other two tribes I had called upon, she was expecting me. She wrote as she spoke about the Cabecar culture, which was even more helpful. I took extensive notes and copied every symbol she recorded. I found the Cabecar language easier than others to pick up, and I wondered if it was because the roots somehow seemed entrenched in Asagi.

I was eager to learn more, to ask questions, and grateful to Vosega —not only had he made introductions for me on that first day, but he had temporarily opened a volcanic tunnel so that, in order to visit the village, I would not need to trek up and down the mountain in the traditional way. Not to say that the journey through the lava tube was easy; it was not. But it prevented me from having to navigate a path to and from the secluded village by myself.

On the second day, I emerged from the tunnel and took a few moments to admire the altar that the locals had constructed for Vosega. It was made of large stones and raised about three feet from the ground. On top of the rounded altar stone lay an assortment of corn and legumes, and beside those were some small figurines and several woven wreaths.

I then made my way back to Tulaswaga's farm. She was busy working when I arrived but stopped what she was doing and came over to give me a hug, a gesture that I was certain was not native to her people. I wondered if she worked all this land by herself, because I had yet to notice anyone else on her compound.

She escorted me into her dwelling and proceeded to tell me more stories. I listened intently, sure that there must be answers to my larger questions about the summit in our interactions together. By now I had to assume these leaders were instructed that upon my arrival they follow a precise protocol.

I wondered who the instigator of these proceedings had been. I was starting to feel like this was all so much bigger than what I had initially suspected. This was bigger than Alistair, it was older—it seemed divined somehow. *I could let my mind get lost down that rabbit hole*, I thought, but not right now, *not whilst I need to be present and listening for clues*. I prayed to Malarin—that the bigger picture would reveal itself someday.

OPHELIA

"Eyok?" Vosega asked as I walked into the hall. I was still waking up and wasn't completely lucid. I absentmindedly nodded in agreement, forgetting that this was an actual ritual I'd just agreed to, and that it required exchanges and expectations. The prior day's story had left me frustrated and haunted. It was all I could do to brush it off and fulfill my end of the eyok. If Vosega knew he was catching me off guard, he didn't allude to that with his expression.

I meandered to the round hearth and sat down in the seat I 'd grown accustomed to over the last few days and adopted as my own. I looked around; there was no sign of Lucas or Elias.

Lost in thought, I jumped when Vosega set down the mug of gilly mead and a cheese plate on the table beside my chair. "Sorry. I didn't mean to startle you," he said, flashing a sheepish smile as he sat across from me in his massive lounger. "I cooled the gilly today—it should be a suitable temperature to drink now.

I took a few silent sips. It was delicious. Warm, thick and sweet— but not too sweet. The flavor reminded me of warmed peanut butter with a dash of cinnamon. You couldn't taste the alcohol at all; it just tasted like comfort in a mug. Vosega patiently stared at me. My grogginess was sloughing off and it occurred to me that it was probably my turn to start the eyok ritual with a story, though I had no idea what story I'd share.

"You will share this morning's first story," Vosega said. It was not a request, it was a statement. "I will ask the question," he added.

Apparently, the fog of the morning wasn't completely gone. I'd forgotten that, as my host, Vosega decided what he wanted to hear. I, however, hadn't gotten to decide what he shared with me.

"Yesterday you shared with me about your grandmother Lilith and your mother Eleanor. Today I wish to hear about your father." My face must've reflected my exasperation, because he followed the statement up with, "Whatever you know about him."

At least it'll be a short story, I thought. "I really don't know much at all," I began. "My mother didn't talk about him—she refused to elucidate on any part of that time in her life."

"Well, then it will be a short story, but I would like to hear what you know. Since you are full Conduit, perhaps I can detect who your father might be from what little you know," Vosega suggested.

I tried not to roll my eyes. *So a large, shirtless man in a volcano is going to tell me more about my father than I've known my entire life?* I thought. *That would be a story to tell the grandchildren.* I sighed and decided it was useless to protest. I was pretty sure I was in some eyok contract at this point.

"Well, I think my mother was living in Texas at the time of my conception. She was young—seventeen. Her adoptive parents had just passed away in a car accident and she was floundering, as was to be expected." My eyes went to my hands. I was suddenly sad for Eleanor's loss, and hoping she was doing well, and that she was happy.

"What part of Texas?"

"Laredo, near the Mexico border." I was going to continue with what little I had left to say on the matter when I heard a door open and shut. We both looked to the hallway. As the silhouette moved closer to the entrance, I realized it was feminine, and my heart began fluttering in my chest, frightened it could be one of the two women— Nandi or Vivienne—stalking me. Vosega stood and spread his arms.

"Vos!" a little voice shrieked and a delicate female with long sandy hair streaked across the room and jumped into Vosega's arms. She began showering him with kisses and I started to feel uneasy for an entirely different reason. I heard Vosega whisper something in her ear and she jumped down, her cheeks a pale pink from blushing. She shot out her arm as she walked up to me.

"So sorry. I am Oya." I took her hand and shook it gently.

"No need to apologize. I'm sure you didn't realize Vosega had company. I'm Ophelia. I'm friends with Lucas." I smiled as I spoke.

"Lucas!" she said, almost aghast, as she pulled her hands to her chest. "Lucas is here? Where?" Her eyes scanned the room.

"He arrived four nights ago," Vosega answered, then Oya began rambling in a language I didn't recognize, not even as Asagi. Vosega replied to her many times as she spoke while I stood there, captivated by their dynamic. I grabbed my gilly mead and sat down to enjoy the show; it was like watching a foreign film. I guessed that Oya was surprised Vosega had not told her we'd arrived, and maybe he was explaining why he hadn't asked her to join us. Oya looked a little hurt and almost a little frightened as she spoke. Then they both abruptly stopped and turned to me.

Oya spoke first. "I didn't mean to disturb eyok. I only just returned from Venezuela. It has been several days since I have seen my Vos. Please continue." Without further ado, she was now seated lackadaisically on Vosega's lounger, with her legs sprawled over him and her own mug of gilly mead.

"As I told Vosega," I started again, a little flustered, "there isn't much to share." I took a moment to gather my thoughts while I took a long look over Oya. She had to be younger than twenty when she consummated. Her skin was caramel-colored and her hair was a long golden tan—it almost sparkled in the firelight. Her body was tiny, especially beside Vosega's, but she was curvy, with large breasts, round buttocks and shapely legs. She wore some beaded necklaces around her neck and large dangling earrings in her ears. Her attire was minimal and very similar to Vosega's—leathers that barely covered her feminine assets and exposed her perfect waist. Needless to say, she was sexy as hell. I cleared my throat and started from the beginning, since I hadn't gotten very far anyway.

"Well, Oya, Vosega asked about my father. The sum of what I know is, my mother was living in Laredo, Texas, when I was conceived. She had just lost her parents and was disheveled, trying to find her footing in a life without them. Eleanor—that's my mom—was working at a café and living out of her car when one of her regular customers offered her a place to stay on his ranch outside of town. I don't know what happened out there or who she met, but I get the impression from our limited conversations about it that that's where she met my father. He could've been the regular, for all I know. Aside from that, I know I get my red hair from him, as well as the wild curl—I only know this because as a child, whenever my mom would try to tug through the tangled mess, she would mutter under her breath about how much she hated it, and how it reminded her of him."

I paused and looked at them both. Although I didn't know Oya, I could tell something was stirring behind her eyes, some semblance of recognition.

I made a mental note and continued. "I guess I have one more incident, if you wanted to call it that. We were living in North Dakota at the time and Eleanor was married to Les, a real jerk. Anyway, she was working at a local café part time—mostly the morning shift. I'd hoped for months that she'd leave Les—he was abusive to her—but she wouldn't listen to me. Then one afternoon she came home early from work in a panic. She wouldn't tell me what was going on, but I heard her yelling at Les when he came home from work that day. She was begging him to leave with her. She said that she'd seen my father and that he would hurt us—that he may hurt me. She was screaming and crying and begging him to come with us. But Les refused and beat the crap out of her before he went to bed that night. I thought that was the end of it. I tried to fall asleep; I'd seen him do worse to her and she'd stayed. But whatever she saw at work scared her into action. As soon as Les passed out, she packed us both a bag and we left in the middle of the night. As a child, I figured she'd simply had enough, but looking back on it now, it was more likely that seeing the man she assumed was my father scared her into leaving, afraid he would find us."

They both stared at me blankly. I hadn't shared that story with anyone, and as I rolled it over and over in my mind I felt this twinge of fear and realization: Eleanor had been abused for years by Les, but the possible sighting of my father had her fleeing to the hills. *What could he have done to her?*

Oya spoke first. "Ophelia," she began. My name sounded funny in her odd accent. "What year were you born?"

"1990, why?" I asked.

She turned to Vosega, ignoring my question, and began rambling in that bizarre language. She was yelling as she stood up. Vosega responded with minimal words and calm tones. Oya continued, sounding as though she was building in agitation. She pointed to me several times and pulled at her hair dramatically. I looked on, horrified, afraid that something I'd said was offensive. I wished that Lucas or Elias were there to help me—perhaps they knew the language the couple were speaking. After a good five minutes of Oya shouting and pointing, but not addressing me, Vosega interrupted her.

"I am sorry, Ophelia, will you excuse us for a few moments? Oya is unmistakably worked up about something and I would like to speak with her privately."

I just nodded, still unsure of what I'd said or what had happened. I looked down at my hands, and when I looked up again they were gone. I sat there in stunned silence, mindlessly sipping on my gilly mead.

ELIAS

I got back to the chateau just before noon. I was eager to see Ophelia; typically, just the sight of her eased my nerves. I was slightly alarmed, however, when I entered the hall and it was empty. The fire appeared well tended, but there was not a soul in sight. I cautiously moved down the hallway, wondering if this was foolish worry. *But was anything a foolish worry these days?* I reminded myself.

Ophelia's door was closed. I knocked on it and heard movement on the other side. Her faint voice called, "Come in."

She was sitting on the bed, her head in a book, when I entered. "Good afternoon," I smiled. She set the book down—and her face lit up with the smile I found felt like home.

"Is it afternoon?" she said.

"How foolish of me. You have been down here too long. You probably do not even know what day it is, let alone the hour. Would you like to go for a walk?" Then her face really lit up with unadulterated excitement.

"Really?" she squealed.

"Yes, really. Perhaps we could practice some sparring too. I could use the exercise." I beamed as she leapt off the bed and wrestled to get her shoes on.

"Me too!" she said. "I feel like a slug!"

She got ready hastily and we stepped into the hall. "Where is Vosega?" I asked.

"I don't know. Oya showed up this morning, and then they started fighting during our eyok, and I haven't seen them since." There was something in the way she said the word "fighting." I sensed she was not telling me everything. But I had learned not to push her. Lucas was quick to jump on everything, and I saw the way it tested her. I did not want to treat her that way. I would let it be and she would share it with me when she was ready.

"I will leave him a note," I said, "in the event he should return and be concerned." I tried not to let my frustration leach into my voice. I knew Vosega felt that his fortress was safe enough, but leaving Ophelia unattended was troublesome. I would need to discuss it with Lucas later.

I wrote a quick note and turned to Ophelia. "Shall we?" I gestured for her to lead the way, curious which exit she would choose. She decided upon the westward staircase, which led to a beautiful grassy meadow, not far from a hot mineral spring. I knew Ophelia had eyed it when we first arrived, during our chateau tour. I wondered if she would insist on bathing since we were so close. My mind was drawn to the idea of seeing her naked body; I had to shake my head to dislodge the beautiful visual I had created.

We walked in silence until we ascended into the sunlight. It was a beautiful day—warm and humid, with a slight breeze.

"What a perfect day," she asserted.

"Indeed," I agreed. "Lead the way." There were no real trails; thanks to Vosega, the national park had been closed due to volcanic activity a few years earlier. Even if it were open, no one would be stomping around these parts of the mountain. Any designated trails were at least a mile from us.

"This way," she pointed and began trekking over the shrubbery and through the foliage. As I suspected, it was in the direction of the mineral pool.

"I think I remember there being a small open area here, perfect for a sparring match." She winked at me as she looked over her shoulder.

Does she have a clue what that look does to me? I wondered. If she did, she was coy enough to disguise it.

After just ten minutes of walking, we came upon an oblong grassy area, just large enough for two people to fence. She kicked off her shoes playfully as she stepped onto the thick lawn. Then she ran over to the opposite end and put on a mischievous smile. "Are you ready?"

"The pertinent question is, are you prepared for combat, Ophelia Banner?"

She gestured a come-hither motion with her hand. "Bring it on."

I crouched and growled a soft, joking snarl. She laughed and mimicked me. This was only the third time we had sparred. I had been too busy visiting villages to practice with her. We both advanced and began the dance best described as dueling.

I wish I could say it was flirtatious and intimate, but I could not. When Ophelia practiced, she was serious and intent. For nearly two hours we sparred. I also wish I could say that I let her win, but she justifiably won three matches and gave me a proper challenge the five that I bested. She had been studying vigorously, and her form confirmed that it was paying off. But there was something more, something I could not put my finger on—the very thing Lucas had described. It was more than training. She was faster, stronger and far more capable than she should have been. He was right, we had reason to be concerned. She appeared to be escalating her skills at an alarming rate. And we still did not know exactly what a Sulu was capable of. The thought created a hard knot in my stomach. *How could we keep her safe and not hinder her growth?*

"I'm a mess," she said, interrupting my pondering. We were both winded when the duel was over, and sweaty—very sweaty.

We were lounging in the grass staring at the sporadic clouds when she spoke up. "Race you to the hot spring?"

Before I could answer she was on her feet, darting through the landscape. I had no choice but to follow. I would decide what to do next when we got there.

I fell in step with her as she ran and giggled. I could not help but laugh at her jubilance. The bath came upon us quicker than I had expected. I had been so wrapped up in her smile that I had not thought of a good reason not to join her. She did not wait for me to have any hesitations either. As soon as the pool was in sight she began stripping. First her top, then her bra, then—I looked away. I stopped and let her finish undressing without my vagrant eyes upon her. I had to remind myself that I was not some childish virgin—but then again, this was different than any love affair before it. This was my Atoa, my other half, and the mere thought of it demanded respect.

She gingerly stepped into the bath, the water was steaming about her face by the time I turned around.

"I thought Europeans weren't modest," she teased.

I took a deep breath. "I am not necessarily European," I stalled. "My family had homes all over the world."

"Well, whatever you are, you stink. Come join me." She plugged her nose playfully to mock my odor.

"I would not want to muddy the waters," I said, trying to figure a way out of this, but the truth was I wanted it. I was already getting hard thinking about it. But I could not tell her that I could not get in because I had an erection. It was now or never.

"The water is perfect, and I won't judge you if it gets a little cloudier when you get in." She smiled at me again and I knew I would not refuse her. "Wear your underwear, prude."

"I am no prude! What happened to the young woman embarrassed by her nakedness after a close encounter with a friendly spider?" I teased.

Her cheeks flashed red. "I was more mortified by my reaction than my nudity."

I was not entirely convinced that was the truth, but I had already decided I would join her.

It was time to show no fear. I took off my shirt and it was her time to feel flustered. She blushed and turned away. I let myself enjoy that for a moment, and then slowly took off my shorts. I did not wear trousers, so that settled the modesty question. She did not look back at me as I slowly folded my shorts, goading her to take a peek. I took my time stepping into the warm water. It was perfect.

Only after I was completely immersed did she bring her eyes to meet mine.

"It's nice, isn't it?" she insisted.

"Lovely," I concurred.

We sat there in silence for a long minute.

"Elias." She paused. I knew a question was coming next.

"Yes, Ophelia."

"Do you know anything about my father that you aren't telling me?" I had no idea how she came to this question. I was taken aback but tried not to show it on my face.

"No. Why do you ask that?"

"Today, during eyok with Vosega—well, Oya got upset after I told her the few facts I knew about my dad. I couldn't understand what she and Vosega were talking about, but Vosega had asked me about my dad, and after I shared the whole *three* things I knew, she began rambling in some language I didn't recognize. It was not Asagi, trust me. Anyway, she rambled and yelled and pulled at her hair and pointed at me. I don't know what I said."

I waited a little longer, because sometimes when Ophelia ranted like this, she would pause, then pick back up. When I was certain she was not going to carry on, only then did I answer.

"I know nothing about your father or his origin. But perhaps Oya does. I will bring it to Lucas' attention and we will see what he believes happened," I assured her. "Ophelia." She looked up from her hands and met my gaze. "Whatever upset Oya has nothing to do with you, even if it pertains to your father."

She nodded.

LUCAS

I heard their voices long before I saw them. Olly laughed and I found myself picking up the pace. I caught wind of her scent on the breeze and I picked up my pace again. Sulfur also wafted through the air, and I realized I was near the small mineral bath she'd told me that Vosega showed her during her tour that first day. *Is Olly in the bath? With Elias?* My sprint was now urgent.

I turned the corner around one of the many giant boulders that cluttered the landscape and saw her pulling up her pants. I felt like I got the wind knocked out of me and my face got flush with anger. I swallowed hard, took a huge breath, and did my best to look casual as I stepped out of the shrubbery and into view. We'd agreed to take the pressure off Olly—to stop competing for her affections—and here this asshole was, taking a dip with her.

I cleared my throat. "Did I miss an opportunity to skinny dip?" I asked in my best breezy tone.

"Shit! You scared me." Olly jumped as she pulled her pants up the rest of the way. I found Viraclay to her left and shot him a death stare. Olly laughed nervously. "Actually, you did miss a good soak, but there wasn't any funny business. Just two people washing the sweat off their bodies after a good spar." She put her hand on my shoulder. "As always, Elias was a complete gentleman." She flashed me her brilliant smile. Her hair was wet and stacked on top of her head in a soaking bun.

"Always a gentleman, huh?" I flashed him another wicked stare. "Was the bath your idea?" I spun her around and cradled her shoulders in front of me.

"You know it was. I'd been pining for that mineral bath since we saw it four days ago. I practically had to beg Elias to join me."

I squeezed her tighter. "You wouldn't have had to ask me twice."

"I know—because you're a pervert," she teased, then pulled away from me as Elias moved toward us. I fought back the urge to punch him in the fucking face. She took one step closer to him and gestured toward him playfully. "Whereas Elias here is extremely old-fashioned, almost prudish. How your two behaviors are so drastically different, when you're the one who is hundreds of years old and he is my age, is beyond me."

"Just lucky, I guess," I grinned.

Elias spoke up for the first time since I'd entered the clearing. "I was shamefully battered with a manners baton as a child. Regretfully, it does not appear that I can break the habit." He was now beside her and I felt my blood boil with jealousy. "Never the matter. Fortunately for us, Lucas is here to keep us all playfully on our toes. How was the perimeter run?"

I bit my tongue and tasted blood. I had two options here—or three, rather. Beat him now and upset Olly, berate him now and upset Olly, or play nice now and berate him later—this was the best scenario, I knew. So I chose the third option. I took a second to think of what I would say later, and it gave me some solace.

"There's no reason to suspect we've been followed here, yet," I said, pulling Olly in close to me and pressing her body to mine. "I guess that means we can continue to spend time with dear old dad. How has the old bastard been treating you?" Olly said nothing. I pulled her back from my chest to look her in the eye. I saw that Elias was looking at her attentively too. Something had happened. Of course something happened, I realized. That explained why they were out here to begin with. "What happened?" I asked.

Olly still didn't meet my gaze.

"Ophelia Aleacia Banner, what happened? Tell me now before I go ballistic on Vosega, that self-centered offensive asshole. I knew we shouldn't have come here. What the hell was I thinking?" Olly stopped my rant and grabbed my arm. I had already been mindlessly walking toward the chateau entrance.

"Wait," she said. "He didn't do anything. We were in the middle of our eyok when Oya showed up." She was holding tightly to my arm.

"What? Oya is here? Now?" My head was reeling. "He couldn't even have the decency to ask her to stay away while his son and his friends visited for a few days? After I haven't seen him in centuries? This is unbelievable." I clenched my hands into fists.

Olly continued. "They didn't do anything—but when Oya got here and I shared the few details I know about my father, well, she seemed to get upset and then they left the room. I was alone until Elias got home around noon."

I turned to see Elias' face, and he confirmed what I was feeling. Fury at the prospect of Vosega and Oya leaving her alone.

"I'm going to speak to my father *right* now!" I said forcefully. Olly grabbed my arm again.

"Wait. I think it was my fault. I said something that upset Oya—concerning my dad." Olly's eyes were pleading. "She began speaking in this weird language, not Asagi, and then I could tell Vosega didn't want to upset me. So he asked to be excused."

I turned to face Ophelia dead-on and grabbed her shoulders with both of my hands. "Let me explain something to you about Oya. She needs to have my father's undivided attention, so much so that she made up a language that only the two of them can speak." I saw slight recognition flash across her face; I hoped I was getting through. "Are you following me? The bitch was probably peeved when she walked in and saw Vosega alone with another woman. She made up a wild excuse to get him alone by starting some argument. I remember these tactics from when I was a child. Trust me, this has nothing to do with your dad, or you, or anyone else but that manipulative bitch." I kissed Olly on the cheek and moved her aside. "Now, I'm going to speak with my father privately. Take the long way back to the chateau, please." I said the last bit to Viraclay, and then I was gone.

~

I ENTERED THE CHATEAU TO FIND IT EMPTY. *BUT IT CAN'T BE EMPTY*, I thought. *Vosega never leaves this mountain.*

"Vosega!" I paced in the large entertainment hall and watched the water bubble periodically in his personal hot bath. I thought of my mother and my blood boiled. "Vosega!"

I turned to pace another lap and he entered the room.

"Yes, my son?" He put his hand up. "Before you say anything, I have already asked Oya to leave."

"What was she doing here?" I growled. "You can't spend a few days apart?"

Vosega stepped closer and I stepped back. I was moments away from physically attacking him. Rage and frustration from years of disappointment was surging through my body and taking over my senses.

"I didn't know she was coming. Last I saw her we had made plans for her to return to my mountain on the next full moon. She missed me, however, and decided to surprise me with a brief visit."

I scoffed. "I guess she got her tryst after all." I let all the venom I had bottled up leach into my voice. "You left Olly alone. I trusted you with the woman I love, and you left her alone!"

"She was always in earshot. I never left the mountain." He said it coolly, and it dug deeply under my skin. It reminded me of the day that my mother died. He couldn't get to *her* quick enough from his mountain.

"Oh, but you *did* leave Ophelia wondering how she offended your hot-headed bitch of a mistress," I accused.

"I admit that Oya was ill-mannered with Ophelia, but those are some very ugly descriptions."

"What was her problem? She got upset because you were spending time with someone else?" I demanded.

"Perhaps seeing Ophelia here caught her off guard." I watched Vosega's body language as he spoke. There was something he was dancing around. Something was making him squirm.

"What are you not saying?" I stood still and waited for the truth.

"Oya asked about you—she was surprised to find out you were traveling with companions." He knew I would rather vomit on him than entertain the thought of Oya's phony concern.

"I hope you politely told her to fuck off for me. While you're at it, please feel free to do so yourself." I brushed past him, hitting him hard on the shoulder. "She'd better not come back while we're here, otherwise I'll have words with her. And I need you to apologize to Ophelia. She doesn't deserve being in the middle of your drama—she took it personally."

I was gone before he could say anything else.

ELIAS

*S*ix days of making my way to the Cabecar village. I had all of
the characters of the language written down at this point
and was now learning more vocabulary and how to properly
pronounce words. I was quite sure that I had what I needed to translate the Cabecar parts of Alistair's journals. However, unlike the first
two villages I had visited, where my contacts seemed to have day-by-
day plans for me, Tulaswaga did not appear to have a prescribed
agenda. And I was not certain when it would be the right time to
leave. I still had so many questions, but I was frustrated to find that
often my inquiries were met with a question in and of itself. It was
urgent to continue the mission, but I needed to trust my intuition, and
it said, *Stay—just a little longer.*

As far as any of us could tell, we had not been followed to Costa
Rica. But I felt it was only a matter of time before we would be
tracked down. And, again recalling Lalee, I knew I did not wish to put
anyone else in danger.

But something inside me knew I had not found what I was looking
for here—yet. So I returned to the village once more.

OPHELIA

*V*osega was contrite. "Before we enter eyok this morning," he started, "I must apologize for Oya's behavior yesterday."

I began to object when he put his hand up. "Please let me continue. I was already unhappy that she behaved in an uncouth manner in your presence, and disturbed our eyok. Lucas brought it to my attention that you felt to blame for this disturbance. I would like to assure you that you were just witness to a lovers' quarrel."

I looked at him suspiciously. "Why did she keep pointing at me and pulling her hair?"

"Oya was taken aback that I had visitors, and she tends to lean toward the dramatics when she is upset. I assure you, my dear, you are charming, and it is Oya's loss that she was too troubled to enjoy your company."

I had to hand it to him. He had a way with words, that Vosega. "I'm sorry Lucas yelled at you," I said. *I did feel to blame for that.*

Vosega waved it off. "Nonsense. Fathers and sons find themselves in discord often." He smiled at me in such a way that I felt completely at ease.

He was moving on too. "Now, may we participate in a proper eyok this morning?" he asked. "I want to know how you got the nickname Olly," Vosega said cheerfully.

"It's not a very long story." I admitted. Come to think of it, I didn't know if I had any long stories.

"No matter. Please share and feel free to elaborate for an old man's entertainment."

"Well, as my mother tells it, I started talking at an early age— around 11 months."

"Is that early?"

I shrugged. "I couldn't tell you. She made it sound that way. Anyway, I was forming sentences, and for the most part was extremely understandable." I laughed to myself, thinking that might be the only time Eleanor ever said I was understandable.

Vosega caught my inner chuckle and inquired about it. "Please tell me what is funny."

"It may not make a lot of sense to you, but my mother and I didn't have the best relationship." He raised an eyebrow. "She was difficult at times, and I tried my best. To make a long story short, she very rarely found me pleasing or 'understandable'—more often than not, it was as though we were speaking two different languages."

Vosega nodded. "I see. I can understand." He laughed. "I find you very understandable!"

We both laughed at that, and when the laughter subsided, I continued. "Eleanor says that I was a stubborn child and that I refused to say my own name. I decided my name was Olly. Over the years it just stuck, no matter how many times my mom tried to get me to go by Ophelia. Now I go by both, but maybe it was always about challenging her, or her challenging me?"

"That was a very short story," he said, then paused. "May I ask you something?" I nodded. "Do you love my son?" The question caught me off guard. I thought about my answer.

"I do, very much. He's my best friend."

"So you don't love him as a companion?" he asked.

"It's complicated," I sighed. Vosega just nodded, obviously aware that I was the monkey in the middle of the two men I loved. But bigger than that, in many ways, once I met Elias, there was never a question of choice; I was destined for one man and we both knew it.

Vosega was silent for a moment, then he spoke quietly. "I met her once, his Yesi." That was the second time I'd heard her referenced by a nickname.

"But Lucas said he hasn't seen you since he was fifteen...?" The statement came out more as a question.

"He hasn't, really. Sometimes I would watch him from afar, and I knew he knew I was there. I watched him grow up that way. He was born stubborn and determined, like water, like his mother—and apparently like you." Vosega winked at me. "He was always meant to find his own way. The building of the canyon by the river is far more laborious and magical than the formation of the mountains by the earth." Vosega shook his head slowly. "If Lucas wants to build a divide, by Chitchakor's strokes, there will be one."

"So then how did you meet Yessica?"

"She called on me. I was here, as I have been for the last seventy years. She wanted to connect with Lucas' father—understand me—to perhaps better understand him. It was three days before she disappeared."

"Lucas doesn't know about this?"

"How could he? This is the first time we have spoken in nearly 850 years. My son is brilliantly bolshie." I couldn't argue with that. He went on to explain. "The Kraus family, along with Yesi, were traveling through on their way to Hanoi. They had spent some time in Argentina but felt like it was time to move once more. I don't know how she knew where I was; I suspect that Lucas had told her the indicators of my presence. No matter how she found me, she did and I will forever be grateful for it." He looked at me. "Does he talk about her?"

I shook my head. "Not often. It seems to hurt him. I mean, of course it hurts."

"Yes, but it's no way to live, trying to forget those you lose. We have to remember them, build shrines to them in our memories. He will see that someday—or at least I can hope he will see that someday."

He looked off in the distance above my head for a moment. "I had the pleasure of spending several delightful hours with her. She was a joy to be around. She told me all about their adventures, how they had met, their favorite places to travel. She brought life back to this old man."

"How did Lucas and Yessica meet?" It felt too informal to call her Yesi. I didn't know her.

"I will do my best to tell it as she did." He smiled a warm and excited smile. "First you must know what both of them were up to before their meeting. I'm not sure what Lucas has told you about our last engagement, but he was fifteen when he decided to set out on his own." I noted that Vosega either didn't know why or chose to ignore the reason his son felt so dejected—enough to leave. "We were traveling through the lands of the Ghurid Dynasty—what is now Pakistan. I had no idea where he went, but I should have guessed it was somewhere where he could learn the skills to defend himself and vent some of his angst. He joined the Varangians of Constantinople under the name Alpin. The Varangians were mercenaries shipped from Scandinavia. They were paid exceptionally well for their skill set."

"What was their skill set?"

"Death, with no mercy—they were utterly lethal. Lucas has always learned quickly. After his mother died I started to train him in combat. With the Varangians he was able to execute his training and pick up new aptitudes. He served in the guard for fourteen years. Until the fall of Constantinople in 1204, when good old "bushy brows" couldn't hold onto the Byzantine Empire." I thought about asking who the hell bushy brows was but didn't think it was necessary for the story, or else Vosega would've elaborated. "Lucas travelled northeast and found himself in the battle of Rodosto, in February of 1206. Bulgaria seemed as good a place as any to spend a little time while he sorted out where he wanted to go next, so he stayed put for a while."

"Lucas was how old at this point?"

"Alpin," Vosega winked, "was a spry thirty-one years of age."

I'd always wondered exactly how old Lucas was when he consummated.

"Meanwhile Altani—that was Yessica's birth name—was born in Mongolia to Mr. Khan himself. She was his daughter, with his beloved consort Chiangi. Once Genghis had consummated with his Atoa, Borte, he decided it was necessary to have as many children as he could with unconsummated Conduits. At the time, it was how you expressed power and assurance of your legacy in the human world. He had countless children, but Altani was always his favorite daughter after she saved her younger brother from a would-be Tartar assassin. However, her presence was not appreciated by Borte, the empress, so Altani was to be married off the year that Khan was coronated as the emperor, during the Kuraltai.

"The night before her wedding, Khan came to Altani's chambers and begged her to take to the Silk Road, to find her Atoa. He wanted her to find true happiness, he loved her so much. I think he also knew they would meet again someday—he had huge plans for his empire. It would take him over one hundred and fifty years and nineteen lifetimes to expand, and then finally lose, the empire he built."

I put my hand up. "So you're saying that Genghis was *all* the Khans? They weren't his children and grandchildren, but in fact *him*?" I wasn't that shocked to hear this was the case, I just wanted to make sure I understood Vosega correctly. I'd resigned myself to accepting the "awe factor" of the Conduit world. This meant that when histories as I knew them were completely different than what I had been taught, I could acknowledge the occurrence without making my head explode with questions and disbelief. It was actually way easier than trying to wrap my brain around the truth.

"Yes, that is exactly what I am saying."

I nodded with understanding. "Proceed."

"Altani took her father's advice and fled her nuptials. She was young, and the world was a different place for young women than it was for young men. But she was fortunate enough to meet a small caravan full of families on the road. They agreed to let her join them until they reached Constantinople. When they reached the Black Sea, word had spread about the tumult occurring in the deteriorating empire, so Altani headed north as soon as they made port. The twenty-six-year-old Altani found herself in Rodosto shortly after the battle, trading what few spices she had left and feeling unsure about where her future would take her. Alpin ran into her outside of an ale house—she was being berated by a drunk Bulgarian horde. It was love at first sight." Vosega smiled. "I wish I could say they lived happily ever after." His smile faded. I saw a tear cascade down his cheek.

"I wish it ended that way too," I said, realizing I truly meant that. I loved Lucas enough to know that he deserved to be with the woman he was meant to be with.

Just then we heard a door open, we passed a knowing glance between us. I got the hint: for now, this should stay between us. When Lucas entered the room to our conspiratorial silence, he looked nervously at the two of us before speaking.

"Why do I feel like you were sharing my awkward baby photos with Olly?"

We laughed, maybe a little too hard, which didn't assuage his anxiety. But Lucas was willing to blow it off if we were. He grabbed a mug of mead and sat down next to me.

"Want to wrestle?" he asked. Now that I knew a little more about his history, I was more eager than ever to learn from the best.

I nodded enthusiastically. "Let me go change."

"Perfect. Let me drink a couple of these." He downed his cup and got up to grab another while I skipped to my room.

ELIAS

*I*t had been another informative day with Tulaswaga—but something crucial was amiss. I simply could not put my finger on it.

I was nearly back to the mountain entrance when I saw a young woman at the altar. I had never seen anyone actually participating in a ritual there. She was chanting and dancing of sorts. She gave me a sideways glance when she saw me approach, but she did not stop what she was doing. I quietly filled the distance between us, then stopped, admiring her enthusiasm as she carried on. After a few moments she stopped the chanting and dancing. She removed a hefty sack from under her skirt and gingerly opened the bag, reached in and withdrew a large handful of something. I stepped a hair closer. She began another chant while letting a fine black sand fall from her hand in a circle around the altar.

My heart skipped a beat. I knew that black sand—I had some of that black sand. I shuffled in place like a young child that had to use the loo—attempting a thin veneer of patience as she finished her ritual. When she completed a circle for the fourth time, she stopped and closed her eyes.

I still said nothing, not sure if she was truly finished with her ceremony. After a long moment she opened her eyes and turned to walk away. I called to her as she was replacing the bag, back under her skirt.

I pointed at it and asked in broken words what it was.

She rambled off several Cabecar words in quick succession, then pointed at the volcano where Vosega resided. I pointed to her bag again and asked as best I could if I could retain some of the sand.

She looked at me hesitantly before reaching in and giving me a handful. I took it carefully, and held it tightly as I ran back to Tulaswaga's farm. I was winded when I entered the boundary of her property. She met me before I reached the structures, concern apparent on her face.

"I am okay," I said in Asagi.

She nodded with understanding.

"Can you tell me—what is this?" I used the Cabecar words I had learned, along with some Asagi, when I was uncertain of the correct vocabulary. This was how we had been communicating for the past six days, and it was fairly efficient.

Her eyes widened. She closed my hand. Holding it, she ushered me into the building where we had been spending most of our time together.

She directed me to sit down on the floor—cautioned me not to drop any of the sand. Her voice was stern and demanding. She had never taken this tone with me before, so I sensed the severity of the situation.

She shuffled around collecting several items before sitting down across from me. She set four kinds of objects in a small pile in front of me—several leaves, a few stones, and two different flowers. She sprinkled some water over the top of the pile and mumbled a few indistinguishable words. Then she gestured to my hand with the black sand, indicating I should create a circle with the sand encompassing myself while including the things she had gathered. I followed her instruction. When the circle was complete, Tulaswaga stood and began dancing and chanting around me, never breaking the circle of sand.

As she danced, I felt something shifting in my body—it was as though elements of my being were suddenly aroused in ways they never had been before. My senses felt heightened and bigger than myself. An electricity vibrated between my body and the earth under me, then transferred to the pile of leaves, onto the flowers and finally through the stones. The current moved to encompass the entirety of the circle. Time seemed to go by slowly but somehow substantially while I was in the circle of sand. I did not know how long the ritual carried on, but when the vibrations finally stopped and Tulaswaga took her seat across from me again, it was dark outside.

We said nothing for a long time. When Tulaswaga spoke, her voice was hoarse. "This is the transformational earth." She pointed at the sand. "The soul of Iriria. The proof that all life moves in circles, from creation to destruction and around again. From destruction comes life." She gestured to the flowers and leaves inside the circle. "Comes strength and longevity." She pointed at the stones. "You are now part of the circle; you have Iriria's soul within you." She lowered her head and blew a break in the sand. She put her hand on my heart. "She lives in here."

Tulaswaga lifted me to my feet and gave me a long, reassuring hug. My body still felt a residual buzz. The closest thing I had ever felt to this type of connection had to be what I used to feel between Ophelia and me, before Lucas stifled our connection with his camouflage. It felt familiar, safe, as though I was more whole than I had been before this night.

"Go, share Iriria's soul with others." She smiled and turned to leave. I followed her out, and marveled at the night sky. Something was vastly different, yet entirely the same.

"How can I ever thank you?" I asked Tulaswaga.

"I will thank you—one day."

I knew my time was done there, so I left with a peace that whatever had just happened was part of what I had been looking for in Costa Rica, that when the time was right I would know how to utilize the "transformational earth," as she had called it. I felt an odd acceptance wash over me. I could not quite explain the intensity of contentment I felt surrounding my encounters at the village. It was as though my spirit knew this was all already ordained to happen, that my role was to simply be present. I had never experienced anything like this before. I had been exposed to prophecies since I was a child, but this was bigger than a prophecy—it was orchestrated—every move I made had been accounted for. I was grateful for the inner peace it provided me, even if I did not understand it. It meant that participating in unknown rituals, receiving cryptic advice and realizing someone had had the foresight to notify these people of my appearance was not to be feared—but instead was confirmation that I was in all the right places.

All of this led me to believe that I would indeed be triumphant in securing a summit location.

LUCAS

Ophelia was already asleep. I'd just met with Viraclay. He'd returned from the village long after dark. Something was different about him; I couldn't place what it was. I didn't care, though, once he said the three words I'd been waiting for—'time to leave.'

It was just me and Vosega in the hall now. "We'll be leaving tomorrow," I said as I poured myself another cup of mead. I had to admit my old man knew how to brew some good drink.

"Where will you be going?" Vosega asked behind me.

"I don't know yet—Viraclay plans the travel around here," I scoffed.

"Will you come back to visit?"

I turned around to face him. "Probably not." I moved toward the fire and sat down.

"I see. Well, may I have a moment of your time at present then?" He sat on a bench opposite me. "We both know you have been avoiding me during this stay."

I didn't respond to the accusation. There was no need. "I have a minute."

"I will speak swiftly. Oya was traveling in Norway when she ran across a pod of assassins." My eyes rolled at the mention of her name, but Vosega didn't skip a beat. "Amongst these assassins was a pixie. Oya overheard the conversation between them; they were comparing conquests and defeats. The pixie told a story about ambushing a Conduit in Iceland thousands of years ago during the mating migration. He said it was a hit ordered by a private party, separate from the Nebas." I was sitting up in my chair now, stunned. I began shaking.

He continued. "He went into details about the order—it convinced me that this story is not a work of fiction. He said it was supposed to be an annihilation job—they were expected to take out the whole family..." He paused. "But something went wrong, and aside from himself the rest of his team was killed." Vosega let a small smile flash across his face. "I suppose I did that. But I am grateful this one got away and has a big mouth, because I haven't properly avenged your mother's death—if this is to be believed."

I downed my mug of mead and got up to give myself a refill, replaying the revelation I'd just heard in my mind. As the information sunk in, I began considering it more deeply. I wondered when pixies became lethal assassins. Vosega sat patiently.

When I resumed my seat, I spoke. "What do you want me to do with this information? I mean, how the fuck do you want to proceed with hunting this asshole down?" I finished my second mug.

"I have been attempting to track down leads," Vosega replied, "but I have been out of circulation for so many years that many of my connections have disappeared, been murdered or are in deep hiding. I have tried to determine a motive for anyone who might have wanted to eliminate our family—if it wasn't related to the war, as it would seem, then I am afraid I have no idea why anyone would want any of us dead." He put his face in his hands and rubbed his eyes. "You were just a boy. We were not challenging anyone's territory."

"Let me get this straight, *Dad*, you are bringing this to my attention because you want me to hunt down leads, because you won't get out of this fucking hole?" I gestured around me.

"I have tried," he said, somewhat feebly. "I don't know how the world works anymore. Many of my friends are gone, presumably dead." His demeanor changed. "I will go with you," he asserted.

176

I put my hand up, barely containing my anger. "Wait. I'm not even going to consider pretending to be Sherlock and Watson together, sleuthing and solving crimes. I just want to be clear as to why you haven't done something with this information yet. How long have you had this intel?"

"Forty years."

My face got hot. "You didn't think to get a hold of me sooner?" I stood up and started pacing. *He was such a coward.*

"It's hard to track down a son who doesn't want to be found, especially by his father. That is why I started to make my whereabouts more known, hoping you would find your way back to me." Vosega stood. "You have every right to be angry, hate me even more, if that is possible. But you did come find me, and now you know."

I was fuming. It wasn't a good time for me to try and communicate any further. It would just end badly for both of us. "I gotta get some air," I said, and went to leave. Then I turned back to face him. "I will hunt this piece of shit down."

"Will you at least tell me who hired the hit when you do?" he asked.

"You will know," I said coldly. Then I left.

OPHELIA

I watched as Elias shook Vosega's hand and Vosega pulled him in closer for a hug. It was interesting to see Elias' resistance to affection. I wondered if he was always that way.

"You are making your father proud," Vosega said as he squeezed him tighter. "You are making the Pai Ona proud." Elias patted his back, in that awkward way that many do when they are acutely aware of sincere flattery and intimacy.

"Thank you, Vosega, for your kind words and exceptional hospitality," Elias replied.

"You are welcome in my mountain anytime, young man." Vosega gave him one last pat on the shoulder, then gestured to me. "Please come here, Ophelia."

I gladly stepped in front of our half-naked Adonis host. I was sad to say goodbye to him, but not his bare chest—it was too distracting. "I'm going to miss you!" I said sincerely, then threw myself into his arms for a hug.

"You see, gentlemen, this is how you embrace." Vosega grinned. Elias, somewhat embarrassed, retreated to his room for a moment to collect the rest of his things. Lucas sulked in the far corner.

Vosega held me tight, then pulled me back to face him. "I will miss you too." Then his voice hushed. "You are special, my dear. Trust your heart. There's enough love in there to right any wrong and envelop this whole world with compassion." He pulled me in again and then spoke even quieter. "Take care of my son. He needs your strength. I would not tell him these things; it is all I can do to get him to stay in a room with me for more than a moment. But I will tell you. He has goodness in him, masked by fear and loss—and I know you can see behind the mask."

"I do see his goodness," I whispered in response. Then I squeezed him one more time. "Goodbye, Vosega."

"We will meet again, my dear." He smiled at me as we detached, turning his attention to Lucas. "A parting hug, my son?"

Lucas ignored him entirely, looking to me instead. "Are you ready, Olly?" he asked just as Elias entered the hall.

"Yeah," I said as I turned back to Vosega to give him a sympathetic look. He just shook his head in a dismissive "Don't worry about it" way, then we left.

WE WERE BACK ON ANOTHER PLANE. THIS ONE WAS NOT AS LUXURIOUS as the one we'd taken over the Atlantic from Costa Rica to Paris. We had to stop to fuel up in Bosnia on our way to our final stop, India.

"Make it quick, Olly. We're just filling up the plane, not sightseeing. We need to get out of here as soon as we can." There was urgency in Lucas' voice.

"Got it." I gave him a thumbs-up as I scooted into the small airport convenience store. I wondered if that was what they called it in Bosnia. *A convenience store, perhaps a market?* I giggled to myself, confident that the local word for either of these establishments probably sounded very different than anything I could have imagined. I'd overheard Elias speaking to the gasoline attendant as I entered the building; the language was sharp and thick with syllables.

Thankfully the universal signage for "restroom" was easy enough to locate on a door near the back of the shop. I reached for the knob, but it was locked. I walked over to the employee at the counter, a solid woman with unruly gray hair flitting about her face. Her eyebrows were dark and framed big green eyes. She had a square jaw that might have been attractive on a man but was distracting on a woman.

She gave me a once-over. I smiled. She didn't smile back. I pointed to the restroom, then played my best game of charades, gesturing turning a knob and then maneuvering a key into the lock. She grimaced and spoke a few mumbled words that I didn't understand. Then she abruptly turned around and walked behind a curtain.

I stood there for a minute, not sure what to do. A door open behind me, and I realized someone was exiting the bathroom. I hurried over, not bothering to make eye contact; I was feeling a bit out of my element.

I took care of business and washed up. When I opened the door I noticed that there was a community board of sorts in the hall. A large poster caught my attention. On it was an image of ruins atop a steep mountain. The ruins were comprised of three walls of stones that, while somewhat dispersed, held tight to the peak's cliff faces. A fourth wall looked more like a jetty. The terrain was rocky and strewn with grass and shrubbery. There was one distinct structure left looming over the remains.

I gasped and inhaled sharply, I ripped the poster off the wall. I braved the front counter again. As I stood there, the older woman peeked around the curtain, then yelled three or four words I was unfamiliar with.

"Excuse me?" I said, trying my best to be polite but feeling a pressing need to find out more, and quickly, before Lucas came in to harangue me.

A young man barreled around the corner, out from behind the curtain, as though he'd been pushed. He hollered back to the lady, then politely said, "Yes, how may I help you?"

I sighed in relief. "Where is this?" I asked, pointing at the poster. "What does this say?" I aggressively pecked at the writing above and below the image with my finger.

He looked at me oddly but answered. "It is a tourist flyer. To visit

Stjepan Grad near the town of Blagaj, here in Bosnia." I looked at him inquisitively, trying to sort out my own thoughts. He continued. "The village isn't far from here, only kilometers away. Do you want to visit?"

"Yes. I mean, maybe. May I take this?" I asked, feeling flustered.

The young man turned around as if to make sure the woman behind the curtain wasn't watching, and nodded.

I stared at the poster intently. *Was I going mad? The remaining* structure of the Stjepan Grad ruins looked like the image I had in my mind of Hafiza. I was wondering if I was just so desperate to see her again that my mind was playing tricks on me, or if this was really all that was left of her—which made no sense. These ruins were obviously a tourist destination and potentially thousands of years old. *What does this mean? Are Elias and Lucas lying to me about what happened? Are they concealing even more from me?* I needed time alone to think about it.

I looked at the poster once more, wondering if this could truly be Hafiza, then quickly folded it and stuffed it in my pant pocket. For now, this would be my secret.

I put on my best smile, bounced out the exit, then jogged to the tarmac where the small plane was parked. Both of them were standing there—Lucas with his arms crossed, Elias casually leaning against the nose of the aircraft.

"Sorry, there was a line for the potty," I explained, hoping they hadn't noticed my interaction with the young man at the counter.

"Another thirty seconds and I would've stormed the store," Lucas kidded, but I suspected there was more truth in that statement than he wanted to admit.

"No storming necessary." I smiled. "I'm right here." Then I almost surprised myself by adding a roundhouse kick and landing directly in front of Lucas, missing his face by an inch. "Besides, I think my lessons are paying off. Don't worry—I can take care of myself."

Lucas' eyes got wide and then he rolled them dramatically. Elias muffled a chuckle. I decided to follow his lead and laugh.

"After you, gentlemen." I waved at the door. I could tell Lucas wanted to say more, but he decided to hold his tongue. I was sure he had lined up some snarky comment about not playing around with my safety.

I was glad they bought my cheery demeanor; I didn't want to get into a spat about possible lies and deception until I had more time to rest and study that poster. Who knew? Maybe I was wrong about it. We'd been traveling for many hours; I was beat.

I climbed in the back while the two men manned the cockpit. As I strapped myself in, I looked at the back of their heads, thinking about how different they were. By all accounts I would say Lucas was the more playful of the two, but he could be so much more intense. Elias was a constant. He laughed, but was always vigilant and on alert—I usually sensed his concern, though he rarely voiced it. Lucas was always reminding me about how he was watching out for me. Considering what had happened to his Atoa, Yessica, I wondered if that was to make himself feel better more than to remind me that he was at my guard. Elias carried the weight of the world on his shoulders. It was evident in his eyes. Lucas would just as soon carry me on his shoulders, right out of here or harm's way—or more likely, as far away as he could from Elias.

All of this was a distraction from my itch to pull out the poster and start shouting theories, questions and accusations. My leg literally itched where the paper was folded in my pocket. I just needed a few more moments to examine the picture and refine the image in my memory of the castle I'd grown to love, and even call home.

ELIAS

I was pleased enough with our accommodations in Jammu, India. Our flat had been recently renovated and had all the necessary amenities—air conditioning, clean running water, a very nice kitchen and good bathroom facilities. We were in the city center, a few blocks from the main market. I had travelled through India many times as a child. I knew Jammu was a fairly well-tended city, since it relied on tourism more than most. The city itself was nestled between two beautiful mountain ranges. The weather was not optimal —it was hot, with oppressive humidity. But this was where my mission had next taken us.

I was certain I had tracked down the right village this time. There were very few clans in northern India. These particular Bhil people were so secluded that their existence was considered legend among many of the locals.

I had purchased a motorbike for transportation; it would assist me greatly on my journey up into the neighboring mountains. Lucas and Ophelia would be able to get around adequately on foot.

I warmed some water for tea. The kettle began to shriek as Ophelia entered the kitchen. She had been acting peculiar since we started the second leg of our trip from Costa Rica. I wondered what was keeping her on edge. Lucas followed behind her—I watched him carefully as well. He, too, had been acting irritable, even more so than usual. Perhaps all this travel really was getting to them. This had been my lifestyle for years, basically all of my life. My time in San Francisco had been the longest I had stayed put since I was eleven.

"Did you sleep well?" I asked Ophelia.

"Fine." She was curt.

I turned to Lucas. He noticed her short response as well but appeared to be lost in thought about something else.

I took the kettle and poured it over my loose-leaf tea, then offered, "I procured up some vada this morning."

"What's vada?" Ophelia asked. She picked up one of the small cakes off the plate I had set on the counter, and looked at it curiously. "It looks like a donut."

"They are a fritter made out of lentils. Try one, please." I watched as she took a bite and smiled.

"Hmmmm… they're good," Ophelia said with a mouth full of food.

"I am glad you like it. There is a market just down the road with all kinds of street food and produce. Plus, a colorful array of textiles and jewelry." I walked over to the table and sat. They both followed me and took the other seats. Lucas reached for a vada and smiled in approval as well.

"Soooo… can we go spend some time at the market?" Ophelia asked hopefully.

"I will be gone most of the day," I started. As I expected, she already knew that.

"Yeah, I was talking to Lucas. I figured you were busy with your 'secret errands.'" She said the second part mockingly. There was something in her tone that had me curious.

"I kind of have an errand to run as well. Maybe a couple of days' worth," Lucas conceded.

I looked at Lucas, now extremely intrigued, but before I could inquire, Ophelia interjected.

"Oh, now you have secret errands too? How convenient." There was more sarcasm in her voice.

"No secrets, but possibly a wild goose chase, so before I say anything, I'd like to investigate a few leads," Lucas said defensively. "Besides, Elias has been running around for weeks with a top-secret mission and you haven't given him any shit."

He was throwing me under the bus. I did not care about that, but I did worry that whatever he was up to could put all of us in danger.

"Should I be concerned about this secret errand?" I asked as benignly as possible. He turned a venomous gaze on me.

"Should I be concerned about your fucking 'mission'? You've almost gotten us killed more than once already!" Lucas pushed back the chair and got to his feet. "If you must know, I just need some time to process my visit with dear old dad, alright? Is that okay with both of you?" He looked at Ophelia as he spoke.

I saw her stare soften; she was buying this story. I was not.

"Sorry, Lucas." Ophelia stood beside him, and put her hand on his shoulder. "I'm sure this has been hard for you. Take all the time you need." She sat back down.

I did not say a word. I was afraid my suspicion would betray me. Lucas sat down in silence.

"Alright," Ophelia started, "so you two have things you need to take care of. Would it be too much to ask to allow me to be a tourist for a while?" She looked eagerly at both of us as she spoke.

"No, that isn't an option," Lucas asserted.

Now Ophelia was on her feet. "This is ridiculous! You expect me to sit here by myself while you two run around all day? I'm tired of the secrets and the seclusion. I've been a good sport. Do we have reason to believe we've been followed here yet?" She looked at both of us intently.

I shook my head and Lucas said no.

"Don't I have this magical hairsy charm that gives me some supernatural GPS power?" She twisted the bracelet between her thumb and index finger.

I nodded again, but Lucas was ready to start his counterargument. He reached for the hairsy charm. "We don't know how this thing works, and we won't know if we were followed until we're spotted."

Ophelia interrupted him. "That's bullshit. We haven't seen Vivienne or Nandi for three weeks and over two countries ago. I've been practicing combat with both of you. Before that, I had lessons from Ying. I've been beyond patient. I'll be no safer here sequestered alone than I'd be in a public place where I could at least create a diversion."

I could not argue with her logic.

She continued, her voice escalating with each word. "I challenge you!" She pointed at Lucas. "Let me show you I can take care of myself at least long enough for you to locate me with this stupid tracing device." Once again, she played with the charm.

Lucas smirked at her with a devilish expression that implied he thought this was foolish, but he would entertain her to shut her up. "Fine! Let's wrestle, Olly. But if I win, you stay put. This *is* ridiculous," he scoffed. "We just want you to be safe."

She snorted. "This war is coming—you can't hide me from it. Let me live a little while I still can. Let me have some control over my day-to-day life." She stopped and thought about something. "If I win, I get to go to the market by myself and you *can't* join me, even if you want to. You don't have the option to say no. This is my ticket to freedom."

"As you wish," Lucas growled. He was confident he could best her. It was a risk, because he knew she was Sulu, capable of amazing things —more importantly, she was capable of the unknown. But he was betting she had no idea how to utilize any of her skills. "When this is over and I've proven you need to listen to us," he said, "because you're not ready to defend yourself, I don't want to hear about you being on your own again."

I still said nothing. It was not that I wanted Ophelia to be left to her own devices; it was that I suspected her resolve. I also agreed with her, that the war was coming. She would be in the thralls of it at some point. I wanted to keep her safe, but I understood the vexation of seclusion. Up until this point I had not grasped her feelings of isolation. I empathized; I had been sheltered by protective parents most of my life. It did not matter that I knew they meant well. Upon their passing, I have been isolated by this quest and the necessity of secrecy.

I hated the solitude. Lucas on the other hand loved seclusion, so he could not wrap his mind around her resistance. In addition, there was another element to his protectiveness. He was still holding on to the woman he had protected in San Francisco. But Ophelia was no longer that woman.

The house had a rooftop deck. The two of them marched up the stairs to it while I followed. The tension was palpable as we emerged into the open air.

Ophelia took a position opposite Lucas. I backed up to the far corner, where the air conditioning unit hummed.

"Don't think I'll take it easy on you. You need to understand the threat you'll be up against on your own," Lucas explained before he crouched.

"By all means," Ophelia said. She curtsied, then ran at him.

She leapt up a few feet in front of him, attempting to plant a spin kick on his right side. He moved quickly, quicker than she could have assessed. There was a blur of movement. Now Lucas was behind her, reaching for her neck. She somehow anticipated his whereabouts, though, and ducked just in time for him to lurch forward. He stumbled slightly on her huddled form but recovered quickly, of course, and pounced over her, landing directly in front of her. She stood and met him with a right jab to his cheek. I heard it make impact. Lucas was not throwing any punches; he just wanted her to see she could not defend herself from the speed of a Consu.

He proceeded to sweep his left leg, dropping her to the ground. She quickly scrambled to her knees—steadied herself, preparing for another launch in his direction. Lucas picked up his pace yet again and was once more behind her, reaching for her neck. Right before his hands met her flesh, a deafening scream escaped Ophelia's mouth. I saw Lucas' face go ash white. Everything stopped. It was as though even the wind felt the impact of her scream, and with it came the startling realization that she was manipulating the shield she had created around herself, thus immobilizing Lucas'. He was still frozen from shock as she turned to face him. She inhaled, and the pressure of the combating shields subsided.

"What did you do?" Lucas shouted.

She looked past him to me. I stepped up to both of them and put my hand on her shoulder. "Ophelia, what did you do?"

"I proved I can take care of myself," she said calmly as she brushed off my hand and walked back down the stairs.

OPHELIA

I sat on the end of my bed, shaking. The truth was I had no idea what I'd just done, just as I had no idea what I did in the fencing hall with Ying.

When Lucas was about to get the drop on me, my angst spilled over and I harnessed something beyond me, yet somehow inside of me. In that instant I felt my being expand, and within the umbrella of expansion I recognized new sensations. My fingertips burned, the air tasted thick with emotions, and a palatable shield rebounded off my skin, advancing on Lucas' gift and driving it away. *What is happening to me?* I worried. *Is this what they are referring to when they say they can't tell me what I am?*

I was so angry, so tired of all the secrets and all of the detention. I leaned over and riffled through my bag until I felt the small leather satchel Rand had given me in my hand. Then I moved my hands to the folded piece of paper with the image of what I suspected to be Hafiza. I held both items fiercely. They represented some weird sentiment of control for me. In all honesty, I knew they were just small fragments of my life I felt were my own. I hated this feeling. It was silly. It was childish, and in a way it made me feel further secluded.

I stood, my knees nearly giving way. It was time to share what I had, to lay my cards on the table and hope Lucas and Elias would do the same.

I stepped out of my room and walked into the kitchen. No one was there. I walked aimlessly through the unfamiliar house but all was silent. I was alone.

LUCAS

I was shaking as I sat at the bar. It wasn't far from the apartment. It was a dive, just the way I liked them. I ordered a beer. It arrived warm. I didn't care.

I couldn't believe I'd just given Ophelia her ticket to freedom. *I practically handed it to her on a silver platter*, I scolded myself. There was nothing I could do now, unless I tied her up. But after what she'd just displayed, that probably wouldn't detain her for long either. *What does this mean for her detection?* I wondered. *Can I keep her safe?* And, most worrisome, *Is she diminishing my powers as hers gain momentum?*

I thought about my shield; it didn't feel any less potent. *What do I really know about Sulu?* It was a myth, an old wives' tale among the Conduit community. My mother had told me a story once, when I was seven years old. She said her grandmother heard that a Sulu existed when the first strokes were painted. That this Conduit was so powerful that the other Conduits feared him or her. They didn't understand where the Sulu's copious gifts came from. Now I understood what my mother meant. I trusted and loved Ophelia, but I didn't understand what was happening to her, or how it was affecting me. *No one can know about this*, I told myself. *They might harm her out of fear of the unknown.* This was exactly why I couldn't antagonize her anymore; I couldn't risk someone else witnessing her power. She made it evident that I wasn't to follow her to the market—that I needed to give her some space. And so I would. My gut ached at the thought of it.

I had to let this go, though. She'd proved she could defend herself. I downed the warm beer and gestured to the bartender to give me another. He brought it over.

I decided I'd put my attention toward something I could control: the investigation of my mother's murder.

I let my mind drift back to the memories I had of my mom. It had been centuries since I let her occupy my thoughts, mostly because it hurt like hell. Everything about my childhood that was pure died that day—died with her. Now I remembered that she would lay with me at night and tell me stories until I fell asleep. It dawned on me that *she* was the person who had introduced me to the fable of the painter's strokes—of our creation. When we were in Hafiza and Aremis shared the story with Olly, I couldn't remember who had first told it to me. I racked my brain that day, but I couldn't place my mother as the story-teller. I had stuffed those memories into a deep, dark, distant part of my heart. It stung so badly to think of her, to miss her still.

I finished another beer, swallowed hard and held back tears. Another woman I couldn't save, another person I loved taken too soon. I let myself wallow for a while, but then I found a reservoir of resolve. *Time to stop crying and whining about more things I can't change and concentrate on the task at hand,* I told myself. *I couldn't save her then, but I can avenge her now.*

I had no idea where to begin the search, though, so I started brain-storming. I didn't see any point in going back to Thule; I doubted I'd find any leads there. Vosega had killed the majority of the pixies that would be able to tell me anything of any value. I wasn't thinking about the ones he'd killed the day of my mother's murder—that news I knew well. He hadn't mentioned this, but I knew he was behind the erup-tion of the Eldfell volcano in 1973, which virtually wiped out the colony of pixies that migrated to Thule every seven hundred and eighty-eight years. If I was hoping to catch what was left of them during their mating brawl, I was about seven hundred and forty-three years too early.

I had a few connections from my mercenary days that could be useful, but at what risk? There was a price on my head, and there's no honor among thieves.

I didn't even have a name to go on, but I did have a pretty good description of the braggart in Norway from Oya. For once, she was good for something.

I pulled out the sheet of paper she'd passed along to my father to give to me. The pixie she overheard was tall for his kind, about four foot eleven. He was thin, with wide shoulders and long, stringy arms. He had wild, shoulder length, grayish-silver hair. She'd said that some strands curled while others were wiry and straight. He wore a black ascot cap. She described his clothes as nondescript, just jeans and a white T-shirt. She'd got one look at his face and remembered that he had a large burn scar that started above his right eye and continued to below his collarbone. His eyes were a pale green. He had a generous mouth, wide and framed with thin lips. She'd said the rest of his features were characteristically pixie—narrow nose, high cheekbones, no eyebrows and a pointy chin.

I turned the paper over and started sketching the description. I was pretty happy with the likeness when I completed it. I stared at it for a long time, trying to memorize the face of my mother's killer.

OPHELIA

I stayed at the house that first day after I was left alone. I could've gone out—after all, I'd won my freedom. But the way things shook down with Lucas and Elias had me feeling vulnerable. It didn't feel like the right time to take on a new country too.

There were groceries in the refrigerator, so I decided to cook up something for the guys, hoping it might smooth things over, with Lucas especially. It was 5 p.m. when I heard the front door open. Elias walked into the kitchen where I was sautéing some onions. He had a bottle of something in his hand.

"Thandai?" he offered. I had no idea what that was.

"Sure, why not?" I said. Elias smiled that smile that made everything feel all right.

He poured us two glasses. The liquid was milky white with brown flakes in it. We raised our glasses. "Salute," Elias said, and I nodded as our glasses met. The Thandai was lightly sweet and, as to be assumed by its color, creamy. I liked it.

After he took a sip, Elias asked, "How was your day?"

I turned back to my onions. "I've had better. What about you? Did you find what you were looking for?"

He leaned against the counter beside the stove where I tended to

194

my meal preparation. "I found a good resource. I am still seeking answers to the riddles in the journals I showed you."

I supposed he felt like that was some sort of transparency on his part, but it was all so vague, and I was aware I was hearing the bare bones of what he was really up to.

I looked up at him, met his gaze—something I tried to avoid most days. This was the man I was supposed to spend eternity with, and he couldn't be forthcoming with me. *What does this mean?* I wondered. I looked into his green-gold eyes for answers that I knew he wasn't going to give me. He saw that I was searching for something. I wanted to reach in further—to tear his wall down. I knew in that instant he would actually let me. I leaned in closer, inhaled his scent.

He returned the gesture, and I felt the faint remnant of the electricity I used to feel so vividly before we were both strapped down like Fort Knox by Lucas to prevent detection. I leaned in further still, until our lips were almost touching.

I could sense the shield I had around me—my own barrier—lift ever so slightly and push outward, as though it was trying to encompass Elias, bring him in with me. Unlike earlier that day, it wasn't anger fueling me, it was desire. I knew I could control it.

Just as my barrier was about to reach him, the moment was interrupted when we heard the front door open. The moment passed.

I didn't see Elias move to create distance between us, but I felt the air shift around me. By the time Lucas entered the kitchen I was back tending to the onions and Elias was gone, presumably in his room.

Lucas came up behind me. He said nothing.

"Can I help you?" I asked as I turned around. He was intimately close to me. He grabbed me by my waist once I was facing him.

"I'm sorry I'm such a protective dick," he said as he stroked my lower back with one hand and brushed through my hair with the other. "I just love you, and I couldn't bear it if something happened to you. I couldn't forgive myself." He pulled me back from his chest and looked me in the eyes. "I love you so much."

"I know," I conceded. "I love you too."

"I can give you some space." He said it hesitantly. "We've got this hairsy thing, right?" He plucked at the bracelet.

"I'll be okay." Lucas wasn't convinced of that, and I couldn't blame him after what happened to Yessica. But I wasn't her, and these weren't the same circumstances.

"You definitely have some cool tricks up your sleeve," he said, smiling at me. "What was that?"

"I don't know, but I can promise you it will get triggered again if someone threatens me," I said confidently. He looked at me for a long, hard moment.

"I'd feel better if we understood how this hairsy thing works. Will you humor me?"

"Of course I will." I pulled his torso back to mine and hugged him enthusiastically. His arms felt like home. "Can we play with the charm after I'm done with dinner?"

"Deal. I'm going to go shower. How long until it's ready?"

"Maybe forty minutes."

He gave me a thumbs-up and headed down the hall.

LUCAS

ere we are, back on the fucking rooftop, I thought. I hoped this time it would end a little differently than it had earlier that day.

Viraclay leaned against the doorjamb, waiting for us to practice with the charm. I hated his nonchalance. He was playing some game here, I just knew it. He couldn't possibly feel good about this scenario either.

"Alright, I guess I'll start by rubbing the braid together the way Fetzle showed us in the shuttle," Olly suggested.

"It's as good a place as any to start." I shrugged.

She rubbed the bracelet together. I saw and felt nothing, but she perked up with a smile. "I can see where you are." She giggled and didn't take her eyes off the charm.

"Of course you can. I'm right here."

"Not like that. Hurry. Go run to a room in the house." She was talking fast, as she often did when she was excited.

I sped to the half bath in the hall. I waited there for a moment before returning to the roof.

"You were in the half bath." Olly smirked.

"Impressive." I raised an eyebrow. "Could've been a good guess."

She took her eyes off her wrist for a moment to glare at me. "Alright, let's see how far this thing transmits. Go to the market."

"Done." I took off east, leaping from the roof to a narrow alley between buildings, then darted through the streets. I passed unknowing pedestrians, who simply felt a waft of air around them. I followed the trail of vendors to the very last one, then quickly made my way back to the apartment, all in under a minute.

"You hit the main drag through that alley then ran for three blocks east, made a right turn and continued down that street until you hit the bazaar, where you ran the length of the vendors and returned the exact same way you came."

Elias spoke up. "She did not remove her eyes from the charm the entire time you were gone."

"Well let's see if we can make it more than a mile." I ran about ten miles away, then thirty, then fifty—and in the last test run I had her stop activating the charm for twenty minutes, at which point I was nearly eighty miles away. She was able to determine exactly where I was relative to her, in addition to how I got there.

"Well, this is all fine and dandy, but how do I see where *you* are?" I asked, pointing out the obvious.

"Maybe I need to untie it and put it on you?" Olly suggested. She began to fiddle with the knot I had made.

"If I may make a suggestion?" Elias walked over and put his hand on her busy fingers. I felt my jealousy swell up, but I shoved it aside; this wasn't the time.

"By all means," I hissed. *Okay, I guess I didn't shove it aside real well*, I thought. As usual, the levelheaded Viraclay ignored my tone and continued.

"Perhaps..." He paused. "It is whatever guard you displayed this morning that has you hidden from Lucas' sight."

Olly chewed on that idea. I, for one, was curious to see if she was going to be able to manipulate it on cue to test the theory. She didn't say anything but her face got hard with concentration.

"Lift your shield at the same time, Lucas." She said it calmly, but there was something else in her request. Regardless, I did as she directed. I lifted my camouflage to encompass the house and not just the individuals in it. Then I could see it clear as day—she had a very solid shield around her, identical to my own—but not mine. She was breathing heavily as she extenuated herself in order to lift the weight of it. I remembered when I first started playing with my gift—that was exactly how it felt for me. But this was bigger, because she wasn't consummated yet; she didn't have the strength of a Consu. It was miraculous. She pulled it further and further from her body until she enveloped me. Enclosed within her shield, I felt exposed. Really exposed. I wanted to replace my own armor. I almost demanded it.

She began activating the charm and I could see her clear as day. It was like there was a string that bound our two bodies in my mind's eye. I could just follow it to her.

"Replace your shield," she told me. I gladly did as she commanded. I could still see her. The charm still worked, even with my gift in place —but hers had to be down for me to see her. *What does that mean? She can block magic? Can I block magic?* That was definitely something to consider later.

"I can see you!" I beamed at her, and quick as a whip, she responded while simultaneously snapping her own shield back into place.

"Of course you can. I'm right here."

"Smartass." I laughed as I picked her up and squeezed her tightly in my arms. "You have no idea how excited this makes me." I spun her around and noticed Viraclay had dismissed himself. I bet it pissed him off that I just made one more connection with her. It would infuriate me if the tables were turned. I laughed out loud—it was a win-win for me.

"But just so we are clear," I said, "we don't need to lift our shields completely. I want you to stay hidden. I just need you to expand it a little beyond your own skin."

"Yeah, yeah, I get it," she said cavalierly. "Keep the shields on, and if I need you to see me, I just pull mine back a little."

I beamed at her. "Have I told you lately how brilliant you are?" I squeezed her a little tighter.

OPHELIA

"Can you guys cover cleanup duty?" I asked. "That little exercise exhausted me—or maybe it's the Thandai catching up with me. Either way, I'm ready for bed."

"Yeah, go to bed," Lucas said as he kissed my forehead, then he turned to the kitchen as we trailed off the stairs down from the rooftop. I realized I didn't know where Elias was. It didn't make a difference to me at the moment, but he hadn't said goodnight, and that wasn't like him.

Still thinking about the test with the hairsy charm, I made my way into my room. It was on the bottom floor—the only room on the bottom floor. The ground was tiled a rich brown shade, so the floor stayed fairly cool under my feet. The walls of the room were painted a pale green, not quite pastel. The bed frame was oversized, with ornate carvings in a rich mahogany-colored wood. I had my own bathroom and a large closet that stored three pairs of shorts, five tank tops and some undergarments in a bag on the floor. I definitely couldn't complain about the accommodations.

I walked to my bag. Again, I pulled out the poster and Rand's pouch. I'd planned on sharing these items and my theories about them with the guys after dinner. But now I was back to second-guessing my decision. The truth was I wasn't tired at all—I was plagued with questions.

It may be silly to be holding on to secrets from your only allies, but I was now more convinced than ever that Lucas was guarding some very important secrets of his own. I'd seen glimpses of it twice before. Once when he took his shield down, when he and Elias wanted to convince me that the Conduit world existed, and a second time when he dropped his shield to let me know how he felt about me. Both times I'd detected secrets, something deeply hidden—something he was guarding.

Tonight, I'd felt his fear of exposure. It was as though I could see the dark chamber he hid his secrets in. It was right there in front of me, and I knew that if I wanted to, I could open the door. But his fear, in turn, terrified me.

What is Lucas guarding so fiercely from me? What do these secrets mean? How can I share my own secrets when I'm not sure about what he is hiding? Should I tell Elias what I saw?

I had felt an immediate wall erect around my heart upon sensing Lucas' secrecy. I realized I didn't know what he was capable of, and for the first time ever, I wondered how that could affect me. For the time being, I would wait to share this with either of them—wait to figure out what I was missing. Not just from Lucas, but from the bigger picture about this mission Elias was on as well. I needed to trust my companions, and I desperately wanted to—but something in my gut demanded that I wait just a little while longer to share what I knew.

LUCAS

J had some ideas of where the local mercenaries might hang out. When I was running in less-than-tasteful circles, I'd heard about a place, a local inn, in the heart of Delhi. The owner didn't ask questions and served all kinds of clientele. I preferred my privacy when I was traveling, but many nomadic hires liked having company for a night. It was my best bet at producing a lead.

Now that I knew Olly could "phone" me with the hairsy charm if she suspected any trouble, I felt comfortable traveling the 375 miles to Delhi, which meant about an hour's run for me. I geared up with some extra cash and a change of clothes—in the event that I got dirty during this chore. I left just after 11 p.m., which meant that Olly would be asleep for the majority of the time I was gone, plus then I could catch the nighttime patrons, as well as the morning patrons, and be back in time for tomorrow's dinner.

Elias was still up when I left, but he didn't ask where I was going, and I wouldn't have told him anyway. *I like this unspoken agreement we've developed*, I thought as I shut the door.

ELIAS

*L*ucas had left the night before. He had yet to return. But I decided I would not question his whereabouts until I had cause to. Ophelia assured me when she woke that she was still very adamant about maintaining her independence, so I left her to it.

As I had hoped, I was lucky enough to find the correct Bhil village on my first attempt. It was smaller than any of the other clans I had engaged with before—there could not have been more than ten people in the confines of their secluded portion of the world.

The elder I met upon my arrival was friendly. Although he was toothless, he was able to clearly speak two languages. One was ancient, with similarities to Asagi, just like in the other three villages. The second language, Gujarati, was even easier for us to converse in, since I had studied it while I was keeping an eye on Ophelia in San Francisco.

The tribal elder was named Rajahish. He was warm, almost as warm as the vibrant colors the tiny clan wore. They were all adorned in bright yellows, deep oranges and eye-catching reds. I was immediately at ease in his presence. I appreciated the casualness and assurance I felt.

I explained that I needed to learn the symbols he used to write their language, and he was all too eager to assist. We sat in his hut of wattle and thatch while he drew symbol after symbol with red chalk on the ground.

As I was leaving that evening, I noticed a small bowl full of crystals near the door. I pointed at them and asked their purpose.

"To see the magic that hides in plain sight," he replied. I thought about the three crystals I had on my person, Alistair's crystals. I was certain this must be their origin. I reached into my satchel and withdrew them. As I let all three fall into my hand, Rajahish mumbled words I did not understand. He closed my hand around the crystals and looked into my eyes intently.

"Put these away. They will have a place when it is time to reveal the truth of Varuna. Until then, keep them safe."

I nodded and replaced them back into my bag.

As I turned to leave, he spoke up once more. "Tomorrow we will share some of our own truths."

I made my way back to my motorbike, all the while considering what I had gleaned on my journey thus far. I had now linked the three bags of seemingly random items I had found in Alistair's study to three of the five villages.

Which led me to wonder: Was I either missing two items, or was it that only three villages were truly relevant to my search? I had accumulated so many new questions since this quest began: *Why these villages? What do I have to do with this grand orchestrated plan? Who knew I would be visiting these tribes? Are the men and women who represent gods to these tribes all the same people—Varuna, Moai Kavakava, and Sibu? Are the rituals I am partaking in just as important as the languages I am collecting?* I felt frustrated with the inquiry at times, content with a steady faith at others, and acutely aware that the cooperation from the tribes was integral to this investigation—so if I wanted to maintain open lines of communication, I needed to play by their rules—even if I did not understand them.

LUCAS

I'd been sitting in the lounge of the Parkesh Inn, nursing drinks, for nine hours. So far, I'd seen a mangled powrie walk through the door, two hobgoblins and a nymph—none of which were in a talkative mood toward each other, and certainly not to me.

I didn't need a pixie to waltz up—but I did need someone in the mood to chat. This wasn't the type of crowd you asked questions in. In fact questions got you killed, so I was hoping for a couple of lonely conversationalists to happen upon this place, at which point I'd eavesdrop, or if I was lucky, join the dialogue. But at this rate it wasn't looking good.

Mercenaries are an odd group. They trust no one, but also fiercely defend each other's privacy—it's that combination that enables the loose alliance of these individuals to coexist. When I frequented these places I began to respect the assassins' code; it kept things simple. None of this banding together shit Viraclay was attempting. I ordered another drink just as two Conduits entered the lounge. I was grateful to see that I didn't recognize them, and they appeared not to recognize me.

I sipped my whiskey, waiting to see if the two Conduits would strike up a conversation, but they didn't. They simply sat at the bar in silence.

It was going to be a long day. I looked at my watch. It was nearly 9 a.m. I needed to stretch my legs. I decided to run a few miles, then make my way back to my stool—it would only take a couple of minutes.

OPHELIA

"*O*h shoot!" I blurted out as I saw all of the groceries topple from the bag in my hands onto the ground. The throngs of people continued to maneuver around me in the market.

"Here, let me help," a soft voice volunteered.

"Thank you. I'm just so clumsy sometimes," I said, flustered. I looked up to see a woman with brilliant bronze skin beaming at me.

"Aren't we all?" she said gently. We quickly collected the groceries from the ground and replaced them back into the bag. Once we were both back on our feet, the stranger offered her hand. "Hello. My name is Talia."

I kindly took it and introduced myself. "I'm Ophelia. But you can call me the clumsy shopper." I laughed.

"Ophelia will suffice." She smiled. "I haven't seen you at this market before," she said as we strolled slowly through the crowd. "We don't get many Americans in these parts."

"Guess my accent gives me away, huh? Yeah, I'm pretty new to the area. I couldn't resist a good local market adventure, though. This place is great. The smells alone are intoxicating." I took a deep whiff.

"I couldn't agree more. What brings you to India?" She looked at me inquisitively.

"Curiosity, I guess." I didn't look at her while I fibbed. I knew I needed to be extra cautious with anyone I met. I was well aware there were still assassins on our tail but I was craving some good old-fashioned friendly chitchat.

"Well, be prepared to walk away with more questions than answers," she replied. "This country in amazing, but a mystery in many ways."

"Thanks for the warning. What about you, what brings you here?" I asked, attempting to conduct my own character investigation, to vet this "Talia" to make sure she was harmless.

"My husband. He loves this country and its people. We always make our way back here at some point during the year."

I was quickly taken with her serene demeanor. I was so hungry for female friendship that I soon found myself saying, "Want to grab a tea?" I blurted out the invite before thoroughly thinking through the consequences. I had a brief moment of regret, then decided I deserved a little normalcy. I could defend myself if need be, and Talia looked really normal—none of my spidey-senses were going off. Tea in a public market was harmless, *right?*

"Sure. I will show you my favorite little place," Talia said. She led me some way down the road to a hole-in-the-wall café.

As we sat down, I finally had a moment to take in how beautiful she was. She was tall, slender, and her skin was perfectly sun-kissed. I wondered where she was from, because although she had a Brittish accent, her appearance suggested different origins. Talia's hair was a warm black. It cascaded past her shoulders in a thick, straight mane. Her eyes were brown, but exotically shaped, and sat upon high cheekbones that looked like they had been chiseled perfectly to fit her face. Her petite nose sat above plump lips that housed perfect teeth and an inviting smile. When looked at in her entirety, she was an exquisite woman.

She caught me staring and cleared her throat.

I turned beet red. *How embarrassing, I make a new friend, then get caught gawking at her.*

"Sorry," I choked. "I was lost in thought."

"No problem. I ordered you the same tea that I usually enjoy. I hope that's okay?"

"Thank you." The cashier served us our tea. She reminded us to wait while it steeped.

"Are you traveling alone?" Talia asked. I definitely had not thought through exactly how I'd answer these types of questions when I asked her out for tea. I didn't want the whole conversation to be a lie. That would feel terrible—even if she never found out the truth.

Still, I needed to maintain boundaries while I assessed her properly.

"No, I'm traveling with my roommate and an old family friend," I said. That was a stretch about Elias, but my description of Lucas was pretty spot on. There was no need to explain that I was traveling in a love triangle between two men, running from assassins while hunting down answers about a summit.

"Neither of them is a lover?" she said coyly. *Way to hit the nail on the head, Talia.*

I hedged. "I think both of them might appreciate the opportunity to make our relationship more... but it's complicated." I averted my eyes.

"Enough said," she smiled. "We can move on to a less complicated conversation. What part of the States are you from?"

I appreciated her casualness. It made her seem innocuous. She wasn't pushing for answers. I liked the vibe I got from her. I resolved that I would continue to be vigilant in our conversation, but enjoy myself—I deserved that. Days of seclusion had taken their toll on my spirit. I let my shoulders relax.

"Originally, I was from Chicago, but spent the last few years in San Francisco. What about you?"

"I travelled all over, but New York City was my home for the longest. Thank God I didn't pick up that accent though!" We both laughed and spent the rest of the afternoon comparing notes on our favorite cities across the U.S. It was one of the best days I'd had in a very long time. We agreed to meet at the market again the next day.

As I skipped home, riding the elation of the conversation with a new "normal" acquaintance, I wondered if I should share it with the guys. I was afraid they would tell me I couldn't continue to see her. It had already been hard enough to convince them I could handle the market by myself. *Maybe I'll keep Talia to myself for a while until they realize I'm not an infant,* I decided.

LUCAS

Six days of this shit! Running back and forth from the apartment in Jammu to the crappy hotel in Delhi. I didn't mind the travel; I was just impatient for a lead. I felt like the bartender might be getting suspicious, too; most patrons came back around after a few years of absence—not six days in a row.

The worst part was that all I did all day was think about what Ophelia was doing—*was she safe?* Viraclay and I'd decided after Hafiza fell that the less we had to trace the better. This meant we chose not to employ cell phones. I was regretting that decision. *I'd love to shoot Olly a text right now,* I thought. Instead I was left wondering.

If somehow I was able to distract myself from thinking about Olly, it meant I was probably thinking about my mother. I had very purposefully repressed her memory all those centuries; it was painful, raw—needless to say, I felt extremely vulnerable when I acknowledged those emotions. The last thing in the world I needed to do was feel exposed while I was attempting subterfuge.

The whole idea of this undertaking was beginning to feel futile—yet I persisted. I sat in the corner today, away from the bar, as if that would make me any less conspicuous. The lounge was deathly dim and dreary, with absolutely no windows, since it was nestled in a conveniently located basement below the inn. The furniture was dark. There were three lights in the entire space—one that lit up the alcohol behind the bar, another that lit the way to the bathroom, and a third just above the entrance. That was it.

I happened to look up just as four thuggish Yeren walked in under the entry light, followed by a slimy looking Nakki—I got a clear visual of their faces. The Yeren all looked similar, with slightly different shades of hair framing their eyes. All four were nearly eight feet tall, with long tresses and longer beards. I'd never seen Yeren dressed before, but these were—I supposed it was to hide their furry ape-like torsos and long extremities while mingling among society. The Nakki, also known as a water nymph, was in human form, but I could tell what she was right away. She reeked of an old salty harbor. The closest ocean was hundreds of miles away. Her skin shimmered in a scale-like fashion, and there was a slickness to her hair, as though she had been rolling in slobber from a Saint Bernard. She was scantily dressed—the extreme opposite of her entourage. Her nipples were barely covered by a bikini top, while her ass hung out of the back of teal latex shorts.

My eyes followed the group to the bar, where they ordered drinks. Luckily for me, they found seats easily within earshot.

I sank a little deeper into my chair. My heart was racing, I didn't want it to give me away. I took some slow deliberate breaths and a long sip on my beer.

"Tits! Grab my drink, will ya?" one of the Yeren shouted. *Her name is Tits? You've got to be kidding me,* I thought.

When she replied, her voice was nasally and abnormally high. "Shit, Noptir, next thing you know you'll be asking for a blow job."

"Not a bad idea," Noptir agreed. The rest of the Yeren laughed at this disgusting excuse for flirting. *Could you even call it flirting?* I wondered.

Tits sat down next to Noptir. I was sure there was something going on under the table. No one was going to acknowledge the whereabouts of Tits' missing hand.

"Fuck this line of work—but it beats living in a cave," a deeper voice spoke up. They all lifted their glasses in unison in agreement.

For a long moment it was silent. I worried the talking was over. Another less-polite noise filled the silence, along with some very audible moans. The deep-voiced Yeren spoke up again, probably so he could continue to ignore the hand job Noptir was getting at the table.

"Where are you off to next, Fliwick?"

Fliwick's voice was soft, feminine, and I realized she wasn't a he. Yeren women got the shitty end of the deal on that one—just as hairy and large as the male Yeren, they were indistinguishable. "I'm working for a rich asshole in Atlanta. He wants me to off his wife. It's the third one I've done." She shrugged. "But he pays well."

There was a final long groan, then both Noptir and Tits adjusted themselves in their seats, now ready to participate in the conversation.

"I'm heading to Uruguay. I hear there's some good contracts down there," Noptir said as he took a swig of his beer. "What about you, Poo?" I had to hold my breath in order to not laugh. Tits and Poo —*what a classy bunch!* I felt Poo glance in my direction, so I took another sip of my beer, trying to choke down the chuckle completely.

"I don't know. I like it here in India," Poo said. "I may stay around for a while, try and drum up some work." I wondered what their job here was to begin with; *what would you need four strong, gigantic beasts and a water nymph for?*

Tits spoke up next. Boy, was her voice irritating. "I'm heading to Split in Croatia. A friend of mine, an old pixie named Zeric, says a lady with my talents could get a lot of work down there. He's coming to get me in a week."

Noptir interrupted. "Tits, you ain't got friends—or talent." He laughed heartily at his joke.

Tits leapt onto Poo's lap and straddled him aggressively. "Want some company tonight, Poo? I just recently cleared my schedule—and apparently I'm looking for friends." Poo, amenable to the offer, grabbed Tits by her hair and shoved her mouth on to his as she gyrated feverishly on his lap.

I had a feeling the scene was going to get hot and heavy for a while, so I quietly slipped out of my seat and snuck outside. *I'll wait here,* I decided, *where I can see them leave.* They were most likely staying at the inn. I'd figure out where Miss Tits was staying and pay her a visit. Tracking down a pixie would be the best lead I could possibly get.

Then I had a sudden twinge of anxiety. *What if Elias wants to leave India before Zeric arrives?* I needed to have a reason to stall.

ELIAS

*W*e were going on almost two weeks in Jammu. I was certain I had all the answers I would get from Rajahish. I had taken detailed notes on their language and was starting to be able to decipher entire words in Alistair's journals.

I would have moved on after a week, but Lucas insisted that the normalcy was good for Ophelia. He said that this independence was bringing her back to life. To some extent I agreed with him. She was glowing, possibly the most content I had seen her in some time, so I agreed to stay on. Meanwhile, Lucas was uncharacteristically absent. I had asked him twice already what he was tending to, but as expected, he told me to literally fuck off. I considered pressing it, but Ophelia appeared unconcerned with his daily forays. Admittedly, I appreciated the reprieve from his constant hovering. Most importantly, I trusted that he would never leave Ophelia's side if he felt she was in danger.

We had no reason to believe we had been followed to India, but I was ready to move on in my investigation. I *needed* to move on. I was so close to obtaining the characters for all of the five languages I sought in order to complete my translations.

I decided that today would be my last day visiting Rajahish. I found myself melancholy at the prospect of not seeing the kind old man's toothless smile ever again.

I approached the clan slowly, drawing out the inevitable goodbye.

Rajahish and his wife were husking corn by their home. He smiled as I approached, and I felt a deeper pang of loss. He stood when I was close enough to touch, then took my hand and shook it vigorously.

"Today is the day," he said in Gujarati. My own Gujarati had advanced quite quickly while immersed in the language. I rather enjoyed the way it rolled off my tongue.

"Today is the day," I affirmed, not certain we were talking about the same things.

"Come, Viraclay." He said my nickname with great reverence. We had gotten to know each other very well over the past two weeks. "I must show you one last thing."

I followed him into the house.

"Shall I sit?" I asked.

"Please. I am preparing my favorite tea for you." He set too small clay bowls on a wooden table in front of where I sat. "I must tell you a truth," he said. The he brought over a pot of boiling water and poured the contents into each bowl carefully.

"By all means."

He sat down across from me. "This truth may have you thinking less of me, because it means the other truths I told you were not final."

I leaned in closer. "I could not think less of you, Rajahish."

He looked at me with squinted eyes. "That is a truth that is not final as well." He took a sip of his tea. "I am not Rajahish, I am Alistair."

I shook visibly as I took my own bowl into my hands. *What is he saying?* I had never referenced Alistair's name in his presence.

"That is an odd name for an elder of a Bhil clan," I said, "but if you say that is your name, then I must believe it." I tried to sound casual, but I was taken aback.

"I am the descendant of a god," he stated coolly.

"I believe that," I asserted.

"Do you?" he asked. "Do you believe in Gods? Or do you placate an old man?" His tone was still casual.

"I believe you believe in Gods—and so they exist, Alistair." He looked at me through squinted eyes once more.

"My name is not Alistair, I *am* Alistair. Therefore, I am the son of a God. Or as you would see it, the son of a man I believed was a God."

I stared at him for a long moment before I spoke again, realizing I was not on the same page as him. "Am I a God?" The question came out of my mouth before I could ponder its consequence.

"You are the son of Gods, are you not? What is a God, but something to believe in? Something to hope for, to connect with, to bring life and joy into the world. It is a circle. You are a son of Gods, and I am the blood of a God. It is all the same continuous thread. These truths will be of great importance someday. What you think you comprehend now will be of little meaning later."

With that, Rajahish stood up and moved toward the door. "Today we say goodbye, but do not worry. We will find each other again. We are all part of one thread, of one circle."

I left my tea on the table, embraced Rajahish's shoulder as I left, but I said nothing. He had said what he needed to say. And I had not the slightest idea of what any of it meant.

Once again, I left with more questions, but most importantly, I left with the crucial answers I desired—a complete catalog of the Bhil language.

OPHELIA

For nearly two weeks I'd been meeting Talia at the market, then enjoying a cup of tea over innocent chitchat. It was divinely normal. I was loving it.

"Okay, Ophelia, I've let you off the hook about the whole guy *thing* for long enough. Give me some details, dear," she said as she smiled mischievously.

If I am being honest with myself, it would be nice to have another woman's opinion on the matter, I thought. I'd need to keep out the whole part about destiny and being hunted while in the middle of a three-thousand-year-old war. But I figured everything else was fair game. I chuckled to myself.

"What am I missing?" Talia asked. "Does this mean you're ready to give me some details?"

"Yeah, I guess I am. But you first. You haven't told me very much about your husband. What brings you guys over here? I know you said he was from the area. Does he have family here still?"

"There's not much to tell. We've been married for what feels like forever. Huan is incredible—the most valiant, kind and compassionate person I've ever met. He would do anything for anyone. He is from China originally, but we met in Turkey. We were both traveling.

He was selling rare stones to merchants. I was just passing through the city where we met. It was as if the world stopped and everything changed for us the moment our eyes met—and we've been together ever since." Tingles ran down the back of my neck as she spoke. I thought about my first encounter with Elias, how it felt like the world stood still. I could see on her face what Huan must mean to her. Their bond was evident, although I'd never even met the guy. Talia was lost in her own thoughts.

"So, you two just come here to enjoy the culture?" I asked.

"Huan spent much of his childhood in India. His father had an affinity for the Indian culture, he loved Bhiluda and this area of Rajasthan. I guess the area has grown on me as well." She smiled a genuine smile. "Enough about me. I am just an old married lady. Tell me about these men."

"Well," I began, "both of my travel companions are pretty incredible, in different ways, of course. Lucas and I've been friends for a couple of years now. We lived together in San Francisco for a while. It wasn't until Elias came into the picture that Lucas made it apparent he had feelings for me that consisted of more than just those of a buddy. I feel like I really know Lucas. We have a long history. He was the first man in my life that I ever felt safe to be myself with. He is strong, funny, sexy… We share a lot of laughter and it's easy to be with him. Sometimes he's a little protective, though, and he's definitely a jealous guy." I paused. Talia gestured for more.

"Elias, on the other hand, is just irresistible to me. Both men are attractive, but something about Elias is downright addictive. When we met, it felt like my world kinda stopped. The way you described meeting Huan. But I don't know if I like that feeling of being out of control. That's how I feel with him, like I'm out of control, or that I could devour him—possibly worse, let him devour me. I feel like if I opened my heart to him, I would never get it back. I would have to succumb to our connection."

"Oh honey, it sounds like you're in a pickle," Talia admitted. We both laughed. But I almost wanted to cry because I *was* in quite the quagmire.

"So, what does your heart say?" she asked. "Do you love them both?"

"I believe I *do* love them both, just differently. The big problem is, we're stuck traveling together for a while and I don't want to hurt either of them."

"I see. In other words, you won't listen to your heart until you're sure you won't hurt one of these grown men? Emphasis on grown men." We laughed again. "Look," she said, "I can tell the situation is even more complicated than you're sharing with me. Call it a sixth sense." She put her hand up. "Don't worry—I'm not offended. I won't pry any further. But if I may give you some advice..."

I nodded to let her know I was open to that, so she continued. "Not everyone gets to have that world-stopping love; it's rare, and even those who find it can lose it. I can only speak from my own experience, but that isn't something you just pass by. If this Lucas guy really is your friend, he'll understand that. Maybe not at first, but he will someday, and if he's lucky he'll find his own world-altering connection."

"I know you're right. I guess I still need to mourn the future I saw with Lucas at one point."

"Ophelia, you need to abandon your pride. From what I heard from you, you're just afraid of being out of control. But control is overrated. Why don't you let fate take the wheel for a while? You might find you'll enjoy the ride a little more."

"Jesus," I said with admiration. "Has anyone ever told you that you're a straight shooter?"

"All the time," she said with a smile.

ELIAS

"*L*ucas is still occupied?" I asked when I saw her lying on her bed. She scrambled to sit up. As she did, I saw her stash something behind her back.

"Oh, I didn't hear anyone come in," she said. I heard the crinkling of paper.

"My apologies. Did I interrupt something?" I replied, feeling a little awkward. "I will come back later." I began to leave, but she insisted I come back into the room.

"You're not interrupting, Elias. It's something I've been meaning to show you. Come sit down." She patted a hand on the comforter beside her on the bed.

I took a seat. I had noticed her evasive behavior since we had arrived in India, but I felt as though she deserved her privacy. After all, I had my share of secrets, as did Lucas.

"Please share." I smiled at her. She looked away modestly. She then pulled out the piece of paper she had hid behind her. As she unfolded it, I noticed the fold lines were deeply cut, as if she had pulled it out to look at it many times before this moment. My curiosity intensified. She handed it to me. Once I saw what was on it, I did not feign surprise.

"Where did you get this?" I asked.

"When we stopped in Bosnia for gas, on our way here. Remember where we fueled up the charter plane?" She thought my hesitation was confusion. I understood exactly where she found the poster advertising the fort; I was merely wondering what she made of the image and why she felt the need to keep it secret.

"I remember," I said. "What does this image mean to you? Why were you concealing it?" I kept her gaze as I spoke. I felt as though I must have failed her somehow, that she desired to hide this from me. *To what end?*

She sighed loudly. "Is it Hafiza?"

"Yes, it is."

She put her head in her hands. "I don't understand. This fort is in ruin—and not from an explosion, but from decay. If this is how it's been for hundreds of years and tourists are in attendance every day, then where were we?"

"Before I explain, may I ask again—why did you conceal this?" I put my hand on her shoulder and held my breath while I waited for her response.

She stood up and began pacing as she spoke. "Because at first I felt like an idiot, like I didn't know what was going on, that my memories must be wrong, that this wasn't Hafiza." She pointed at the poster. "Then I thought I was lied to. I wondered why you guys didn't explain this to me thoroughly, why was I still in the dark. I felt like everyone around me has secrets, and maybe this could be mine. Maybe knowing something that you guys thought I shouldn't know, or couldn't know, gave me some semblance of control over this situation."

She put her hands up and gestured to her surroundings. "We agreed we would approach our situation as a team, but instead you're off running 'secret errands' all day long while Lucas 'protects' me from the world I belong in. He keeps me so guarded I can't experience anything. What am I fighting for if this is my life—a woman in a gilded cage?"

I said nothing, not certain if she was done venting. I wanted her to get it all out, so I could understand, so we could fix it.

"The truth is," she continued, "secrets just made me feel more secluded—more alone." She collapsed back onto the bed. But then she abruptly sat up again and tugged at the nightstand drawer. She pulled out a small leather pouch.

The air in my lungs expelled rapidly. By the look on Ophelia's face, it scared her. My heart raced violently in my chest. *Where had she found this? What is it? Did she steal it from me?* I immediately dismissed the last thought—she would never do that. My hands shook as I reached for the small parcel. She gladly handed it over.

"Rand gave this to me the night Hafiza fell under siege. I have no idea what it is or its meaning."

I untied the leather string that held it closed, exposing several fragrant leaves. I pulled them closer to my nostrils and inhaled. I knew that smell. I touched their red surface and quickly realized they were not leaves but rather petals, from a flower. My mind was racing, tracing backwards while thinking ahead all at once. I knew that smell from my time with the Tukano Tribe and Reedta in Colombia! I took another whiff. Yes, I was certain that was the smell, but I had seen the flowers only as a powder. I remembered on one of my visits Reedta kept repeating the word "Loktpi" as he threw some of the red dust into the air.

I was mulling this all over when Ophelia brought me back to the present. "I know I should've shown you sooner," she said apologetically. "I wanted to. But after I didn't tell you at first, it never seemed to be a good time. Then I began feeling like the secret gave me control—blah, blah, bah." She rolled her hand around in a continuing circular motion. She seemed to be rambling a bit. I wondered if my silence was starting to concern her.

"Are you mad at me?" she finally asked, looking into my eyes. I could see she was remorseful—relieved to get it all off her chest.

I took both of her hands in mine. "No. I am sorry that you have felt secluded and confined. I am so sorry that I have driven you to secrets. We are going to rectify that, this evening—I promise you. And if you will trust me once more, I promise to never betray that trust again. Will you forgive me?"

She squeezed my hands, then threw her arms around my neck. She was close to my right ear as she spoke, so her voice was soft. "I forgive you, Elias." She pulled back and put her hand on my cheek. "Let's not keep secrets."

Relief washed over me. This was repairable. "Never again," I said as I leaned in to kiss her cheek softly.

OPHELIA

*G*etting everything off my chest was such a relief. I was never one who appreciated secrets. It probably went back to years of hearing about the contents of everyone else's deep, dark, skeleton-filled closets. I'd always done my best to keep my own closets clean. I hadn't realized how much my concealment had been weighing on me.

After I was done spilling my guts with Elias, he had asked me to dinner so he could share some things with me. I wondered if that was to keep his own disclosures from being overheard by Lucas.

As we walked past the market he explained that Fort Blagaj was indeed Hafiza, that the tower I recognized was part of her structure. He said that unlike structures in the human world, a Haven is invisible to mortal eyes. There are incantations that have to be performed for the Haven to appear, and for you to gain entrance. He compared it to an alternate plane of existence, but he seemed unsatisfied with that analogy, because a Haven is *in* this world as we know it. It's just that the magic that's imprinted on it only allows it to be seen or found by those who are invited, or who know the incantation required for the place to materialize. He listed many places around the world that were Haven sites.

This discussion led right into his explanation about his current mission. This time, when he described the task he had in front of him, he held nothing back. He told me about his father, Alistair and the leather pouches that he himself had been carrying around. He theorized that the pouch Rand gave me was part of the same set. He thought that Rand may have known that he had the other three items, and that was why he'd passed the fourth onto me during the siege—he knew that I'd unite it with the others somehow.

I again felt bad for keeping it from Elias after he explained how he'd been trying to connect the items to the indigenous people he was meeting.

We sat in the small restaurant he'd chosen for hours as he dove into every detail of his findings, such as his strange but welcoming visits with the community leaders. He even told me, with some reluctance, about what happened to the first tribe, on Easter Island. He didn't want to frighten me or make me sad but was holding to his word of transparency.

When I asked him about the conversation I'd overheard between him and Lucas in Colombia, I saw some hesitance, but after a moment of wavering he described their suspicions about me being Sulu. Elias confessed that he didn't know much about what it meant to be Sulu, and that it had been centuries since anyone had claimed to be one or known of an individual that possessed such powers. He promised that when he learned more, he would illuminate me.

As we walked back, I thought about my meeting with Aurora, and what she'd told me. I wondered what she had told Elias. A private reading from an Oracle seemed like something that should be kept secret, maybe the only thing that should be concealed from others. Consequently, I decided I would consider asking Elias about it another time.

I reached for his hand as we walked. He happily took mine. I wanted to feel the familiar "electric" sensation I'd felt when we'd first met, but it wasn't there. Nonetheless, his touch felt comfortable, secure.

It was a beautiful night for a walk, so we took our time getting home. When we passed the market, I thought about Talia and stopped. I dropped his hand as I turned to face him.

"There is one more thing I haven't told you about."

Elias raised his eyebrows.

"I have a friend. Her name is Talia. I met her at the market two weeks ago. She's been a blessing of normalcy. We've been meeting for tea after I've walked around the bazaar each day."

He only nodded. I wondered what was going through his head.

"I am sure it has been nice to have ordinary conversations," he finally said. "I trust your judgment that she is of good character." He continued walking. I followed.

"She's very sweet. I'd like to say goodbye to her before we leave, if I can. After all, it was she who insisted I stop trying to control things and let fate take the wheel." I smiled as I thought about our conversation. I was eager to thank her for the sound advice.

"Well, in that case, I must meet her to shower her with my sincerest gratitude."

"You could!" I said enthusiastically. "I mean, if you want—you could meet us around three tomorrow at the café?"

"I would love that," he said, then paused. "Are you certain you are ready to leave? India, that is?"

"After hearing about what you're trying to achieve, yes, I'm ready to leave, to do my part to help you find the answers you've been searching for," I assured him.

"Very well, I am happy to hear that. I am certain Lucas will be too." He stopped. The mention of Lucas' name prompted him to add something I'd expected would come up. "Lucas cannot…"

I put my finger to his mouth. "I know. I won't say anything." The words stung as I said them because Lucas was my best friend, but that friendship had been one-sided at times—and deceptive at others. There was something major he was hiding from me—from everyone. I loved him with all of my heart, but he was holding onto the friendship we'd had in San Francisco. He wasn't ready to move forward into the relationship we could have—as equals. I hoped that over time this would change, but until it did, I knew there would be a void between us. I knew he was aware of it too, although I think he blamed the distance on Elias.

"Oh, Lucas," I sighed as I leaned into Elias' shoulder. I took a deep breath and let it out slowly.

LUCAS

I'd been surveilling Tits' room on the third floor of the Parkesh Inn for seven days. Her activities were pretty basic —food, sex and a lot of baths. Poo was the last of the Yeren to leave. He'd departed India three days before, so she was left to her own devices. She'd replaced him with several strangers. Around 11 a.m. each day she would make it to the lounge for a drink. Fortunately for me, she was a talker. She wasn't talking to me, but that made no difference. I just had to listen. I stayed in the deepest shadows of the lounge at this point for two reasons: the first being that I didn't want anyone to get suspicious of my ongoing presence, the second was to avoid being picked up on by Tits. She literally molested any man that was in arm's reach; I knew that on the day the pixie scum arrived this would be advantageous for me. But until then, I shuddered at the thought of her slippery nymph hands anywhere near my body.

I waited, and I watched. I knew from her conversation with the bartender that morning that she was expecting her friend to arrive late the next afternoon.

"Are you sure you don't want to take me up on my offer, Lido?" she said to him, attempting to purr, though it sounded more like a whine to me. "I'm only in town for one more fabulous night. I could take you places you have never been, my man." She leaned over the bar, and one of her breasts fell out of its tiny excuse for a top. *What a circus*, I thought. But I could see how this behavior worked on solo mercenaries and hit men; they were lonely. There were days on end without companionship except for the unsavory company of one's own hand.

I thought about my years on this side of the fight, after Yessica died. It was an easy way to let off some steam, to work through my rage one job at a time. Then there was Vivienne. My memories with her were a combination of regret, terror, and to be honest, arousal.

I shook off the memory—that bitch chose the wrong side, now she wanted to kill Olly. I was further brought back to the present by Lido's deep baritone voice.

"Tits, put that shit away. I don't have time to visit your little room of horrors. I'm working a double." She frowned as she sat back down on her barstool and simultaneously stuffed her tit—*Yes, pun intended*, I thought—back into her top.

"All I need is five minutes," she grumbled while taking a sip of her martini.

I leaned back in my seat, considering my plan. *The pixie asshole will be here tomorrow afternoon. That means I could be Tits' distraction tomorrow morning at eleven when she came to the lounge for her daily martini. This is working out better than I thought.*

ELIAS

*A*s I got my things in order before we left India, I reflected on my conversation with Ophelia the night before. The only thing we had not broached was the prophecy. After sleeping on it, I decided it was time she knew. I felt our bond getting stronger, and I wanted her to know, and understand, why we could not immediately dive into an intimate physical union—why we could not consummate. I could not trust my own heart to not carry me away as our connection deepened.

I had told her I would meet her friend Talia in the afternoon. When she had first mentioned Talia the previous night, I had to stop myself from panicking. I knew it was not safe for Ophelia to be forging new relationships. But I had the sense to steady my nerves because I realized she had already been convening with this woman for two weeks; if she were our enemy, she would have acted by now. I felt I could support Ophelia in going with her to say goodbye.

She had been packing her own things as I left that morning, and for the first time in days Lucas was still at the house when we woke. I was relieved, because I needed to inform him of our departure. Our paths hadn't crossed in several days.

I had much to do before the appointment with Talia. For one, I had to pick up the IDs that we'd missed collecting in Hanga Roa; fortunately, I had arranged for them to be forwarded to Jammu in the event that no one picked them up on Easter Island. We were running out of viable aliases that would not be easily flagged by a watchful eye, so I was eager to collect the package to buy us more time.

I also had to arrange our transportation to our next and final stop: Russia. I had uncovered a small settlement of Khakas people in the Altai Mountains. I was optimistic that they might offer the final linguistic translations I needed. It would be a starting point, nonetheless. I had found an elite train service that would get us most of the way to Russia. I thought we could rent an entire luxury cabin for that segment of the journey, then perhaps we could lease a car for the final leg.

The post office in Jammu was a bit unruly when I arrived. After about an hour of my waiting in lines while enduring confusion, the workers were finally able to locate my package. I felt true relief surge through me; traveling under an entirely new set of documents helped assuage my fear of our detection.

From there I made my way to a travel agent who worked in my preferred dealings: cash.

LUCAS

$\mathcal{I}$ decided to make Olly breakfast when she woke up, since I was home for the first time in a long time. She was glowing this morning. I was instantly concerned that in my absence I'd missed something, that I was losing her. I instinctually grimaced at Elias when he wandered into the kitchen.

"We will be leaving first thing in the morning," he said. "I am making arrangements today." It wasn't a question, it was a statement. He had honored my request to stay longer, so I couldn't object. It put more pressure on my interrogation of Zeric tonight, though. I wouldn't get a second chance to get answers from that asshole pixie —*If he has any answers to begin with*, I thought.

"Alright. Olly, you ready to leave dear old India?" I asked. She smiled at Elias first, then turned to me to answer. *Yes*, I thought, *I am giving them far too much time together.* Her camouflage had made it difficult for me to detect that their bond was getting stronger. *Fuck!*

I couldn't allow my attention to be divided; it was either I played interference with Olly's love life, or I focused on hunting down the coward behind the hit on my mother.

"I'm ready for the next adventure," she beamed. I wrapped up the eggs I'd been scrambling and served them to her on a plate. I left the rest on the stovetop. *Viraclay could get his own damn eggs.*

He didn't bother. Instead, he grabbed his bag and went to the front door. "I am off to make our travel arrangements," he stated, then left. That was fine by me.

I pulled a chair up nice and close to Olly at the table as she ate. We chitchatted like old times. I realized how much I'd missed spending time with her. If the pixie interrogation wasn't fruitful, I'd wait to pursue my investigation until we were in less jeopardy. I felt a pang in my heart. *When will that be? Will it always be the three of us?* I couldn't wait that long— I would find a way to juggle my time between Olly and my investigation.

One step at a time, one day at a time, I reminded myself. Someday we would have a small piece of normalcy. Other Conduits managed less-turbulent lifestyles. We'd get there, maybe after Viraclay's summit, I tried to reassure myself. But it felt half-hearted, even in my own head.

Olly finished her eggs and cleaned the kitchen.

"Want to practice some combat?" I invited. I had an hour to spare.

"Sorry, I have an errand to run," she chirped. "A couple things to wrap up before we go." She must've seen the dejection on my face, because she came over and put her hand on my arm. "Maybe in Russia? We'll need to find ways to warm up in the Siberian tundra," she said excitedly.

I playfully caressed her lower back. "I like the sound of that."

She swatted at my hand then shook her finger at me. "You know what I mean."

"What?" I said innocently. "That's what I meant, combat lessons— you work up a sweat that way." She smiled at me knowingly and sashayed down the hall. *There really is a pep in her step this morning,* I thought.

After a few minutes she re-entered the kitchen. "I'm on my way out. See you tonight?" she asked as she grabbed her bag. I noticed it was her larger bag, the one we travelled with. She saw me glance at it and said, "I have some stuff I want to get at the market."

"I'll be here in the morning when you wake, I said. "I have some things to wrap up today as well." She waved goodbye and made her way out the door. I took a deep breath as I walked to the window.

"I have a place in her heart that Viraclay can't touch," I reminded myself out loud. I watched as she walked down the street until I couldn't see her anymore. I considered following her for a moment, then changed my mind. There would be time to bridge the distance between us. I needed to focus on the plan for that night.

I jumped in the shower. Took my time packing my things, so they'd be ready for our morning travels. I decided to peek into Olly's room, snoop around a bit. All of her belongings aside from her clothes were gone. I had to assume she'd taken them with her. *Has she been doing this every day since we got here? Taking her journal along with whatever else she had in her bag with her to the market?* I walked up the stairs and picked through Elias' room. Same thing—absolutely nothing. I thought about myself. I did the same thing as these two. *Can I blame them? Are we that paranoid of each other or just always ready for an ambush?*

As though on cue, the hairs on the back of my neck stood on end. I smelled someone in the house. I bounded down the stairs. She caught me on the last step. She was a woman in snake's clothing, or rather just a huge fucking snake—a basilisk.

"Where is your pet?" I heard Vivienne's voice hiss through the snake's teeth.

"Fuck you!" I spat.

She let her elongated serpent tongue trace my earlobe. "Lucas, your bounty is not nearly as large as the Unconsu whore's or Elias Kraus'. Stop being a tease. Tell me where they are, and I will make your death swift."

"You won't get anything from me, bitch. Stop wasting your time. Let's get to the bottom of this the only way we know how, with a good old-fashioned brawl. And not one of these bullshit fights where you change from one creepy monster to the next. Just you and me in our original skins, with no flashy fireworks."

235

"Nice try, Luey," she hissed again. Just then, the westward wind picked up—I felt it move through the house.

"Oh, how convenient. I just caught her scent," Vivienne said as her basilisk's body tightened around my torso. "You stay here, lover. I'll bring her back to finish her off in front of you." Then she sunk her fang deep into my shoulder and everything went dark.

OPHELIA

"We'll be leaving tomorrow, Talia. Off on another adventure. I'm going to miss you and our tea time." I squeezed her hand on the table.

"I'm going to miss you too," she said. "This has been so much fun—building a friendship with you. We will stay in touch, right?"

I nodded as I choked back tears, because I knew that was a lie. I had to cut all ties the minute we left.

Now she squeezed my hand. "Don't cry. There are so many ways to connect, it's ridiculous."

"I know," I reassured her.

"Just promise me one thing. You won't let your pride or your need to save others get in the way of your heart and true happiness."

I reluctantly conceded. "Yes, but…"

She put her hand up. "No 'buts'. Promise me."

I nodded, remembering how natural, how good I'd felt last night with Elias. "I promise." I paused, then asked, "Do you believe in destiny?"

She considered the question before she answered. "I do. I believe I'm sitting here, with you, right now because we were destined to become friends." A smile spread across her face. I closed my eyes for a moment, letting myself consider once more how easy life would be if we all just believed we were on the path we were meant to be on. As flawed or as beautiful as it was.

While my eyes were closed, I felt Lucas' shield disappear. Terror suddenly seized my body. Something had to have happened to him. My eyes instantly welled up with tears. I squeezed them tighter.

My hand unconsciously moved to my bracelet. I withdrew any shields I was carrying directly on myself. I rubbed the hairsy charm vigorously, but still there was nothing.

"I need to go," I said abruptly. I looked down at my bag, quickly wiping my eyes. I didn't want Talia to think I was a lunatic. "I need to go now. Something is wrong," I blurted out. I still didn't look at her, afraid I'd see that same expression I used to see on others' faces when I had an 'episode'—when I would involuntarily channel *their* emotional roller coasters, resulting in me acting as erratic as hell. Before I found out what I was, before I knew my 'curse' was a gift. That look, I didn't want to see that look.

"What's wrong? Can I help you?" There was sincerity in her voice. I finally looked at her as I threw my bag over my shoulder to leave.

I couldn't believe what I saw. I tried to stand up from my chair and I inadvertently took a couple of steps back at the same time, stumbling as I stared at Talia. She was glowing—she was a Conduit.

A million questions swarmed my head. *Does she know who I am? Was it a coincidence that we met? Is she a Nebas, or a Pai Ona? Did she hurt Lucas?*

"Ophelia?" Concern was strewn across her face. "Are you okay? Can I help?"

All the strange sensations I'd felt when fighting with Lucas flooded back to me. This was what I was capable of seeing when I wasn't hiding behind camouflage. I could feel a wave of her alarm wash over me. I didn't need to look around to feel the curiosity of the other patrons in the café. I noticed that the metal, all the metal in the room, faintly shimmered in a menagerie of color. My senses were heightened, charged. I could hear the goings-on in the kitchen—smell the sweet spices from the bazaar a block away in the air. My fingertips felt warm, as though they were being singed by a candle flame. All of this happened within a split second, then I drew my attention back to Talia. *If that is even her real name.*

I focused so intently that I felt the shield I'd been manipulating block out all the other distractions as it shrouded me. It dimmed the shimmer radiating from Talia's beautiful caramel-colored skin. I wasn't fooled, though; this shield was the very mechanism that had disguised her true nature from me to begin with.

"Who are you?" I challenged, squaring my shoulders, preparing for conflict. The other café patrons were slowly taking their leave, sensing the tension in the air.

She said nothing as she eyed me inquisitively, realizing in that moment that something had changed about me.

"Please don't make me ask again, Talia. Who are you?"

"Today I am Talia," she said, "but people have called me Nandi." I felt my knees get weak in the way that they do when shock hits you so hard you feel like you've been beaten with a ton of bricks. I let down 'my guard' while trying to grab a hold of something—her intent, my bearings, maybe even the ability to put my best foot forward in a battle, if it came to that.

"But..." was all that came out. I looked at her again. All I could feel emanating from her was admiration, guilt, shame and concern. Not the feelings of an enemy. *But she is my enemy, isn't she?* She was the woman who had abducted me at Hafiza, who'd almost killed me. Who has been stalking me for weeks now.

I was still staring at her with disbelief when I saw her demeanor change. Her emotions morphed into fear, bewilderment, ferocity and resolve in an instant. She put her finger to her mouth.

In another instant she was by my side. I seemed to see her move, but somehow didn't—she was so quick.

"Vivienne has found you," Talia whispered. "She is close. I will explain myself after we get you safely out of here. Will you trust me? Use your gifts—can you trust me?" *How does she know about my gifts?* I wondered. She reached for my hand, and I realized she was opening her mind to me. I dove in, just as Rand had taught me to. All I could see was that she intended to save me, that she cherished my friendship and that she had no ill will towards me.

"Yes, I trust you," I heard myself say, and decided that I really did. Everything in my gut told me so.

Talia reached behind her head as she recited words I didn't understand. She gently placed that same hand behind my right ear while reciting several other words I couldn't compute. I felt a sharp tingling shoot from behind my ear into every cell of my being—the sensation was similar to your foot falling asleep: painful, immobilizing and ticklish all at once. It was gone as quickly as it came on. The next thing I knew I heard a voice inside my head. Talia's voice.

"I shared my Rune with you, Ophelia. Only you can hear me. We can communicate this way during the confrontation so that Vivienne does not know our next move." Physically, Talia's lips didn't move, but her head nodded gently. "Activate your voice by touching the Rune behind your ear," she instructed.

I looked at her shocked, befuddled and scared. I rubbed behind my ear.

"Can you hear me?" I simply thought the words, and she replied.

"Yes. You just need to think of me as you speak them. I can only hear your thoughts when you address them to me. Do you understand?" she asked. I nodded.

I focused my thoughts back to being my own. I was about to encounter the Conduit who ambushed Aremis, who killed my friends, destroyed Hafiza, murdered an entire village, and now who must've done something to my Lucas, possibly killed him. Anguish and fury swelled in my chest.

The door swung open. I was grateful all the other patrons, and even the café attendant, had left the building.

ELIAS

I was impressed at how quickly I had completed my 'To do' list. I walked back to the house pleased with the arrangements I had made in Russia. I felt it would be a nice house for us to hole up in for some time, if need be.

It was not until I turned the corner that I saw the front door ajar on our flat. I realized something was gravely wrong. I ran in and saw feet sprawled on the floor at the bottom of the stairs. I could tell they were not Ophelia's, but any opponent that could oust Lucas could have already killed her. I knelt beside him, shook him violently, but he did not respond.

"Lucas!" I yelled. No need for hushed tones—anyone who could dispatch his defenses could hear I was in the house already. I shook him again, desperate for a clue as to what happened. I let his body fall limp onto the tile floor and took some deep breaths. After composing myself, I quickly scoured the house, confirming Ophelia was not here. Nor was the intruder. *Think, Elias,* I told myself. *Where is she?* Through the panic, I remembered the tea shop she had told me about, where she met with Talia. I looked down at Lucas' body, torn between carrying him with me and leaving him here. I personally did not care if whoever did this to him circled back and finished the job. However, Ophelia would not forgive me if I left him here to die.

I threw his useless body over my shoulder and ran as fast as I could with a nearly hundred-and-eighty-pound man on my back.

OPHELIA

I n front of us stood a tall, beautiful woman with long, wavy auburn hair. Her frame was curvy and muscular. She wore a gold sari that exposed her defined abdomen. I felt an intense animosity rolling off Talia. She wanted to tear Vivienne apart, and I suspected this fury ran deeper than my protection.

Talia spoke in my head. "She is a shape shifter. She prefers mythological beasts. I can delay her transformations with my gift by muffling her senses and discombobulating her process but make no mistake—this will be hand-to-hand combat. Can you fight?"

"I can," I assured her through our connection.

"Let me keep her attention as long as I can. She will underestimate you as an Unconsu."

Before I could agree, Vivienne spoke up. "Nandi, Nandi, Nandi—what a treat, that I happen upon you here." She swept her arms wide, gesturing to her surroundings. "You have been a tough bounty to collect, my dear." Vivienne shook her finger in our direction. "I feel like it must be my lucky day. First Lucas…"

I lurched forward involuntarily, which caught Vivienne's eye. "Oh, look at this little Unconsu. So feisty," she said, pointing a finger at me then dancing it around like you would to a child. "Just a feisty little thing."

I really didn't like this woman. I was sure Talia was right—that she would underestimate me. I expanded my shield to encompass Talia under it. Dividing my focus, I let my senses accelerate beyond the protective space I'd created. I saw the metal in the room. I had the sense that it somehow felt me. I put one of my arms behind my back casually, and rubbed my fiery fingers together. I felt sparks fly between the pads of my fingertips. *This must be a gift I absorbed from all the time I spent with Aremis,* I surmised.

The thought of Aremis further fueled my anger. My focus sharpened even more intensely. I could taste emotions in the air. I inhaled the flavors with every breath, pairing the intents of Vivienne and Talia. I was acutely aware of each woman's desires, perhaps I even had a minimal insight into each of their next moves. Like the shadow I'd seen before Ying when we last fenced together, this vision was a fraction of a second ahead of the women's actions.

I took all of this in, in a second or less. I was ready for this—fueled by rage, which turned out to be a very effective accelerant.

I decided to ignore Vivienne's taunt; responding might give something away. I heard Talia's voice in my head. "I will swing right, you flank her on the left. And Olly—do not hold back."

We all began to move. Talia acted first. I watched as Vivienne kept her gaze on my friend—the opponent she felt was the greatest threat. Vivienne's body began to tremble and shake, small movements turned into convulsions. I felt Vivienne's confusion as Talia muffled her transformation process.

This gave me a moment to identify a weapon, while at the same time I saw Talia pull a small metal rod from under her sari. As soon as the pole was clear from her body, it expanded, quadrupling in size until it was nearly eight feet long.

Talia didn't hesitate—she swung her weapon, planting a significant blow to the side of Vivienne's pulsating head. A fierce growl erupted form the now-indistinguishable form.

I hastily skidded behind the café's counter, my senses telling me that something I could use to defend myself would be found there.

They didn't disappoint. I reached down under the surface where my hand found an unsheathed talwar sword. The sword curved upward and was very sharp. When I returned to Vivienne's left flank, I was shocked to find a Chimera where she once stood. The beast was hideous. It had a lion's body and head, a tail that slithered and hissed at me—but most disturbing was the goat head that grew from the back of the lion's thick torso. The goat's head was swiveling, so Vivienne could see all angles of the room, all the threats.

Talia's voice manifested in my head once more. "She breathes fire."

Shit! I thought. *How do I fight that?* Then the tail's nasty little snake head darted at me. I swung the sword as I leapt to the left, its fangs just missing me. But my blade had hit its mark. The goat head screamed as my sword swiftly beheaded the serpent. Then it laughed. "No matter," I heard Vivienne's voice say. "It grows back." Sure as shit, right before my eyes, the nasty green snake tail sprouted a new head, hissing a wicked laugh.

My attention was redirected back to Talia as I saw her bound out of the way of a massive flow of fire expelling from the lion's enormous mouth. I simultaneously dodged the snake again, while planting a blow to the base of the goat's neck, wondering if this appendage grew back as easily.

ELIAS

I heard the fray long before I reached the tea shop. I quickly scoured the neighboring buildings, finding a small nook behind a street vendor and in front of a low overhang on a clothing boutique. I dropped Lucas' limp body in the shaded space. *Live or die, he can stay here for the time being,* I thought. The old woman manning the street cart gave me a strange look but said nothing.

I withdrew the Dirk of Inverness from its sheath. I had forgotten to replace its invisible cloak charm after I had cleaned the blade last. This eliminated the element of surprise, but in this moment that did not matter to me.

The noises from the shop had gotten louder, more animal-like. There was no time to waste. I ran across the street and ripped open the door.

My brain took a moment to catch up with what I saw. Ophelia was closest to where I stood. Behind her was a huge beast with three heads. But perhaps even more unexpected was Nandi. I stood for what felt like an eternity, attempting to assess the situation. *Is Ophelia fending off two Consu at once?*

I saw Nandi land a successful blow with a staff to the beast's huge lion head. The lion roared, spewing fire back at Nandi, but she swiftly maneuvered out of the way.

I had distracted Ophelia with my interruption, leaving her vulnerable. Just then, the beast's serpent tail glided toward her, fangs poised for a bite.

I was six feet away, too far to stop the assault. As I stood helpless, Nandi flew through the air and landed atop the beast, striking the snake so brutally that it went limp. She took the beast's goat head in her arms and twisted the neck so swiftly, I thought it would come clean off, but instead it, too, simply went slack. She then sprung off the back of the beast, taking her place beside Ophelia, and I realized —*Nandi is protecting her.*

OPHELIA

*E*lias' presence distracted me for just a moment, but it would've been enough to kill me if Talia hadn't been there to save my life.

Elias was now at my side, as was my friend.

"Viraclay," Talia urged, "get her out of here!" He instantly took my arm but I resisted. I couldn't leave her, especially after she'd just saved me.

"No!" I insisted. "We can take her. The three of us can end this."

A deep roar shook the café. Vivienne whirled around, sending chairs and tables flying. "End me?" She laughed, first with the lion head, but as the other heads reanimated, it was a chorus of laughter. "I will kill the three of you now! *I* will end *this*!"

She spewed a wave of fire and the three of us dove in different directions. I ducked behind a fallen table. Elias lay nearest to the door, his dagger three feet out of his reach. Talia was on the other side of me, maybe six feet away, crouched and poised again for attack. Vivienne began to saunter toward Elias, her large paws kicking debris out of the way as she walked.

Talia launched herself in the air once more, her staff spiraling above her, the energy of the weapon increasing with each round. When it hit Vivienne's spine, there was a loud crack.

Vivienne reeled on her feet, faster than you would think a beast of that size could move.

I was between Vivienne and Talia now. I pointed at Vivienne with my sword.

"You killed my Lucas. I will end you," I said defiantly.

Her head cocked curiously. She laughed once more. Elias was on his feet behind her, eyeing his dagger on the floor, assessing how quickly he could get to it. I raised my blade. I felt Talia follow behind me...

...Just as the door flew open.

LUCAS

I came to in a small alcove between a street vendor and a storefront. I was foggy, but I could hear the fight. It snapped me back to the present threat. I sprang up at Conduit speed, alarming the old woman behind the cart, but I was gone before she could see what happened.

I threw open the door to the tea house. At first my eyes didn't understand the scenario in front of me. *Nandi and Vivienne?* Olly was between them and about to be killed, right in front of me. I saw a dagger on the floor. Without hesitation, I picked it up and lobbed it in the air, confident it would hit one of the threats, giving me time to kill the other.

Nandi was simply staring at me, a medley of emotion crossing her face: disdain, loathing, and pure hatred. In that moment she paused long enough to distract her from the battle—to keep her still for just a second longer than she would have ordinarily.

Vivienne moved slightly as she prepared to heave a wall of fire at Ophelia. The dagger missed her by a hair. Almost simultaneously, I saw Olly's body fly across the room as the dagger struck Nandi's right shoulder. Nandi faltered slightly, uncharacteristically tripping on her own feet.

I leapt over to Olly, but she was looking back at Nandi and Vivienne. Meanwhile, Elias picked up the sword Ophelia had been wielding. He plunged it into Vivienne's back. It didn't stop Vivienne from pummeling the stumbling Nandi with waves of fire, however, as she thrashed around, trying to dislodge Elias' blade. Nandi's body began flaking into ash under the onslaught of flame. Everything seemed to stop when I heard a scream—the most piercing scream I'd ever heard in over a thousand years of walking this earth

Ophelia put her hand up, and somehow commanded the fire that was engulfing what was left of Nandi's body. She redirected it to the Chimera beast just as Elias lost his grip on the sword and was sent spiraling through the air, landing behind the counter. Vivienne ignited and was incinerated by her own flame—just as Nandi had been.

Small fires filled the room atop several piles of ash that littered the devastated café.

OPHELIA

"She's in shock!" Lucas shouted. He was sitting with me, our backs against the wall. I couldn't speak, I didn't know what to say. Talia was dead. It had happened so quickly.

I looked at my hands. They were shaking. I saw Elias kneel beside the place where Talia's body had been, where now there were only ashes. He reached down and picked up the dagger Lucas had thrown at her. It was still intact. *But how could that be,* I wondered, *after being exposed to such intense heat?*

I stood up and walked over to him. "What is this weapon?"

"It is a Rittle. It is indestructible," he said. I remembered the story Vosega had told me.

Lucas was beside us, examining the dagger as well. "What? I thought they were all gone—vanished."

"My mother gave me this one," Elias said. "It is called the Dirk of Inverness. It stupefies its victims—paralyzes them." Elias was looking into my eyes, apologizing for my loss. My knees buckled. Lucas' throw of the dagger had immobilized Talia so she couldn't get away from the onslaught of fire. I started to breathe hard and fast; I was having a panic attack. Lucas grabbed a chair. He put it under me. I let my face fall into my hands, then put my head between my knees.

What a terrible way to go. That's why she'd left me with that last obscure message. She knew she couldn't move, that she wouldn't survive.

I heard whispers. Elias was telling Lucas that Nandi had saved my life. I moved my hands to cover my ears and replayed what she, my Talia, had communicated to me via her Rune in those final moments.

An image of the Ragunathji Temple had filled my mind as clear as day. Under a small shrine was a slender compartment with a thin box. "The answers you seek are there. It will explain everything." Then her voice was abruptly cut off as her body was consumed by flames.

I'd been so angry in that moment, something had welled up inside me. I imagined shrouding Vivienne's body in flames—and just as I envisioned it, it came to be. The burning in my fingers had accelerated, then I projected the flames onto her body. It had all happened so fast that I didn't even have time to think about what I was doing—it was over, and they were both dead.

What is happening to me? I wondered. *And why am I not afraid?* Then I thought about my friend. *Why did Talia have to die? What answers did she think I sought?*

I didn't have the answers to all those questions, but I knew what I had to do next.

PART III

LUCAS

"This isn't a good idea!" I asserted.

"I don't care what you think is a good idea. I lost a friend. I need to say goodbye. This is how I'm choosing to do that." Ophelia looked at both of us as she spoke.

Elias hadn't objected, but he had to have reservations about this too. After what had happened at the café, we needed to get out of India, *now*. We'd gone back to the house to grab my things and Olly's clothes, but now it was time to go.

"Didn't I prove I can take care of myself?" she asked.

"That's what you thought you proved by befriending the woman who tried to abduct you at Hafiza, and participating in a standoff with Vivienne?" The words came out of my mouth before I had a chance to evaluate what I was saying. I could tell it hurt her, but it wasn't the time to coddle. We could talk more about this later, once we were far away from here.

"I don't like your tone, Lucas Healey." She narrowed her eyes on me.

I stepped back and let my shoulders relax. My temper had flared because I was scared for her, but I needed to be reasonable right now. "Olly, this isn't a battle of wills," I said, and meant it. "We need to keep you safe and get the hell out of here immediately. We don't have time for some Hindu ritual. You aren't even Hindu, and neither was Nandi —or Talia—or whatever you called her."

Elias spoke up. "Lucas is right, we need to depart posthaste. However, I believe Ophelia deserves her farewell to Nandi. On her terms." So much for reasonable. My agitation escalated again, as it always did when Elias began giving me orders. "Escort her to the temple, Lucas," he said. "I need to rearrange our travel plans, to move them up to today. Meet me at the train station in forty-five minutes. I will also spend some of that time covering our tracks."

I decided it was futile to argue with both of them. "Let's go," I said to Olly. I headed toward the door and waited patiently for her to grab her bag that she'd recovered from the café, before following her outside.

"I'm sorry, Olly, really, I am," I said as we walked. "About everything. About Nandi. About not being there. About arguing with you a second ago."

She said nothing, she didn't even look at me. The divide between us just seemed to get bigger by the day. I stopped in the middle of the street. "Are you even listening to me?" I said, grabbing her by the shoulders.

"Yes, Lucas, I hear you. I'm just dealing with things my own way. Just like you're dealing with them in *your* own way. Right? That's what you're trying to say?"

I pulled her in tighter. "I love you, Olly. I was just so scared when I thought I'd lost you."

She hugged me back. "I was scared when I thought I lost you too."

After a minute she pulled away, and we continued our walk in silence.

We reached the Ragunathji Temple steps. I began to follow her in when she stopped me. "I want to do this alone," she told me. "Go scout the temple, then give me a moment to mourn in my own way, please."

I hesitated, then ran in and quickly returned, gesturing with a wave that it was good to go. I sat down on the steps while Olly slowly ambled inside.

How am I going to fix all of this? I needed to stop being so hotheaded; I could tell it was making things worse. I thought about what I'd seen less than thirty minutes ago in the café: Nandi, Vivienne —Olly in between. I was sure I was going to lose her just then, but then she did something miraculous. *She controlled fire.* I realized that Ophelia was more powerful than we knew, as well as highly capable of taking care of herself. The thought hit me like a sledge hammer. *What does she need me for?* I felt my eyes start to burn—I wasn't sure I could hold back my tears. I heard her feet shuffle behind me.

"You're done?" I rubbed my eyes before I stood to face her. "That was fast."

"I didn't say it would be a long goodbye."

"Well, let's hope Viraclay moves as fast as you do."

ELIAS

$\mathscr{I}$ watched her from across the elaborate train car. She appeared to be all right, but it was hard to tell; she wore her own masks now. I looked around the cabin. It was a little over the top for my taste, but I supposed the facilitators of this sort of travel wanted to impress their upscale clientele with sumptuousness. Crystal chandeliers hung from the ceiling, lighting a large common room with deep mahogany paneling that came halfway up the wall. There were two overstuffed couches draped with chenille throw blankets along with ornamental pillows. A small corridor led to a full-sized bathroom with a shower. Opposite the bathroom was a bedroom with a queen-size bed. All the windows could be blacked out, so the occupants could sleep comfortably anytime during their travel.

My eyes made their way to the wet bar where Lucas was stationed, drinking his heart's content of vodka. He stared at Ophelia intently while she looked out the window.

How would I know if she was not okay? I wondered. *Would she confide in me?*

I replayed the confrontation with Vivienne in my head once more, and felt the fear well up in me again—I had been certain she was going to be killed. That could not have been further from the truth; she was magnificent. She was like nothing I had ever seen before, consummated or otherwise.

The words of the prophecy rang in my head: "From ashes she will rise. And those who lived before her will question what power was before they witnessed her supreme virtue."

Just then Ophelia turned to face me. She smiled, her perfect mouth sweeping upward into genuine affection. She moved her gaze to Lucas.

"Is there any wine over there?" she called out. "Or did you drink it all?" She stood and walked over to stand beside Lucas' slumped form.

He perked up upon her approach. "I bet they have an overpriced Cab in here somewhere." He shuffled through the cupboards until he presented her with a bottle of red wine. "I'll pour you a glass."

"Perfect. I'm going to get in the shower." She patted at her shirt covered in ash. Particles wafted in the air around her.

From ashes she will rise, I thought once more.

OPHELIA

J had my bag in one hand and my glass of wine in the other. I leaned against the bathroom door until I heard it click closed then sat on the toilet and placed my glass on the countertop, hoping it wouldn't fall from the rhythmic sway of the train. I rifled around in my bag until I found Talia's journal. *Back to having secrets*, I thought.

First, I looked at the book closely. It was leather, bound by a thin leather string so long that it wrapped round it twice. I moved it around in my hands. There was nothing remarkable on the back of the book, but the front had several things going on. I ran my hand across the darker markings that seemed to be indented into the leather itself; I'd never seen anything like them before. They looked decorative, similar to paisley designs, and in no particular order. Some of the markings over-lapped onto each other. Within the random markings were two metal inlays, one above and one below a small, oval brownish-gold stone. I ran my fingers over the inlays then traced the stone. It all looked very old.

I unbound the tie. When I flipped the pages, they opened up to a single sheet of folded paper with my name written on the front. As I took out the paper, I noticed on one side of the book-marked page there was a strange language I didn't recognize. The other side was neatly written English. I flipped through the pages once more. Sure enough, the whole first half before the bookmarked page was in the strange language, whereas the pages that followed were in English.

Odd, I thought. Hopefully Talia's letter explained what I was supposed to do with the journal. I could only trust that it held the answers she had intended to give me, and that I understood them. I started reading.

My dear Ophelia,

I know this must seem so strange. I am sorry for lying to you. I was certain you would know who I was if I had told you my known name. It is true, people call me Nandi. Before Nandi it was Sabiya, before Sabiya it was my birth name, Arsinoe. I liked the named Talia, though, and I will cherish that I got to share that name with you and our friendship. Because although you did not know me by my true name, you were my true friend.

I can only hope that you will trust Talia, your friend, because the story I am going to share is fantastical and I am confident contains some facts you would sooner like to ignore or dismiss, but I promise they are truth.

I hope that by getting to know me better you will believe me. I ask that you read the account I have written for you from beginning to end. Do not jump ahead to the final pages. I've included every detail that I can recall, in a format that I hope will read as if I'm here, imparting to you the story of my life. I do this not only so that you may truly get to know me, but also perhaps so that you may glean some insight that you can use yourself someday. Not many know my story as intimately as you will by the time my journey is through. Which I must assume it is, if you have found this letter.

I must beg of you, do not cry for me. I am with my Huan, wherever that is—somewhere across the River Tins. I have missed him for so long and welcome the finality that death must bring. I am grateful that I had a couple weeks of your time, to get to know you. I am convinced that a soul like yours can only save our people. I have no doubt that the prophecy will be fulfilled with our salvation, and that you are that salvation.

I have much to explain. You must be accumulating more questions as you read on. I promise all will be revealed.

The last thing I want to say is I am so sorry for attempting your abduction when you were residing in Hafiza. I never meant to hurt you or frighten you.

Please do not share this information with anyone. It is for your safety that I ask for your silence. It will all become clear, I can promise you that. I will not forsake you.

Stay safe, friend,
Your Talia

I PUT THE LETTER DOWN AND REPEATED HER WARNING IN MY HEAD. "IT is for your safety that I ask for your silence." *Safety from what?*

ESTHER

*T*he tea shop was destroyed. Small pyres of ash continued to smolder.

"This is a pity," Yanni admitted. "Vivienne was so reliable. Who will we ever find to replace her?" He walked over to me, took my hand in his. "I am sorry, dear, I know you found her particularly useful."

"I did. I am disappointed," I whined. "This is inconvenient."

Yanni kicked a chair exposing a long staff. "Maybe it is not all lost, my love. What on earth is this weapon?" He picked it up to examine it. As he did, it folded upon itself into a small, compact baton.

"Curious. What an extraordinary object," I said as I took it from him, tossing it back in forth between my hands. "Now, how do we expand it again?"

"Mechanics are beyond me, but we will bring it back to the compound where it can be thoroughly assessed." I nodded in agreement. He took the staff from my hands, tucking it into his belt.

"They cannot be far beyond our reach. Look at this place. Fires still burn. Who can we get here fast enough to hunt them down?"

Yanni kissed my cheek tenderly. "Do not worry yourself about these things. I will pursue them from here," he assured me.

"But darling, you are one and they are three," I reminded him as I moseyed into the back of the store.

"One Consu and two Unconsu, versus me. They haven't a chance." Yanni was confident as he spoke. I had to agree that his skills went unmatched by most—but so had Vivienne's.

The kitchen was so *quaint*, with a simple stove for heating water and several jars of dried leaves. *Oh how the rabble live*, I thought.

I heard muffled sobs as I approached the end of the counter. A young boy was huddled in the corner, shaking.

"Oh, darling," I consoled him. "Have you been here all this time? Did you witness this fray?"

He nodded.

I looked over my shoulder, giving Yanni a come-hither smile. I combed through my long black hair with my fingers as I resumed my interaction with the boy.

"Do you work here?" I outstretched my hand to pull him to his feet. He gladly took it as he shook his head no.

"What is your name, child?" I asked in my gentlest voice.

"Najish."

"You speak good English, Najish." He smiled at me. His body had stopped shaking. I gestured towards Yanni. "This is my partner."

Najish smiled at him.

"Do you know what happened here?" Yanni asked.

Najish shook his head no.

"You saw nothing?" I cocked my head at him ever so slightly. "Nothing at all?" I walked him toward the devastated café's seating area.

Again, he shook his head no.

"Then why are you so frightened?" Yanni inquired from behind us.

"I heard things. Monstrous things," Najish stuttered.

"Aw, I see." I gave a knowing glance back to Yanni. He pulled the staff from his belt. "It will be hard to forget those noises. You will live a life of terror, of anxiety. That is no way for a boy to live," I assured him.

Najish's eyes widened. I turned to face him. "That is a life of desolation. We would not want that for you, Najish." I smiled as Yanni raised the baton above the boy's head and struck down hard. His body crumpled to the ground.

"Darn," I sighed. "I had hoped that engaging it in combat would activate its expansion. Oh well."

LUCAS

S
he was finally sleeping when we got to the house in Russia, so I carried her in. She must've been exhausted because she didn't move even as I laid her on the bed that Viraclay indicated was hers. I slipped off her shoes and shut the door quietly.

I looked around the new digs. It was nothing spectacular. Just another house in another country. There was no art or warmth about the place, just a building for shelter.

Viraclay was in the kitchen when I came out of Olly's room.

"Do you think we are safe, for a time?" he asked earnestly.

I thought about it for a moment before answering. "As far as I know, yes. We knew we were being tracked by Nandi and Vivienne. They're both dead." The buzz I'd gotten from the vodka on the train was gone, and I was left wondering what the hell had happened back at the café.

"What was Ophelia doing with Nandi?" I asked.

"I cannot say. I do know that Nandi introduced herself to Ophelia as Talia, and they had been meeting for the last two weeks. Therefore, it is safe to say Nandi did not intend to abduct or harm Ophelia, or she would have done so."

"But why?" I said it out loud, even though it was more an internalized question.

"To what end, I do not know. And it would seem, with her passing, we will never know."

My mind was jumping from one conclusion to the next, but none of them made any sense. I needed some air after being on that train.

"I'm going to go for a run. Check out the lay of the land." I headed toward the door then turned around. "I hope we're okay for the time being. I don't know how they found us, twice. But it will take Esther and Yanni time to get a new assassin in place." I shut the door behind me.

At night the air was cool, fresh, being that we were so close to the mountains.

I had so many questions. *What did Nandi want with Olly? What is Olly capable of? I missed my chance to confront that damn pixie. How will I restart my investigation into my mother's murder?*

ELIAS

I had decided the night before, while Lucas was out as Ophelia slept, that I would honor the agreement Ophelia and I had made in India to only share truths between us by inviting her to join me while I made contact with the Khakas people.

I had left a note for Lucas that he was free to take the rental car if he wished to amass essentials for the kitchen. I was happy when I woke up to see that he had felt so inclined.

Ophelia was in the kitchen making an egg concoction when I got out of the shower.

"Where is Lucas?" I asked.

"Off running secret errands." She waved the spatula in the air wildly.

She wore a long T-shirt that fell just past the curve of her buttocks. I found my eyes being drawn to the shirt's hem as she raised her arm. She turned around and I quickly averted my stare, but she had caught me.

"My face is up here, mister," she said playfully.

I cleared my throat. "Of course." I held back a smile.

"Eggs? I made enough to feed a Russian army."

"Indeed."

She dished me up while I poured a cup of coffee. We sat side by side at the counter, eating quietly.

"Would you like to join me today?" I asked. "In the spirit of transparency." I thought she would be excited by the invitation, but when I turned to look at her I saw hesitation on her face. She chewed slowly, buying time.

"Yes, I think that'd be great." She took her eyes away from her plate to meet my gaze. "Is this because you're afraid to leave me alone again, after what happened at the café?"

I put my hand up. "No. I assure you, you have proven beyond a shadow of a doubt in my mind that you are very capable of defending yourself. This is simply for the sake of lucidity, so that you may feel a part of this journey and in control of your life."

Her face fell back to her plate. I sensed she wanted to say something else, but she chose silence.

She quietly said, "You're kind," nodding, still not making eye contact with me. "Can I have thirty minutes to get ready?"

"Certainly," I agreed. "I will clean up. Thank you for breakfast."

She excused herself from the room as I stood there considering what I was missing in that exchange. Perhaps I would learn more during our outing that day.

OPHELIA

*I*t would only take me fifteen minutes to get ready; that gave me a few moments to read some of Talia's journal. I'd hesitated to say yes to Elias' invitation because I wanted to invest some time reading, in understanding what Talia thought I needed to know. But I also felt compelled to spend time with Elias, ever since our evening together in Jammu, where I gave into just being with him—to being honest with him.

I did a mental eye-roll because here I was, with secrets, all over again. *This is different though, right?* I'd promised Talia I would honor her wishes.

I pulled out the journal and put it on my lap. If I was being really honest with myself, I'd have to admit I was also scared of what I might find in those pages. *One day at a time*, I thought.

I opened the book and dove in.

I decided to start from the beginning—of my Conduit life, that is. It all began the day that I met Huan, in the year of 41 BC.

My name was Arsinoe. I was a leader of my people, daughter of Ptolemy XII and sister to the great Cleopatra.

It was a beautiful day. The Mediterranean Sea was calm, eerily calm. I, on the other hand, was anything but. I felt as though I couldn't breathe. It had been this way for days, ever since my sister had sent me away. I was aboard the Razbunator, a filthy Roman ship navigating its way from port to port as it plodded towards the final destination—my final destination. I was to be paraded around as Caesar's captive and then locked up in the Temple of Artemis in Ephesus. It was a tactical win for all parties involved. My sister Cleopatra desired my disappearance, so that I had no claim to her throne, while Caesar required a public humiliation of a prominent Egyptian after the attempted coup. I was the obvious, consequently convenient, recompense.

The captain and his men had been unusually polite, but I attributed that to the fact that I was soon to be on public display. Bring the goods back undamaged, so to speak. Once the demonstration was made, I would be fair game. It was even more likely that my parade was to be more or less a public thrashing.

It wasn't that I had never been assaulted before. I had sustained plenty of beatings and had been molested a few times during the civil war and political uprisings. However, I had heard stories about the captives of Ephesus and the Temple of Artemis. Stories that travelled as far as they did to meet my ears were never good, and most likely true.

I had been looking for my Atoa for years, but war along with power struggles continued to take center stage in my life. I had started to believe it just wasn't in the strokes for me. It was almost a comfort to think it would all be over soon. The struggles, the searching.

We arrived in Ephesus at dawn. I was taken to a bathhouse and allowed the opportunity to cleanse myself before Caesar himself visited my chambers. He gloated as he assured me that he would not be strangling me as he would usually do to someone of my status. This did nothing to assuage my anxiety; captivity sounded worse than death.

I was trumpeted about that evening. My hands were tied behind my back while I was pulled behind Caesar on his horse. My feet bled from the three-mile walk without shoes. My wrists burned and chafed from the ropes. I had fallen a handful of times; therefore, I had been dragged behind Caesar's horse for several feet at a time, so my robes were tattered and bloody from the gashes in my knees and the road burns.

I had not bothered to make eye contact with the jeering spectators, except for those who threw rocks. I made a special note of each of their faces, in case I ever got free from my captivity.

We were nearly to the steps of the temple when something tugged at my heart, demanding I look up. I met Huan's eyes. They were deep, dark—merciful. I immediately knew who he was to me: he was my other half, my Atoa. Recognition was written on his face as well. It was as though the world stood still for both of us in that moment. My feet refused to lead me away from him. I fell once more and was dragged the rest of the way to the steps, where Caesar himself spat on me before doing the honors of hog-tying me then hauling me into my prison.

273

My mind was racing. How could I get to my partner, my stranger with the dark eyes? After Caesar threw me into a small chamber, barely larger than a closet, I thought he would have his way with me. But apparently, I was too thrashed to be mounted so he called in a couple of priests, demanding I be washed up. The two of them scurried away in opposite directions.

Caesar left the room, at which point I let myself breathe and pray. I prayed that by the grace of Chitchakor's strokes I might find a way to get out of that place to have the opportunity to see those eyes again.

I licked my lips and tasted blood mixed with sweat. I wondered how bad I looked. I felt elation and desperation, simultaneously—miraculously numbing the pain.

The two priests returned with a large water basin, some oils and several towels. They gingerly began unbinding my body. Soon I heard Caesar's heavy walk. I saw his burly frame in the doorway. I heard the shuffling of feet behind him; his personal guard was mobilizing.

"I have an emergency matter to attend to," he said. "See to it that she is washed before I return. I will leave four of my guards here. And do not be fooled by her feminine form—this woman has commanded armies." Caesar disappeared, and I was alone with the two naïve priests.

They removed all of the ropes to clean my wounds. They modestly cut the robe I was wearing because the blood had dried to the garment. When I was naked, they thoroughly scrubbed my body and rinsed my hair, then wrapped it up into a thick, heavy bun atop my head.

I said nothing during the bath. I did my best to seem withdrawn and broken. They handed me a clean robe to wear as they bandaged my feet. It was then that I decided to make my move, afraid they would lock me in the room until Caesar returned.

I began coughing violently. One of the priests commanded the other to fetch me a glass of wine. As he waddled out, I moved quicker than I ever had before, fueled by the prospect of seeing my Atoa outside of those walls. I used the rope that was on the ground and a towel they had used to clean my body. In less than ten seconds I had gagged the remaining priest and bound him, leaving enough rope to repeat the same knots on the second holy man when he returned. I continued to hack, to muffle any noise. I had no desire to hurt either of them; they had been kind to me.

The second man returned with a large glass of wine. I took the goblet swiftly from his hands, gagged him, showed him his colleague I was easily detaining just behind the door, and gestured for him to stay quiet. He shakily complied. I tied the two priests back to back and thanked them for their kindness as I slipped out of the room.

There were two guards stationed a few feet from the door. I didn't have a weapon, but I was very effective with hand-to-hand combat. They both came at me with their swords drawn, but their armor made them slow. I ducked and swung my leg around, tripping one of them while rolling backwards to miss the other's blow. I was about two feet from the guard on the ground, so I go to my feet and planted a shattering blow to his right calf. I heard the bone splinter as he writhed on the floor in pain. It was easy enough to take the sword lying beside his cowering body.

I danced around his friend. These two were clearly not Caesar's finest soldiers; I was able to dispatch them in less than five minutes. The remaining guard let me lead our stance. By the time he was preparing to lean into the fight, I'd relieved him of his sword with a single blow, struck his chin with a high kick and watched him crumple into unconsciousness.

I wondered where the two other guards were as I grabbed the second sword. I approached the back of the temple, hoping to have a clean escape. Certainly, I figured, there must be another way to get in or out of the building.

I reached a narrow hallway with no light and had a moment of hesitation. I heard movement in the shadows so I lifted my weapons to greet whoever was coming. I was going to handle this head-on.

Two eyes manifested in the dark, and my heart sped up. His eyes—he had found me. I dropped my swords and ran into the dark passage. I heard a sword being sheathed before I reached him. We collided and found each other's mouths. For a long yet somehow too brief a moment we let our tongues get acquainted. Then Huan pulled me away, and spoke in Asagi.

"We need to get out of here quickly," he said. "I killed the other two guards, but the distraction I created must be contained by now." His voice sounded so familiar, like I had always known this stranger holding my hands, shuttling me through the dark to safety.

I followed him as we spoke. "What distraction?" I asked.

He chuckled before he answered. "I lit the local guards' stable on fire." He paused. "Don't worry, no horses were hurt. I let them free first." We were both giggling in the dark. Eventually we reached a door that had been effectively demolished. Beside the remnants of the door lay a third guard.

I looked at my rescuer in the moonlight. He turned to meet my gaze.

"What is your name?" I asked.

"My name is Huan," he said, as he caressed my cheek gently. "I will never let anyone harm you again, Arsinoe."

I memorized his features that night, in the dim moonlight. He had shoulder-length hair that he kept tied back out of his face, except for the perfect wily few strands that pestered him so but framed his cheeks perfectly. He was from the Orient; it showed in his exotic-shaped eyes and large, wide cheekbones. His nose was small for his face, but his mouth made up for it, with thick lips and a broad smile. Words do not do him justice; he was glorious.

I PUT THE JOURNAL DOWN AND THREW MYSELF BACK ONTO THE BED. I thought about my collision with Elias in Chicago while I was visiting Eleanor two years prior—how it had moved me that day. I remembered the way his golden-hazel eyes haunted me for so long after that. I'd felt more alive in that moment, when we met, than I had at any time leading up to it.

Even now… When I let my guard down, I returned to that intense state of being whole when I was near him. It was intoxicating then and now.

I wondered what would happen if I gave in to this feeling. It was more than just desire—it was completion. As I let down my guard with him, I felt gaps in my being fill, like the mortar between bricks. That was the lure, the bait that was reeling me in. I wondered if he felt it too.

I thought about Lucas, about how this would hurt him. I loved him, for entirely different reasons—he was comfortable, he was my friend. But this thing with Elias was so much bigger, and that scared me to death. Now, when I thought of Lucas I also thought of the deep, dark secrets he was keeping from me, and that too froze me with fear. I was afraid of Elias because he was being honest and letting me in—I was scared of Lucas because I realized there was so much I didn't know.

LUCAS

I determined the night before, during my run, that there was nothing I could do about Nandi having infiltrated Olly's life, and the truth was I was glad she was gone—there was no love lost between us. I also couldn't slow down or prevent the transformation Olly was going through—all I could do was help her through it. Support her if she wanted it and wait to see how it all unfolded.

The only thing I could control was tracking down leads on my mother's hit. I was torn. I saw the connection between Viraclay and Olly getting stronger in my absence, but I knew she and I had a connection that he couldn't touch—true friendship.

Since seeing Vosega and allowing myself to remember my mother —remember her goodness along with the terrible way I lost her—it had been consuming me. She had been the first person I loved and the first person I'd lost. I needed to get to the bottom of her murder. I was willing to forfeit a short period of time with Olly to have closure.

I had one old acquaintance in Mongolia, since Yessica and I had spent time there frequently. I wasn't exactly excited about seeing him again, and I knew he'd be equally unenthused about my appearance on his doorstep. But we deal with the hands we're dealt.

Olly, Viraclay and I were staying right where the borders of

Mongolia, Russia, Kazakhstan and China meet. The house was nestled in the Altai Mountains, so that Elias could go hunting there for natives. It was a three-hour run for me from there to the capital of Mongolia, Ulaanbaatar. I suspected my contact was still there; I couldn't imagine him choosing another part of the country, away from the political hoopla he loved.

I arrived at his last known residence around 8 a.m. It was a Tuesday, so I wanted to catch him before he ran off to work, or whatever he did during the day. I knew when I arrived that he still lived there; I could smell him.

I climbed the estate fence and quietly snuck up to the back door, avoiding the armed guards at the formal entrance in the front. He was one of the only Conduits I knew who still insisted on being in the public eye, despite the danger it put him in. On one hand, I had a lot of respect for the guy—it took balls. On the other hand, I suspected he'd paid for his fame with some pretty seedy favors. He would need to in order to not be executed by the Nebas.

I went to knock when the door swung open.

"What are you doing here, Lucas? You are not welcome here." The thick man stood in front of me, practically filling the doorframe. He wasn't tall, but he still had a demanding presence. He wore a suit; he must have been getting ready to head to the capital building, just as I'd expected. He had a thick head of black hair and a round face.

"Come on, Genghis, you aren't excited to see your son-in-law?"

"No," he said plainly. "And no one calls me that anymore."

"Only those who know and love you."

He sneered at me. "And you are neither." He put his arm against the doorframe. I thought it was promising that he hadn't swung at me yet.

I heard a sweet female voice come from behind him. "Let him in, Borjigin. You know he won't go away until you give him whatever he wants."

"Hey Borte!" I called around Genghis' shoulder. "I bet you look as beautiful as ever."

She scoffed in disgust.

Genghis moved aside. I took a few steps into their massive kitchen. He shut the door and shoved past me. I followed him into another cavernous room that appeared to be a study. Borte sat in a large armchair. The chair backed up to a wall of books. She was reading one in Portuguese. That was fitting, considering her talents. She was a Linguist; that is, she could understand and manipulate languages. The way Yessica had described it, it was as though Borte could understand every word ever spoken, like an immediate translator. Better yet, she could distort the words so that others could also understand the foreign language. That wasn't as useful now that we had Google Translate, but when Genghis built the Silk Road and expanded his empire, it was integral.

"Doing homework, I see?" I teased.

She shot me an annoyed grimace. She was not a very warm woman. She'd never cared for Yessica either. Genghis favored Yessica above all his other children. It didn't help that Borte and Genghis had never had a child together. The history books will say different, but history is written by people who want humanity to believe a certain story, not the facts. The fact was, they didn't have a child when they consummated, and Borte resented her husband's choice to create heirs with Unconsu to insure his legacy—she took it out on his hordes of offspring, especially his favorites.

"What do you want?" Genghis asked as he took a seat behind his large oak desk. I took the seat opposite him.

I put my hands on the desk. "Nice setup here, Genghis. Two terms as Prime Minister, and two terms as President. Not a bad gig. How do you do it, though? While the rest of us have scampered about hiding in the shadows, trying not to get extinguished by the Nebas."

His face got red. I felt his invisible fog of influence trying to infiltrate my senses. If I wasn't shielded, I'd be groveling at this moment, begging him to lead me—to God knows where. He was the original politician. His gift worked on humans effectively, and depending on the potency, it could be very powerful with our kind as well. My shield had always protected me from it—come to think of it, maybe that's why the guy never liked me.

"Put that fog shit away, Genghis. There was no way I was coming in here unguarded." I waved at the air.

He shrugged. "It was worth a shot."

"You come here to accuse my husband?" Borte interjected.

"I wouldn't dream of that. I'm just wondering if he may know how to get in touch with any of the local unsavory types," I proposed.

"Oh, you are ready to return to your mercenary ways?" Deep resentment was seething in his voice. "The very ways that killed my daughter."

I had to take some deep breaths to maintain my composure. Losing it right now wouldn't help me, and the truth was that the Khan here had no idea what was going on when Yessica died. He was too busy with his political campaigns.

"Maybe that's what I'll do," I said. "Turns out the good guys don't pay as well—but you know that, right?"

He stood up. "Get out!" Rage was making him tremble. "I don't deal with the Nebas."

I stood too. "You aren't the Nebas, but you must feed them something to keep your powerful public lifestyle." I gestured around the room. "I'm looking for someone who's been hiring hits on entire families. It's not Yanni or Esther, so it must be someone in your position. Playing both sides, bartering lives in the shadows."

Genghis didn't bite. He wore the perfect poker face. I threw my fist on the table. "I don't care what you do to keep Borte safe. I wish I could've done the same for your daughter." I paused for a moment, regaining my composure. "I just need a lead. This is your country; you must know where the repugnant spots are." I kept his gaze in the silence that followed.

Once again, Borte broke the stalemate. "Give him this, Borjigin. Let him be off where we can hope he finally meets the great painter at the River Tins as dust."

Khan finally threw me a bone. "I don't allow unsavories in my country. I do, however, ignore their passage through the north. They are not allowed to linger, so you may find establishments that cater to their kind on either side of my northern border." He looked, exasperated, at Borte, then back at me. "Now leave here and do not come back. Otherwise those subterfuge alliances you speak of, the ones that don't exist, may somehow be alerted of a specific bounty that is loitering outside my walls."

I said nothing as I let myself out.

OPHELIA

$\mathcal{I}$ was exhausted after spending the whole day trekking around the countryside with Elias. I could sense his frustration; he'd hoped we would have a more fruitful search, that we'd find the tribe he was looking for, but we came up empty handed.

After arriving back home, we ate in silence, then I excused myself to retire to my room for the night.

Again, I realized that I had enjoyed Elias' company. We were just getting to know each other—we were building a friendship. I found that he was intelligent and witty; I hadn't gotten a chance to see these qualities in him before. It was like he'd hidden them in front of Lucas. I wondered why that was.

I pulled out Talia's journal from my bag. "Let's see what I can read before I fall asleep," I mindlessly said aloud.

Huan was from a very different upbringing than my own. He and his father, Ruit, were very close. His father shared with Huan his predilection for travel and learning about various ancient cultures. You see, even as a young man, Ruit had visited small tribes; that was where he met Huan's mother, Nil. She was the holy woman of the nomadic people in what is now the Northwestern part of China. She was not

Ruit's Atoa, but they shared a bed and she became pregnant. Huan never met his mother; she died in childbirth.

So it was just the two of them. For many years Huan and his father travelled from country to country, visiting small clans of local people, untouched by the inertia of society. It was during their journey to Morocco that Ruit met his Jezebel, his Atoa. Huan was sixteen years old at the time. Seeing the love between Ruit and Jezebel incited Huan's own desire to be whole, so with a heavy heart he took to the Silk Road and began to make his way in the world, trading on his own.

As I said, he was bartering rare stones when he found me. He had crossed the Erythraean Sea and was passing through Ephesus during our first encounter.

So there we were, two new Consus, in love. With Huan I got something I had never had before, a family. Ruit and Jezebel had Almus. Almus found Inca and they begot Alistair. Ruit insisted that his sons and their families meet at least once a year in one of his villages. We called them "his villages" because the people that inhabited them worshipped him, and his teachings and magic was interwoven into their foundations.

And because I can be factual, the truth was he had fathered children within the villages. This was all before Jezebel, of course.

My family still brings such joy to my heart when I think about our retreats together. Alistair loved the simplicity of the villages; it was such a wonderful way for him to grow up. Almus and Inca spent much more time with their parents after Almus spent a span of time in Hungary, uniting the tribes there. He discovered power was not for him—he preferred the unassuming lifestyle that his father and mother engaged in.

Huan and I valued the retreats, the time spent with family, but found that we also appreciated our time alone together, away from everyone and everything. We had several quaint cabins around the world that we could hole up in for months at a time. It was a wonderful time in my life, before the first open battle, before we were truly touched by this war.

MY EYES WERE GETTING HEAVY. I TOOK A MOMENT TO IMAGINE THE WAY Talia and Huan lived. *Could I live that way? Will I need to?*

I WAS STARTLED AWAKE BY A CHEERFUL "KNOCK, KNOCK, KNOCK!"

It was morning. I wiped the drool from my chin and replaced Talia's journal to its hiding spot.

"Come in," I said groggily. Elias entered my room with a cup of coffee.

"Did you sleep well?" he asked as he handed me the warm brew.

"Yeah. I think so. I don't even remember falling asleep." I took a sip. He had made it just the way I liked it. With all his grand plans and ongoing errands, I hadn't even realized that he'd paid attention to little things like that. I internally blushed as I considered how thoughtful that was. "How about you?"

"I slept as good as could be expected." He turned to the door. "I am preparing breakfast. Take your time, but please feel free to join me when you are ready."

He shut the door. I took a deep breath. *Could he be any sweeter?*

ELIAS

$\mathcal{W}$e drove back home in silence after another failed attempt at contact with a second clan. It had been two days since we arrived in Russia, and still we had nothing. The other tribes I had previously visited had known I was coming, welcomed me. Yet thus far I had been stonewalled by the two local Khakas tribes that I thought perfectly fit the previous people's characteristics: small populations who had settled in a secluded location and lived in an extremely traditional manner. I was so close, but I was hitting a wall.

"You seem frustrated." Ophelia looked at me inquisitively. "Can I help with something?"

I kept my eyes on the road as I spoke. "I do not think so. I am afraid I miscalculated something. My projections were wrong, and I have no idea what I am missing. Russia is too big a country to be wandering about seeking small pockets of indigenous tribes." I did not want to sound too discouraged, but the truth was, I was at a loss.

She put her hand on my knee. "It sounds like you need to get away from the job for a bit. Maybe stretch your legs? Lucas is gone again; he said he would be back after dinner. I've been wanting to get my hands on some Russian vodka." She smiled at me coyly. "What do you say? Let's park the car at the house and walk into town. Be my escort?"

I looked at her. She was so physically striking, with a genuine spirit, and playful at heart. Here she was, tagging along with me. It occurred to me that, for the first time since my parents had passed, I felt true connection to another; I no longer felt isolated. "How can I refuse an offer such as this?" I played along. "I will gladly escort you." We pulled into the drive not five minutes later. I threw my satchel over my shoulder. Ophelia grabbed her own bag as I locked the car.

I had chosen a small village called Aktash for us to reside in during this leg of the journey. It had one tiny market, where the roads met right in the middle of the village. We got strange glances from bewildered residents who did not expect any strangers in their corner of the world.

The market had meats, along with rice. We stocked up on both. Ophelia found a locally distilled bottle of vodka with no label, but the smile from the shopkeeper insinuated it was a good purchase.

Once we were back outside, Ophelia gestured to the vast Siberian wilderness around us. White rocks with huge crevasses jutted about while snowcapped mountains spanned the horizon. "Why do you think the tribe we are looking for is here?" she asked.

"The gentleman who turned me onto the various tribes we have been investigating around the world said that he recognized some of the script from the Khakas of Northern Asia. My maps led me here."

"I see. But there are more populations of Khakas, perhaps elsewhere?" she asked.

"Yes, of course. Many more," I agreed.

"Well, why don't we do some research, investigate what other populations might meet the characteristics you're looking for? I can do research—I went to grad school after all." She smiled optimistically.

"Our resources are limited," I told her. "I have an encrypted laptop we may be able to use, if we are fortunate enough to get internet service." I thought about what I had brought with us; it was not much. I had been so confident in my conclusion. I hated hubris, and here I was, victim to my own haughtiness.

She hooked her arm in mine. "We can do this, Elias," she said, encouraging me. "We make a great team." For a moment I felt the shield around her dissolve. The intense electricity between us vibrated in the crook of our arms. Arousal traced its way all the way down into my genitals. Then, just as quickly as she had exposed our connection, it was gone.

I looked down at her grinning face. "I cannot guarantee we will achieve much progress if you keep up with that sort of behavior."

"I know and I agree—I just wanted to see if it was still there," she said with a smile. She unhooked her arm and started jumping up and down in place. "Last one to the house has to take the first shot of vodka!"

"My hands are full!" I protested.

"Duh, that's the only way I have a chance in hell of beating you." She took off and I chased after her, making sure to stay a few feet behind.

OPHELIA

"*D*inner's ready," I said as I set the table. I actually wasn't confident in the meal I'd prepared. The house didn't have a rice cooker, and I'd never before braised the type of beef we'd purchased.

Elias sat in silence as he took a bite of both the rice and the meat. I waited expectantly.

"Well, how is it?" I asked.

"It is delicious," he said after he swallowed. I picked up my fork to carve a piece of the meat, plopped it in my mouth and nearly gagged on how dry it was.

I threw my napkin on the table and spoke, my mouth full of food. "You liar! This is inedible!" I stood and spat the contents of my mouth into the trash. When I turned around Elias was hiding a grin.

"I thought it was lovely."

I laughed out loud. "Shut up!" I grabbed the unlabeled bottle of vodka from the counter and lobbed it at him. He caught it without hesitation. "Let's drink our dinner instead," I said.

He gave me a childish smile and shrugged his shoulders. "If you insist."

"Let's play Quarters," I suggested as I grabbed two shot glasses from the cupboard.

"Quarters?"

"You've never played Quarters?" I gave him a bewildered look.

"No."

"Give me two coins." He fished out two rubles from his pockets.

"Are you afraid of cooties?" I asked.

"Whose cooties?" He was a little wary.

"I don't know, those of the people who have touched this money." I rolled one of the rubles between my fingers.

"Not particularly."

"Good. We won't have to play the sissy way with two glasses, then." I proceeded to explain how to play the drinking game of Quarters. "You bounce the quarter—er, ruble—and try to get it into the shot glass, like this." I demonstrated. "If I get it in the glass first, you drink the shot. If you do it first, I drink the shot. Got it?"

He nodded. "I think I will be rather good at this game," he said confidently.

"We'll see. You can go first then, big shot," I teased.

His ruble hit the table and Elias made it in on his first try.

"Beginner's luck," I taunted, then downed the shot of vodka. But it wasn't luck, I realized, because he made it in almost every time. We had to make up some new rules to ensure I didn't get too drunk. We added all kinds of silly tricks and bonuses, and a while later I realized I hadn't laughed that hard in a very long time.

Elias and I stayed up until 1 a.m. Lucas never came home. I was so tired, but I was having too much fun to throw in the towel. When I finally stumbled to bed drunk, I couldn't see straight enough to read. I promised myself I would get back to Talia's journal in the morning. As I lay there in bed, I realized that the more time I spent with Elias the easier it became to succumb to our connection. And the more I connected with him, the less room there was for Lucas in my heart. I no sooner finished the thought than sleep took me over.

~

LIGHT HIT MY FACE, FORCING ME TO CRACK OPEN MY EYES. *OH BOY, I'M not ready to get up yet*, I thought. Instead, I rolled over in my bed and shoved my hand between the box spring and mattress. I pulled out Talia's journal and fanned through the pages until I found where I'd left off.

You may wonder, my dear Ophelia, how I came to find you in India. Let me shed light on this mystery. As you know, I had been watching Hafiza very closely while you stayed in the Haven. When I was sure I could not breach the fortress, I had to find another way to get closer to you. Viraclay is a very crafty young man, but in this day and age so much of what we do can be traced. I am no technology genius myself, but my dear friend Astor is quite adept. He ascertained that Viraclay may be preparing to depart from Hafiza after tracking an elaborate postal shipment. So, when I realized Elias had sent several packages to several locations around the world, I knew I had to follow the lead. Astor was able to determine through cyber sleuthing that a previous alias Lucas had used was scheduled to fly on a red-eye into Chile, and then on to Easter Island.

I have to give Viraclay credit—he had several red herrings in place, but it was that alias that let me know where you were in South America, and then again in India. If Lucas had succeeded in getting the package on Easter Island, I would have lost you, at least for a while.

So it was that I was destined to meet you, by the grace of Malarin's strokes.

MY HEAD HURT. I PUT THE JOURNAL DOWN AND PLACED MY FINGERS TO my temples, massaging them gently. I couldn't concentrate. Coffee was a must. I stumbled to the kitchen. Elias was up, looking like he had not participated with me in annihilating that bottle of vodka the night before.

"You look like hell." He handed me a cup of coffee.

"How do you look so good?" I asked.

"Trust me, I hurt on the inside." He smiled. "Come here and I will help your head before we begin our research."

ELIAS

*A*fter breakfast, Ophelia and I agreed to engage in further research of the Khakas populations in the surrounding areas.

We were sitting on the living room floor. I was re-reading the demographic information I had compiled, while she was marking the populations on a map as I read them off.

"Elias," I heard, followed by her classic pause, which meant she was figuring out how to formulate her question.

"Ophelia," I answered, followed by the same pause. *I am getting good at reading her*, I thought, though she did not seem to notice.

"Why didn't I notice any Conduits before that day I arrived in the castle and Lucas revealed himself?" she finally asked. "I mean, they glow. I must have met other consummated Conduits before that moment, right?"

I had thought about this before as well. "I cannot be sure of who you have or have not met, but we know you at least met Yanni before our encounter. Did he glow?"

She shook her head rapidly. "He was creepy as all get out, but no, he definitely did not glow."

"I would postulate, then, that our encounter must have ignited something in you. Immediately after that, however, you were shrouded by Lucas' shield, thus effectively smothering out any new sensations."

She did not say anything for a long moment.

"That makes sense. And now I shroud myself," she admitted.

"Indeed. Does that make you feel safer?"

"I think it does. I've spent most of my life feeling so exposed. Maybe that will change someday." It sounded like she was speaking more to herself than to me.

"Perhaps it will," I agreed.

Another fifteen minutes went by before she spoke again.

"Could *you* always see the glow?" she asked.

"Yes, I could. But I grew up very differently than you." I did not know why, but when I referenced her childhood I always felt like I was pouring salt in a wound. I could see her emotional wince when I mentioned it, and it broke my heart.

"Ain't that the truth," she said, looking up from what she was writing on the map. "Thank the strokes you found me."

I laughed out loud because it was the first time I had heard her reference Malarin, and it caught me off guard.

"Thank the strokes," I agreed.

LUCAS

The establishment I found near the northern border of Genghis' turf was very different from the one in Delhi. It wasn't a bar or a hotel—it was merely a junction. A fork in the road. All walks of life moved through it, picking up rides or jobs, or both. *I'll be hard-pressed to overhear any clues that might give me a direction here,* I thought.

The portal was disguised as an abandoned train station at a remote convergence of the Russian and Kazakh borders. There was no reason for any normal human being to be out in this area or be concerned with an old dilapidated building there. Transport portals were different from troll portals; they bounced between four set locations. Troll portals could navigate to and from anywhere in the world.

I entered through the east entrance. Instantly, I was swarmed by moving bodies.

"Watch out, asshole!" a woman's raspy voice hollered.

"Move it, cocksucker!" a deep gravelly voice spat as a large figure hurled into me, sending me flying across the room. I landed with a thud against the adjacent wall. No one even paused at the encounter. I dusted myself off and looked at what I was working with. It was like a hive, with various creatures hustling about. But the arrival of two pixies—one pudgy, and the other skinny—caught my attention. I didn't have time to think; I just acted.

I leapt high into the air, landing directly in front of the hobbling pair. They both jumped, startled by my sudden appearance.

"I have a job for pixies," I said forcefully. "Are you available for hire?"

"Who's asking?" the fat one growled.

"I am, dick," I hissed back.

"And who the fuck are you?" the stringy one asked. "More importantly, why should we care?"

"I have a water sprite infestation at my place in the Marshall Islands," I said. Both of their faces lit up, although they tried to hide it. But I knew how much pixies loved raping and killing water sprites. It was like dangling a rib eye in front of a dog—they would go for it every time.

"You're a long way from home, buddy," the fat one said. "Besides, you look like a capable man, equipped to take care of some little girls who play in the water."

"Yes, I could do it," I said. "But my daughter loves them, and my wife would kill me if I upset our baby girl. So it needs to look like the order didn't come from me. Do you get what I'm saying? They need to just disappear."

They looked at each other, then back to me. "Sounds like an easy gig, but we're on our way to a job already," Skinny said as he tried to push past me.

"I'll sweeten the pot," I said. I didn't want to lose them. "I'll throw in the whereabouts of a nymph I know in Tanzania. She's still a virgin." At that, Fatty grabbed Skinny's arm. I knew this would seal it.

"Talk amongst yourselves, gentlemen," I said. "I'll be right over here. I stepped a few feet further from the stream of foot traffic.

After a minute or two they walked over. Skinny looked at me sideways while he spoke. "This job we're headed to will take us two days. We'll take the contract if you can be back here to set us up forty-eight hours from now."

I jetted out my arm to shake on it. "You have a deal."

They both ignored the gesture. "You're weird man, but this is too sweet of a deal to pass up," Fatty said as they found their way back into the stream of traffic. Then they were gone.

OPHELIA

I didn't have a lot of time to myself since I'd been joining Elias on his forays so today I got up extra early to do some reading of Talia's journal before Elias and I continued our research. We were going to head into the city of Kyzyl to get more information for his quest.

It was during our visit to the village where Huan was born, where his mother was honored, that Ruit told me about the Loktpi. Ruit was an Alchemist—he received and transferred energy. Sometimes he created magical objects or spells. Other times he moved portals or constructed Runes.

Pardon me if the following is something that Viraclay has already explained, but I find it fascinating in Ruit's case. You see, as Conduits, our gifts have nothing to do with the gifts of our parents. Our mother, for example, could have been a Healer, and our father a Calentar, and we may develop seemingly random gifts, such as that of manipulating trees.

But our mortal progeny—our Swali children—always express gifts that come from their Conduit heritage.

Consequently, Ruit's Swali children all manifested magical gifts and the ability to create spells as well as magical totems. This in turn made them the holy people of their tribes. He had five Swali children in total. Each of them were very gifted shamans—as were their children and their children's children, generation after generation blessed with a fraction of Ruit's gifts.

Herein lies the truth of the Loktpi: Ruit created the Loktpi. He also created the myth surrounding the

Loktpi, to protect its true origin and his Swali kin.

What is the Loktpi, you say, and what does this have to do with me?

The Loktpi is a powerful portal key. It can open any door, circumvent any deterrent or ward, and allow

passage to any Haven. As soon as he created this magic, however, Ruit realized the severity of the

consequences should it fall into the wrong hands. So, he immediately hid it in plain sight, within his

children. The powerful portal key is activated by his bloodline blessing sacred items. The items are

different for each tribe, but all of them hold significance for those people.

Forgive me for this next part, but during one of our tea dates you left your bag on your chair while

excusing yourself to use the restroom. I snooped inside, where I saw that you had a small leather sack

full of the fragrant psychotria elata flower. This flower is sacred to the Tukano Tribe of Colombia; they

grind it into a powder and use it during all of their important rituals.

I do not pretend to know how you acquired the flower, but I know what Viraclay is seeking, and it wasn't

until I saw the flowers in your bag that I realized what I needed to do. The Loktpi would give Viraclay

the necessary advantage for finding the safest place to hold a summit, plus the resources to open the

location to others.

A Loktpi? Elias hadn't mentioned a Loktpi.

I was thinking so deeply about all of this that I was startled and almost screamed when I heard a tap on my door. I quickly stuck Talia's journal back into my bag and walked to the door to unlock it.

LUCAS

I had a whole day before I met with Dumb and Dumber again, aka Fatty and Skinny, so I was optimistic that perhaps I could spend some quality time with Olly.

I waited until a reasonable hour, then poured her a cup of coffee and went to bring it to her in bed. When I got there, the door was locked. *That's not like her*, I thought. I tapped on the door, and after a couple of moments she appeared.

"You locking the monsters out?" I gestured to the knob.

"Maybe," she said wryly. "Is that for me?" She pointed to the coffee.

"Yes, as a matter of a fact, it is." As soon as I handed it over, she pushed past me, shut her door and headed into the kitchen. I followed close behind.

"No secret errands today?" she asked. I ignored the sarcasm in her tone.

"No, so I thought maybe we could go for a hike? Like old times, but with a little different backdrop." I didn't see any reason why she would refuse the offer.

"If I go, will you tell me what you've been up to?" she bartered.

"No..." I started, surprised at her confrontational tone. Her facial expression turned icy. "Not yet," I finished, then paused, determining what if anything I was willing to share. I didn't know if my investigation was dangerous—I couldn't add more targets on her head.

But I decided to give her a tiny clue, just to satisfy her for the moment. "It pertains to my mother," I said, "and before you push further, once I know it's safe, I'll let you in on everything."

She stood there for a long, silent moment, considering before she spoke. "I've been helping Elias with his research," she said. "It wouldn't be fair of me to just bail on him." I didn't know if my face showed it, but I was immediately crestfallen.

Just then Elias appeared in the kitchen. *Speak of the devil*, I thought.

But he surprised me. "I overheard Lucas' proposal. I think it would be good for you to get out," he told Olly. "Besides, I need to accumulate more information. Since we were just planning on heading into Kyzyl and popping into an internet café, you needn't stare at a computer screen with me." He was leaning over the counter as he spoke to her. She watched him intently. My time away had given them additional time to strengthen their bond. I'd seen it in India, but now it was even more evident. My heart twitched with jealousy.

"Are you sure?" she asked him.

"I am certain," Viraclay said, then looked at me. "I will need the car. Is that a problem?"

"No," I quickly replied. "I'll carry Olly if she can't handle the journey." I walked my fingers up her arm. "A little piggy back ride never hurt anyone, right?" She scowled at me while brushing off my hand.

"I can walk," she said brusquely, then got up and moved down the hall to her room, where she again shut the door.

Elias said nothing while he puttered around the kitchen. I sat there feeling like a rejected schoolboy. By the time Olly came out of her room, I was prepared to do whatever it took to get back into her good graces.

"Ready to go?" I stood up eagerly.

She nodded. I watched as she walked over to the fridge, pulled a couple of waters out and stuck them in her bag. She looked to Elias. "Bye. Have a good and productive day. We'll work on what you find this evening."

"Indeed. Have fun." He waved at her. She paused. I could see her contemplating something. She walked over and hugged Viraclay around the neck, tightly. I saw his hesitation but sensed that his reaction was more for me than feeling any kind of reservations about being affectionate with her.

"Be safe," she whispered in his ear.

"I will." He pulled her away, perhaps worried this would ruin the truce we'd been comfortably abiding by. "Now go, have fun."

I wanted to be mad at him, but I couldn't. This was partially my own doing, and the rest—well, I had to accept that Olly could decide who she wanted to be with. But goddammit if I wasn't going to remind her of how much fun we used to have together.

OPHELIA

*L*ucas and I had a great time on our hike. It was actually nice to finally get some quality free time with him, especially out in nature. We were both so relaxed and happy, and our trailside banter flowed easily. It reminded me of why I loved him so much. All the stress and tension of late had overshadowed our bond—the good things in our relationship. I'd been spending so much time with Elias that it was easy to forget that what I had with Lucas was special in its own way. I still felt this distinct distance in my heart, that little wall—there to remind me that I only knew one side of Lucas. But there was more. Lucas didn't trust me enough to share everything with me. So I had constructed my own boundaries. For now, we'd have to live with them.

I KEPT MY TOWEL ON AFTER MY POST-HIKE SHOWER AS I SAT ON MY BED. I took out Talia's journal.

To be clear: there are five tribes, thus five ingredients that you must have blessed to obtain the Loktpi.

Ruit arranged for each of his family members to have a full set of the blessed constituents. We each stored our Loktpi in a different form. Some of us went so far as to store it in different places. Huan had his fused together and held it around his neck, in the form of a medallion. I left mine in the safekeeping of a friend. I cannot say how you came upon your piece, but I can tell you where you can find my Loktpi. Huan's birthplace is in Northwestern China, and his people are now called the Tartars. Five hundred years ago I charged a woman named Lis to keep my components safe; she will have long since passed. But her family will have kept it secure. When you get to the village, you will need to find Lis' family and say these three words for them to hand off the parcel to you: "Aseal mettop Loktpi," which literally translates into "Sacred is the Loktpi."

They are expecting a woman, so it must be you who goes. They will not present it to Elias.

I have included the precise coordinates to the village below. Only after you visit the village, after you see you can truly trust me and that I speak in truths and with honor, only then can you move on to read my final entries. Please honor this request. It is pertinent that I have your unwavering trust.

I SNAPPED THE BOOK SHUT. I COULDN'T BELIEVE IT! THIS WAS WHAT we'd been searching for—the location of the Khakas tribe that Alistair frequented. Elias had mentioned that "Tartar" was another name that they went by; maybe that's why we'd missed this particular population.

Just then I heard a knock on my door. "Coming!" I called out, still excited.

"Is this a new thing?" Lucas complained. "I don't even think you locked your door in San Francisco."

"I deserve a little privacy, don't you think?" I argued. I was still in my towel when I'd cracked the door. "I just got out of the shower."

"Olly, at this point, I have seen it all," he smiled coyly.

"It doesn't mean you get to see it again. What's up?" I asked.

"I realized I have to take care of something. Do you feel comfortable here, alone, before Elias gets back?"

I rolled my eyes. "Yes, of course. I'm all good." I pointed at the hairsy charm. "I'm all wired up, remember?" I started to snap my fingers. "Plus I have this parlor trick." I pulled back my shield to give my fingers room to do a little magic. As I rubbed the tips together, tiny sparks manifested between them. I'd been practicing this in private and was quite pleased with the result.

Lucas' eyes got big. "Alright," he acknowledged. "I just wanted to make sure." I could tell he wanted to say more but he left it at that and turned to walk away.

I started to shut my door, then hollered "Be safe!" down the hall to him. I shut the door.

I ran into the bathroom. I couldn't wait until Elias got home, to tell him my good news.

LUCAS

*I*t occurred to me while I was on the hike with Olly that I knew exactly how I'd extract information from the two stupid pixies I had arranged to meet with the next morning. It would take a few preparations, however, to make it perfect and go off without a hitch. First thing I needed to do was get to Montreal.

OPHELIA

"We're looking in the wrong spot, talking to the wrong people!" I blurted as soon as he entered the house. I'd been sitting on the couch, waiting for him.

"What do you mean? Ophelia," Elias replied. "I researched this for months. The Khakas people live here, in Siberia."

"Most do," I acknowledged as I walked into the kitchen, holding a map I'd been studying. Elias followed. I unfolded the map onto the kitchen table and pointed out a spot. "Here, there is a small population just outside of Qiqihar, China."

He looked at the map, then pulled out a stack of papers from his bag. "These are the leads I conjured up today."

While he sifted through his information, I explained why we hadn't seen them earlier. "This particular clan identifies themselves exclusively as the Tartars, I said. "I think that's why you didn't have them listed in your first list of potential tribes."

He stopped his busywork when he found what he was looking for. It was a single piece of paper with demographics for the Khakas in China. He read it, and afterwards he looked up at me with pure adoration in his eyes.

"You are brilliant—simply brilliant." He beamed at me with that smile I loved. "How did you discover this fractured population?"

I was happy Lucas wasn't there because I was going to go with a strategy that I knew wouldn't easily work on him, but might with Elias.

"I can't tell you that right now," I said. He looked back at me apprehensively. "But I need you to trust me. I'll explain, when I can. After I fulfill a promise to a friend."

His face went from curious to worried. I spoke up again before he could start hammering me with questions. "I'm fine, Elias. I'm safe. I just can't explain right *now*." My eyes were pleading. "But can you please trust me?"

He stared at me for a long minute, then took my hand in his. "Yes, I trust you."

I actually didn't even need him to say it; I already knew deep in my soul that he trusted me. He trusted me with the fate of his quest. He trusted me without needing to control everything. He trusted me with his heart. And I, in turn, completely trusted him. I let that sink in.

LUCAS

here they were, Tweedledee and Tweedledum, right where they said they'd be. I was ready: in a black market I knew of outside of Montreal, I'd procured a small piece of Indra's net. I wore gloves as I rubbed the invisible strands between my fingers. All I'd have to do is touch them with it and they'd be unable to move. *It cost me an arm and a leg, so it had better be worth it,* I thought. Once they were incapacitated, I'd discreetly transport them to the small shack I'd leased outside of Oskemen, in East Kazakhstan.

"Hello, gentlemen!" I greeted them with my most charming smile. "How did your job go?"

"Fine. It's done," Fatty responded curtly.

"I don't think I caught your names the other day. I'm Alpin. And you are?"

Skinny reluctantly answered. "I'm Vrec, and this is Jiop. Did you arrange for transportation?"

"Yes. I have a friend who is a troll. She has agreed to grant us passage on her shuttle."

"Ugh, I hate trolls. You know I hate trolls, Vrec," Jiop the fat one groaned.

"Shut up, Jiop," his wiry pal replied. "Just think about the sprite and nymph pussy we have waiting on the other side. Where is the troll?" Vrec demanded impatiently.

"Follow me," I said as we stepped outside the junction. In the dawn's light you could see a small line of trees in the distance. "This way." I pointed to the trees. When we reached the tree line I turned to address the pixie scum. "Fetzle will be on her way shortly. Please put your hands here in mine for safe transport." As soon as they placed their disgusting palms onto mine I tied the net around their wrists. They froze, stiff as a board.

"What is this?" Vrec shouted. "Is this troll magic?"

"No, I'm afraid not. This is a small piece of Indra's net. Most of the magnificent creation has been dismantled and destroyed, but I was able to secure this little piece on the black market. You see, Indra created it to detain her enemies. You two aren't going anywhere until you answer some questions." As though on cue, Fetzle's large silhouette appeared in the shadow of the largest tree. "Fetzle!" I called out.

"FetzleisheresforLucassayshisneeds." Fetzle fired off the words as the two stupefied pixies looked on, their mouths open.

"Fetzle, we need to get to Oskemen," I said. "Can you please shuttle us? By the way, these two pixies don't like trolls."

Fetzle leaned down so that she was inches from Vrec and Jiop's faces. "Fetzledoesnotthinkspixiesverygoodseither," she declared, as she spat a huge, thick ball of mucus onto their heads. I held back laughter, afraid it would offend her. "Fetzlethinksweshouldgo."

I nodded in agreement and took hold of Fetzle's finger and Vrec's arm.

We arrived at the shack minutes later. "Thank you, Fetzle. I'll give you the net of Indra and the other payment we talked about on my return shuttle."

She didn't say a word as she disappeared back into the tree we'd arrived in.

I threw the two belligerent pixies over my shoulders, careful not to loosen the net wrapped around their wrists. The shack was small, as well as completely secluded. There wasn't a soul around for miles. Light filtered through the slats of wood that made up the four walls.

"What do you want?" Jiop mumbled.

"It's simple. I want to know about a hit carried out on Thule in 1185."

"We aren't part of that herd; we would be dead if we were. They were wiped out in the migration of 1973—when the fucking volcano blew," Jiop said desperately.

"Really? All of them were wiped out? The entire herd?" I looked at Vrec, who was staying suspiciously quiet.

"Personally," I continued, "I'd like to let both of you go virtually unscathed. But I'm prepared to do whatever it takes to get answers." I moved to the left of a small table in the far corner of the shack and pulled out a long rod of iron. "I've heard that pixies, such as yourselves, don't care for iron. When it touches your skin, it feels like acid burning through flesh. Evidently, it doesn't kill you. It just feels excruciating." I waved the iron rod around in the air. "Is that true? Shall we find out?"

I took the broad end of the rod and gently touched Jiop's bare shoulder. He wailed violently as his skin bubbled and hissed on contact with the metal. "How about you, Vrec? Give it a go?"

"My cousin Oricen survived," Vrec uttered.

Jiop looked at his companion accusingly. "You knew and you let this bastard burn me?!" he moaned.

"Shut the fuck up, Jiop. You were saying, Vrec?" I demanded.

"Oricen didn't go on the 1973 migration," Vrec continued. "He knew something would happen to the herd. He asked my father to lock him up. Because, as I'm sure you know, we can't exactly just *not* go—it's guttural, instinctual to follow the herd's migration during mating season." He stopped and looked at Jiop. He could see that his mate's skin was still sizzling.

"Continue," I pressed.

"I don't know what else to say. My dad locked him up, the rest of his herd died, and that's it. I was sure glad our herds are chosen by our mother's side. That could've been us, but Oricen is a second cousin on my dad's side."

"Where is this Oricen?" I figured he had to be the scarred pixie Oya had described to Vosega.

"Fuck if I know. He is a lone pixie, no herd. Some solo loser," Vrec ranted.

"He's family," I said. "Pixies know where their family is." I took a step closer with the iron, ready to make contact with Vrec's skin.

"That shit fuckin' hurts, Vrec. You'd better just tell him," Jiop inserted.

"Yeah, you'd better tell me, Vrec." I bounced the iron rod in my hand as I stepped a little closer.

Panic-stricken, Vrec was scrambling for something. "Last I heard he was in Ireland. Fucking some Celtic deity. That's all I know. I swear."

"How long ago was this?"

Vrec looked at Jiop. "They're going to kill me if they know I betrayed family."

"I think you should worry about one thing at a time," I said as I gently grazed Vrec's cheek. The skin blistered and smoked while he screamed in agony.

"It was only three weeks ago," Vrec whined.

"Thank you, Vrec." I turned my back to them as I thought about what this meant. A location just three weeks ago was a good lead. Even if he had moved on, I could track him down.

"Are you going to let us go?" Jiop pleaded. "We gave you what you wanted."

"I don't see why not. I have no more use for you." I put down the iron rod and headed for the door.

"Well, what about the net? You promised it to that troll," Vrec shrieked.

"I did. That's very considerate of you. Thank you for reminding me." I continued to walk out the door. "I need to settle that payment."

I stepped outside, placed my medallion on the nearby tree roots, recited the bidding and waited for Fetzle to appear.

"Fetzlethinksthatsfast." She looked at me speculatively.

"You're right, Fetzle. It might be a record for me as far as interrogations go."

I collected the pixies from inside the shack and set them in front of Fetzle as she waited patiently. "As promised," I said grandly, "two pixie snacks and one Indra net. Savor them."

"OhsFetzlewills," she said as her finger and thumb snapped off Jiop's head with one quick gesture.

ELIAS

The next day Ophelia returned with me to Kyzyl to prepare our travel arrangements to China. The coordinates she had mysteriously given me were close to the city of Nehe. I chartered a plane to fly us from Kyzyl to Qiqihar—the largest city closest to Nehe. From there we would rent a car to drive to a cluster of yurts I had read about slightly east of Nehe on the Laolai River.

I was hoping that Lucas would be back by the time we returned from Kyzyl, but he was not. I was anxious to get moving, ready for this piece of the puzzle to be at its end. Ophelia and I had packed our things. We were sitting on the couch in silence.

"There's one more thing," she said. Her tone was full of trepidation, which in turn made me uneasy. "I have to visit the village alone."

I turned to face her, allowing my shock to be completely evident on my face. "Is that a fact? Why would that be?"

"I still can't tell you yet." She rubbed her hands together nervously.

"This is all per your mysterious informant's instructions?"

She nodded. "Remember, Elias, you trust me." Her voice was warm and assured, but serious.

I broke our eye contact to face forward. She was right. Just the day before I had told her I trusted her, and I had meant it. But maybe that was not enough. Maybe I really needed to believe it. And to trust myself that I would be making the right decision to place the fate of the mission in her hands. I knew this was part of committing to someone. Commitment also meant letting go of our ideals of control.

I took her hand in mine. "You are right, I do remember. I trust you, completely." It felt good to say the words out loud. I had not been able to put my trust in anyone in so long, I had not realized the extent of that burden. She smiled at me, the genuinely sincere smile she only shared when she felt connected.

The front door opened and we quickly released our hands back to our sides. I stood as Lucas entered the room.

"We have a new direction," I said. "I believe I have been looking at the wrong group of people here in Russia. I have reason to believe that in fact we need to relocate to the Northeastern part of China." It came out faster, shriller than I intended.

"Really? I can't say I'm entirely surprised," Lucas said as he came in and took a seat beside Ophelia. "You were getting pretty lucky with your other hunches."

They were not exactly hunches, but it was useless to explain my research to Lucas. "I have been very fortunate thus far, yes."

"Well." He was not addressing me at all. He grabbed Ophelia's hand and kissed it. "It pains me to do this, but I have to run an errand that will take longer than a day, and it's definitely not in China." Lucas touched Ophelia's cheek and turned her face to meet his. "Can you live without me for a week—max?"

She playfully brushed his hand aside. "Oh please, I lived without you for years, Mr. Healey." Then she pulled his arm around her shoulders. "But I'll miss you terribly." She gave me a sideways glance and a wink. She knew exactly how to assuage his fears. "Is this more about the secret mother errands? Do we get to know where you're going?" she asked.

"Yes… and absolutely not," he asserted.

"Will you be safe?" she asked, genuinely concerned.

"I'll always come back to you," he said as he leaned in closer to her body to kiss her on the forehead.

"Well, then I guess it's settled," she said. "I give you my permission to go." With that, she popped up from the couch. Lucas was immediately beside her, tickling her sides.

"Your permission?" he teased. "How did I get so blessed!" She laughed wildly and begged him to stop. I had to repress my jealousy at this very public display of affection between them. Even though she and I had deepened our bond, they had something Ophelia and I had yet to develop—friendship.

OPHELIA

$\mathcal{E}$lias was asleep. I watched his head bob around where he sat. I personally couldn't sleep on planes without some sort of sedative.

I really wished I could, because I was anxious to read further into Talia's journal. It was all I could do to not get up and take a peek while Elias was out. I looked at his face. His features were relatively symmetrical and defined, but not sharp. He had a strong jaw, distinct cheekbones and a dimple when he smiled that drove me a little batty. His sandy blond hair was a little longer, too, these days. I liked it.

My eyes made their way to his closed eyelids. I could imagine what lay within. I knew his golden eyes like I knew the feel of my own skin. I was mesmerized by those eyes. His lids twitched and I wondered if he was dreaming. *What does he dream about?* I thought. *Maybe I can get a little taste?*

Before I knew what I was doing I was stretching my shield to encompass Elias. I let the various sensations flowing from him flood my body and my mind. I let our connection vibrate between us, I dove in. It felt natural, like I was supposed to share this type of intimacy with him.

I could sense his anticipation, perceive his yearning. I couldn't see what he was dreaming about, but it tasted good on my tongue. Desire, gratification—profound connection. I was being swept away by it, but he stirred and I was startled back to the present. I felt shame in my intrusion. I replaced my shield, but ruminated over what I'd discovered inside his head, inside his heart.

Is that what consummating would feel like? I believed I was ready to ask the question I'd been avoiding.

LUCAS

I'd arrived in Ireland the day before. *What is it about this country that's so appealing?* I thought. I decided that it was the people; they were so rich in character. *I love their beer too,* I considered as I took another swig. I thought about Olly—wondered what I'd come back to. Viraclay was getting closer to her every second I was away. My only solace was that I knew what we had was special. Our relationship was based on friendship; that would always be there. Maybe when I got to the bottom of all of this business with my mother, I'd share it with Olly and it would make us closer. For the time being, I had to focus on the answers I presently sought.

"You were saying, Gemma?" I reminded the pretty blonde bartender of the conversation we'd been having on and off for the past hour. She'd been bitching about an odd customer that would come in just before closing every night. She described his grey stringy hair, black ascot hat and nasty facial burn with contempt.

"I'm just saying he's a rightful stook," Gemma said as she continued to wipe the bar in front of me. "Another round?"

I was going to be there a while, waiting for the "stook" to show up around closing. "Please do me the honor, my lovely lass," I said. She shook her head in playful disgust.

OPHELIA

My hands were shaking violently as I approached the village. I knew nothing about these people—not their language nor their culture—certainly not what they might think of me. I knew they preferred to be identified by the name Tartar rather than Khakas, because that was how Talia referred to them in her writings to me. Elias had given me a brief rundown of what he knew, but I was so nervous that it had gone in one ear and out the other. I'd never done anything like this in my life, and I definitely didn't want to mess up the mission.

I just kept repeating the name Talia had given me over and over in my head: Lis, Lis, Lis, Lis.

I tried to distract myself by admiring the gorgeous countryside, vast grasslands that nestled up to huge mountain ranges, with streams and rivers that wove through the plains. I was deeply aware of the similarities in landscapes between this part of China and the Siberian plains we'd just left. It occurred to me that we'd lucked out with the season. It got very cold here in the winter, but July was beautiful.

I saw the yurts ahead of me. They were far more primitive than the ones we were staying in beside the nearby river. These structures were covered with animal hides, not some water-resistant vinyl.

Smoke billowed from the center of the largest structure, while the others formed a semi-circle nearby. I counted a total of seven. I was about fifteen yards away from the closest of them when someone spotted me.

A boy began waving a stick high above his head, scaring the sheep in front of him into scattering. I waved back, not sure if it would be a sign of aggression or of greetings. I nervously adjusted my bag on my shoulder.

The young man started to jog in my direction. I noticed he was short—maybe four feet tall. I thought I could probably take him, if need be. I shook the thought out of my head. *What am I thinking? That isn't an option,* I scolded myself. *Just give them the name.*

I started yelling, "Lis! Lis! Lis!" The boy paused for a moment. A huge grin swept across his face as he picked up the pace until he was at my side. He was wearing a deep indigo robe with an orange sash. I realized his stick was a herding staff. His black hair framed a cherub-like face with big cheeks. He couldn't have been older than fourteen.

"Lis?" I repeated.

He nodded and yelled, "Lis!"

I let my shoulders relax a little. *This was a good start, right?*

We reached the first yurt. A woman with a baby strapped to her back peered out of the entrance flap. I waved, and she quickly retreated back into her home.

The young man chanted "Lis!" until we reached the largest structure. He pulled the flap back to expose the circular center of the yurt. I stepped inside, not sure what to expect.

"Welcome," a husky voice said, and I screamed. *He'd scared the shit out of me.* I turned to see a man of medium build, shirtless, not two feet from me.

"I'm sorry, you scared me," I said as I peeled my hand from my chest, where it was clutched to ensure my heart didn't, in fact, stop beating.

"My apologies. Please sit by the fire." He gestured to a pile of sheep's wool. I took a seat.

"You speak English?" I asked.

"I do. I was taught by my grandmother, who was taught by her grandfather, and so on. As were all the descendants of Lis." He took a seat across from me on his own pile of sheep's wool. "My name is Wailee, blood of Lis."

"My name is Ophelia," I said, then closed my eyes and recited the critical saying in my head before I said it aloud. "Aseal mettop Loktpi."

Wailee's eyes widened. "Aseal mettop Loktpi."

We sat looking at each other for several minutes before Wailee spoke again. "Let it be time to perform the blessing." He stood, walked over to a basket full of dried brown and tan-colored leaves. "But first I must confess something and ask for your forgiveness, wise Ulus Ophelia."

Is he calling me Ulus? What is an Ulus? I went with it.

"Forgiveness for what?"

"There was another that came before you. A man. He knew the Loktpi. My great grandfather knew the prophecy spoke of a woman. But the man said he knew of the prophecy. He recited the song and said he was an old god, an original son of Nama." Wailee looked down at his hands shamefully. "The man took the original Loktpi. My grandfather said he already had the blessing."

Questions, so many questions. *Who is the man that has beaten me to it? Who is Nama? It could have been Ruit, right?* Before I could ask any of these questions, Wailee continued.

"Today and tomorrow I will perform the blessing on you, give you the sight. Then I will bless the Huanan." He put his hand in the basket full of dried vegetation, pulled out a handful, then replaced it in the basket. "When you leave, you will take the writing of Huan." He picked up a traveling from his table.

Huanan and writings of Huan? There was no doubt I was in the right village. I had to admit I was nervous about this blessing ritual. I wondered if the prophecy he spoke of was *the prophecy*—the one Elias had heard from the Oracle—or just a local cultural one. So many questions.

"Take off your bag," he said. I respected the tone of the command. I didn't ask any questions. "Then resume sitting." He adjusted the pelts I was sitting on so that there were only two.

Wailee collected a few items from around his yurt and placed them in front of me: some leaves, a couple of stones, and some flowers. He splashed water onto the pile while chanting words I didn't understand.

Wailee handed me the basket of dried plants, then walked in a circle around me including, the pile of items he'd collected within the circle. "Trace my steps with the Huanan," he said, and I did as I was told. I created a circle around myself and the items with the Huanan from the basket. As soon as I finished making the circle, Wailee began dancing and chanting around me.

I watched him intently. As I did, I felt this odd sensation take over my body. It was like my rhythm was changing. If all the parts of me previously moved in their own way, they were now all in sync somehow. With every step he took, with every movement he made, I felt more and more in tempo. The pulsating rhythm consumed me—I felt it expand and contract and build into a crescendo, loud and pounding in my body and deep into my soul. I don't know how long the blessing lasted; time was distorted, like when you meditate.

When it was over, Wailee stood above me, careful not to break the circle. "Today you became blessed by the earth. You have the unbreakable energy of life, death and the never-ending circle of both. It will stay with you always." He knelt down to brush the Huanan away. He reached for my hand and helped me up. "Take this." He handed me the scroll. "Let it be that my grandfather's soul rests, that he no longer exists in dishonor for his mistakes."

I didn't know where the words were coming from, but I found myself saying, "Your honor is restored."

Immediately Wailee began to weep, while I excused myself.

I RETURNED TO OUR YURT AND TOLD ELIAS ALL ABOUT THE BLESSING and the scroll, and he told me all about his similar experience in Costa Rica. He decided he'd make dinner for us, so I stepped into my room for a moment to read more from Talia's journal.

We were very happy. Spending years together, sometimes alone, other times with Ruit and the rest of the family. We passed centuries in this way, blissfully ignorant of the war around us. We could afford to be— we were either in seclusion or quietly enveloped in family and community.

I have thought back on these years with a fondness, as well as with a resentful hindsight. What if we had concerned ourselves with the matters of the world sooner, before the war came to our doorstep?

Isn't that the way of the world, though, to turn a blind eye until we have no choice? We enjoy the safety of the nucleus of our families until the nucleus is swept into the frenzy society generates when no one is watching. It is a wicked irony that Dalininkas assembles into his strokes the fatality of ignorance and our innate desire to succumb to it.

So it was that we succumbed to ignorance and only lifted our heads from the sand when we were struck with fierce loss: the disappearance of our patriarch, Ruit.

It was nearly a hundred years ago. I remember the night well. The evening Almus contacted Huan with his suspicions about their father's absence.

Almus explained that Ruit had told Jezebel he was going to travel to Alaska for a week to visit his old friend Lester. This was not uncommon; it was uncommon, however, that two weeks after his arrival he went silent. No communication, not with his wife or sons, not even with his beloved grandson. They were most alike, Ruit and Alistair. Both truly loved the indigenous people and their tribes.

Almus travelled to Alaska only to find Lester dead. Lester and his Atoa had been brutally slain, their entire home burned to ash. Almus was convinced Ruit had gotten away, although we had no reason to believe that.

But still he insisted, and indubitably we all wanted to believe this, that Ruit somehow survived, that he was in hiding. Jezebel's reasoning was that if they had both been ambushed Ruit would have contacted one of us, just to say goodbye. It could have only been an instant, but he would have let us know of his demise. I understood her thought process. With the Runes Ruit had given each us, it would have only taken an instant to send a distress call or a goodbye.

Ruit's Runes were one of his greatest creations. It was like a walkie-talkie for the family. You simply stroked the symbol and imagined one of the eight of us that bore the mark. It was brilliant and amazingly useful for a family that travelled around the world. It was how we knew when and where to congregate each year.

But by the same token, if he was alive, we considered: why did he not use the Runes to communicate now? Huan and I both were devastated. We believed he was gone. That was the day our ignorance had betrayed us. We could no longer ignore the war that had been raging; it was time to pick a side and defend our family.

Almus convinced us to meet with Sorcey and Cane. Viraclay's parents were empathetic, truly heartbroken for us. Cane was already assembling small factions of Pai Ona to determine how to proceed. During this meeting Almus planted a seed in his brothers' mind, perhaps even through his gift of implanting dreams. I don't know the depth of the inception, but the notion drove Huan until his dying day.

Almus believed Ruit was a captive of the Nebas, and that he could be saved. He convinced his brother to start a private operation. It needed to be private because, even then, we suspected a traitor.

Huan had a useful gift; he received truths. He could ask a question and demand the honest answer. You were compelled to tell him the complete truth. It made for a very honest marriage, I assure you. Sometimes I thought it was in jest that the two of us were created for each other. Malarin had a sense of humor because my gift allowed me to fog and distort memories. Thus, the truth of the individual could be bent. It was a fun family game: One of us would say a phrase to another and then I would distort its memory in the brain. At which point Huan would interrogate the person until he could find a way to get enough clues to guess the phrase. Mind you, this was before television or board games—we had to entertain ourselves.

In the game of war, truth was very valuable. Especially when the truth could lead you to the discovery of a captive Pai Ona.

"OPHELIA!" ELIAS CALLED FROM THE KITCHEN. "DINNER IS READY." I put the journal away but was left with a nagging feeling I couldn't put my finger on.

I walked slowly down the hall between our yurts and took a seat at the table.

"Are you hungry?" Elias asked. I took a long moment to respond. "Ophelia, are you okay?"

"Yeah, I'm sorry," I said. "I'm just distracted. It was a strange day."

"Indeed. You are so brave to take on this errand." He stopped what he was doing and made eye contact with me. "I am so proud of you and so very honored to be sharing this journey with you." The sincerity poured out of him; it caught me off guard.

I found myself getting choked up. "I—I'm honored that you trust me and are willing to share it with me," I conceded. But the moment was too heavy for me. I decided to break it up. "Now, what does a girl have to do to get a drink around here?"

ELIAS

I waited until Ophelia left the next morning before I unrolled the scroll she'd brought back. Her encounter the previous day sounded incredible. The blessing experience reminded me of my own in Costa Rica. She was leaving some things out, however; I felt her reservations. But I believed she would explain more to me in due time.

This scroll was marvelous; it was a key to the Tartars' written language. Every symbol I would need to complete my decoding of Alistair's journals was right there.

I pulled the three journals from my bag, along with the four codes to the other languages I had transcribed over the last few months.

We were so close. The summit location would be revealed in these markings. I was certain of it.

OPHELIA

*D*ay two with Wailee was very similar to day one. He performed a different ritual, we walked, and he talked about how all of life is cyclical: we live, we die, and our remains give fruit to more life.

I could follow his train of thought. I liked the simplicity and beauty in it. I liked him as well—he had a modest and honorable demeanor that I'd not encountered among many others.

At the end of our session I was sad to say goodbye, knowing that the next day would be the last time I saw him; he had told me that this would be the extent of our time together.

I was eager to get home, however, to hear what Elias had learned from the scroll. He was in the shower when I got back, so I escaped to my room for a few minutes of reading.

For twenty years Huan searched while I followed. If he heard of a Conduit presumed dead or mysteriously gone missing, we tracked down anyone who saw them last, at which point Huan asked questions, learning as much truth as he could. When we were done, I would scramble the memory of our time there so that the individual would not remember our visit or be able to share it with another Truth-sayer. Over that time, Huan and I agreed that some of the disappearances seemed to be abductions, not

murders. But there was no proof, nothing to justify our theory. Just inconsistencies. Why publicly slay
one family and privately dismantle another, we wondered.

But Huan had grown tired of chasing the rumors, the crumbs, for clues. I saw his unease before he
shared with me his intent.

At one point, Almus and Inca met us on the road to Nigeria. My gut ached with intuition; I knew this was
going to fuel Huan's frustrations. Almus planted a seed. So it was that he came to me that night, after
spending the day with his brother, and he told me of his plan to infiltrate the Nebas. He would start as an
interrogator—a bought henchman—and work his way into the close syndicate of the Nebas.

I pleaded with him that night, begging, "Huan, stay. Huan, why must you leave me? Am I not your
family? You said you would keep me safe forever."

And just as he did the night he rescued me from Caesar, he caressed my face, telling me, "My love, you
are my heart and my soul, and that is precisely why I must uncover this truth. If there are captives, their
release will be the undoing of the Conduits who imprisoned them." He kissed my forehead sweetly.
"Their undoing would insure your safety, my Arsinoe's safety."

I HEARD THE SHOWER TURN OFF. I WAS TORN BETWEEN CONTINUING TO read and seeing Elias. My heart won the battle. Elias' room connected to mine through a common yurt with a kitchen, dining room and lounge area. I excitedly ran to the kitchen to pour us a drink so we could hang out on the couch and he could tell me about his day.

As I situated myself in the living room I thought about the love that Talia and Huan had. It was so deep—so passionate. Sitting there, waiting for Elias to come out, I realized I could have that too.

I could have Lasteea. We could consummate.

LUCAS

Two days and the little fucker hasn't shown up, I thought, getting frustrated. Gemma was building up her own frustrations with me: she was starting to wonder why we hadn't fucked yet, considering the way I was hanging around. *How should I explain that I'm in an incredibly convoluted love triangle with the woman I love, and that I wanted to save myself for her—in case she decided to choose me?* If she didn't choose me, I would be too heartbroken to entertain Gemma in the bedroom anyway.

I looked at the clock; it was 1 a.m. *Maybe it is time to frequent another bar,* I thought. I pushed off from my stool.

"See you tomorrow, Alpin." Gemma called as I strode out the door. I didn't bother to respond; I wasn't coming back tomorrow night.

I ambled down the street, thinking about what my next strategy would be, when I heard a woman squeal. I stopped, waiting to hear if it was out of pleasure or pain.

There was heavy breathing. I heard muffled noises and hard rocking against something wooden. The noises came from between the two buildings to my left. Another squeal pierced the air—this time definitely not out of pleasure. I sped down the narrow alley to see a young woman pinned to the wall, her mouth covered by a grayish-green hand. Her skirt was up around her waist and his pants were down to his ankles—he was thrusting and gyrating against her body. She couldn't see me, but he sure as hell could.

"Let her go," I commanded. The face that turned to meet mine was scarred and ugly. He smiled wildly at me, and I saw his pointed pixie teeth.

"I'm almost done, man," he growled, then sank his teeth into the woman's bare shoulder, the pixie equivalent of a playful love bite. The rage boiled over in me. I ripped between the two of them.

In a second I had the young woman's clothes composed. I whispered in her ear. "Go! I will take care of this. This man will never attack anyone again." She screamed as she ran back to the main street.

"What the fuck, Conduit asshole?" he yelled. "Since when do you meddle in pixie affairs?"

I grabbed him by his exposed cock. "Since when is it okay for pixie assholes to rape young Irish women, Oracin?" I squeezed and pulled his member until he squealed like the poor woman he'd been assaulting.

"Wait, wait wait," he winced. "Do we know each other?" That confirmed he was my guy. "Was she yours?" he said. "I didn't know."

I squeezed a little harder. "She's no one's—definitely not yours for the taking. Maybe I'll just remove your junk and this won't be a problem ever again." I dug my fingernails in until I felt blood trickle between my fingers.

"Wait, man, I won't do it again, okay?" There were tears streaming down his face, glistening over his scar in the moonlight.

"Why don't you wait to get your kicks until the herd migration, you piece of shit?" I growled in his face. I was positive I had the right guy—but this would doubly verify it.

"I can't, man. My herd died in a freak volcanic eruption forty years ago. It's just me. I can't live the next 2,000 years with blue balls." He was squirming in my grip, but there was no way he was going to be able to break free.

"You're part of the Thule herd?" I asked. He nodded. "I need you to listen to my next three questions very carefully," I began. "I'm only going to ask them once, and I need an honest answer. If I don't think you're being truthful, I'm going to dismember you and feed you your filthy cock, one bite at a time. Am I making myself clear?" He winced and nodded vigorously.

"Who hired you to assassinate the Conduit family during the migration of 1185?"

"You expect me to remember that far back? I don't fucking know, man!"

"Wrong answer." I felt flesh tear under my nails. One of his testicles fell out onto the cobblestones. He howled in agony. "You have another testicle. Are you that hungry tonight?"

After some profound cursing, he drew his attention back to me.

"I don't know who hired the hit. All I know is that it was supposed to be the entire family, but they didn't tell us it was a Vulcan's family. We got the wife, but missed the kid. The father chased us down and killed everyone but me." Sweat was streaming down his face and I realized he might pass out, so I squeezed the wound shut to stop the massive bleeding. "Gave me this scar, see?" He jutted out his chin.

"Who took the order?"

"Some pixie named Kino. He died with the rest of them—like I said." His breathing was shallow as he spoke. He was definitely going to die. I just needed answers before that happened.

"Focus! Who did Kino usually work for? The Nebas?"

"No. Kino knew some guy who worked regularly with some other powerful Conduits. I don't know their name, I swear!" His heart was beating erratically by now.

"Who was this guy? Was it a pixie?"

"No, it was a hobgoblin." His head swayed to one side. I shook him slightly. "I think his name was Clive," he panted. Then his head went completely limp. I felt a few final twitches take over his body.

"Fuck, I always let my temper get the best of me!" I scolded myself aloud.

I kicked the corpse and rolled the name Clive around in my head.

OPHELIA

I was in Cape Cod visiting my friend Astor when I received his first correspondence. I remember the moment I realized it was him. I couldn't breathe. It was as though the world had tilted on its axis. Astor thought I was having a stroke. He hurried to my side as the color renewed in my face.

"Nandi, what is it? Is he gone, is Huan gone?" Astor asked as he took me by the shoulders. I put my hand up, beckoning his silence.

Ophelia, when you first receive a visual communication from a Rune that you were not expecting, it can be like suddenly going cross-eyed. Visual communications are different than audio ones. You need to close your eyes to absorb the image. It can play out either like a movie or still images, depending on how skilled the communicator is. Huan was very good at projecting his messages, audio or visual. I closed my eyes, and soaked up the image of my husband. It was the first time I had seen him since he had left me seven years prior, when he'd embarked on his covert pursuit of the truth. He had told me before he left that it might be years before I would hear from him, but that if he were ever to be discovered, he promised he would let me know—he would say goodbye.

I held my breath wondering if this would be our last words. Astor sat beside me, holding my hand. Huan was looking at himself in a mirror. He smiled at me that radiant smile. His hair was longer, unkempt. I winced when I saw a long, fresh scar across the right side of his face to his chin. It was nearly healed, but it had to have been bad for there still to be any evidence on his face.

"I miss you." His voice rang in my head, and tears swept down my cheeks.

"I miss you too," I said, "more than you know." His smile grew bigger. He moved away from the mirror to sit at a table. A note had already been written in his hand. It read as follows.

My Dear Nandi,

I am making progress. True progress—more than we have made in our twenty years of searching. I have done things that I am not proud of. Should these acts make their way to your ears, forgive me. I have saved more than I have harmed, trust me.

I stopped reading and said very assuredly. "Of course I trust you." He nodded and I continued reading the letter.

I have waited so long to reach out because there are those among these villains who express gifts of telepathy, possibly more. I do not want to risk revealing myself or putting you in danger. Understand that our communication will play out in short sentences, letters or shared visions. It is the safest way to keep our connection secret. Please do not reach out to me, because I never know who is listening. When we are through, I ask that you boggle my mind. That way I am not at risk of being interrogated. I love you. I believe someday we'll recognize this period in our lives and the sacrifices we make for the betterment of all of our people.

Stay safe and out of sight.

Then he burned the paper and I disorientated his memories.

J thought about the time when Talia had spoken to me in my head at the tea house, with her Rune. I remembered how it felt, how strange it was. Thinking about her voice brought back the terrible image of her death—I hadn't given myself time to really mourn her. To absorb what had happened.

The journal made it feel like she was still with me, like we were pen pals exchanging letters and stories. But she wasn't here. I didn't hold back the tears this time. I cried long and hard. When the crying stopped, I rinsed off my face and prepared myself for another goodbye.

MY BLESSING HAD FINISHED THE DAY BEFORE. *TODAY I'LL RECEIVE THE Huanan leaves, the last piece of the Loktpi puzzle,* I told myself.

I kept finding myself wondering who had stolen Talia's Loktpi; I couldn't wait to mull this over with Elias. I had to keep it to myself until I finished reading the journal, though, because that was what Talia had asked of me. I would never get to thank her for her gift, for the gift she was giving all of us. My eyes welled up with tears again as I thought about it. *At least I'll have the time to finish reading the journal now that this part of our mission is over,* I thought.

I knew Elias would be so relieved when he discovered what we had in our possession. Lucas would be happy this whole wild goose chase was over, I was sure of that. *Maybe we could all settle somewhere safe for a while,* I mused. Between Lucas' shield and my developing shield, we'd be able to go undetected. Meanwhile Elias could finish his arrangements for the summit and we could start changing the direction of the war. I allowed myself to feel real hope.

"Ulus Ophelia," Wailee interrupted my train of thought. I stood as he approached. "I have completed the ritual. You may take the Huanan. It is a fungus; don't get it wet until you need to."

I didn't know what that meant, but it had all seemed to come together as needed so far. I took the small leather pouch containing the Huanan. "Thank you, Wailee." I gave him a slight bow. "I won't be returning tomorrow, as you know."

"Of course." He bowed back. "Remember, all things move in circles. You move in circles."

I smiled at him, put the Huanan fungus in my bag and began the walk back to our yurt compound.

ELIAS

While Ophelia said her goodbyes to the Tartar tribe, I was able to decipher the entire codex that Alistair used. The rotating codes had a very specific sequence. I had all three, including the cadence he used to move onto the next code. I had converted my yurt into an office in which I hung the maps I had taken from his study, along with the key for the codex. Now I just needed to systematically translate the contents of each journal.

I heard the door open and close. Ophelia was back. I met her in the living room.

"How was your farewell?"

"It was sad, but good. He gave me this." She handed me a small leather pouch—the same dimensions as the others I had collected and that Rand had given Ophelia.

"What is inside?" I asked as I opened it. "A dried fungus?"

"They call it Huanan. It is sacred to the Tartar people, just like all the other bags to their respective tribes." She fell back onto the couch as she spoke.

"Are you alright?" I sat beside her.

"Yeah. I just have so much to talk to you about, but it isn't time yet." She put her hand up before I could respond. "I told you I can't talk about yet."

"Well you have been of great help to me on this journey, Ophelia. I cannot thank you enough." I put my hand on her leg and felt her barrier melt away with my touch, along with all our inhibitions.

She took my hand in hers. "When we find a place for the summit, when we unite the Pai Ona and the Poginuli, things will get simpler, right?"

I noticed she dropped her guard when she wanted to know the truth. "Not at first," I told her. "It will most likely get more complicated. But eventually, yes—we will create a new, safer world for our kind."

"How can you be so sure?" I felt her hand gently caressing my palm, the electricity radiating between us.

"I have to be," I said. She leaned forward and put her mouth to mine. Her tongue traced my lips before sliding between them. She tasted like nectar, sweet and fragrant. She moved her hand to my lap, where she walked her fingers to my aroused penis. My head was clouded with lust. It took all that I had to pull away. I could not give in now. Not when we were so close to changing the tide of this war—to changing her future. My words came out breathless, labored. "Ophelia."

She put her finger to my lips. "Call me Olly," she whispered.

"Olly, I want this more than anything—but..." Before I could finish her wall was back.

"This has something to do with the prophecy, doesn't it?" She stared at me knowingly.

"How do you know that?" I asked.

"I felt it, just now. Your thoughts are coming clearer to me, formulating in sentences instead of just feelings."

"I see. When did this develop?"

"Just now. We need to talk about this prophecy."

"Indeed, we do." I adjusted myself more comfortably on the couch, assuming she meant now.

But she surprised me. "It can wait," she said. "Let's deal with the summit location first."

She stood. I watched how her hair fell over her shoulder as she turned to leave the room.

"Elias, I want you too. But I can wait." She smiled coyly as she entered the hall.

OPHELIA

J threw myself on my bed face down—overcome with sexual frustration. I almost marched back out there and demanded a detailed description of the consummation process. Because at this point, from what I could tell, it was escalating into a downright sexual frenzy every time I let my guard down. I thought about what I'd glimpsed in his head about the prophecy. It was brief, a snippet of a thought. But his feelings were laced in fear—fear for me, for my safety. Truth be told, that was why I couldn't deal with diving into the prophecy right then and there; I wasn't quite ready to hear what had him so afraid for me. I could go back out there, and I was sure he would answer all my questions—but instead I reached for my bag, for a welcome distraction.

For forty-nine years we carried on this way, with brief calls. Huan had started disclosing the small clues he was discovering, indicating that some of the Nebas had their own suspicions about certain executions. But everything began and seemed to end in rumor and insubstantial speculation. Huan was confident it would amount to something, that the small pieces would connect and uncover a bigger picture.

It was during one such exchange that he came across a name that was ancient, and potentially explanatory for the dead ends. A Truth-sayer rarely found this much ambiguity. Something or someone had to be causing the obscurity.

He wrote the name in large letters on the bathroom mirror. I looked at his face through the image. He looked tired. Even with ageless skin, I could see my Huan was exhausted. I was beginning to get resentful of this mission, of his absence. He felt my discord in our connection.

"Did you write down the name?" his voice asked gently in my head.

"Yes. Vita. Do you know it?" I responded.

He shook his head. I let mine hang lowly in the reflection he could see of me.

"I am getting close to something. Trust me. I love you."

"I love you," I repeated. That was my cue to work my magic and befuddle his mind. We disconnected. A few days later Huan called on me again. This time without words or messages, but just to include me as a witness to a discussion he was having.

Lucas Healey's face filled my mindsight. It was dark in the room where they spoke, but I knew his face. Huan's voice was hushed and calm. "Why are you here, Lucas?"

"To uncover what happened to my Yessica." Lucas' eyes began to well up with tears, and my heart wept for his loss.

"What do you think has happened to her?"

"I think she could be being held captive somewhere."

"Why do you think that?"

"I don't know. I just fucking do—I couldn't forgive myself if I didn't at least track down the assholes who killed her."

"How did you get into the Nebas' confidences so quickly?"

"Everyone knows I'm a renegade. They think I just want to kill people, that I'm so angry that I want to hurt everyone. It doesn't matter their side."

"Is that true?"

"Probably. I can't see straight without her." The tears were readily streaming down his face now.

"What will you do if you find her?"

"I will kill them all and set the other Pai Ona free."

I felt Huan's head turn and saw they were in a long, dark passage.

"Shield your mind. They are tangling thoughts up somehow. Do not trust anyone. Now run!" Huan said urgently to Lucas.

I saw that he was running as well, that Lucas was no longer with him.

Huan was in my head. "Someone is coming. I am so close, my love. This passage leads to a chamber that only Yanni and Esther can open. They beckon others down here often, but never me. I stopped Lucas before he could be escorted into the chamber. He's just arrived, a few days ago, to the compound. I had hoped I could question him before he had a chance to be secluded. This was better than I had imagined.

We have an ally, and I will be able to confirm my suspicions that they are manipulating thoughts

somehow when I speak to Lucas again. I must go. I will be safe. No one saw me. I love you."

"I love you too." I let my chest fill with a medley of emotion: hope, fear and sadness, all blended

together. I completed my disconnect with Huan and thanked Malarin for his strokes.

I WAS IN A BIT OF SHOCK. *LUCAS? LUCAS KNEW HUAN?*
I put the journal down when I heard a car pull up outside.

LUCAS

$\mathcal{M}$y flight got in early, for once. I guessed I would make it to bum-fuck China by dinner. My driver drove like a bat out of hell; I appreciated that.

The yurt complex Elias rented had several units clustered together, connected by adjoining catwalks. I tipped the driver generously and headed to the building that had the lights on. I wasn't done with my search, but at least I had a lead to follow: Clive, the goddam hobgoblin.

I opened the door. "Honey, I'm home!" I shouted.

Olly's head peered from around the corner of an adjacent hall, and her face lit up.

"You're safe!" She made a running start and leapt into my arms for a hug.

"Returned safe and sound, just as I promised." I kissed her cheek.

Viraclay entered the room as I put her back on her feet.

"Was your errand successful?" he asked casually.

"Yes, I think I could call it a success." I directed my focus back to Ophelia. "How has China been?"

"Great! I met a local tribe." She yammered on excitedly.

Elias interrupted. "Olly, would you like me to prepare dinner?" My ears perked up. He had never called her Olly before. *I'm away for three days and now he is calling her by her nickname?* I didn't like it. I glared at him.

"Yes, please," she answered as she ushered me over to the couch to talk about her experience with the local shaman. We ate and enjoyed some wine I'd brought back from the duty-free store at the airport in Ireland. After dinner Viraclay excused himself. I was relieved to have Olly to myself for a while.

We played a game of Four Corners—a card game we'd played often in our apartment in San Francisco.

"When did Viraclay start calling you Olly?" I meant the question to sound nonchalant but was aware it sounded snide.

"*Elias...*" she emphasized his name. "...is welcome to call me by whichever name he chooses. We're close enough now that I think it's appropriate for him to decide if he wants to use my nickname. Your turn."

"Oh, you're that close now?" I asked. I knew the moment I said it that it wasn't going to go over well.

She put her cards down and stared at me until I met her gaze. "Lucas, what are these secret errands you go on?"

"I can't tell you that; it would put you in danger," I argued.

"Really? More danger than I'm in already? Elias shares things with me. He tells me the truth. About the people he knows." She gave me an exceptionally dirty look and continued. "About the places he goes. He even tells me about his life before I came around, without being forced to. He is my friend."

"Just your friend?"

She looked at me sternly. "For now."

The two words sent me into a tailspin. I could feel anxiety mixed with frustration bubbling up inside me. I was losing her; maybe I'd already I lost her. But instead of being able to tell her how sad the prospect of her with another man made me, I exploded.

"For *now*?! What does that mean? So, you have chosen?" I got to my feet. "Elias runs around for months, keeping you in the dark about his daily to-dos. I decide to pursue my own interests, and I'm no longer in contention for your affections? How is that fair?"

Now she was on her feet. "That is not how it went. I love you, too, Lucas. You know that."

"You *love* me?" I scoffed. "Really? But I'm so easily replaced by the amazing Viraclay. Do you even know what love is?"

Tears streamed down her face. "And *you* know what love is? You had the love of your life—your other half—and yet you stand in the way of that gift for me? Yes, you do know what love is, Lucas Healey! But you can't possibly love me and expect me to deny my destiny, the opportunity to be whole." She wiped away her tears as she ran down the hall. I wanted to follow, but my pride wouldn't let me. Not yet. I turned to the door and ran as hard and as fast as my legs would carry me.

ELIAS

I knocked on the door again. "Ophelia?" I listened for her response. When she did not demand I leave, I took that as an invitation to come in. She was lying on the bed, her back to me. I climbed up beside her and stroked her back gently. "Are you okay?"

"Lucas, he's just so…" She trailed off.

"I know. But he does love you deeply." I brushed at her hair with my fingers, pulling it from her tear-stained face.

"He's so secretive."

"That, he is." I pulled the last strand of her wild strawberry-colored hair from her face, tucking it behind her ear. That was when I noticed the odd marking. I stared at it, thinking that perhaps she had a tattoo I was not aware of. I examined it closer. It was not a tattoo, it appeared to be burned into the skin. It looked familiar. It flooded back to me— the image of Alistair rubbing the same mark on his finger the night before he was murdered. "Ophelia, where did you get this mark?" I ran my finger across it; it was smooth.

She sat up and did her own prodding investigation. "What mark?"

I swiftly collected a mirror from the bathroom drawer. She fiddled with it until she could see the reflection in her bedroom mirror. "I don't know what that is." There was fear in her voice. "Have you ever seen anything like it before?"

I looked at it closer. "Once, on Alistair—the Conduit I found murdered, whose items we have been researching from."

Recognition washed over her features. "It's a Rune. A form of communication between Conduits. Talia had given it to me when Vivienne attacked us, so that we could coordinate our tactics."

"Curious." My mind was percolating with ideas. "How does it work?"

"I don't know." She replaced her hair to cover the Rune. "She just touched behind my ear, then told me to touch it to activate it, and told me that we could speak to each other within our minds."

I saw she was holding something back, but I did not press it. "I will do some research," I promised, "—when I can, of course."

She nodded. I took her by the shoulders. "How are you doing?"

"I'll be fine." She brushed it off. "I'll feel better after a shower."

I left the room with an offer that should she need to talk, she knew where to find me.

OPHELIA

I poured myself some wine and returned to my room. We would be traveling again the next day. I couldn't deal with another confrontation with Lucas before we left. I crawled into bed to read.

The leads went cold once more. Lucas and Huan built an alliance, although in hindsight they were driven by two very distinct fuels. Lucas was full of hate and anguish from his loss, while my Huan was still filled with hope and love. Four more years passed, and Huan was never called to the room, not once. Over the four years, Huan and Lucas took every moment they could to strengthen Lucas' shield so that he may guard himself from whatever manipulations were occurring. They practiced with Huan's influence over him, until the day came when Lucas could guard himself enough to lie to my husband, the Truth-sayer. His shield wasn't impenetrable, though. If the interrogation persisted, it would falter. But it was a breakthrough, nonetheless.

No more than three weeks after their triumph, Lucas was beckoned to the chamber. He had had an especially trying errand that day. I don't remember what it was, only that he came back agitated and exceptionally paranoid. In the middle of the night, Huan summoned my attention.

He was talking faster than usual. "Lucas came back from the chamber," he said, "and he hazily remembered a person in chains. Thick, heavy chains."

I turned my focus inward. Where was Huan? What was he doing? He was in the dark passage. He was running.

"I don't have much time. I saw Esther and Yanni leave the compound a moment ago. Lucas has promised to keep them at bay should they return hastily." Huan pulled his large copper medallion up so I could see it in his vision. "I will use my Loktpi. Stay with me, love, but in silence and if..."

I stopped him. "It is not this day."

He reached the door. It was massive, of a medieval origin, with brass fittings fastened with iron studs. Huan pulled at the lock. As expected, it didn't come ajar. He placed his medallion with the power of the Loktpi at the lock and recited the incantation he was taught by his father. We both inhaled deeply when the door unfastened. All of this happened in a matter of seconds, faster than you could tie your shoe. In the center of a circular room stood a chair, and in the chair was the naked body of a limp woman. Her dark hair was matted over her face. The moisture in the air pooled on her skin; even in the crevices of her elbows, water glistened. The room was lit by a single candle, flickering above her head in a small iron holder. Huan rushed to her side, lifted her head in his hands, brushed away the clotted hair. Her face was dirty, her features indistinguishable in the shadows.

"You are safe," he said. The woman said nothing. "Vita?" Huan whispered the name so quietly I wondered at first if she had heard him.

Her eyes moved first. She lifted her head from his hands. "Vita," he said it again.

Awareness came to her face, but she didn't know the stranger in front of her.

She still said nothing. "How long have you been here?" he asked.

The woman could not resist Huan's gift for eliciting truth. "Since 1687," she said calmly.

Huan closed his eyes in disgust, then asked, "Is there anyone else down here with you?"

Vita shook her head no. I felt Huan's disappointment. He was hoping to rescue many more. I felt the shift in his resolve.

I could not be silent. "You can't do this, Huan. If you let her go, they will know it was you, and the last seventy years will be lost!" I said desperately. "What about your father? What if they catch you?"

"She is a prisoner, and I am here to release the imprisoned," he said sternly in my head. "I would want someone to do this for you."

I knew I had lost him. He was going to do this thing; he would save her no matter what I said.

"I love you!" I shouted in his head.

"This is not goodbye," he said. "Now leave me. Clear this conversation and leave me. I will reach out again soon." I saw him use the Loktpi once more. The chains that bound Vita fell to the ground. She crumbled into his arms.

LUCAS

I ran for miles, beyond borders. I just kept running, my thoughts bouncing back and forth between my mother's murder and Olly's words.

I knew the hobgoblin Clive was my best bet in moving forward with the investigation of my mother's death. *But how can I connect with hobgoblins,* I wondered. They were notoriously tight-lipped. Which was what made them perfect for that kind of work. I'd seen a couple of the wretches in Delhi, but seeing one and engaging with them were two different stories. *I must have some connection,* I thought, as I replayed every moment I'd ever been in the company of one of the creepy creatures.

It occurred to me that I did know a guy in Prague who hired them frequently, mainly for flesh consumption, after financial deals he'd made had gone bad and he needed to dispose of the evidence. I vowed to reach out to him tomorrow.

I stopped and turned around—now that I had a game plan for one of my problems, I needed to deal with the other. Olly's words had stung, but I had to admit the truth—she was meant to be with Elias. *Unless something happens to him.* I smiled at the brief thought. I knew I couldn't stop their connection, and it wasn't fair of me to even try anymore.

I was only making it harder for her. I was denying her what Yesi and I had. *How could I do that to her?* It was time for me to give her my blessing and step aside. It was time to let her be happy.

I felt suffocated by the words as they came to mind. I was barely able to breathe, my eyes stinging. The tears that followed came out in massive, unrelenting waves as the reality of that loss shook my entire body.

OPHELIA

J didn't care that I needed to get ready to leave China in the morning. I stayed up into the wee hours of the night, riveted by Talia's journal; I needed to know what had become of Huan.

I had been crying for nearly seven hours straight when I felt the Runes tug at my consciousness again.

Huan was standing, facing me in a mirror.

"My love, my dearest Nandi. As you suspected, Vita's release became complicated and I am afraid there is no way to circumvent the ill-fated outcome. I was able to successfully release that poor woman, but I have been exposed. They are coming for me. Know that I love you with all of my being, and that I will be with you—always. You will know I am there when you see the flutter of a butterfly's wings or when a branch brushes your cheek—that will be me, my strokes." He turned as he heard the door behind him open. I noticed the lavishness of the room he was in. There were thick velvet drapes adorning tall, oversized windows, and large, overstuffed chairs with detailed rich embroidered patterns littered the space. Then three figures entered the chamber: Lucas, Yanni and Vivienne. When I saw Lucas I had a flash of hope. He could save him—he could save his friend, my Huan.

I felt a calm, a peacefulness wash over Huan. He had resigned himself to his execution. Anger, sadness and desperation welled up in my chest, but I couldn't flood him with these emotions in his final moments.

So I swallowed hard and wrapped my beloved in feelings of love and devotion.

I felt a tear well up in his left eye. He squeezed it back and took a deep breath.

I heard Yanni ask, "How long, Huan? How long have you been conspiring against us?" He circled Huan as he spoke, but Huan did not move a muscle. He simply stared between Lucas and Vivienne, who both stood before him. Yanni laughed boisterously, so loud I almost jumped. "You have been doing my bidding for over seventy years. Have you wasted seventy years of your life?"

My mind tried to wander. I had a million questions racing through my brain. But once again, I locked them away. I had the rest of my life to get to the bottom of my queries. In that moment, I needed to be present with my Huan—in his last moments. I choked back the tears in my eyes and the sobs in my chest.

Vivienne spoke now. "Does it really surprise you, master Yanni? Consider all of the disgusting Pai Ona he let slip through his slippery little hands. Perhaps he was letting them go—warning them of our approach." With that, she kicked Huan in the calf. I felt the piercing pain fly up his thigh. Huan buckled and fell to his knees.

"The question is, was he acting alone?" Yanni hissed. "You have a very useful gift, Huan; you make others speak the truth." Yanni shook his head disappointedly. "Tsk tsk tsk, such a useful gift. It is why you were considered so valuable in the field." Yanni took Huan's face in his hands and squeezed his jaw so that the mandible disconnected from its joint. The sound of bone fracturing filled my ear drums. Then he tossed him aside.

Huan didn't make a sound. Yanni continued. "I am so frustrated this day. Because of you, not only have I lost Vita, who spread lies, but now I have lost you—who exposed truths." Yanni kicked Huan in the ribs where he knelt. My love did not cry out, but I felt another huge surge of pain.

Vivienne hauled him up to his feet and demanded, "Look your master in the eyes when he speaks to you."

"The question is," Yanni said, "did you act alone?" He was once again circling my beloved. "We never took you down to Vita's quarters. It seemed a moot point to try to instill lies into a Truth-sayer. Or worse, perhaps you would get truths from her." Yanni laughed again. Huan looked at him with pure disdain. When he looked up, I caught a glimpse of Lucas, and I wondered why he said nothing, did nothing.

"I thought it was risky to let you work with others, considering your talents," Yanni said. "And you were often so clumsy at finishing the job, as Vivienne here has pointed out." He gestured to his left at the monstrous woman. "Now we know it was all a ruse, and that my suspicions were warranted. Still, there were many who didn't get away, weren't there? How does your conscience deal with that, honorable Huan?" Yanni sneered at the word honorable.

For a long moment there was silence in the room, as though he was letting the question sink in. Vivienne interjected once more. "We must find out if he was working alone."

Yanni chuckled as he casually walked over to her. "Patience. I am getting there." He backhanded her with such force, she stumbled two steps backward.

"Sorry about that, Huan," he said coldly. "As you know, she is always so eager. What she doesn't

understand is that it isn't as simple as interrogating the interrogator. We don't have another Truth-sayer in our coterie. Your people have a natural air of 'righteousness' about them." Yanni hung his head once more. "Which makes this all the more saddening. Now, we could hunt down your pretty little partner, Nandi. Oh, the things I could do to her." Yanni rubbed his hands together maniacally. I felt rage wash over Huan, but he knew better than to react. It would simply feed Yanni's desires.

Yanni turned to Vivienne. "I suppose that's what I would have you do, dear—hunt down Nandi, force him to talk. But see, that would take time, a lot of time. If we have a traitor, we must flush them out now."

Yanni strolled over to Lucas, who had been stiff and silent the entire time. "Wouldn't you agree, Lucas?"

Lucas nodded somberly.

"You were closest with him. Were you not?" Yanni flippantly gestured to my husband.

"We spent time together between jobs." Lucas' voice was steady. It revealed nothing. Perhaps my Huan was the one who'd been fooled. It occurred to me that Lucas' shield could have been there the entire time, that he was bait for Huan. To reveal Huan's ultimate intentions.

Yanni walked back to Vivienne. "You see, my dear, it is nearly impossible to get an interrogator to confess. It is far easier to get the Truth-sayer to reveal his allies on his own, with his own talents." The tenor in Yanni's voice changed; it was demanding and violent. "Vivienne, put our dear friend Lucas to the test."

She walked over and gruffly escorted Lucas so that he was facing Huan dead on, so there could be no mistake as to who Huan was asking the questions. I felt Huan's surge of anxiety for his friend, who worried that Huan himself would expose Lucas' alliance with him. Huan didn't want to hurt Lucas, didn't want to betray him.

But my own suspicions were mounting. This test would either expose Lucas' treachery—an alliance with Huan—to the Nebas, or it would reveal his manipulation of my husband. Huan felt confident that Lucas could withstand one, maybe two questions without revealing the truth. But their exercises had never successfully pushed his shield beyond two questions.

"Huan, be a doll and ask Lucas if he has conspired with you against the Nebas," Yanni commanded. Huan had a moment of hesitation, but thought if he didn't ask they would know; it would be better to let Lucas' shield work for him and eliminate all suspicions. I felt Huan conclude, 'I could save one more person...' My heart was breaking as I followed him through this thought process. I wanted to shout, fight or run.

"Lucas Healey," Huan began, "have you conspired with me against the Nebas you serve?" His voice was steady, purposeful, the way it was when he projected his gift.

"No," Lucas replied.

"Well, that's that!" Yanni brushed his hands together as though it was all wrapped up. Then he stopped

351

and put his finger to his lips. "Wait. I have a couple more questions. Huan, ask Lucas if he knew where Vita was, and how she was assisting us?"

Huan repeated the question, and again Lucas replied no.

"Just a couple more, I promise," Yanni said. "Then we can put this messy business behind us. Ask him if he was ever your friend or ally?" Yanni got very close to both of their faces for this question.

Huan swallowed hard. "Are you my friend or ally?"

With ice cold eyes, Lucas replied, "No."

My blood chilled in my bones. They had never successfully accomplished three deceptions. Had they been successful this time? I wondered. Or was this actually the truth?

"Perfect," said Yanni. "And now, one more, just to make sure Lucas has a higher vocabulary than the word 'no'. Ask him if he would kill any of the Nebas, given the chance."

Huan knew how Lucas would answer this question. It brought him peace. I felt it wash over him. His voice was now clear and calm in my head. "I love you. Promise me you will not let ignorance sway you any further in this lifetime, and when we meet in the next, we can share our stories."

I couldn't be strong any longer—even my thoughts were coming through in thick sobs. "I love you," I told him. "I will avenge you."

Huan interrupted me. "Don't avenge me, my love—avenge truth. Don't let all of my works here go to waste. But stay safe, stay vigilant. We do not know who our friends are." Those were the last words he said to me.

Huan directed his focus to Lucas. "Lucas Healey, would you kill any of the Nebas, given the chance?"

Lucas answered with more intensity in his voice than he had previously. "Yes, I fucking would."

Both Vivienne and Yanni erupted in laughter as though it was the funniest thing they had ever heard.

"Oh, Lucas, that is why we love you. You are a raging bull. We just need to point your fury in the direction of our opponents." Yanni put his hand on Lucas' shoulder. "Speaking of killing... Do away with him."

I saw Lucas' hands reach for my Huan's face, heard the unmistakable tearing of Conduit flesh, then felt a deep and devastating darkness.

I DROPPED THE JOURNAL. MY MOUTH WENT DRY. *WHAT DOES THIS MEAN?* I felt lightheaded. *Lucas killed Huan?* There must be a reason. I compelled myself to read on. I didn't want to. I had to.

ELIAS

*I*t had been an hour since I checked in on Ophelia. *Perhaps I should see how she is doing,* I thought. *I will just finish this last page.* I completed the final sentence, and read over what it said. I had been working backwards in the journals, hoping the more recent entries would have valuable information about the summit's location.

Finally, here it was, in my hand—Alistair's findings and conclusion.

"After ruminating and researching," it read, "I have concluded The Cathedral will be the securest and most appropriate venue for the Kraus summit. Rajahish is the current keeper. He can share the way the Loktpi will open the portal."

My hands were shaking as I read and reread the translation.

Rajahish is the keeper? Have I been that close already, when we were in Jammu?

And The Cathedral? I thought. *I had believed that was only a myth.*

OPHELIA

*O*n I read. I couldn't stop until I'd learned everything I could from Talia's journal.

So now you know how my Huan met his demise. At the hand of Lucas Healey, in the coterie of the

Nebas. But I still had to know the truth of it—did Lucas kill him to save the cause, or was he a snake?

It took me several years to track Lucas down. He served as a mercenary for the Nebas for at least

another decade. Once he was no longer in service to Yanni and Esther, it took more time than I expected

to find him. It is difficult to find someone who doesn't want to be found, especially when their talents

allow them to hide in plain sight.

So it was that I finally discovered his whereabouts in South America. But just as I arrived to confront

him, to ask him the questions that were plaguing me, he switched gears entirely and voyaged up to San

Francisco, where I first saw you.

I intended to confront him there, but then I saw him meeting with Viraclay. This was very interesting to

me, considering that it was no secret that Elias suspected Lucas had a hand in his parents' murders. The

two of them despised each other. My curiosity stilled my action. Instead I simply watched. I watched as

you and Lucas built a life together. I watched him fall in love with you. I watched how he coveted you. I

watched when he would secretly meet with Viraclay.

I watched for a year and a half, until one night I saw the confirmation I had been waiting for. You see,

the Nebas thrive in a loose alliance. Mercenaries are not paid in gold or money; we have lived lifetimes

and have thus acquired mounds of wealth. More wealth than any one person could spend.

354

No, the Nebas need something greater than wealth to align them—they barter in time, in life and death. When a Nebas hunts and kills another Conduit, they receive a pardon for their own life, or for those they love. By killing a Pai Ona you spare your own death warrant, temporarily.

The price on Lucas' head was high; he'd left the Nebas with unsettled debts, and in a cloud of suspicion. Yanni and Esther had made it clear that finding him would promise centuries of time free of their menace.

Or perhaps the bounty on Lucas' head was all an elaborate story to reinstate Lucas back into Pai Ona confidences so that the real prize could be claimed: Viraclay.

The night before you were swept away to Hafiza, I saw Lucas meet with Yanni. I don't know what was said, but the next day Lucas left you alone for the first time in all the days he had been in San Francisco. He withdrew his shield and exposed your location, as well as Viraclay's. You two were sitting ducks. I watched in horror as Yanni approached the apartment Elias had been residing in, and Huan's words rang in my ear, "We cannot stay ignorant of this war any longer." I thought about the prophecy and knew that the loss of Elias would eliminate any chance of peace for our people, as the prophecy foretold. I couldn't watch all hope disintegrate in front of me and do nothing. I mustered all of my strength and projected mass confusion; I discombobulated Yanni's senses. He knew someone was manipulating him, but before he could sniff me out or reinstate his coordinates on Elias, he caught wind of something else: you.

I didn't intend to put you in danger. I didn't know your virtuosities at the time. Please forgive me. By the grace of Malarin's strokes, you were spared. I knew you and Viraclay were in danger—that Lucas had betrayed you both and that he was entrenched in your lives. I followed you to Bosnia and devised a plan to get a hold of Lucas. When I abducted you from Hafiza, I never intended to harm you. I wanted to lure Lucas out of his safe haven. I hoped to destroy the traitor among you. When my attempt failed, it became harder to breach the defenses.

When the siege happened, I took out as many Nebas as I could from the rear as they approached the fortress. I wish I could have done more, but I couldn't gain entry. I have no idea how they could have done so, except that Lucas must have permitted some access from within.

I am so sorry to have to expose all of this. I know how much you love him, how he saved you. I saw him fall in love with you, so I don't understand why he has forsaken you. All I know is that you are brilliant and special and meant to change this world, but you cannot do that with treachery in your midst.

Forgive me, for everything.

Your friend,

Talia

LUCAS

I was about fifteen minutes from the yurt complex when I caught his scent. It was faint, but distinct. It was Yanni. He was here—in Nehe.

OPHELIA

y eyes welled up with tears. I put the journal down, then picked it back up again.

I reread the entry for a fifth time, shaking my head in disbelief. *How could Lucas do this? Why would he do this to me?* My hands were shaking. I tasted acid on my tongue as my body tried to react viscerally by vomiting. I swallowed the upheaval and replayed that night— months ago, another lifetime ago, in San Francisco. Everything had felt so foggy that evening, like I'd been looking through a muddy lens.

Realizations wash over me as I concluded that Talia must be right. This time I couldn't hold back the vomit, and I heaved all over the floor.

I heard a door open and froze. *Would it be Elias or Lucas? What would I say to either of them?*

The hair on the back of my neck stood on end. I felt my fingertips go numb with anxiety. I'd been preparing myself to fight, to confront our enemies, but I couldn't have prepared myself for this. I felt tiny, wounded and lost all at once. My bedroom door swung open, and I flinched. It was Elias.

He was immediately at my side. "What is it? Are you ill?" He was examining my body. I handed him the journal but said nothing. I sat at the end of the bed, wide-eyed, waiting for his response.

As Elias read, I heard another door open. This time both of our bodies stiffened, knowing who it was. In a moment, Elias was in front of me, guarding me.

"We need to get going, now!" There was an urgency in Lucas' voice as he entered the house. He entered my room, assessing the situation but not knowing what to think. "We need to go. I detected Yanni," he said.

I got to my feet but decided to stay behind Elias. I could feel the fury rolling off him as he glowered at Lucas.

For a tense moment Lucas said nothing—we all said nothing. Elias had taken on an offensive crouch and, without thinking, I noticed that Lucas had begun to mimic him defensively.

I took the journal from Elias' hand and casually stuck it in the back of my pants, as it suddenly became clear exactly how I would handle this.

"It was you," I said calmly, looking at Lucas.

Lucas turned to meet my eyes, bewilderment clear across his face. "What? What was me?"

I waved my hand. Immediately, all of the shields were down, both mine and his. Alarm replaced bewilderment as he felt the shift. "Olly, what are you doing?" he said.

I put my hand on Elias' shoulder as I stepped out from behind him. Without any barriers, I could feel it all—every pointed feeling in the room: rage, fear, questions—thousands of questions from both men.

"I know what you did, Lucas, what you have done. You were the one who disclosed my location in San Francisco to Yanni and Esther. It was you who dropped the wards, which allowed the Nebas to infiltrate Hafiza and kill our friends—kill people who trusted you! To kill Aremis!" I stepped closer still. I was yelling at this point, my own disbelief and ire swelling inside me.

I was directly in front of Lucas, staring him in the eyes. I reached for his arm so he couldn't hide the truth, so I could see it all. His body was trembling. He was scared. Somehow in all of this, I still felt an overwhelming outpouring of love toward me. He didn't pull away. In some way, I think he wanted me to feel it all, as though that might excuse his actions, his betrayal.

"Did you kill Huan?" I asked. The question took his breath away. The memory flashed across his mind. I saw that he did. I saw the whole scene—the heartbreak, the hurt. I saw Huan fall. If that was true, I knew then that it all must be true. He couldn't deny any of it.

He tried to explain. "It wasn't that way, Olly. Huan knew he had been made and he asked me to kill him swiftly so they wouldn't find his connection with Nandi and track her down. He begged me to kill him. He was my friend."

"That, he was," I said callously. "Did you love him?" A tear fell from my eye as I realized he did, but it made no difference.

Lucas said nothing. I heard a growl sneak out of Elias' mouth behind me.

"Did you tell Yanni where I was, that night in San Francisco?" My voice was shaking as I asked the question. I gripped his arm harder.

"I told Yanni where Viraclay was!" he spat. "I wanted him gone. I wanted our lives to stay as they were. I knew Yanni would track down Elias if I left the area, which would take him out from under my shield. Yanni said he would let me go; I didn't tell him that I was guarding you for Elias—just that I had been camouflaging the rotten prick in San Francisco."

Lucas looked past me, to Elias, and I wasn't sure I'd be able to hold Elias back if he decided he'd heard enough. "Something went wrong," Lucas continued, "and when I pulled my shield back, Yanni detected you instead. I didn't know what you were at that time—I didn't know that you would be more detectable than Viraclay. I wouldn't have risked it!" he said, exasperated.

I knew it was true. I saw his intentions plain as day, his remorse for putting me in danger.

"What about my parents? What about Hafiza?" Elias spat. He couldn't hold back any longer. I thought he'd already demonstrated amazing restraint as it was. I held tight to Lucas. I felt bafflement then recognition roll off of him, but before we could press on, there was a calamitous sound from somewhere in another part of the complex.

"We need to go!" Lucas shouted. "Yanni has found us. I will make this right. Please trust me." Lucas' eyes were pleading. I didn't have time to think or react, because the sound got closer and Elias grabbed me. Without thinking, I reinserted the shields.

I was scared. Confused. And angry.

ELIAS

*R*age—pure unbridled rage—surged in my veins. I wanted to kill him, right now—rip him apart.

It was the panic in Ophelia's voice that anchored me.

"Get your things," I said and hesitantly left her alone with that monster, that villainous fiend. I moved with lightning speed, collected everything I had been working on and threw my bag over my shoulder, just as there was another thunderous noise. It was the sound of Yanni overturning the yurts in the compound. I entered the room to overhear Lucas warning Ophelia.

"Whatever you do, Olly, whatever happens. You cannot." He grabbed her by the shoulders, shaking her. "You cannot show Yanni your abilities. Do you understand me?"

She did not respond. She was in shock. I interjected. "Lucas is right." I did not look at him when I spoke, afraid it would send me back into a hurricane of fury, and for the moment I needed him to help get her out of there alive. "Yanni cannot know your gifts. No matter what happens. For the safety of everyone, you must be discreet." Another ominous noise rang out in the night sky, this time much closer. "We need to go," I said, handing her her bag.

"Is it just Yanni?" I asked Lucas through bared teeth, resentful that

ASHLEY HOHENSTEIN

my parents' justice needed to wait a moment longer. Infuriated that I had to communicate with this man in any other way besides fists.

"I only detected him," Lucas replied as we raced through the second corridor. We were nearly to the last yurt and the rental car that was parked just beyond it when we heard the distinct sound of crushing metal, followed by splintering wood, as the rental car collided with the last yurt.

"Hurry back the other way," Lucas said as he turned. We had Olly between us. When Lucas opened the door we had just come through, we were met by a wall of fire. The yurt we were in was all that was left of the nine that had been clustered together. Smoke billowed into the remaining circular structure. There was a loud cackle on the other side of the thin vinyl wall.

"Come out, come out, wherever you are!" We heard another shrill cackle. I looked at Ophelia. She was still in some sort of shock.

"We will get you out of here," I assured her. Still, she said nothing. The three of us backed up to the center of the room.

"I will huff and I will puff and I will blow your house down!" Yanni taunted. The wall to our right tore open to reveal his silhouette in the smoke. Lucas flanked my side, the two of us creating a defense between Yanni and Ophelia.

"Good day, gentlemen!" Yanni bowed. "Fancy meeting you here."

"Fuck you, Yanni!" Lucas shouted back. "You aren't welcome."

"Well, that's just rude, Lucas," Yanni said as he began slinking to our right. We countered to the left. "You are not a very good host. Perhaps that's why we never became fast friends."

"On the contrary, Yanni," Lucas sneered, "I think I realized what a puppet you were centuries ago. No real man respects a husband who can't do a thing without his wife's permission." Lucas stood erect.

I pulled the Dirk of Inverness from my sheath and invoked the invisibility charm.

"Yeah, that must have been it. I like friends with balls." Lucas gestured to his scrotum, then crouched again.

Yanni cackled. "Well, you know what they say—happy wife, happy life." Yanni leapt toward us and I pulled Ophelia just out of reach.

362

Lucas stepped the opposite way and planted a solid kick to the back of Yanni's head.

I heard the crack. On a human, that blow would have been fatal, but in this case it simply slowed our attacker down.

Ophelia grabbed my arm. "I can help," she whispered.

Yanni laughed. "Isn't that sweet, gentlemen. Your pet desires to assist you. Adorable."

Lucas' voice bellowed over the crackle of the fire. "No need to worry, Olly. I got this asshole. This has been a long time coming."

The fire had completely consumed the vinyl and was working its way through the building's structure. Yanni had not just been tearing down the other yurts—he had been building our pyre. We were surrounded by huge flames.

Once again Ophelia tugged at my shirt from behind. "I can extinguish…" she began, and I put my finger to her lips, but it was too late.

"You can what, my dear?" Yanni had turned his back to Lucas and now had his complete attention focused onto Ophelia. He advanced, and I crouched, ready to incapacitate him with one little cut of the dirk.

Lucas flung himself onto Yanni's exposed back. "Get her out of here!" he demanded, then yelled, "Olly, I love you!"

I saw no other way. I sheathed my weapon and threw Ophelia over my shoulder. Once I was sure I had her held tight, I dove through the flames—focusing on the patch of dirt I saw free of fire in front of me.

Her screams were all I could hear, her bloodcurdling screams. She kicked and tore at my grip but I held fast, sure that if she broke free she would run back into the torched rubble.

"Lucas! Lucas!" she screamed. "I love you! Lucas!"

I just ran. When she could no longer scream, she continued saying his name in whispers, "Lucas."

PART IV

ELIAS

I watched her. She had not spoken since the previous night. Her eyes were like red sapphires from the endless tears. Her cheeks were stained with striated lines of soot and ash. I wanted to comfort her. I knew what he meant to her but I could not find the words. I sensed the distance between us. She was barricading herself. I was at a loss—I could not fathom what she was going through.

I had run for fifteen miles, until we reached Nehe. When we made it to the city center I stopped the first car that passed us and offered them four thousand dollars in American currency if they would drive us to Qiqihar.

We lucked out, because they happily agreed.

When we arrived in Qiqihar, I had us dropped off at a shuttle service that usually frequented the Qiqihar airport. I negotiated with the driver to take us to Shenyang, traveling through the night. Again, with a lofty amount of money, they conceded, despite the driver's uneasiness about our disheveled appearance.

We were still two hours out from the Shenyang airport. I would need to pull out more cash in Shenyang—then I would get Ophelia situated in a nice hotel and carry out my plan to get us back to Jammu by the following night.

I looked out the window, then back at Ophelia. I had no idea how we had survived, and without a scratch on either of us. I was certain she had something to do with that. Olly had guarded us from the fire. I only hoped that Yanni had been destroyed, that Lucas prevailed and that she may see him again. I personally wished that they both were terminated in the fire, but for her peace, I had to hope Lucas had survived—he would not escape justice either way.

I watched as she rubbed the hairsy charm on her wrist, but it brought her no comfort. So I assumed the worst—that the connection was gone because Lucas was dead. If Yanni was not taken by the fire, I surmised, Lucas had done enough damage to detain him temporarily —otherwise we would not be here.

ESTHER

I walked up to the smoldering rubble. I smelled him. He had
been here. He had found them, like he had promised.

I knelt beside the remnants of a vehicle; the metal was scorched
and blistered. The fire had burned out of control for some time before
the local humans got it doused. The landscape was charcoal from the
destruction.

"Mistress, he isn't here," Akiva asserted from across the remains.

"But he *was* here," I said. "I know my beloved's handiwork. The
question is, where is he now?"

"Mistress?" Akiva called to me again.

His presence was irritating me. "Did you come to assist me?" I
roared. "Or are you useless? Because I dispose of useless things." I
stood to face him.

"I am anything but, I assure you. Let us see what is in the debris,
shall we?" Akiva raised his hands and anything that wasn't ash
hovered in the air.

"That's more like it." I walked amongst the items suspended a few
feet above the ground, the charred earth clinging to my dress. I very
much liked the way the ash stained the red fabric. It was destruction

and beauty melded together—a pure unfiltered representation of life and all of its reckoning.

I stopped when I saw the ring. It was directly in front of me, floating in my path. It was a defining moment. A proverbial fork in the road. Everything changed in that instant. I swiped it where it perched. It was his ring. It was my beloved Yanni's ring. The token I had given him the night we consummated. He would never have abandoned it.

The metal was warped, contorted into a hideous vestige of the original piece. I fell to my knees. Our lives flashed before my eyes and I knew the tearing sensation I had felt the night before had been his soul leaving this world.

Akiva rushed to my side. "Mistress, what is it?"

I swallowed hard. I couldn't let anyone see the weakness I felt. I knew it was my Yanni; I knew I had lost him. It was why I'd taken to this journey. When my heart stopped less than twenty-four hours earlier, the sensation was unmistakable. It was disorientating—as though my being had been sliced in two and my insides carved out and lit on fire. It had all happened in a moment, and then the terror was gone, replaced with pure desolation. Driven by extreme dread, I demanded Akiva aid me in tracking my beloved down.

I said nothing as I placed my hand upon his shoulder and hoisted myself up.

I seized control of Akiva's body. With his gift, I hoisted every piece of shrapnel within a five-mile radius into the air.

Then with every ounce of my being, every cell in my body, I screamed, a monstrous scream until all the air left my lungs. As I howled, I projected the wreckage as far as it would go, destroying every person, building or thing it came into contact with.

Akiva stood motionless, waiting for me to instruct him or emancipate him from my control.

"We will kill them all," I proclaimed. I let the gaping hole in my soul be filled with pure rage. "We will kill them all."

OPHELIA

J pulled my knees to my chest. The shower had cleaned the stench of the fire from my body, but it also seemed to wash some of the fog away from my thoughts, illuminating the harsh reality of the situation, leaving me numb. Lucas was gone. My Lucas was gone. Our last interaction had been filled with discordant words and unanswered questions.

Lucas had been the first person who ever took care of me, the first anchor in my life. He had been my safe place.

He'd also betrayed me. But I still loved him so much, and he was gone. A million emotions ran through me as I played with the hairsy charm once more.

His essence was absent. There was just a void. I swallowed back the tears. It was all made worse by our last argument, even before our final confrontation.

He knew I was falling in love with Elias; he knew he would lose me. I swallowed again but this time it did nothing to hold back the tears.

~

The door to the hotel suite opened. Elias came in, food in one hand and fresh clothes in another.

"I brought you something to eat." His voice was soft, gentle.

"I'm not hungry."

"It has been two days since you ate anything."

"I said I'm not hungry." I met his eyes then looked away. Somehow my feelings for Elias felt like a betrayal to Lucas. I knew I wasn't thinking straight, but it was all so messy, so broken. "I'm sorry," I said.

He sat on the foot of the bed. "Okay, you can eat when you are ready. I am going to get in the shower. Our flight is in three hours." He got up and headed toward the bathroom.

"Elias?" I called. He stopped and turned to face me. "Was this in the prophecy? Did you know he would die?"

Elias sighed. "No." He paused. "Would you like to read it?"

I nodded.

He walked over to his bag where he pulled out a folded piece of paper. He placed it in my hand and resumed his seat at the end of the bed.

I unfolded it carefully. It was obvious it had been unfolded and re-folded several, possibly hundreds of times.

My eyes scanned the words before starting from the beginning.

The strokes have foretold, a day will come when a child is born of miraculous conception. Through the will of his parents he will confound us all. But with his creation follows mass destruction. His path is hers. From ashes she will rise. And those who lived before her will question what power was before they witnessed her supreme virtue. The union of the two will either offer salvation or annihilation of the world as it is and will ever be. The dance they dance will determine if her rise gives way to her death or if her virtue brings peace among the chaos.

I SET THE PAPER ASIDE. "I'M EITHER GOING TO KILL EVERYONE OR SAVE everyone?"

"It is a heavy burden to bear. It is why I did not wish to share it with you." He leaned in closer, but I scooted back. I wasn't ready for his comfort. He understood and retreated. I looked at the prophecy in my hand once more.

"Can I keep this?"

"Of course. It is yours." He rose from the bed.

"Elias." I thought now was as good a time as any to get it out there, to be on the same page. He stood waiting for my question patiently. "This prophecy only has merit if we consummate, doesn't it?"

"Yes," he answered solemnly.

"So we can't possibly—it would put too many people in danger," I asserted.

"It would seem so." He knelt beside the bed. "This is why we need to unite the Pai Ona. If the way of this war changes, perhaps the way of the prophecy will as well."

"But we don't know that, do we?"

He shook his head no.

I let the gravity of that sink in: *We may never be together.*

Elias stood once more.

"This may seem like a silly question," I asked. "But does consummating include making love? Marriage?" I just wanted to rip the Band-Aid off all at once and know what we were really working with here.

"I have never consummated, clearly, but I understand that it is a union of souls, lives and bodies simultaneously—so yes, our intimacy is…"

I stopped him there. "I get it." I threw myself back onto the bed and took to playing with the hairsy charm again, searching for any sign of Lucas.

ELIAS

*O*phelia had filled me in on Nandi's journal and the Loktpi while we travelled to India from China. We just had one more piece of the puzzle left.

Rajahish sat across from me once more, just as he had a week or so earlier. His toothless smile brought me little comfort this time. Ophelia stayed outside the hut.

"I need the ritual to create the Loktpi," I said. "We have all of the blessed ingredients." I showed him the pouches and their contents, then watched him, not sure how he would respond.

"It would seem you do." He looked at me intently, and I saw the wisdom behind his eyes. "You will need the girl." He nodded toward the door. "She was blessed as well."

"Yes, she was."

"It was not a question." He got up and pulled a clay pot from a shelf. He showed me the basin of the bowl. It had an odd marking in the center. "Combine the sacred items in here. Splash water, sprinkle dirt, ignite with fire then share your wind until the flame is extinguished. The ritual must be performed at the highest point of Bhangarh, at nightfall."

"Alright. Anything else?"

He handed me the bowl. "The gatekeeper has a temper. It would be best if you performed the ritual quickly."

"I thought you were the keeper."

"I am the keeper of the portal, not the keeper of the gate. He is testier than myself."

I nodded. "Thank you for your advice." I got up and bowed to the old man.

Then he whispered something to me. "Elias, her soul is in anguish. Souls in anguish cannot be trusted." Rajahish's eyes darted from me to the door. "There will come a time—very soon, I am afraid—when she must pick a side."

I bowed once more but said nothing. I knew Ophelia's soul, and she would get through this.

"One last thing," he said. I turned to meet his stare. "That is the last Loktpi that can ever be made. Alalli died. She was one of the pieces. Her whole tribe died. We can never be whole again. Our father, our creator, he stored the necessary fragments of his creation in his children, and their children. Our blood was key to the Loktpi's duplication, and now part of that bloodline is gone. Only four parts remain. Do you understand my words?"

I nodded and winced at the thought. "I do. The pieces of the Loktpi were in Ruit's Swali children. Alalli's piece of the key is gone. It can never be reassembled again. The ingredients can never be blessed."

"You understand."

I agreed and turned to go.

"Hold tight to your key," he reminded me. "There were only eight ever made, and we do not know who commands them." I saw hesitation cross his face before he spoke again. "When the time is right, you may want to reassemble your Loktpi into a more easily transportable structure—such as a medallion or token. You must activate it first, in order to transfer its power. As the portal keeper, I may assist you— when you are ready."

I paused as I considered the consequences of there being several other keys out there, and how this may affect the summit—then realized I needed to first confirm that we could enter The Cathedral. I remembered that Ophelia had said Huan wore his Loktpi around his neck; this must be what Rajahish was referring to. I would definitely be returning to create a practical form in which to transport the Loktpi.

"Goodbye, Rajahish," I said solemnly. I know we will meet again." I ducked out of the hut.

Ophelia was standing just outside the door when I exited, and I hoped she had not heard his foreboding words.

"Shall we?" I said as she followed in step with me. "Bhangarh is just a day's drive. We will set out tomorrow morning."

OPHELIA

*W*e took our time getting out of Jammu and on the road to Bhangarh. It was fine by me, since I hadn't been sleeping well for the past few days.

On the drive there, Elias explained the ritual and gave a vague warning about The Cathedral's gatekeeper. I didn't think he intended to be vague, but rather truly had no idea what the warning really meant.

We arrived around 4 p.m. I was surprised to see flocks of tourists navigating in and out of the ruins of Fort Bhangarh.

"We are going to find the largest Haven in the world inside a tourist attraction?" I said skeptically as we approached the gate.

"Hafiza was a tourist attraction," Elias reminded me.

We followed the line of people as they entered through the fort's entrance. A cheerful looking woman stood under a sign that read, *No Entrance After Dark*. Apparently, if you missed the sign, her purpose was to remind you of this fact.

It was beautiful. The fort was nestled into a mountainside, its stone a shade of a rich brown. Its architecture was impressive, with huge arches and tiered columns, creating a feeling of true magnificence.

"If no one is allowed here after dark, what's the plan?" I looked up at Elias as we walked.

"We will wait, hide and make our way up there," he said as he pointed to the final tier, which was poised ominously over the grassy yard we were presently standing in. "In the interim, shall we pop in for a tour? Learn what all the fuss is about?"

"Sounds good to me." We pulled a classic tourist move and fell a few feet behind an English-speaking tour guide.

"Bhangarh Fort is one of the most haunted places in the world," the guide announced. "The locals believe that the fortress is frequented by an old, dark wizard named Sinhai. The wizard fell in love with the beautiful princess Ratnavati. The princess of Fort Bhangarh didn't share the sentiment. Ratnavati rejected Sinhai's advances. So, he developed a plan to bewitch the princess with a love spell. He concocted the potion and poisoned the young princess' drink. But Ratnavati suspected the wizard and his scheming. So, when presented with the drink, she cast it aside, where it hit a boulder. The boulder, bewitched by the potion, followed Sinhai and plowed him over, killing him, but before the dark wizard met his demise, he cursed the fort and its inhabitants. Only a short while later, the fort fell under siege, and all ten thousand residents, including the princess, were killed." After the story followed a flurry of questions from the tourists.

"I think I heard enough," I told Elias. We agreed to do some exploring on our own, attempting to find the easiest access to the roof of the highest structure.

Close to six that night, the tourists began funneling out of the complex of ruined buildings. We found a small inlet near a staircase we'd located in the highest building. We snuck in there and waited for a while.

When it appeared all of the other tourists were gone, we crawled out from the inlet. I heard the gates being locked below.

"Do you really think this place is haunted?" I asked Elias.

"Most likely, yes," he said as he pulled out the items we would need to perform the ritual.

"Haunted by something so evil, they won't let people be on the grounds at night?"

"It would seem."

"Should we be concerned?" Anxiety welled up in my chest. "They described some visitors disappearing after dark."

"I heard that. I also read about several disturbing incidences concerning the poltergeist that wanders around the fort at night," he added mutter-of-factly.

"What you're saying is that we should be concerned?"

"We should be on high alert." He looked at his watch. "We have approximately forty-five minutes before sundown. I suggest we make our way to where we need to be, so that we can begin immediately and avoid bodily harm from said poltergeist." He picked up what he had pulled out of his bag in preparation, and looked at me. "After you."

I climbed the stairs as quickly as I could.

We reached a door. It was locked. "Pardon me," Elias said as he handed me the bowl with its contents. He proceeded to kick the door in. I was impressed. We ran up a second flight of stairs that came out behind the building, onto the mountainside.

"I think we should climb up to where we can hoist ourselves onto the roof," he said, looking at the setting sun. "Quickly would be best."

He didn't need to tell me twice. I scaled the mountain until I found a suitable spot to scramble up and over a stone wall onto the building. I took the bowl from Elias once more while he managed his way onto the roof—quite a bit more gracefully than I had.

The sun was sinking lower and what felt like faster than before.

Elias pointed at a spot where there was a slight incline, making it higher than the rest of the structure. "We need to get there."

We ran across the top of the building. Elias set the bowl down. "As soon as the sun disappears behind those mountains, we will begin."

We both watched with a laser-beam focus until the last bit of yellow light sank out of sight. Instantly the air around us got cold.

"Elias, do you feel that?"

"Shhh. Focus, Ophelia."

All the hairs on the back of my neck stood on end. A shadow elongated over Elias' face—there was something behind me. A deep voice rumbled and growled in my ear. I was too terrified to turn around.

Elias heard the predatory sound. He looked up from what he was doing. Even in the fading light, I could see the color drain from his face. His hands began to shake as he worked to untie each of the leather pouches and pour the contents into the clay bowl.

I felt an ethereal arm take hold of my right shoulder.

"Work faster!" I urged him. I couldn't mask the terror in my voice.

Elias emptied the last item into the pile. "Splash the water!" he shouted, then he dove over my shoulder. I moved to where he'd been. When I looked up I was horrified to see he was wrestling with a huge black mass of shadow and fangs. I took my eyes away to complete the ritual, shakily splashing the water, followed by sprinkling the dirt we'd collected earlier. I was distracted when I heard Elias cry out in pain. His shoulder was impaled by an enormous fang, and his body was flopping around like a rag doll as the monster tried to dislodge its tooth from Elias' torso.

"I will be fine!" he yelled. "Finish the ritual!" Just then his body fell seven feet onto the stone roof. I pulled a match from the matchbook and lit the contents of the bowl on fire.

Elias was attempting to crawl back to where I was. "Blow on it!" he called.

I blew on it, but nothing happened. "It's not working." I ran over to Elias and got him to his feet. The monster grabbed me by the neck and I was hoisted into the air. I couldn't speak. The pressure around my neck was constricting, my vision was starting to blur around the edges, just as I saw Elias lean down and blow on the small, dancing flames. All went dark.

My body was falling, or perhaps floating. Until it wasn't. Elias grabbed my hand.

His whisper was so soft, I wasn't sure I heard anything at all. "The Cathedral."

I opened my eyes. It was like nothing I had ever seen before. I repeated, "The Cathedral."

GLOSSARY

Alalli~ The Asagi word for mother.
Atoa~ A Conduit's other half or partner.
Asagi~ Conduit language.

Chitchakor, Malarin, Dalininkas~ The master painter and creator of all life in the world.
Conduit~ A semi-immortal being that expresses extraordinary powers when consummated with their other half, or pair. Upon consummation Conduits no longer age. Conduits are always coupled as a receiver and an imposer.
Consu~ A consummated Conduit
Covening~ The act of Conduits gathering to perform the ancient magic.

Dalininkas, Chitchakor, Malarin, ~ The master painter and creator of all life in the world.

Elemental~ A Conduit that can manifest or create the earth, wind, water or fire.
Eyok~ An ancient morning ritual that includes a guest and a host

sharing stories. It is customary for the host to start the ritual with a story of their own choosing. The host can then ask their guest to share a story of the host's choosing. It is customary for the ritual to last the entire length of the guest's visit. The purpose is to share Conduit history and build each Conduit's legacy

Gilly Mead~ A breakfast mead produced by Vosega. It has less alcohol and is fermented differently than other meads. It is served hot.

Haven~ A place of ancient magic, often a safe house.

Imposer~ A Conduit that can impose their will or energy onto another being or object.

Lasteea~ A connection and feeling deeper than love.
Loktpi~ A magical key that can dissolve any wards and unlock any door, revealing the location and passage into any Conduit Haven.

Malarin, Dalininkas, Chitchakor, ~ The master painter and creator of all life in the world.

Nebas~ Evil or 'bad' Conduits who most likely align with Esther and Yanni, either in secret or openly.

Pai Ona~ The 'good' Conduits, those fighting to unite and end the war.
Paksyon~ A small congregation of Conduits, who are usually participating in covening.
Pealatunic- The Asagi word for magic.
The Pierses~ Sister books that contain ancient magic spells.
Poginuli~ A broken Conduit, an individual Conduit whose partner has been slain.

Receiver~ A Conduit that receives or absorbs another object or being's energy.

The Rittles~ Weapons forged with magical poisons that inflict severe injury.

The River Tins~ The magical river where your colors can be cleaned, according to the creation myth of the Conduits.

Soahcoit~ A consummated Conduit pair.

Sulu~ A beacon of energy, often in the form of a group of Conduits. In rare occasions, it is an **individual Conduit** that creates an energy vortex.

Swali~ A human that has some Conduit heritage, or a demi-god.

Tulaswaga~ The Asagi word for gift.

Unconsu~ A Conduit that is still mortal and has not been consummated.

Vulcan~ An earth Elemental Conduit that has the power to control and manifest or create volcanic activity.

FORSAKEN MAP

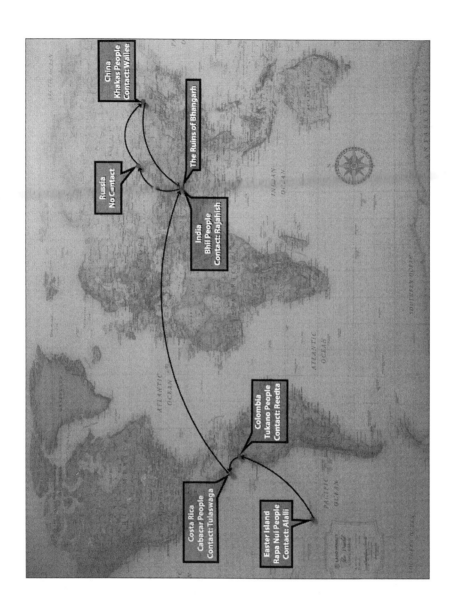

China
Khakas People
Contact: Wallee

Russia
No Contact

The Ruins of Bhangarh

India
Bhil People
Contact: Rajahiish

Colombia
Tukano People
Contact: Reedra

Costa Rica
Cabacar People
Contact: Tulaswaga

Easter Island
Rapa Nui People
Contact: Alalii

PEDIGREES

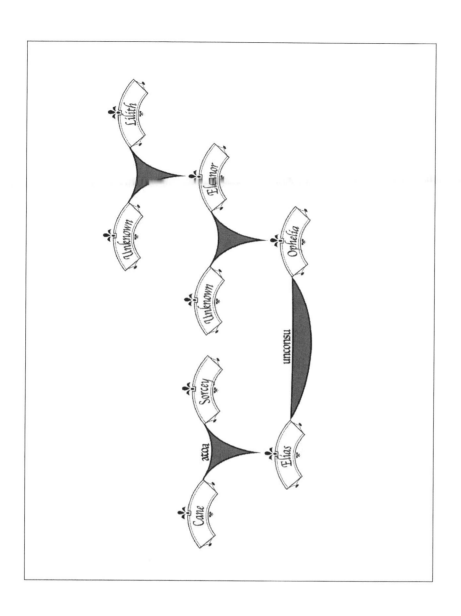

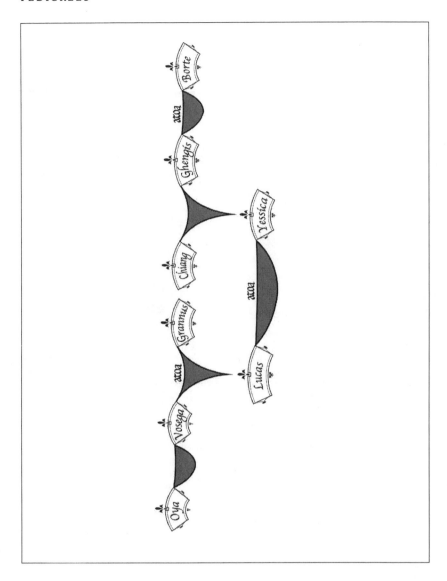

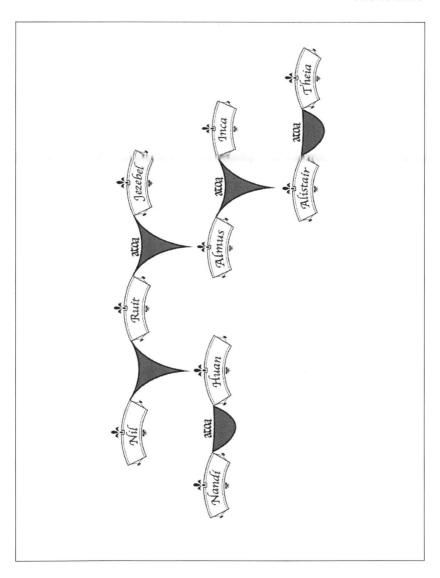

ACKNOWLEDGMENTS

I need to start by thanking Erik for his continued support and unwavering belief in me.

He also took an active role in the production of *FORSAKEN*. He designed and formatted the pedigrees and the map, for readership ease.

To my beta readers, I appreciate the time and effort you ladies put into making me a better writer. Specifically I want to thank Jen, Alicia, Aunt Becky, Aunt Yvonne, Michelle, Rebekah and my weekly writing buddy Rachelle.

A gigantic, colossal, enormous, thank you to my editor Ella Medler for polishing *FORSAKEN* up and making it the best version it could possibly be.

I also want to show my appreciation for Cherie Fox who designed my whimsical cover. She is truly talented.

Just because I can, another shout-out to my dog Franky for being my furry writing friend when I needed it the most.

Lastly, to my family and friends who continue to cheer me on and keep me focused—you are amazing!

CAN'T GET ENOUGH OF THE CONDUIT CHRONICLES?

Take a moment to pop over to my website:
https://ashleyhohenstein.com
While there you can sign up for my Readers Club and get FREE Bonus Content instantly!
By enrolling in the Readers Club, you get instant access to a short story. This prequel gives Rand's perspective of what happened the night Sorcey and Cane died.

A NOTE FROM THE AUTHOR

I want to say thank you so much for taking the time to read *FORSAKEN*. *The Conduit Chronicles* has been a dream of mine for many years. I am so excited to take you on this journey and introduce you the Conduit world.

If you would like to get the latest publication news for the series, please visit my website and make sure you join the Readers Club to get a FREE Bonus Content. Learn what Rand saw happen at the Kraus compound the night that Sorcey and Cane died.
https://ashleyhohenstein.com

THE GATEKEEPER & FALLEN are now available on Amazon and through other major online retailers. *THE GATEKEEPER* is a short story, written to build and enrich the Conduit world. *FALLEN* is the third installment of *The Conduit Chronicles*.

If you enjoyed the book, please take the time to review it on Amazon.com or Goodreads. I am so grateful that you took the time to read *FORSAKEN*. I would love to hear what you liked about the book.

ABOUT THE AUTHOR

Ashley Hohenstein lives in Northern California.
Ashley has been a massage therapist and health educator for seventeen years. She has owned several businesses and has found entrepreneurship to be dynamic and fulfilling.
She was an avid reader at a young age and enjoyed getting lost in other worlds. Her dream has always been to become a published author. *The Conduit Chronicles* came to her on a backpacking trip through Europe. It took seven years to get the book written and published.
If you want to learn more about the author visit her website:

https://ashleyhohenstein.com

Be sure to pick up the next two books in The Conduit Chronicles series. *THE GATEKEEPER* and *FALLEN* are both available for purchase on Amazon and in Kindle Unlimited library.

Made in the USA
Middletown, DE
10 December 2021